BY STEFANIE PINTOFF

*In the Shadow of Gotham*
*A Curtain Falls*
*Secret of the White Rose*
*Hostage Taker*
*City on Edge*

# CITY ON EDGE

# CITY ON EDGE

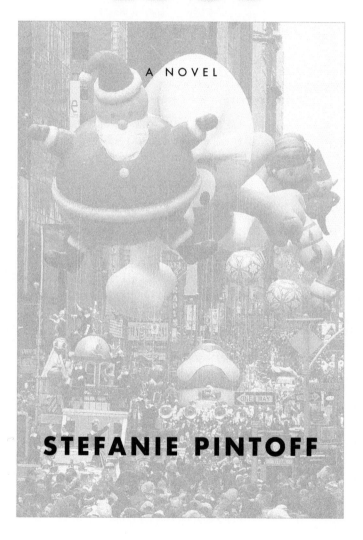

A NOVEL

## STEFANIE PINTOFF

 BANTAM BOOKS   NEW YORK

Copyright © 2016 by Stefanie Pintoff
Maps copyright © 2016 by David Lindroth Inc.

Published in the United States by Bantam Books, an imprint of Random House,
a division of Penguin Random House LLC, New York.

BANTAM BOOKS and the HOUSE colophon are registered trademarks
of Penguin Random House LLC.

Library of Congress Cataloging-in-Publication Data
Names: Pintoff, Stefanie, author.
Title: City on edge : a novel / Stefanie Pintoff.
Description: New York : Bantam Books, [2016]
Identifiers: LCCN 2016027321 (print) | LCCN 2016034168 (ebook) |
ISBN 9780425284452 (hardcover) | ISBN 9780425284469 (ebook)
Subjects: LCSH: Government investigators—Fiction. | Terrorism—Prevention—Fiction. |
Kidnapping—Fiction. | Abduction—Fiction. | BISAC: FICTION / Mystery & Detective /
Police Procedural. | FICTION / Thrillers. | FICTION / Mystery & Detective / Women
Sleuths. | GSAFD: Suspense fiction. | Mystery fiction.
Classification: LCC PS3616.I58 C58 2016 (print) | LCC PS3616.I58 (ebook) |
DDC 813/.6—dc23
LC record available at https://lccn.loc.gov/2016027321

Printed in the United States of America on acid-free paper

randomhousebooks.com

2 4 6 8 9 7 5 3 1

First Edition

Title-page image: copyright © iStock.com/© r_drewek

Book design by Victoria Wong

For *MZP and* CAP

*The line between good and evil is permeable and almost anyone can be induced to cross it.*

—Philip Zimbardo

*All human beings, as we meet them, are co-mingled out of good and evil.*

—Robert Louis Stevenson, *The Strange Case of Dr. Jekyll and Mr. Hyde*

## PART ONE

# INSIDE THE FROZEN ZONE

Fourth Wednesday of November

12:41 p.m. to 6:59 p.m.

# Chapter 1

## 15 CPW

Sometimes the simplest things could be complicated.

Like enjoying an incredible moment.

Perched high above Central Park West, Evangeline Rossi had an unparalleled view of the city from the penthouse terrace. Straight ahead, the park was a fiery swath of oranges, yellows, and reds. To her right, she could trace the Manhattan skyline down to One World Trade Center. On her left, the rooftops of Harlem stretched in a wide arc. It was as expansive as the scene where Spider-Man swings, swirling and twirling, through the canyons of Manhattan. And every bit as dizzying.

*Mind over matter,* she told herself.

But the vertigo didn't cooperate. More than a sensation that played cruel tricks on her, it was a reminder that the brain never controlled the body completely. She was at the mercy of a host of involuntary physical responses—from her rapid heartbeat to tingling skin to skewed and unsteady vision.

Control was just an illusion.

She glanced over to her host. Tall, lean, and unbothered by the fact that he was more than five hundred feet above street level, he let his elbows dangle over the railing edge.

*Damned if she'd let him see her struggle.*

She forced a relaxed smile, even though her world was spinning and her frozen fingers could no longer feel the railing she clutched. The flimsy metal-and-glass-panel was an insufficient barrier, anyway, against frigid, thirty-five-mile-per-hour winds. The temperature on the old CNN billboard might read 43°F, but today's wind gusts had sent the real feel to below freezing.

"You were right," she managed to say. "The view's spectacular."

"It's even better from right here." Tony Falcon's dark eyes turned from the skyline to focus on Eve—and sparked with something primitive.

Seeing only the good-time blonde he'd met over drinks at the marble bar of the Modern, he placed a hand on top of hers—and Eve's every nerve came alive, responding to his warmth. Another involuntary response.

A helicopter buzzed nearby, one of several security measures in place for tomorrow's Thanksgiving Day Parade. Eve steadied herself, glanced down to the street, and saw dozens of officers on foot. Small as ants, they swarmed, and her equilibrium shifted awkwardly again.

"Hope they've got it in hand," he said, shaking his head. "Three and a half million people crammed onto these streets. Every year, it's a miracle when nothing happens."

Eve focused on Tony. She didn't have to look to envision the scene on the ground that created a frozen zone. Garbage cans had been removed. Bags were being searched. Barricades had been erected: concrete stanchions, reinforced by city sanitation trucks filled with sand, each strategically placed to block potential car bombs.

The goal was simple: to erect a secure cordon that would be as impenetrable as a medieval fort.

The helicopter approached, hovering directly above them.

"New York's Finest sure know how to ruin a moment." Tony snorted in disgust. He pulled his hand away, buried it in the pocket of his cardigan sweater with leather elbow patches. He stood, solid and steady—and Eve envied him.

"I'm cold, anyway," she said. "Maybe we should go inside."

"An excellent idea." He moved to open the glass terrace door.

Six steps later, when her head cleared the threshold, she felt a rush of relief.

She found a smile. The illusion of control had returned.

Just inside, she stopped, lingered by a classic black Steinway piano.

Scattered memories fell into place, of practices and concerts—all now seemed a lifetime ago.

"Do you play?" she asked him. She circled the piano, relishing how with every step her balance grew steadier.

He shook his head. "I keep it for guests. Sometimes, the boy." He indicated one of the photos on top of the piano. The setting was a park—and the boy was bashful, poking his head out from behind a tree. The camera had focused on his long, dark lashes.

"Handsome. Your son?" She picked up the frame and studied it. The child appeared to be about seven or eight.

"No. Just a nephew."

*A lie.* The likeness was too strong in the squared jaw. The broad nose. The expression of the boy's mouth. It reminded her there was plenty she still didn't know about her host.

She replaced the photograph. The man liked his secrets—almost as much as he liked his trophies.

The Steinway was just one of many. In the living room alone, Eve also recognized a Klimt, a Rembrandt—and a marble tribute to the female form by Rodin.

She walked toward him. "You've surrounded yourself with beautiful things."

"Life can be tough. Beauty makes it easier to bear."

*Another lie.* If Eve knew one thing about the man who'd invited her up, it was this: He was obsessed with collecting fine objects. When he was a child, he'd hoarded comic books and toy cars. Then he grew up, made a small fortune from a tech start-up, and began an acquisition spree like no other.

Vintage sports cars. Rare works of art. Exotic animals. And women. The harder to obtain, the better.

The fact that he wanted to possess *her* normally would have bothered her. But she liked him—much more than she expected to. Master-of-the-universe types were usually predictable: too one-dimensional for her taste.

Besides, they had things in common. She wasn't his usual empty blonde. In fact, she was a collector, too—though what she collected was information. She observed human behavior and choices. Clues that told her volumes about a person. It was a habit she couldn't kick; didn't matter whether the subject was personal or professional.

From the way Tony moved, she knew that he was supremely confident, a risk-taker. From the clothes he wore, she knew that he favored quality over ostentation. When they talked, he focused on her with an intensity that made her feel she was the only one in the room who mattered. It was seductive—just like the man himself.

A man used to getting exactly what he wanted.

Which probably explained why when she peeled his hands off her thighs at lunch the day before, it only made him want her more.

"I should go." Eve touched her leather jacket, which she'd casually draped on the back of the sofa, and made as if to put it on.

"Not yet." He passed her a snifter of cognac. His hand brushed her own—strong and sure.

*Be careful.*

"It's the afternoon before Thanksgiving," he teased. "Where do you *really* have to be?"

Eve's heartbeat quickened. "Company's coming. I have to get ready."

He reached over and brushed a blond curl from her forehead. His tanned body was solid and powerful under his monogrammed shirt. "Relax. I can have your whole Thanksgiving delivered on Haviland china."

She put down the cognac after taking a small sip. She felt his gaze travel down her chest. She was wearing body-hugging jeans, high leather boots, and a red silk shirt with five buttons. The first was already undone.

She didn't move. She let him stare.

"Stay awhile," he breathed. His fingers traced the side of her face, down her neck, to the deep V of her silk shirt. Then he caught her arm, pushing up her hammered metal bracelet so he could kiss her wrist.

She grabbed his hand—held it—and took a step toward the bedroom.

He followed her six additional steps. Stopped.

With his free hand, he unbuttoned his own Egyptian cotton shirt and let it slip off his shoulders, revealing a smooth chest tapering down to a full six-pack.

Another four steps.

His fingers then made quick work of the buttons on Eve's shirt, which fell to the floor, revealing a low-cut lace camisole.

"Magnificent," he whispered.

Five final steps—and they were in his bedroom.

She took in what lay before her. It was everything she'd hoped to see.

Except for one thing.

By her count, there were three women in the room other than herself: one by Picasso, one by Degas, and another by Klimt.

"You do like unique women," she breathed. He had just kissed her arm—long, slow.

"They mean very much to me."

"But one is missing. The most important Lady. The one you've been telling me about."

"The only woman I want now is you." His breathing was heavy; his hands were moving fast.

But she had seen him steal a quick glance to his right. Where there was a door. It looked like the entry to an ordinary closet.

Eve knew better.

She slid her fingers around his arm. Tugged lightly, pulling him toward the closet that wasn't a closet. "How about something different? Something I'll bet even *you* haven't done before?" She unzipped her left black-leather boot, tossed it aside.

He quirked an eyebrow. "What do you have in mind?"

She pressed her lips to his ear. "I want the Lady to watch." She kicked her other boot off.

He grinned as he flicked the light switch on the wall—and suddenly what had appeared to be a television opposite the bed was revealed to be a computer screen with a security keypad. It required a code—as well as his voice command—before the closet door swung open.

Revealing a safe room.

It was rectangular, about eight feet by fifteen, clad in polished walnut. There was a chaise longue, a fully stocked bar, a four-foot-high steel safe, and an entire wall of masterpieces.

He led her to an emerald-green case with brass fittings that lay on top of the safe. Wrapping his body around hers, he kissed the nape of her neck. And opened the lid.

Eve couldn't stop the delighted cry that escaped her lips.

Inside the case, nestled in a cushion of green silk, was the Lady Blunt Stradivarius from 1721. Named after the granddaughter of Lord Byron, the violin had last sold for nearly sixteen million dollars to an anonymous buyer.

She pulled Tony to the floor, next to the safe, right below the Lady Blunt.

She straddled him.

He took a noisy breath, then seemed to relax. His fingers reached for her blond curls.

"A masterpiece!" she said, intercepting Tony's hand. She casually slipped the metal bracelet from her arm. Clapped it around his wrist. And activated it by pressing a small remote in her pocket.

The electromagnetic handcuff instantly bound Tony to the base of the steel safe with a force stronger than twenty-six men.

His eyes widened with surprise. Definitely not the good-time blonde he'd expected.

Eve was on her feet before he could react. She snatched the case holding the Lady Blunt. Enabled her earpiece.

And called for backup.

One minute, thirty-two seconds later, they were not alone. Three officers in body armor had joined them in the safe room, guns raised.

"Anthony Falcon, you're under arrest," she began calmly. She never lifted her eyes from his chest. He was like a dog: less threatened when no one made eye contact.

"FOTTITI!"

Tony's accent wasn't as charming when he cursed.

"On charges related to the theft of over one hundred nineteen million dollars' worth of stolen art and musical instruments," she finished.

"YOU BITCH!" he snarled.

The agents assisting Eve surrounded him. Deactivated the electromagnetic cuff still attaching him firmly to the steel safe. Pinned his arms behind his back.

First he resisted; then he looked around. Sized up the situation. Regained control of himself.

He was outnumbered and there was no way he could win. But he was a fighter who, even in retreat, was already planning his next battle. "Who are you? What's your real name?"

"You lost. Do this the right way, Tony."

"There's nothing *right* about this."

Eve's three agents marched him out of the bedroom.

But before he was through the door, he wrenched his head back toward Eve.

His face was twisted with menace when he said, "I have eyes and ears all over this city. I'll be in touch."

Eve shrugged. "Guys always say they're going to call. Then they never do."

**VIDOCQ FILE #A3065277**

**Current status: ACTIVE**

**Evangeline Rossi**

Nickname: Eve

Age: 34

Race/Ethnicity: Caucasian, Italian

Height: 5'5"

Weight: 117 lbs.

Eyes: Hazel

Hair: Blond

**Current Address:** 350 Riverside Drive (Morningside Heights).

**Criminal Record:** None.

**Expertise:** Behavioral science and criminal investigative analysis, subspecialties in kinesics and paralinguistics. Seasoned interrogator and hostage negotiator.

**Education:** Yale University, B.S. and M.S., Clinical Psychology.

**Personal**

**Family:** Mother, Annabella, deceased. Stepfather, Zev Berger, recently deceased, former CIA operative.

**Spouse/Significant Other:** None.

**Religion:** Agnostic.

**Interests:** Addicted to crossword puzzles. Concert-level pianist. Avid runner who has finished four NYC marathons.

**Profile**

**Strengths:** The stepdaughter of a CIA spook, Eve was born into the business and is dedicated to her work, believing that it makes the world a better place. Her instincts and training give her insight into the criminal mind that most agents of her age and experience do not possess.

**Weaknesses:** A perfectionist. She likes control and does not delegate well.

**Notes:** Popular within the ranks following successful resolution of a hostage crisis at Saint Patrick's Cathedral (case history #667533) but increasingly less of a team player since moving her offices into the mansion she inherited from her stepfather.

*\*Assessment prepared—and updated—by ADIC Henry Ma. For internal use only.*

One hour later

## WJXZ REPORTS

Good afternoon! This is WJXZ News with Gwen Allensen reporting from the Upper West Side, where all the balloons—not to mention Macy's workers, street vendors, and of course New York's Finest—are getting pumped up for tomorrow's Macy's Thanksgiving Day Parade.

A number of tourists have braved the sleet and bone-chilling winds to watch this annual event. I've been talking with Sara and Francesca, high school seniors from Cincinnati, who have been snapping pictures as this big blue creature behind me is inflated: Papa Smurf. Do you know it takes ninety minutes to inflate one of these giant balloons?

FRANCESCA: This is so cool! Can we get a selfie with you and Papa Smurf?

GWEN: Only if you promise to catch my good side. Seriously, you can see all the activity behind me. Everyone here will be working overtime, throughout the night, to get ready for the main event.

The numbers tell the story: Tomorrow's parade is going to feature more than eight thousand participants—including cheerleaders, dancers, singers, clowns, and eleven marching bands—in addition to eighteen giant character balloons (like Papa Smurf here) and two dozen floats. Sara and Fran-

*NEWS NEWS NEWS NEWS NEWS*

cesca tell me they'll be part of it all tomorrow, performing with the show choir from their high school—

SARA: That's Briar Woods High—and we'll be on the *Spirit of the Midwest* float, in the first section of the parade!

GWEN: All of us at WJXZ wish you good luck, girls. Now back to you, Bob.

# Chapter 2

Giant Balloon Inflation Area — West 77th
to West 81st Street

Everyone loves a parade.

But not Allie Donovan.

Not today.

Not just because she had passed two cops in full body armor—standing with submachine guns hoisted, right across the street from a vendor selling cotton candy, stuffed animals, and balloons.

A plush Hello Kitty purchase later, she continued walking—totally freezing to death!—in the kind of sleet and wind that had already turned her favorite umbrella into a mess of broken spokes. It was the fourth Wednesday in November and she was right outside the American Museum of Natural History—together with a bunch of news reporters, police, parade workers, and street vendors. All gathered at the staging ground where the giant balloons were being inflated.

This used to be a neighborhood secret. Not anymore.

Now the crowds came from all over. In another hour, Allie would see lines snaking around the museum, people packed like sardines, at least ten deep. It no longer attracted just Upper West Siders pushing bratzillas in double strollers. There would also be suits from the Upper East Side; yoga lovers from TriBeCa; granola-crunchers from Brooklyn; and slow-moving vacationers from flyover states. They would all keep coming, over the next seven hours, as eighteen giant characters sprang to life—from Paddington and Pikachu to Sponge-Bob and Spider-Man.

But right now Allie could still move—and so she did. She cut through the traffic, weaving left and darting right, passing Snoopy

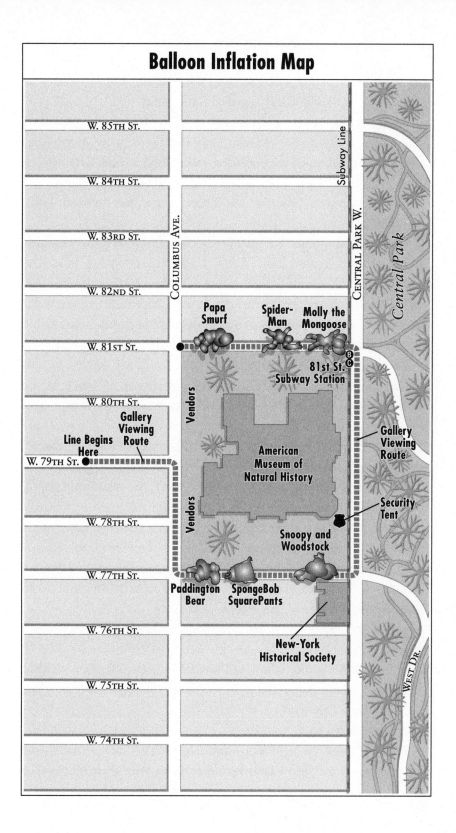

# Balloon Inflation Map

and Woodstock. They were bursting with helium but covered with net—itching to fly but sandbagged to the ground.

She passed the silver gas tanks that lined the park blocks, their black hoses feeding the balloons, making them grow bigger and bigger—until eventually they stood as tall as a New York City brownstone.

Then she stopped. Someone she'd been desperately trying to avoid had just seen her.

The woman under an oversized golf umbrella was charging straight toward her—a pink plastic smile frozen on her face. The crowd parted in front of her like she was Moses crossing the Red Sea.

They were smart to get out of her way. Because even when she wasn't wearing a black raincoat and boots with heels like stilts, Gwen Allensen always reminded Allie of a burnt matchstick.

Brittle—and prone to snap.

Allie clutched her broken umbrella and shrank as much as she could, deep into her bright purple rain slicker, silently willing Gwen to go away. She thought for the gazillionth time how it was stupid that her dad actually liked this woman. Then she thought of the advice Sam, their driver and all-around protector, had given her.

*Treat her like you would an annoying bee: Just stand still and let her buzz on by. That's how you don't get stung.*

Sam didn't like Gwen, either. Since he was a grown-up, he wasn't allowed to say so, but Allie had figured it out. Sam normally talked a mile a minute, but he clammed up the moment Gwen entered the car.

Gwen was already shaking her head. "Allie, what did you *do* to that umbrella?" she scolded, snatching it away.

Allie's heart sank. *Nothing,* she thought. *The wind ruined it, no help from me.*

She pulled her hood tighter and watched Gwen pull a new one out of her vast black-patent bag. It was drab olive green—ugly and small—and she offered it to Allie.

Allie made no move to take it.

With a *tsk-tsk* noise, Gwen reprimanded her. "You already look like a drowned rat! Most girls would *want* to look their best if they knew they were going to be on the news with their dad."

Allie wasn't most girls. Never had been and never would be. And who said she wanted to be on TV?

Today was what Dad called a command performance. That meant she had to show up, shut up, and smile—because he was dedicating Macy's newest balloon and all eyes would be on her. If she didn't look happy about it, people would notice—and talk—and it would be all over the evening news and tabloid papers.

"When I was your age, I *cared* how I looked!" Gwen continued.

Allie stared at a lipstick smudge on Gwen's teeth—neon pink staining white enamel—but she only said *Thank you* and took the umbrella. That was one of eight safe phrases she used in conversation with Gwen. The others were:

*Yes, please.*
*No, thank you.*
*Hello.*
*Goodbye.*
*I'm fine.*
*I'm not hungry.*
*Can you close my door, please?*

The phrases were polite—but without more, they were what Sam called conversation closers. Apparently, they discouraged dialogue and shut down social interaction, which was normally considered a bad thing—since part of growing up meant having the ability to talk politely and at length with people you couldn't stand. But Allie was in no hurry to grow up—and no one could shut down a conversation better than she could.

Today, she got lucky. Gwen saw a celebrity she wanted to interview, and suddenly she was off, jostling umbrellas and blowing perfumed air kisses.

Allie disappeared into the throng, and that was when it hit her: *Something is wrong.* She saw too many adults, not enough kids.

But she shook off her sense of foreboding as easily as the water from her raincoat. She thought: *I'm only upset by Gwen.*

She kept moving, stopping to gaze at the lifeless balloons. Hello Kitty had yet to take shape. The Aflac duck was a blob on the ground.

She turned the corner at West Seventy-seventh Street and walked past three local TV stations, their reporters and news vans all flanking Central Park West. Next was central command, where two dozen officers and a Homeland Security crew huddled in animated conversation under their tent.

Her eyes drifted briefly to her dad, who was wearing his dress uniform and his tensest expression. She recognized two of his advisers and the Counterterrorism team—and heard snatches of conversation. Phrases like *threat level orange* and *close Central Park West.*

Her gaze flicked to the park—and more armored cops carrying machine guns.

The traffic light turned green. Buses and yellow cabs flew by, wheels spinning through puddles and wipers thrashing double time.

Except the nonstop traffic wasn't the problem. The people were—dozens of them, coming on foot, arriving too fast. They were coming by subway, arriving in hordes.

*Too many adults, not enough kids.*

Allie walked faster and went left, where the balloon Dad was going to dedicate—Molly the Mongoose—was still a lump. She had admirers already gathering—fans of the wildly popular *Go and Find Out,* an educational cartoon based on the mongoose's motto.

Spider-Man was up next. Surrounded by blue slicker–clad helium workers, the giant balloon slowly started to take form. A separate team of nine inflators, all drenched in canary-yellow Macy's raincoats, struggled with his slippery upper body, finally connecting it to the silver tanker-truck parked in front of the Beresford. The gas started pumping—and in a matter of minutes, Spidey's long, stretched-out hand began to reach forward.

From an apartment at the Beresford, seven floors up, early Christmas lights twinkled and blinked. Foreheads were pressed against every glass window. How lucky they all were, Allie thought. They got a full view of the action but from a warm, dry, safe spot.

Dozens of cops were staring straight ahead, stone-faced.

Allie kept moving, because she didn't like these crowds. She felt better—a little safer—once she'd put some distance between herself and the rest of them.

*Too many adults, not enough kids.*

She passed by Toothless and the Wimpy Kid and reached Columbus Avenue. There more street vendors hawked candy and popcorn and neon glow sticks. And she remembered last year: when her mom bought her a purple wand, all sparkles and light, and it had felt like magic as it glowed.

Her throat closed up tight when she thought about her mom, and she started to choke up—so *quick!* she chased that memory away.

She must have still looked upset. A second later, a cop named Dale, who worked her dad's security detail, caught sight of her at the corner.

"Hey, Allie! You okay, sweetheart?"

"Yeah, just checking out the balloons." She lied without any second thought—because she couldn't possibly admit how much she missed her mom. Or how much the crowds were freaking her out. She'd be brought to her dad, and end up spending the whole afternoon squirming under his watchful, worried eye. Or—total horrors!—he might delegate her to Gwen.

There would be worried looks that meant *Allie's still depressed.* Or *Allie doesn't have a perspective on things.* Then there'd be a serious discussion about how it was very important to *talk to someone.* About her grief. About how holidays were hard.

But Dale's question had rattled something in her chest. She felt it as she drifted with the crowds, taking three steps at a time. Her heart was banging too fast.

A dozen officers were patrolling, their bodies tense, ready for anything.

She dodged different people in the growing crowd. Two women, tall and reed-thin, who wielded their umbrellas like Kendo swords. An old black man who shuffled by, leaning heavily on his cane. Three guys in Cornell sweatshirts, cracking jokes and laughing at SpongeBob. A family of five with a shrink-wrapped stroller who pushed past her, their sons sloshing through puddles.

They were all wet. Shivering. Sleet-shocked.

But self-absorbed.

And Allie had counted six kids. *Why don't I see more?*

She wandered back to Spider-Man. His head was high in the air; his torso still sagged low to the ground.

A burst of wind caught her full in the face. She pulled her hood tight. Caught sight of a woman wearing a Macy's yellow rain slicker, standing by Spidey's fingers, staring straight at her.

*She's going to say something to me.*

Her hunch was all wrong.

A man with a black baseball cap collided into another man in a bright orange-and-blue Knicks jacket. As they veered into her space, Allie half fell on top of a running toddler. She caught herself—just in the nick of time—but his mother still shot her a dirty look and hustled him away among Spider-Man, Molly the Mongoose, and about three dozen people.

She saw her dad fighting his way toward Molly's staging area. He was with people from Wholesome Minds, Molly's production company—or the new rival to Disney, as everybody said.

It looked like he had decided to dedicate Molly ahead of schedule.

The crowds were really growing.

*Not enough kids.*

The sleet was coming down, small pinpricks of ice, and her breath made frost puffs in the air.

Dad climbed onto a podium, grabbed a microphone, and started talking. He said, "New York is *my* city. With more than eight million of us calling it home, we're going to disagree about some things. But the Macy's Thanksgiving Day Parade is one of our oldest and most beloved traditions. The kind of tradition that brings us together, whatever our differences."

Allie only half paid attention; she'd heard it all before.

People who had been wandering among the balloons began to converge on this spot.

Crowding the sidewalks. Spilling onto Central Park West.

Cars honked and lights flashed. Somebody was going to get hit.

Dad was still talking. Saying it was *always an honor* to be here. Praising family. Thanking Macy's. Making jokes about this being the holiday to celebrate America, football, and Mom's apple pie.

Allie couldn't listen; she had to tune out. She knew it was his job. That the top cop had to say the right things. Had to work to heal what the press called the city's *divisions*. But she hated seeing her dad so politician-fake.

*I don't like crowds. Not ones like this.*

Her last hunch—about the woman staring—had missed the mark.

But her hunch about the crowds? That suddenly became all too real.

Police officers started yelling; they wanted spectators to form a line.

No one listened.

Another round of people emerged from the subway. More crowds, all gaining momentum. Soon joined by a small group of angry voices from Central Park West.

*Police scum! Killer cops!*

*NYPD! KKK!*

All around her, cops assumed defensive positions.

The chants were ugly. Because people tended to use hurtful words when they were upset. But Allie also thought: Sometimes people were mean. Like at school, when the popular girls called her *Dumb Ass Allie.*

Another shout: *No more racist pigs!*

Allie knew that *pigs* was a bad word for *cops,* so this couldn't be good.

Dad's advisers inched closer to him. One climbed onto the podium. She saw him whisper in Dad's ear.

The crowd began to chant. *Don't shoot! Don't shoot! Don't shoot! DON'T SHOOT!*

Dad always said it wasn't easy policing more than eight million people. Sometimes the NYPD got it wrong and people got mad. Usually they blamed him.

He was talking fast now, though his words were drowned out by the crowds.

*Too many people, not enough kids.*

More police reinforcements came. Outnumbered. Outmaneuvered.

They couldn't draw their weapons. There were still tourists. Some peaceful protesters. Some kids. Too many reasons not to escalate the situation.

Allie noticed a hooded teenager raise his fist in the air. He bumped it high, three times, like he was punching the sky. She thought: *He can't be much older than me.*

Suddenly a bottle was thrown. It landed about four feet from Dad. The impact launched a million shards of broken glass.

Then all Allie saw was a mass of moving bodies.

The adviser next to Dad gave a signal. Police officers linked arms to form a human chain. She felt sick when she realized: It was to protect all of them.

Tourists. Officials. Even—especially—Dad.

She tried to move closer to him.

So did the mayor.

Everybody was shoving one another.

Suddenly the mayor was nearing Dad's side.

Allie froze.

The chant was growing louder. *DON'T SHOOT! DON'T SHOOT!*

Police cars were streaming onto Central Park West, sirens blaring and lights flashing. More reinforcements coming.

Meanwhile, Allie was mesmerized by the sea of bobbing heads. Protesters, but some were not the ordinary kind. They didn't care about free speech or "just being heard" or making a political point.

This was a mob.

The mob had surrounded a police car, trying to block it from passing Eighty-first Street.

Rioters rocked it two times.

Three. Four. Five.

On the count of *six,* they toppled it—and the mob cheered wildly.

Helicopters were approaching overhead.

Officers were shouting instructions. They wanted to separate the balloon-watchers from the mob—but in the sleet and wind and the commotion, it was hard to tell everybody apart.

Allie retreated toward Spider-Man. His inflation team was long gone, and only rioters surrounded him now.

She heard a *whump* behind her—as someone stabbed a knife into his polyurethane flesh.

At the same moment, she saw a flash of red and heard a sharp *pop*.

One second her dad was standing, yelling into his radio.

The next she saw him crumple and fall.

There was slick blood streaming down his face. Too much blood. It seemed to be everywhere—even on the mayor, and on Dad's adviser, even on the yellow-cloaked Macy's rep who had been standing, smiling, at the base of the podium at Dad's left.

She wanted to move, but her legs were frozen.

She wanted to scream, but no sound came out.

Most of all, she wanted to refuse to believe this was happening. She was dimly aware of another flash of yellow, then black-gloved hands approaching over her left shoulder, capturing her in a giant embrace. Those hands were sweet-smelling, scented with cinnamon and apples.

Allie was too shocked to resist. She couldn't—so she didn't bother.

She heard a hoarse whisper in her ear. "Don't look!"

She felt a prick in her neck. The putrid olive-green umbrella she had held dropped to the sidewalk.

Her knees went weak and wobbly.

She was being lifted. Then carried.

In the chaos and confusion, no one noticed.

And as she drifted into a warm, fuzzy haze—and the whisper in her ear murmured, "Don't worry, it will all be okay"—she no longer cared.

# Chapter 3

## South of Giant Balloon Inflation Area

Frank García hated some things in life with a vengeance. Hypocrites and ass-kissers. Confined spaces. Beer that wasn't ice-cold.

But most of all? He hated dealing with his ex-wife Teresa.

Didn't even have to see her. A text or email or phone call was more than enough to set him on edge. Any form of interaction was nothing but trouble. Messed him up bad.

Divorce had made Teresa's negative qualities worse: She'd become more opinionated and unreasonable. Plus, the grudge that he bore against Teresa was long-standing and deep: Not only had she done her best to turn Frankie Junior against him, last year she'd even managed to put García in the nuthouse for thirty-nine interminable days. Her lies had convinced a judge to make García's participation in a PTSD treatment program a condition of continued visitation.

Thank God that was over, but today she'd made a stink because he had brought Frankie Junior with him to work. He'd expected complaints that the driving sleet would make the boy sick. But for a change, Teresa had other gripes. "He's too adventurous as it is. Wants to be just like you. He doesn't need any encouragement to fuel his interest in bombs and guns."

Teresa had no idea what it was like to be an eleven-year-old boy. But it was never worth arguing with her. Even though what she was planning to do with Frankie tomorrow involved a much bigger risk.

As part of Eve's secret FBI unit, García had access to the Bureau's Daily Brief. And for the past week, it had been chock-full of threats to the Macy's Thanksgiving Day Parade.

There were plenty of terrorists—from lone wolves inspired by ISIS to the ever-present threat of al-Qaeda.

There were celebrity stalkers—including one nutjob who maintained that if Idina Menzel wouldn't marry him, he would set himself afire when she passed Columbus Circle.

There were radicalized political activists—who would focus on city officials and the various NYPD and FDNY officers who'd be marching in the parade, especially in light of recent tensions over shootings of unarmed men.

And vendetta-seekers—including thirteen former employees of different parade sponsors, each with a significant grudge against their respective corporation.

It was going to be a damn miracle if they made it through and nobody got hurt. Still, Teresa planned to take Frankie Junior to his first Thanksgiving Day Parade.

That was how divorce worked. Teresa had custody of Frankie on Thanksgiving Day—and there wasn't a single damn thing García could do about it.

Not that he hadn't tried. The judge had completely ignored García's plea to intercede. Laughed him out of court, actually, having decided that García was just another conspiracy-theory nutcase.

García understood. Four tours in Iraq and Afghanistan had changed him. His wary nature had gone into overdrive; now he was nakedly suspicious. What Teresa called *paranoid*. Out of habit, he scanned city rooftops for snipers and crossed streets to avoid risking IEDs in garbage cans. He avoided tight, enclosed spaces—which meant he refused to take the subway. The psychologists fretted—and prescribed everything from medication to therapy to an assistance dog. *To help you deal with the stresses of everyday life,* they said.

None of it was his style.

What others saw as a liability, he saw as an advantage. *His* advantage. He wasn't going to let anything dull his edge.

This was his last day with Frankie before the holiday. He'd finish up his check of the parade zone. Then they'd watch some of the balloons inflate, maybe drink hot chocolate to keep them warm in spite of the sleet and cold. Who knew? If he could manage to avoid a panic attack amid all the damn crowds, it might even be fun.

First, he just had to complete his twenty-two-block security screen. The space that stretched from Fifty-ninth to Eighty-first Street. He was focused along the east sidewalk of Central Park West—where aluminum stands formed a tall barrier between the street and Central Park itself. City workers had erected the grandstands about two weeks ago. They formed a temporary scaffolding that rose twenty-four feet high, offering fifteen rows of prime viewing space for the parade.

Tomorrow, invited guests would fill them. Macy's employees. Their families. VIPs. Not to mention holders of special guest tickets awarded by charities.

They were great entertainment for a small boy who loved to explore unauthorized areas.

Frankie Junior was scampering just slightly behind him, clambering up and down the metal bleachers, unbothered by the rain. Playing a solitary version of hide-and-seek.

The skyscrapers on Central Park South's Billionaires' Row were silhouetted against the sky and the park itself was already deserted due to the rain. A half-dozen cops strolled by. A handful of local residents had come out to look at the police cars and news vans. All were enjoying the calm before the parade.

García breathed in exhaust from the cars. Inhaled the steam from a cart that sold pretzels and hot dogs. Savored the aroma from another that sold roasted and candied nuts. Cops were at every street corner. Why did they seem to be keeping an eye on the vendors more than the crowds? Maybe they were hungry.

Frankie Junior caught up to him. "Papa—can I get a pretzel?"

"Get me one, too." García passed him a few bucks. "Extra mustard."

"Nothing better than street food," he said when Frankie returned.

"You eat anythin' else?" Frankie flashed him a crooked grin.

García shrugged. It was pretty much that or the corner diner. Wasn't like he was going to cook.

"I like this better than what Mom makes me eat. Stuff with vege-tables." Frankie made a face.

Just the mention of his ex-wife soured García's mood, so he im-mediately changed the topic. "Your math test come back yet?"

"Nope."

"What about that history project?"

Frankie Junior's brow furrowed; then apparently he drew a blank.

García was interrogating him again, even though it wasn't his in-tent. But normal conversation was always hard. He wasn't much of a talker, and neither was his son.

The sleet continued to drench the crowds.

A street vendor was piping Christmas carols into the air.

García found himself unreasonably annoyed. "Jingle Bell Rock" when it wasn't even Thanksgiving yet? He liked holidays as much as the next guy—but he didn't think they ought to mingle.

He readjusted his mindset. Time to get back to work.

With Frankie Junior in tow, García trolled up and down the bleachers. Checking for wires. Bundles. Packages. Anything that might get past even the dozens of New York's Finest who were swarm-ing around.

Another block and he saw the T-shirt and souvenir vendors. Ev-eryone out to make a buck off the tourists.

So far, so good.

You just had to analyze the terrain. That's what he'd learned from the insurgents. The best IED countermeasure was the human mind. Figure out where your enemy liked to hide—and you'd won half the battle.

It was when he reached West Seventy-fifth Street that he first real-ized something was wrong. That the crowds he was seeing weren't normal. That a mass of people had swarmed into the area—and for reasons having nothing to do with the parade.

At first he thought it was a protest.

Then he noticed that bottles and bricks littered the ground. People ahead were shouting.

At West Seventy-sixth Street, García saw a uniformed cop, radioing for help, sounding desperate. Blood streamed from a split on his lip.

*This was a riot.*

He glanced at Frankie Junior—who was balancing on the top bleacher row, oblivious, still eating his pretzel.

"Come down here," he ordered. "Walk beside me." García positioned his own body as a barrier, protecting his boy.

At West Seventy-seventh Street, García witnessed a medical first responder snap back, narrowly avoiding a rock flung at his face.

*Too dangerous.*

"What's going on?" Frankie Junior reached for García's hand—for the first time in a very long time.

García elbowed through the protesting rioters. Pushed his way toward the museum, stopping at the B/C subway entrance south of Teddy Roosevelt's horse.

"Listen to me," he told his son. "Something bad's happened, so I need you in a safe place. Go downstairs. Take the first uptown subway that comes, okay? The B or the C; it doesn't matter. Get off at One-twenty-fifth Street. I'll text your mom to meet you there."

"I want to stay with you—"

"Not now. Don't lose your backpack. It's got your medicine." García ignored Frankie's look of disappointment.

He knew Frankie was scared, but not enough to trump his excitement. The boy didn't understand that this wasn't the kind of entertainment that anybody wanted. This was pointless. Tragic.

García had always had more than his share of dark thoughts—but he purposefully put them aside where his son was concerned. Frankie deserved a good life—and as long as García lived, he was going to do what fathers did.

Protect his own.

Nobody was going to hurt his son. Not on his watch.

**VIDOCQ FILE #Z77519**

**Current status: ACTIVE**

**Frank García**

Nickname: Frankie

Age: 41

Race/Ethnicity: Hispanic

Height: 5'10"

Weight: 185 lbs.

Eyes: Brown

Hair: Black

Prominent features: Triangle of three tattooed dots on knob of right wrist (the symbol of *Mi Vida Loca,* My Crazy Life, the motto of the Latin Kings); tattoo on left arm (*I will never quit,* warrior ethos).

**Current Address:** 3884 Broadway (Washington Heights).

**Criminal Record (U.S. Army):** General court-martial for involuntary manslaughter, resulting in dishonorable discharge plus forfeiture of all pay and allowances. Sentence: ten years.

*Related: Military record makes clear that he loses respect for the chain of command when a superior fails to meet his exacting standards.*

**Expertise:** Member of elite team of Army Rangers (75th Ranger Regiment). Specialized hand-to-hand combatives expert (including knife-fighting training by experts in Apache knife techniques). Weapons expert and trained sniper.

**Education:** Graduated South Bronx High School.

**Personal**

>**Family:** One of seven siblings (four brothers, two sisters). Two brothers, Jesus and Alex, are current members of Latin Kings. A sister, Emelina, died of lung cancer in 2006.
>
>**Spouse/Significant Other:** Divorce finalized from spouse, Teresa. One son, Frankie Junior.
>
>**Religion:** Devout Catholic.
>
>**Interests:** Devoted to Frankie Junior and his extended family. Passionate about weapons and vintage muscle cars.

**Profile**

>**Strengths:** A warrior who will fight to uphold his personal code of honor.
>
>**Weaknesses:**
>
>- Belief in irrational superstitions is a frequent distraction and cause for concern.
>- Significant risk of PTSD meltdown or alcohol addiction relapse.
>- Isolated and suspicious of others.
>
>**Notes:** A highly skilled individual with serious personal liabilities. García mistrusts alliances.

>*\*Assessment prepared by SA Eve Rossi. For internal use only.*

# Chapter 4

West 81st Street, SW and NW corners

Julius Mason—nicknamed Mace, after his favorite ball player—bounded up the stairs of the C line exit for the natural history museum and came out aboveground on the corner of West Eighty-first and Central Park West. Right where the balloons were being inflated for tomorrow's parade.

*Weird.* Cops were swirling and Spider-Man was a limp heap on the ground. Some wacko must've called in a threat.

Whatever. Mace was feeling good, the rhythm still in his steps from dominating three games of grit-and-grind streetball downtown at the Cage. Even in the teeming downpour, he'd had game.

*Ain't nothin' else like it,* he decided. The pulse. The excitement. The *feel* when the game went white-hot and his ball swished through nothing but net. He'd seen interviews with players describing their mental game, how they thought through this or that move before making it.

*Liars.* Every single one of them.

Streetball was about freestyling. Goin' with the flow, being in the zone, following no real guidelines except those rules that mandated staying inside the faded white lines. Most days, Mace figured all he needed to be happy in life was a hoop and a ball.

His feet pounded the concrete at an easy dribbling pace, crossing the street before he registered that one of those cops was shouting at him.

"STOP!"

Mace halted. Turned. The rain was light now, but the air was heavy with fog. Still, there was no mistaking the nine-millimeter service pistol—a Sig P226—pointed right at him. One of three NYPD standard-issue service pistols.

Problem was: It was being held by a kid in his twenties with a sprinkling of freckles on his nose, a high-pitched voice, and a jittery grip on his gun.

*Just my luck. A rookie cop.*

Mace dropped the ball. It made a *rat-tat-tat* as it bounced into the street.

"S-Stop right there," the rookie demanded. "Don't move. You just breached a blockade."

Mace knew that wasn't right. Sure, Central Park West shut down when the floats started lining up for the parade. But that was hours from now. The blockades never went up before ten p.m.

Then again, he looked around. The rainswept street was almost deserted—except for the cops.

No cars—except the kind with flashing lights.

Stretching down Eighty-first Street, all the balloons sat half-deflated and unattended.

Only a smattering of people. Mainly white. Shuffling into the residential buildings facing the museum.

Plenty of police. But all of them distracted. Gathering evidence behind yellow tape on Central Park West.

Leaving just him and the rookie.

"Easy, man." Mace plastered what he hoped was a friendly smile on his face. "We're good here. What's the problem?"

He kept his hands at his sides. *No sudden movements,* he reminded himself. He was still wearing his layup pants, a shirt bearing his lucky number 17, and a bright orange-and-blue New York Knicks rain slicker. A mesh gym bag was slung over his right shoulder. He didn't think he looked particularly threatening.

Then again, it was a sorry fact of life: Just being a 230-pound, six-foot-seven-inch-tall black man was threat enough to some people. Especially people who carried badges with their prejudices.

"Where have you been t-tonight?" the rookie said and gulped.

They were standing in front of a residential building. The Beresford. A white-glove co-op building that was home to several of the city's movers and shakers—not to mention a half-dozen celebrities and Mace's new girlfriend, Céline. So he knew: On a normal evening, residents would be rushing in and out, asking uniformed doormen to hail them cabs and unload their packages.

Tonight, the building's multiple doors appeared to be locked. Mace caught sight of the doorman inside—watching nervously.

Mace nodded at him—even though he didn't think the man would recognize him. He just wanted somebody watching.

The rain was dripping down his brow, clouding his vision. But he didn't dare move his hands.

He turned his attention back to the cop.

"Look, I get it," Mace said in a smooth, even voice. "You're just doing your job. It's late, something's happened. But whatever's gone down, it didn't involve me."

The rookie's arm was still shaking.

*Keep it cool and calm.*

"I've been playing streetball, West Fourth Street downtown," Mace continued. "At least eight guys can tell you."

"Drop your bag! Hands up!"

An elderly white man with a tan overcoat and a cane shuffled by, making a wide U to avoid Mace and the cop. The cop gave the man only a passing glance.

Where was the cop's partner? Mace wondered. A newbie like this oughta have backup.

He glanced down. The sidewalk was one big puddle. Bad enough that his brand-new Air Jordans were soaked. No way was he sending his bag for a swim.

"Listen, why don't you check my ID? Then you'll see I'm not the guy you're looking for, and we can both get on with our business."

The rookie eyed him skeptically. "W-What kind of *business* do you have in this area?"

"A friend's expecting me at the Beresford for a pre-parade dinner party. It's for some of us riding one of the floats."

"Wise guy, huh? You expect me to believe you got friends at that building and a role in the parade?" The cop's stammer disappeared when he got sarcastic.

"I run No Bull Pit," Mace explained. "It's a dog rescue organization based in Harlem—and we just found ourselves a corporate sponsor. Ace CyberDog."

The rookie looked at him like he'd sprouted two heads.

"You know, the security company," Mace added. "They're also a parade sponsor—got their very own float—and my friend, their CEO, lives at the Beresford. Ask the doorman. He knows me."

"I'm giving you a direct order to drop that bag." The rookie's gun wobbled.

*What the f—* Mace stopped himself. Not just because he knew he'd better not be stupid. Because he imagined Céline, in that black thing she wore, chiding: *You expect to kiss me with that mouth?*

Mace kept his hands clearly visible. But he didn't drop the bag. "Send somebody to check out my story. I'm legit."

Suddenly the rookie had backup. The other cop was a Hispanic man in his thirties with a shaved head and a take-no-shit expression. "Look, asshole, we're not asking again. You're surrounded by cops, and every one of us is pissed off about what just happened. So how 'bout you drop that bag and stick your hands high in the air?"

So much for Mace's stupid idea that a seasoned cop would be more reasonable.

He put his hands up. But he didn't drop the mesh bag. It stayed where it was, slung over his shoulder. "I don't know what happened or who you're looking for, but I ain't your guy. Let me prove that. Check my ID."

Now two nine-millimeter service pistols were trained on Mace. The second was a Glock 19.

"See that bulge?" the new cop told the rookie. "How the left side of his jacket hangs a little heavier than the right? Means he's carrying a weapon."

"Yeah, that's why I'm askin' you to check my ID. You're gonna find my FBI license and carry permit." Then Mace couldn't help himself. He spread his hands wider. "See, we got more in common than you think."

"DON'T MOVE! We're looking for a shooter who matches your exact description."

"You mean I got a twin I don't know about?" Mace forced a big friendly smile. Not because he felt like it, but because he knew it made him look a bit goofy. Less threatening. Maybe humor was the wrong move, but it was all Mace had in his playbook.

He kept his hands wide, up in the air. "Look, I didn't shoot anybody. You hear me?"

"*You* hear *me*. I don't care who you are; you're disobeying a direct order from an NYPD officer. Keep those hands in the air and drop that bag NOW!" The cop—Mace nicknamed him Baldie—definitely had attitude.

Mace racked his brain for a way to defuse the situation. "Can we call a truce here? I repeat, I am not the guy you're looking for."

Neither cop moved. The rookie tightened his grip on the Sig.

Baldie took Mace down without even a split-second warning. His baton caught Mace right in the knees. It was all he could do to keep the gym bag from falling.

He grunted. Felt pavement as a boot kicked him hard, then anchored his head to the ground. He could smell oil and damp and something like vomit.

The bag landed just shy of the puddle.

A hit to his ribs—and his Glock dislodged, scuttling six feet to the left.

Why wouldn't these guys *think*? Guys with guns needed cool heads. That's what kept them on the city's payroll and off the front page of the *New York Post*. Besides, *he* was keeping his cool—even though nothing would feel better right now than smacking his own fist right into the freckled rookie's baby-faced chin.

"Lay flat on the ground!" Baldie shouted.

*One.* He was better than this.

"Don't move a muscle."

*Two.* Mace looked left. People were gathered, watching. Scared. One guy had his smartphone up, filming.

*Three.* He kept his cool. There were plenty of witnesses.

"The last thing you guys need is more bad publicity," he pointed out. "Just check my ID."

Baldie cursed under his breath. His boot pressed harder on Mace's back. The cop was royally pissed off, but he nodded to Babyface.

The rookie leaned down. His breath stank of onions, and Mace tried not to flinch.

He felt his jacket open wide. His right inside jacket pocket unzipped. Soft, fleshy fingers found his keys. His MetroCard. His cellphone. Finally, his wallet and ID.

Babyface pulled it out. Squinted. "You think he's legit?"

"Radio it in," Baldie ordered.

Mace kept his eyes on the ground. Watched raindrops puddle next to his face. Waited. Three minutes, he figured. He knew he was in the system. Once Babyface confirmed Mace was the real deal, he'd be on his way. He'd miss the appetizers, but a three-minute shower and change of clothes and he'd be sitting down by the main course.

One minute.

Two minutes.

Three minutes.

*Taking way too long.*

"Holy crap! You gotta listen to this!" Babyface passed the radio to Baldie.

*Definitely not good.* Mace tried to stay relaxed, keep it casual.

He stared at the ground so hard that its details fixed themselves in his mind.

Four minutes.

Then the cops made a decision.

"Assholes like you'll try anything, huh? Convenient that you forgot to tell us how you've got a rap sheet a mile long." Baldie's voice dripped with sarcasm as he slapped a pair of cuffs on Mace's wrists.

"You ain't no FBI or parade VIP," the rookie jeered. "You ain't got special connections. According to our desk sergeant, you're just a wheeler and dealer who got fifteen to twenty at Rikers."

"Don't know where you came up with that," Mace insisted. "My background's sealed. Part of my security clearance."

A funny noise came from his bag. It put both cops on edge again. Babyface radioed in a second call—this time for backup.

Mace thought: *What's the going rate for wrongful-arrest lawsuits these days?*

Now the bag emitted a high-pitched tone. First, soft and slow. Then more insistent and agitated.

"What the hell's in there?" Baldie demanded.

Babyface unzipped it with his right hand. He didn't say anything. He didn't have to. A small head with beige fur, floppy ears, and a big white patch on his nose poked out of the bag.

The cop's jaw actually dropped.

"He's a rescue puppy," Mace explained. "He's supposed to ride the Ace CyberDog float tomorrow and get auctioned off for charity at Herald Square. I named him Melo, after my favorite Knicks player."

No response. Mace guessed these dudes weren't Knicks fans.

The puppy wriggled his way out of the bag. Scampered over to Mace. Licked his chin. "The mother was tossed out of a car on the West Side Highway," Mace added. "Got hit. She didn't make it—but her unborn litter did."

The senior cop didn't say anything.

"Don't you just love people?" Mace said, bitter.

Baldie stared at the puppy like it was radioactive.

At that point, Mace knew: It was going to be a long night. Because he'd seen cops with that look before.

He glanced down at the puppy, which was now crawling gleefully onto his shoulders. "You took my cellphone, right? There's a number in there for Rossi. Special Agent Eve Rossi. Will you just call her, let her explain everything?"

Then Mace went quiet. It wasn't going to help the situation to say more.

"Make the call," Baldie commanded Babyface. "'Cause I don't want to deal with the damn dog."

A minute passed. Then two.

The puppy nibbled at Mace's fingers and the rain fell.

Suddenly the dog was yanked up in the air.

Mace was hauled onto his feet. Cold metal handcuffs pinched his wrists, and pain shot through his left shoulder. Baldie looked him square in the eye, grim-faced. "Looks like we're going to get to know each other real well tonight. 'Cause your lady don't pick up."

# Chapter 5

## American Museum of Natural History

The block of Central Park West in front of the American Museum of Natural History was now swarming with cops. Their show of overwhelming force had come late—but it had come strong.

First, two busloads of protesters had been arrested and carted downtown. The overturned police car had been towed. The injured had been whisked away by ambulance.

Mounds of trash had been swept from the sidewalks and streets. The museum closed its doors early.

This was NYPD territory now.

And Mace was stuck in the middle of it.

He was not under arrest, but he had been detained as a *person of interest*. That meant he'd ended up in the main rotunda of the museum, sitting on a hard wooden bench next to four ugly-looking dudes. Men who, anybody with eyes in their head could see, looked absolutely nothing like him. At least, not if you really *looked* at them, beyond their basic stats.

Sure, they were each about 230 pounds. Between six-five and six-eight tall. Some shade of black. And wearing some kind of athletic gear.

But beyond that? Absolutely nothing in common.

Which wasn't doing a thing to shut up the guy to Mace's left, who reeked of body odor and was intent on making conversation.

"Wrong place, wrong time, wrong color skin." B.O. Dude pulled a squashed pimento-cheese sandwich out of his jacket pocket. A few

BBQ potato-chip crumbs clung to the bread. Mace wasn't sure he'd ever seen anything less appealing.

"Want half?"

"Nah. Eating shit like that ruins my game." Mace wished the guy would shut up.

"You sound like my girlfriend. She's always doin' yoga and pushing healthy crap. Quinoa. Faro. No beer or pizza or cheeseburgers—any of which I'd kill for right now." He wheezed like the ex-smoker he probably was before taking a huge bite of pimento.

Mace couldn't watch. It really must be a man's world, if a dude like that had a girlfriend.

Meanwhile, the drunk guy on B.O. Dude's other side was arguing with himself, playing with four different skull rings on his left hand. He twisted them back and forth, back and forth, until the ring on his pinkie flew off and scuttled across the floor. He scampered away, giving it chase.

Despite the fact that there was a news team just across the rotunda, a battle-weary cop couldn't resist giving him a knee, hard to his chest. It stopped him in his tracks. Then he fell, spinning twice on the slick stone floor, just like a breakdancer—before yukking up part of his lunch, all over his blue-checkered shirt.

Five feet behind the vomiter, another guy was clearly a druggie suffering from withdrawal. His body had contorted into a strange dance that had no rhythm. His head jerked; his arms swayed; his legs twitched. Miraculously, he did not fall off the bench.

Mace whistled under his breath. This was a new low. He wanted to scream and curse just like his crazy companions. Even if he knew that would just make a bad situation worse.

*Where the hell is Eve?*

Shifting position slightly, he felt the ache in his ribs where he'd been kicked. He was going to have a bruise.

Mace stared up. Took in the Predator and his Prey. The Barosaurus was reared up and angry, about to fight and protect her young from an attacking Allosaurus.

Sort of like the two cops guarding Mace and his new companions.

Both were about as irate as the Barosaurus. Then Mace considered them more carefully and saw that was where any comparison ended.

The older cop had hunched shoulders, a beer gut busting out of his shirt, and hard seen-it-all eyes. He was beaten down—maybe by the job, or problems at home, or a combination of both.

His young partner was a black officer who was trying too hard, hoping a clean shave and a pair of spit-shined shoes would help him move up in the ranks.

Maybe he was right. Maybe it was a game strategy Mace ought to have tried himself at some point during the last twenty-some years.

Mace stared at the black officer. Decided to take a chance. The cop had already delivered Mace's rescue puppy to Céline for safekeeping—a small sign that he actually might care. "Hey, Officer!"

No response.

Mace tried again, a little louder. "Excuse me, Officer!"

This time the man's head snapped toward Mace before he stuttered forward, like he'd been holding on to something so tight, it was hard to let go.

"Help a brother out, man. How much longer is this going to take?" Mace asked.

A shrug. "Can't really say."

"What's goin' on over there?" Mace indicated an area on the opposite side of the rotunda, where a tent was erected and a team of medical personnel clustered.

The cop didn't respond.

Mace inwardly groaned. "Look, I get it," he said. "Something's happened and witnesses ID'd a man about my height, weight, and skin color. Wearing my kind of clothes. But it wasn't me. I need outta here now."

The officer shook his head and shuffled farther away from Mace.

The pimento sandwich guy elbowed Mace to get his attention. "Where you been? Under a rock?"

"I mind my own business."

The other man grinned. "Bad idea if you ask me. There was a mega-protest here earlier. Shots fired—rumor says the top cop got hit bad. Right in the head. Didn't make it."

"So they rounded up the usual suspects. Meaning us. Suspected cop killers."

"That's why this place is locked down like Fort Knox."

*Damn.* No way was he getting out of here tonight unless Eve worked miracles.

From the medical tent, Mace heard raised voices. Several people were shouting at once—but one voice was louder than them all. "I SAID GET AWAY FROM ME."

Mace listened closely—and caught snatches of the conversation. *You need to cooperate with us. It's for your own good. In shock.*

"DAMN IF I'M COOPERATING WITH YOUR RIDICULOUS DEMANDS. YOU BASTARDS BETTER STOP PUTTING OBSTA-CLES IN MY WAY."

The shouting man was no longer lying down. He was no longer surrounded by medical personnel—even if he looked as though he ought to be. His face was streaked with red—as were his shirt and pants—and his hair was sticky with it.

He paced by the main door to the museum, feet a dozen inches apart, hands waving wildly.

Mace stared, incredulous.

He was no more than eight feet away from a ghost. The same ghost he'd just been told had been killed.

Except this ghost was flesh and blood and moving like a force of nature.

New York City Police Commissioner Logan Donovan.

**VIDOCQ FILE #A30652**

**Current status: ACTIVE**

**Julius Mason**

Nickname: Mace
Age: 43
Race/Ethnicity: African American
Height: 6'7"
Weight: 230 lbs.
Eyes: Brown
Hair: Black
Prominent features: Three-inch scar by left ear

**Current Address:** 1889 Lexington Avenue (East Harlem).
**Criminal Record:** Multiple felony convictions—conspiracy to import and traffic illegal contraband. Sentence: fifteen to twenty-five years.
**Expertise:** Clandestine movement of goods across borders. Specialized knowledge of smuggling networks for weapons, narcotics, and exotic wildlife.
**Education:** Attended Bronx Regional High School (Hunts Point, South Bronx).

**Personal**

**Family:** Mother, Dolores. Father, unknown. Brother, Marcus, deceased (gang violence); brother, Duane, deceased (drive-by shooting). Pit bulls—Romeo, Ace, and Danger.
**Spouse/Significant Other:** Currently involved with Céline Bonnot.

**Religion:** Baptist.

**Interests:** Regular player, pickup hoops. Founded No Bull Pit, dedicated to helping rescue pit bulls from dog-fighting rings.

**Other:** Abandoned longtime gang, the Bloods, when they became involved in dog-fighting.

## Profile

**Strengths:** Loves nothing more than the thrill of a close game—and winning it.

**Weaknesses:** Doesn't play well with others. A loose cannon with no respect for authority. Operates by his own rules, preferring instinct vs. planning. Soft spot is love for animals.

**Notes:** His good-natured personality predominates over his intimidating physique. Wants to train his rescue dogs for the FBI K-9 program.

*\*Assessment prepared by SA Eve Rossi. For internal use only.*

# Chapter 6

## American Museum of Natural History

Lights were flashing and cops were cursing—but one sound in particular kept Commissioner Logan Donovan perpetually distracted: the incessant ringing in his ears. It obscured the well-meaning questions of his colleagues, asking if he was okay.

It echoed when he tried Allie's cellphone, to no avail. He tried her four times in quick succession, annoyed that she was being irresponsible. How many times had he told her that having a cellphone at her age was a privilege, not a right?

With a situation on the ground that demanded his best skills—both tactical and political—Donovan had no time for his daughter's disappearing stunt. When Jill was alive, she would have checked with every friend and teacher, shaking down trees and defusing the drama. But he had a city to run—not to mention a police department under threat and millions of tourists to keep safe during one of the year's most high-profile events.

So he made the only decision he'd ever made when forced to deal with his child: He delegated. His first call was to his housekeeper, Jackie, asking her to do what she could from home. His second was to his sometimes-girlfriend Gwen, to convince her to follow up on-site. It was the sort of favor he hated owing Gwen. But she was the kind of woman who knew how to ask the right questions.

With the issue now handled, he allowed his eyes to wander the rotunda, searching for his deputy commissioner, George Kepler. He stopped when a glint of light caught his attention—the reflection of one of his captains' badges. He squinted.

*McDonnell!*

A warrior type who lived for his uniform, yet lacked even a smattering of common sense. No understanding of the kind of pressures the department faced these days. He'd rounded up a group of five men—*persons of interest* in the immediate vicinity following the riot and shooting—who fit the general description of the guy who'd shot him. Donovan's attention focused on one detainee: a large black man, dressed to play ball, who was sitting down—but filled with so much power and energy, he looked like a rocket ready to launch. Something seemed familiar about the man, though Commissioner Logan Donovan couldn't place him.

Didn't matter now. He had no time for reminiscences.

He also saw something else McDonnell was oblivious to: The place was crawling with media, at least a dozen news cameras trained on the activity inside the museum. It was only a matter of time before they decided the men being held were being held "too long." Before they focused on this one's black eye or that one's cut lip—injuries that had been suffered God only knew where. But if the media got hold of it, then the public would whip itself into a frenzy.

Once that happened, then never mind the department: *He* would have a bad name. His detractors would point out how this practice was completely at odds with his vision of community policing. What he called the "protect our city" philosophy—something that, with his considerable charm and ample supply of political goodwill, he had shoved down the new mayor's throat two months ago.

Some leaders threw their weight around like sumo wrestlers, but not Donovan. His approach was more subtle—and far more effective.

He started walking toward where George Kepler was in the middle of a meeting.

An earnest medical tech with a crooked nose—one that looked like it had been broken a half-dozen times—trailed after Donovan. "Commissioner, you don't seem to realize what a lucky escape you've had. Just another couple inches and—"

Ignoring him, Donovan spoke to the two young cops he passed. "Everything under control? Do something about those news cameras, will you?"

Startled, they immediately acknowledged him with a salute—a reminder that he was still in full dress uniform—which was followed by a thumbs-up.

Another issue resolved.

Donovan passed a ruddy-faced officer. "Your new baby letting you get any sleep, Mike?" The commissioner made it a point to remember the little stuff—the birthdays and weddings and high school graduations that marked his officers' lives. It made them feel that he valued them. Then their allegiance was his.

Mike winced. *Too loud,* Donovan told himself.

"Yeah, he's doing great." The heavy bags under Mike's eyes said otherwise. "You okay, Commissioner?"

"Right as rain."

This time, two other heads turned to see what was the matter. *Still too loud.*

The med tech continued to trail him. "You brush it off like it's nothing, but that injury of yours is serious."

Donovan didn't bother to acknowledge him. The medic was badgering him, thanks to the city's legal team. A bunch of bureaucratic worrywarts who operated from a position of fear, constantly terrified that the department was about to get sued.

"People have *died* after getting shot by paint guns," the tech persisted. "You were hit by a pellet traveling three hundred feet per second, two hundred miles an hour."

"Hey, Billy—you did some great work with the advance team this morning," Donovan roared to a carrot-topped rookie.

The young man reacted with a jump. Then a deep blush. "Thanks, Chief."

The med tech stayed right on his heels. "This wasn't just a publicity stunt at your expense—"

"It was an assault," Donovan roared. "Not just on me, but on the honor of every man and woman who wears this uniform!"

The med tech cringed. "The fact that you're shouting is another sign that you've suffered a serious injury. You're fortunate your eardrum didn't rupture—but you've got hearing loss and a concussion."

*Not to mention this damned incessant ringing,* Donovan thought.

"You'll recover faster—and avoid serious complications—if you rest."

Donovan spun to face down the med tech, staring at the man's mangled nose until the smaller man flinched. "Consider your job done. Go file your report; you've examined me and I'm fine. Now, I need to speak with my team."

"Please, Commissioner. Medical evaluations are important work. Sit down—"

"Medical evaluations *are* important. That's why when the mayor's cutbacks hit last summer, I fought for every single med tech to keep his job. Including you."

The folder slid from the tech's fingers, spilling papers onto the floor. His hands shook as he bent to gather them.

Donovan allowed himself to smile, knowing he'd scored a victory. "Now, *sit* and *down* aren't in my vocabulary—and my deputy's waiting." He made sure his smile stayed there as he turned, crossed the steps, and joined the briefing.

George, his second-in-command, was wrapping up the story of what had gone wrong. He had laid out every unexpected turn in the road, highlighting each sharp curve, every blind spot, all the screwups. "A handful of the protesters were legitimate. The others are under arrest—or will be, once we scour the video footage we have."

"We were outmaneuvered and outnumbered," Donovan added. "This riot could've spun out of control, like we've seen elsewhere. Baltimore. Ferguson. Chicago. It's to your credit that you stopped the violence. Because of you, tomorrow's parade will go on."

A cop to the left of the commissioner gestured angrily with hands that were heavily callused—and red from the cold. "Yeah, but I get tired of seeing fires burn and bullets fly and good cops hurt. Because of the media and these damn protesters, every single one of us is a target. Like our job ain't hard enough without people blaming us for everything wrong in our society."

Donovan merely stood, nodding. He meant it to be a signal: His guys had his permission to vent, if that's what they needed. Sometimes the pressures of the job needed a release—even if it meant the official briefing ran off course.

A stocky lieutenant with short cropped hair—dyed a brilliant yellow—cleared her throat. "I'm from a family of cops. My dad was part of the layoffs back in '85. He and the others planned to march across the Brooklyn Bridge in protest. And you know what happened? The same guys he'd worked with, side by side over the years, showed up and chased 'em off. My dad was a good cop—and *he* wasn't allowed to protest. Makes me sick that scum like this can."

"Times have changed, Lieutenant. Plus, this was no legitimate protest. This was a mob. A flash mob." Donovan planted his hands in his coat pockets. *God, if only the awful ringing in his ears would stop!*

His deputy glanced at him sheepishly. "You doing okay, Chief?"

Donovan stared impassively back into George's pearl-gray eyes, determined to show nothing. George Kepler was a stand-up cop, and no one could ever complain that George didn't pull his weight. But he was nakedly ambitious, always alert for any sign of weakness. One of those guys always bucking for the next big opportunity—and in a way that was too obvious and greedy.

"I feel fine. But I sure could use a shower." Donovan grinned. "You make a damn fine-lookin' redhead!" someone yelled out. That drew a laugh from the officers.

Donovan nodded with good humor. "We need to review our strategy for this parade. Make sure it's sufficient to handle what's coming our way. Not just ordinary protesters. And not just those threats targeting parade-goers and participants, though we're monitoring chatter from terrorists and always concerned about lone wolves and celebrity stalkers."

"How many threats are we looking at, Chief?" another voice shouted.

"If you can believe it, less than last year. But we're up to one-thirty-nine and counting. Eight are highly credible, and our Critical Response Unit is split into two teams, both foreign and domestic, closely monitoring them," Donovan replied. "But right now I want to talk to you about the most important one: the one targeting *us.* We've received six anonymous phone calls in the last twelve hours warning us that someone intends to hurt cops at the parade. The first call warned of a man who wanted to shoot some cops. Subsequent calls warned of machete attacks and chemicals—again, directed at police officers, not the public at large. In light of Queens and Ottawa, Philadelphia and Texas and the attack on me today, we have to take it seriously."

"We have a man in custody," George added. "He may or may not be the source of the calls."

"And the calls could be pranks," Donovan said. "But they're reason to be especially alert at all times and back each other up. Be mindful that anything, regardless of how insignificant it appears to be, may be a setup. Rely on your training—and trust your instincts." He focused on the men and women watching him. All looked cold and tired and a little apprehensive. "Before we get down to business, a lot of you look hungry—and I certainly work better on a full stomach. Michaels, why don't you order coffee and pizza for all? Let's everybody take fifteen. Then we'll reconvene inside; I'm going to commandeer a room."

George trailed him to the main entrance, then opened the door before Donovan could reach it.

"We have one more issue to discuss," George said hesitantly, like a man walking on eggshells.

Donovan pushed through the door without slowing. George wanted to grill Donovan about his every ache and pain—and Donovan had no patience for it. Like he wasn't man enough to do his job, despite it all.

"Can you give me half an hour? There's something I've got to do." He kept his voice smooth, though he could sense his temper rising.

There was so much work to be done. He had to be an example to his colleagues—but he especially had to protect his officers on their patch. Territory that, for the next twenty hours or so, was a two-and-a-half-mile route running from the American Museum of Natural History to Macy's on Herald Square.

A staccato of heels striking the stone floor sounded behind him, signaling Gwen's arrival. "Excuse us," he said to George—ignoring his deputy's frown, which sagged the corners of his face with the weight of his worry.

Donovan pulled Gwen aside, thinking again what a singular woman she was—tough and professional, with made-for-TV looks. He would never depend on any woman for his happiness. Still, he acknowledged that Gwen had been the one who made him laugh, who allowed him to dream, who held him together in the days after Jill's death. Somehow, she had even weathered his home situation with grace. At his age, dating someone necessarily involved his kid—and Allie was not a Gwen fan. His daughter had yet to regard his girlfriend with anything other than a thousand-watt death stare.

Once they were alone, Gwen raised a hand to her mouth, as though she was afraid to say the words that needed to be said. "I looked for Allie, like you asked," she blurted out. "Asked around. But I can't find her, Logan. Not anywhere."

He stopped walking. Looked at her, wanting something more. Some additional fact or detail that would transform her words into different ones. Ones he expected to hear.

"Someone must have seen her," he insisted stubbornly.

Gwen shook her head. "No one I can find."

"Did you contact Jackie? Check with my driver?"

"I did. Jackie's still heard nothing. And Sam's already off for the holiday; he hasn't seen Allie since he drove her home from school yesterday."

"What about texts? Emails?"

"Nothing." There was no emotion in Gwen's eyes.

He knew she cared, of course. But she was like him: She recognized a teenage girl's stunt for what it was. You couldn't panic or overreact where Allie was involved. You had to keep a cool head.

Even as you cursed the fact that she made you waste your valuable time.

He pulled out his own cellphone. Dialed Allie's number.

Once. Twice. Three times.

Then four. Five. Six.

At seven, his emotion flared from annoyance to full-blown anger.

He'd just been targeted tonight by violent protesters—the kind who saw him as a symbol of everything that was wrong with the

NYPD. Who blamed him whenever a rookie shot an unarmed man. Or when a couple bad cops who believed they were above the law mistreated a suspect in custody.

He needed to rehabilitate his department's image—while simultaneously ensuring the security of thousands of spectators and performers at tomorrow's parade, not to mention his own officers. Didn't he have enough to deal with?

This wasn't the first time Allie had run off. The fact was: She was a handful. His wife, Jill, at least, had known how to handle Allie's drama. He never had—and Jill's passing had only complicated the tricky teenage issues. If Allie had been a boy, he'd have taken her to ballgames and they'd have watched ESPN together. They'd have talked about the Knicks' new point guard or the Jets' starting lineup. He would have known how to show tough love when there was a problem, how to say *man up,* how to ignore his own guilt and grief.

Instead, he was at a total loss. Allie liked books and taking photos. Things even most girls weren't into. Most nights, she took herself to her room as soon as the dinner dishes were put away. Often he paused outside her door—always closed—and thought he heard crying.

It was possible that he was wrong. He certainly wanted to think so. *His* daughter ought to be stronger and smarter than that. "When I find her—"

Gwen cut him off. "Maybe it's time to face another possibility, Donovan." She put a hand on his arm. "You have more than your share of enemies. Your line of work attracts them."

"You think I don't know that? I was shot at today," he snapped, throwing off her hand.

Gwen stiffened. "There are people who hate you. Personally, not just because you're the top cop. Have you asked yourself whether they might have targeted you today? Whether to hurt you, they might have targeted Allie?"

Logan Donovan shook his head. It was a possibility that made sense to acknowledge but never give credence to. Sure, he had ghosts in his past. Yet he was a leader who refused to be rattled by the skeletons he'd locked in his closet. And a father who refused to let his child drag him into her prepubescent drama.

"Don't worry about it, Gwen," he said brusquely. "You did what you could, and I appreciate that. Go back to work. This isn't your concern anymore."

*I'll find someone else,* he decided.

# Chapter 7

## American Museum of Natural History

Gwen Allensen was deeply worried. She'd known the commissioner for more than two years. Long enough to figure a thing or two out.

First, if Donovan had an issue, medical or otherwise, that might interfere with his job performance, he'd never admit it. The man believed in nothing more than his own invincibility.

Second, if Allie was truly in trouble, Donovan would be the last person to see it. The man had a view of his daughter that was one-dimensional and limited. From growing up with three sisters, Gwen knew it could be difficult, between worries about mean girls and peer pressure and social media. But Allie was different. She never prattled on about pop music or crushes or parties like Gwen and her sisters had. Allie acted more grown-up—and as much as Gwen complained that Allie was sassy, the truth was that behind the smart mouth was a hurt child. One who desperately missed her mother—and had no idea how to connect with her father.

That was why Gwen was worried to learn Allie didn't pick up her cellphone. Or reply to Donovan's texts.

She didn't want the commissioner to know that she'd second-guessed him, so she sent her two assistants to question the vendors and other news reporters. They canvassed the helium suppliers and countless inflation workers in yellow Macy's coats. She herself called around to area hospitals and checked their video feeds from the area. *Nothing.*

So she approached Morris, one of the NYPD tech guys who'd

helped her in the past. "There are cameras at the Beresford, its neighboring buildings, and on every corner of the museum," the techie assured her. "We'll review all footage."

"And keep it on the QT. Don't let the commissioner know," Gwen warned.

The techie's eyes widened in surprise.

"He's not himself at the moment," Gwen explained. She motioned across the room, where Donovan was talking too loudly. Waving his hands wildly.

Several officers were turned toward the commissioner, their faces dumbfounded.

"What's wrong with him?" the techie asked Gwen.

Gwen turned back to face the techie. "Nothing he won't fix, by sheer force of will. The real question is: What would *you* do if your thirteen-year-old child was missing?"

"I dunno. I've got two cats. They need food, a smattering of affection, and their twice-daily medication. It's more than enough for me."

"I'm not asking you to *be* a father. Just *think* like one."

"Well, Allie had to have seen her father shot," the techie hazarded. "She must've been upset, not thinking clearly. Maybe she'd go to a friend?"

"The commissioner doesn't know her friends. Can't name a single one." Gwen shook her head. "It's because Jill was sick for so long. The more her condition deteriorated, the fewer friends Allie asked over."

"Well, if she's like every other kid," the techie said dryly, "she's spending hours on that cellphone of hers; she must have been communicating with *someone*. We just have to figure out *who*." That was the thought that sparked an idea. "If you have Allie's number, I can locate her phone."

Gwen checked her own contacts, rattled the number off.

On the opposite side of the rotunda, Detective Michaels's pizza delivery had arrived. It attracted cops like bees to honey—and suddenly the tech work area was deserted.

Gwen watched as Morris focused his attention on his laptop monitor and called up a new search. It yielded a screen covered with numbers. Even if a cellphone was turned off, so long as its battery was present, it emitted a signal looking for base stations within range. That signal—a "ping"—lasted less than a quarter of a second. But it contained both the mobile identification number—the number assigned by the service provider that was similar to a landline number— and the ESN—a thirty-two-bit binary number assigned by the manufacturer. The latter was what Morris tracked; unlike mobile numbers, it could never be changed.

The screen's string of numbers began flashing fast, blurring into green and yellow psychedelic lines as Morris went back in time, tracking Allie's movements from the moment she had arrived with Donovan at the balloon inflation.

At 1:46 p.m., Allie had been at the corner of Eighty-first and Central Park West. She had wandered around, checking out the balloons. And returned to the corner of Eighty-first by 2:09 p.m.

"The pings go silent," Morris pointed out. "Right here—at two-eleven p.m."

*In other words, right when Donovan was giving his speech,* Gwen thought. *Just before he was shot. Poor kid probably panicked.*

"Here's what I think happened. At two-eleven, I believe she sees the commissioner—hurt," Morris explained. "She drops her phone. And in the chaos and confusion, somebody grabs it. Maybe the battery's fallen out. If not, the person finding it knows enough to remove the battery. Finders keepers is the name of the game. Within twenty-four hours, Allie's phone's going to be nothing but a bunch of parts for sale on the black market."

"That's a great story to explain the missing phone," Gwen said evenly. "But not the missing girl."

The techie looked at her sharply. "Right now it's all I can give you. Look, the commissioner's right not to worry prematurely. In the meantime, we've covered all the bases. As part of the shooting investigation, we have people checking official surveillance. Interviewing civilians with smartphones. We'll be on the lookout for any suspicious activity. If there's a problem, somebody will catch it. But the most likely scenario is that the kid got spooked. Got caught in the chaos of the crowds. Lost her phone."

Gwen nodded, but she couldn't shake the gnawing sense in her gut: Something was not right. But what was her responsibility, really, to a child who wasn't her own?

NEWS NEWS NEWS NEWS NEWS

## WJXZ REPORTS

This is WJXZ News with Gwen Allensen reporting from the Upper West Side.

For viewers just tuning in, we're bringing you Mayor Kelly with an update on the city's response to the protest at this year's annual Macy's Thanksgiving Day Parade balloon inflation ceremony—a protest that unexpectedly turned violent.

*MAYOR KELLY:* Today is a difficult day for me as mayor of this city. My friend and colleague—Commissioner Logan Donovan—was brutally attacked on what should have been a day of celebration and thanksgiving. While the commissioner's prognosis is excellent—and we expect him to make a complete recovery—I do want to update you on the city's response and additional street closures in the area.

*UNIDENTIFIED REPORTER #1:* Have the police identified the shooter or shooters?

*UNIDENTIFIED REPORTER #2:* Do you believe the commissioner was attacked in retaliation for Stan Smith's death while in police custody? Can you comment on reports that Smith was beaten by officers and repeatedly bitten by a police dog—after he had been subdued?

*UNIDENTIFIED REPORTER #3:* Is there any remaining threat to public safety?

*MAYOR KELLY:* This is an ongoing police investigation, so we cannot answer questions that may bear on the evidence. But

I want to assure you: The public's safety is my number one priority. Tonight and tomorrow, you will see a significantly heightened police presence both in the parade zone and throughout the city.

UNIDENTIFIED REPORTER #4: The balloons are still not inflated. Will the Macy's Parade go forward as planned?

UNIDENTIFIED REPORTER #5: Have you received specific terrorist threats targeting the parade?

# Chapter 8

## American Museum of Natural History

Logan Donovan stood in front of the museum's circular membership desk in the middle of the rotunda, jiggling his foot impatiently, and watched the laptop screen on the counter. Behind him, footsteps pounded, phones trilled, and cops shouted orders.

Donovan was oblivious to all of it.

Five segments of video footage had been loaded onto the computer: three by tourists, one by a Macy's worker, and one by a resident at the Beresford.

He had now seen himself shot four times over—though no footage seemed to have captured an image of the two people he most wanted to see. *The shooter. And his daughter.*

"Commissioner? May I have a word?"

Donovan groaned silently as he allowed the woman known as Mo to pull him aside. A tall woman with dirty-blond hair, cut fashionably short, she was the last person he wanted to see right now.

"Tough day all around, huh?" She looked at him with a mixture of respect and pity, but her voice was typical Mo.

He flashed Mo a smile that he hoped would appear warm and friendly.

George had once diplomatically called Mo an acquired taste. But Donovan had been dealing with her for almost a year, and he'd yet to acquire even a basic ability to tolerate her. He was beginning to accept that he never would.

It didn't matter that she'd kept him in his job. He owed her no favors there; she'd have replaced him in a heartbeat, if she could. But with crime rates down twenty-two percent across all five boroughs, Donovan had been far too popular to force out.

"You feeling okay?" Mo looked him over. He felt like a horse being evaluated before the big race.

"Sure," he lied. "Nothing wrong that a shower, a few hours of beauty sleep, and a whole lotta shampoo won't cure."

"That's not what I hear." She started ticking his problems off on her fingers. "I spoke with Medical. You've got a concussion. You have issues with balance. Your hearing has been compromised." She let it all sink in before she added, "And I just heard from George that your daughter's run off."

He felt his body stiffen. "It's been a rough day. But I defy anyone to say I can't handle problems. That's what I do."

"My point is: You've got more problems than usual. And the situation with your daughter?"

He bristled. "Since when is my family anybody's business?"

"You're the top cop in charge of this city, Logan. If you have a runaway situation—"

"Which is pure speculation on your part."

"You would—understandably, of course—be distracted. Unable to focus on your responsibilities to this city." Mo's gray eyes locked onto Donovan's.

He felt as though he was being stalked by a predator he'd underestimated. Now, with his back up against the wall, he needed an exit strategy. One certain to best Mo, who had a clear agenda—and was poised to push it through.

"What's happened to you this afternoon is something no public servant should be asked to deal with," she was saying. "You were representing the citizens of New York—and particularly those of us who want to resolve the tensions that divide our community. The NYPD's taken some real heat these last few months. I want you to know I've got your back on this. On everything."

"I appreciate that, Mo." He found another smile, because it was what she expected.

"We need to keep working together to keep this city safe. And to do that, I need you in top form. Which is why you should take some time off."

"Can't. Not with the parade tomorrow. Not with my own men and women under threat. This is my city, and it's my job to protect it. My daughter will turn up soon—and in the unlikely event that she doesn't, I have good people to help me find her." Donovan just barely held his fury in check—but he kept his voice at a normal volume.

"You've had a rough time since your wife's death. You took barely any leave then. I'd say you deserve a break. And we deserve one hundred percent of your efforts."

He couldn't believe she was trying to use Jill's death—and now Allie's disappearance—to justify forcing him off the job.

"I give one hundred percent of myself every day." He kept his voice even. "Every single day. Including today."

"Except you *can't*, Commissioner. Not when you have so many issues. A lot of people are worried. The medical personnel who've treated you. Deputies who've worked with you for years. The consensus is clear: They say that you're not yourself."

*George.* And after all he'd done for the stupid ingrate.

"You're known for having nerves of steel," Mo continued, "but today, people tell me that you've repeatedly flown off the handle."

They were in the middle of a conversation, but he found himself struggling to keep up. Too many problems competed for his attention. *His pounding head. The infernal ringing in his ears. Allie.* He forced his eyes to meet Mo's.

"The Macy's Thanksgiving Day Parade is a big event for our city," she was saying. "And like every big event, it generates attention from those who want to disrupt it. As you know, this year in particular, we have a number of credible threats to safeguard against. Your injuries—as well as your concerns about your daughter—make you a liability. Given the political climate, we can't take chances."

Donovan's ears were roaring. His head was pounding. But through it all, he realized that Mo was making a power play. She had waited patiently until the moment he was at his most vulnerable. Now she was moving in for the kill.

"Stop right now. I'm no liability. In fact, the security plans that we're implementing—plans that have been in place for months—are *my* plans. And I have the finest police force in the world supporting me."

"Take some time," she insisted. "You've earned it. This is my city—which means the buck stops with me, for the credit or the blame. So I'm taking charge of all preparations for tomorrow's parade. Together with George Kepler."

"Excuse me?"

She was talking nonsense. George was *not* assuming his job. Donovan shook his ocean-filled head, trying to clear it.

"I'm not asking you, Logan, I'm telling you. It's an order. Go home. Take care of your health. Take care of your daughter."

He'd just been played—in a more effective way than he'd thought Maureen Kelly, mayor of New York City, was capable of.

Like hell would he stand for it.

Behind Mo, Donovan saw the deputy commissioner, the deputy mayor, and a host of high-level political officials coming toward him.

He also saw the various news organizations represented, with multiple camera crews in place.

*And Gwen.*

He drew a breath and ran his hand across his red-flaked hair, pointed to her cameraman, then motioned her over. Suddenly there was a great commotion as reporters and news crews charged toward him, practically stumbling over their equipment.

Before Mo could say a word, he introduced himself and seized control of the situation.

"This is your police commissioner. At one-forty-seven this afternoon, during the annual balloon inflation ceremony, there was an unfortunate incident of violence. A small group of protesters incited a riot—and I was assaulted."

He paused—the cameras flashed—and the questions came rapid-fire.

*Commissioner, who are the perpetrators responsible?*

*Commissioner, is it true that you have the shooter in custody?*

*Commissioner, are you uninjured—and able to continue leading the largest, most sophisticated police force in the world?*

Donovan looked directly into the cameras. He kept his answers to the point. His voice at normal volume. He reassured the public about his health—about security at the parade—and thanked the mayor and every other public official in the city for their confidence in him.

In other words, he ignored the infernal ringing in his ears—the tinnitus that was a temporary symptom of his ear injury—and did what he had to do to save his job.

After he ended the impromptu press conference, Mo Kelly, her brows knit in a tight V, sat shivering with anger. He got up and charged across the room, leaving her behind, cursing her with every step that he took.

She wasn't an acquired taste. Just a bad one.

So sour and unpleasant that he wished he could spit it out.

# Chapter 9

## 350 Riverside Drive, Vidocq Headquarters

At 107th and Riverside Drive, the white marble mansion with the sea-green slate roof was one of the city's last freestanding houses. It was imposing at more than twelve thousand square feet, and was guarded by two lion statues. Passersby approached it like it was a rare unicorn sighting—completely unexpected in the urban jungle of Manhattan. Eve, who had inherited it from her stepfather, Zev, simply called it home.

Inside, she had created a work-life space. One where she could work with her team downstairs, in offices outfitted with state-of-the-art technology—or, alternately, escape them altogether on the top floor, where she maintained private living quarters.

That was where she retreated now to take a fast shower. A cake of Swedish salt soap transported her to the sea, and coconut-scented shampoo erased all remaining traces of Tony Falcon. Manipulating people was sometimes part of the job. The fact that she was good at it didn't make her like it any better.

Then she dried herself with an oversized white plush towel and dressed quickly in her normal clothes. A cashmere sweater. Loose-fitting black slacks. Fashionable shoes with a low heel. She towel-dried her curly hair and didn't bother to straighten it.

At last—she was herself again.

Bach—the German shepherd that she'd also inherited from Zev after his death—waited for her patiently, gazing up at her with adoring brown eyes. Eve still wasn't used to Bach's unwavering, unconditional love, but he had certainly made the last year a lot easier. He never judged her. He slept at the foot of her bed each night, then made sure she got up early each morning. He motivated her to exercise, ate her leftovers, kept her kitchen floor clean of crumbs. And since he was a handsome dog, he was constantly attracting attention, introducing her to new people.

She leaned down to pet Bach and unexpectedly the memory of Zev washed over her. The pain of losing him was sharper whenever a holiday or a birthday approached. She blamed the fact that her efforts to investigate his murder had thus far failed. Without closure, she was still figuring out the best way to deal with the fact that—all these days, weeks, months later—she felt alone.

The dog helped.

Work also helped.

Which was one reason why she went to her office now, Bach trailing close behind. She wanted to make sure no questions had surfaced on the Falcon case; then she'd write up her report. Check on her under-the-radar investigation into Zev's murder—and whether any of her discreet inquiries had returned leads. Anything to avoid focusing on Thanksgiving—though even three floors up, she could smell the aroma from the kitchen. *Her* kitchen, which normally was littered with nothing but cartons of takeout. Today it was filled with the scent of apples and cinnamon and some kind of bread baking. It was mouthwatering—and enough to feed a small army.

Tomorrow, she'd deliver the feast to Saint Agnes and join volunteers who fed the homeless—not only serving them, but also sitting down and eating with them. Zev had explained that it was about making a connection that could last beyond the meal. Frankly, she couldn't see the point. There were so many homeless. Shouldn't the goal be about ending hunger permanently, not just on Thanksgiving Day?

She would be turning thirty-five next month. Half a decade from forty. Maybe it was because she was getting older. Maybe it was because she was still working to survive Zev's death. Suddenly doing things that seemed worthwhile was important. And Zev had believed Saint Agnes's efforts were important, so she would do this in his memory.

Her train of thought fizzled the moment she saw the visitor in her office.

Unwelcome. Sitting awkwardly on her cream sofa, taking in the plants and the view of the Hudson River. Waiting—with a cup of coffee in one hand and his ever-present smartphone in the other.

"Henry, what are you doing here?" she demanded—and felt she had every right to. This was a holiday—and he had invaded her personal workspace. It didn't matter that Henry Ma, the assistant director in charge of the New York FBI office, was technically her boss.

He took off his glasses and rubbed his eyes. "Sorry if I startled you."

"You didn't startle me. But really, Henry—don't you have someplace better to be the afternoon before Thanksgiving?"

They both ignored the fact that he probably didn't. As a matter of principle, Eve never asked about Henry's private life. But she'd seen the transformation over the past year: He'd put on at least thirty pounds, his crisp-ironed shirts had become crumpled, his wedding ring had disappeared from his finger, and most nights he stayed late at the office.

"I need a favor," he began.

"It's the day before Thanksgiving," she repeated firmly. "You should have phoned first."

But that was never Henry's style. Just like he would never offer a word of gratitude for the Falcon bust, even though the art thief's arrest had eluded scores of other agents for months. Henry was an "I" guy. A political schemer who had already moved on to his next challenge, looking for—and taking—any conceivable advantage. It was the strategy that had led him to one plum assignment after another—and now, finally, a corner office at 26 Federal Plaza.

Eve, on the other hand, had never learned how to play the game. She was superb at her job but bad at office politics, so her career shot up and down in perfect alignment with her failures and successes. She certainly hadn't developed the Bureau allies who would protect her no matter what.

But recent successes—and her inheritance from Zev—had given her both security and freedom from the bureaucratic bullshit. She'd moved her work out of their former office in the basement of Federal Plaza to this house on Riverside Drive that had once served as a CIA command center. It made perfect sense, given the top-secret and unconventional nature of her unit. And Henry hated the arrangement, because it made her less dependent on him.

"I didn't bother calling," he said wearily, "because I need you to come with me."

"It's Thanksgiving," she repeated. "I'm busy."

Henry looked up in surprise. "You're not cooking."

"I'm supervising a feast."

"You rarely socialize."

"I mind my own business. You ought to try it," Eve said tartly. She was not in the mood to get into any of this right now. Besides, she'd had a few relationships in recent months. No matter that they'd lasted a few weeks at most—or that she'd ended each before it really started. Entanglements got in the way of her work; she accepted that now. She wasn't like other women who felt supported in a relationship; she only felt dragged down. *Because of her job?* she wondered. *Or was it that fierce independence that made her so good at her job?*

She wasn't sure she knew—or cared. The gift of being half a decade from forty was that she no longer felt a need to apologize for the way she lived her life.

"You heard what happened this afternoon at the balloon inflation ceremony?"

"It was all over the news," she replied warily. "Hard to miss. I also saw the report saying it was just a paint gun—and the commissioner is unhurt."

"That's only partly true. Mo called me. She's got concerns."

That meant Maureen Kelly, the newest mayor of New York City. Eve had yet to meet her, but she knew her by reputation: a brash woman with the kind of take-no-prisoners attitude that didn't win her many supporters down at City Hall. The city loved her.

"Concerns about the commissioner," Eve hazarded, "or about the parade?"

"Both. You know how important the parade is to this city, Eve. It has to go forward tomorrow without a hitch."

Eve studied Henry's face. "That sounds like something Mayor Kelly and the commissioner can handle. Not sure how we come in."

"The commissioner is not himself," Henry insisted calmly. "But he's too popular to remove from duty. Deputy Commissioner Kepler is doing what he can to mitigate potential damage. You come in because of the commissioner's daughter. It seems the girl disappeared in the aftermath of the shooting. The commissioner isn't particularly worried; apparently, she's run off before. But someone should be looking out for her interests, as the commissioner won't—or can't. Since Donovan's like the proverbial captain who won't abandon his ship, Mo, George, and I decided a more unorthodox approach is needed."

"Vidocq," Eve said flatly.

"Exactly."

"So are you asking my team to find the commissioner's daughter? Or to confirm her disappearance is unrelated to the parade?"

"I won't lie to you. It's probably a little of both."

Eve opened her mouth to say something she probably shouldn't— and was saved when her cellphone trilled.

She answered. Listened.

"Eve," Henry continued over her phone call, "I know you take pleasure in challenging me at every opportunity, but you really don't have a choice this time. I've got a car waiting to take us to the parade's staging ground."

She slipped her cell in her bag and grabbed her coat. "That was one of my guys." Her smile was merely polite. "Turns out I'm desperately needed at the Museum of Natural History—for reasons of my own. Guess your ride will be faster than hailing a cab."

CLASSIFIED

## VIDOCQ FILE #W19767588

## Current status: ACTIVE

**Henry Ma**

Age: 56
Race/Ethnicity: Asian (Chinese American)
Height: 5'9"
Weight: 211 lbs.
Eyes: Brown
Hair: Black

**Current Address:** 152 Hester Street (Chinatown).
**Criminal Record:** None.
**Expertise:** Behavioral analyst.
**Education:** Georgetown University, B.S.

**Personal**

**Family:** Daughter Julie, age 15. His large family—including four brothers, one sister, and nine cousins—still resides in Hunan, China.

**Spouse/Significant Other:** Divorced from wife, Caroline, following twenty-seven-year marriage.

**Religion:** Active member, First Chinese Presbyterian Church.

**Interests:** Deep knowledge of modern Chinese history. Model train enthusiast.

**Profile**

**Strengths:** A political animal always seeking out the next opportunity or promotion. Succeeds because his ambition is backed up by his ability: He's adept at solving complex scenarios, always thinking multiple steps ahead. Can be relied on to execute, even in the most difficult situations.

**Weaknesses:** Inspires little loyalty in those he supervises because he shows them none. He treats them as pawns in the larger game that he plays—and should he find himself back in the field, he will discover few allies willing to support him.

**Background:** Entered duty as a special agent with the FBI in 1981. After completing training at the FBI Academy in Quantico, VA, he was assigned to the Los Angeles division, where he investigated organized crime, drugs, money laundering, and gang matters. In 2001, he returned to FBI HQ as assistant special agent in charge of the FBI Critical Incident Response Group, National Center for the Analysis of Violent Crime. Henry joined the New York Division in 2009, serving as head of the Vidocq Team until his promotion in 2010 to assistant director in charge.

*\*Assessment prepared by Special Agent in Charge Paul Bruin. For internal use only.*

*NEWS NEWS NEWS NEWS NEWS*

## WJXZ REPORTS

This is WJXZ News with Gwen Allensen, reporting from the parade staging area at the American Museum of Natural History. Right now, I'm talking with Deputy Commissioner George Kepler.

*GWEN:* Deputy Commissioner, is there a real concern that more violent protests like today's may endanger the parade?

*KEPLER:* This city and the NYPD will not tolerate, under any circumstances, efforts to disrupt the Macy's Thanksgiving Day Parade. This is a national event of historic proportions—not to mention a special family day that kids of all ages enjoy. I'm here to reassure the public that they should come on down and trust that New York's Finest are going to ensure their safety.

*GWEN:* I understand a number of arrests have been made?

*KEPLER:* Yes. Most have been charged with disorderly conduct or unlawful assembly. I'm also pleased to report that we've arrested one of the ringleaders responsible for the attack on the commissioner himself. His name is Brock Olsen, a well-known radical anti-police activist from New Jersey. Since this is an ongoing investigation, no further details are available.

# Chapter 10

Parade Staging Area—West 77th to West 81st Street

Central Park West was empty except for the police and a team of Macy's balloon handlers, who were attempting to patch Spider-Man's puncture wound. The balloons would still inflate. The parade would go on.

It had to—because it was too important to New York City. Sure, it ushered in the holiday season and plenty of tourist dollars. But it also symbolized something magical—something larger even than the city itself. Donovan loved being part of that.

For now, the crowds had been sent home—giving him a few hours to regroup and reorganize the troops. He had pulled in an extra eight hundred officers from counterterrorism-related units. Nothing reassured the public like seeing boots on the ground, ready to serve and protect. He would station officers from his elite Emergency Service Unit along the parade route in full uniform—and on its periphery in plainclothes. The air would be filled with not just Snoopy and Spider-Man, but police cameras and helicopters. This would boost the morale of his own officers as well.

*What was he going to do about Allie?*

A mixture of rain and sleet poured down. Guilt and anger darkened the commissioner's thoughts. He needed to focus. Too much—specifically, three and a half million lives—was at stake. Not to mention his own reputation, as fifty million eyes watched live from the safety of their living rooms.

Allie still didn't pick up her cellphone. She'd not been in touch with Jackie or Sam. Damn it: While she'd always turned up later, safe and sound, right now he didn't have time to wait.

*Where could she have gone?*

In the past, she had run to the Egyptian room at the Met. Once, to the old FAO Schwarz on Fifth Avenue. A bench at Riverside Park with a view of the river.

It was a matter of figuring out what she liked: what sort of places appealed to her *this* week. As opposed to last week or last month.

*Has Gwen noticed?* Keenly observant, little was lost on her.

He saw her by the WJXZ News van, interviewing a crew of Macy's workers. From the edges of their conversation, he gathered they had successfully cleaned Molly the Mongoose of the offending paint that had sprayed the balloon when he was shot. Next up was an officer who handled specially trained police dogs.

Gwen's voice was sweet as honey when she called out, "Commissioner, do you have a moment to tell our viewers about the different kinds of security measures in place to ensure everyone's safety during tomorrow's Thanksgiving Day Parade?"

*Damn. No time for this.*

Donovan had never been a patient man, but he was a charmer—and he knew it was the key to his success. All he needed to do was offer the camera a few polite words and his trademark smile—which was not a politician's Cheshire Cat grin but one that put everyone around him at ease. "People should know they're in good hands with Officer Colecchia and his specially trained partner Caesar on the job," Donovan explained, indicating the eighty-pound German shepherd at his side. "Colecchia's a sixteen-year veteran of the force, and he's been partnered with Caesar for the past seven."

It was a gift to be able to remember details like that. Most people couldn't—and it impressed the hell out of them that Donovan kept such facts at his fingertips. He decided that, despite the lost time, this second interview had been a godsend. Mo now had zero ammunition to oust him. He defied her—or anyone—to claim that he was unfit for duty.

After giving a few more sound bites for the camera, he scrambled back onto the street. He would check in with Gwen later. He planned to devote the next half-hour to locating Allie and sending her straight home. That should be sufficient; then he'd be free to devote one hundred percent of his efforts to his officers and his city.

His only child had always been a mystery to him. But he'd better figure out how to find her. *Now.*

Desperation seemed to thicken his words as he yelled at a group of cops, asking if they'd seen his daughter. He felt a flash of anger when they responded only with questions and confused looks.

When he neared Eighty-first Street, he saw a senior detective he recognized. He and John Williams had gone through training at the Academy together. They had been drinking buddies ever since.

"John! Got a sec?"

"You okay, Chief?"

He wished the damn noise in his ears would stop. "My daughter's missing. I can't find anyone who's seen her since . . ." He found he couldn't finish the sentence. *Since I began my speech. Since I got shot with paint. Since I got this damned concussion and started hearing things.* None of these were facts he wanted to dwell on.

"Slow down and start from the beginning," John urged, his voice laced with concern.

Donovan's ears were ringing and his body was shaking and he felt dizzy. His words tumbled out faster than he wanted—but he managed to explain it all.

"So did you finish reviewing all the video footage?" John asked.

God, he was such an idiot. Maybe the paint gunshot actually had messed up his brain. "I got interrupted."

"They're adding more footage, all the time, as they recover it. They're looking for more evidence on the rioters."

Donovan didn't wait for John to finish. He ran into the Homeland Security tent and commandeered a laptop. Opened the NYPD system.

Typed in his passcode. Waited.

Six seconds later, he was rewarded.

Three new amateur videos of his aborted speech had been uploaded. Two were useless. But the third showed his daughter.

It had been taken by someone standing almost immediately be-hind Allie. It showed her standing. Then being swept into the crowd.

The crowds seemed to half carry, half push her toward the en-trance for the B and C subway lines.

At the last second, Allie was near a man in a yellow raincoat. A *Macy's* raincoat. Was she *with* him? Was he embracing her? Carrying her? It almost seemed that way—before the two figures disappeared belowground. Lost in the throng.

Stunned, Donovan asked aloud, "Am I seeing straight?"

Nobody was listening. He took off running until he reached the very spot.

He glanced around. First left. Then right.

Searching.

Almost believing that any moment Allie would be visible, legs moving fast, a bright spot of purple raincoat on a dreary, dull day.

Had the man in the yellow coat been helping her? Had she simply gotten caught up in the general panicked exodus? Was she lost now, aimlessly riding the subway rails? Because she knew nothing about the subway. For security purposes, he'd hired Sam to drive her when she traveled in the city.

He raced down the subway steps, two at a time. When he reached the uptown platform, he saw one of his captains trudging toward him. Taking annoyingly slow steps.

*Gonzales.* That detective seemed to put on more weight every year. He also wore his hair a little too long, just above his ears—and forgot to shave, at least twice a week. Donovan had begun to suspect this was all a sign of trouble at home.

"HAVE YOU SEEN ALLIE?" Donovan asked him. "I saw video footage of her; she was headed down here."

Gonzales cringed.

A dead end. Donovan started toward the stairs to the downtown platform.

"Chief!" Gonzales stepped in front of him. Holding something in his hands. An offering.

*A phone.*

"WHAT?" He was still talking too loud. He needed to fix that.

"We found it under a bench on the downtown platform, Chief."

Not just a phone. *Allie's* phone. Impossible to mistake her iPhone, in its pink case with purple hearts.

Equally impossible to imagine Allie without it. Her iPhone was permanently attached to her body. Like a second skin.

"WHERE?" Donovan demanded. "I need to see," he added, more softly. He could barely make out his words over the ringing, but this time Gonzales didn't wince.

"Down the stairs. Under the last bench."

Donovan stalked toward the spot. What was her code again? She used Tolkien's birthdate. He'd have to Google it.

Turned out he didn't need it. Allie's passcode had been turned off.

And the moment he pressed the power button, he saw: The picture was wrong.

This wasn't Allie's usual home screen. It wasn't the brilliant rainbow she'd photographed their last vacation on the Cape.

It was Allie herself—looking small and frightened and wet, her hands bound together in front of her with plastic zip ties.

But the picture wasn't the only thing that made Donovan's heart wedge in his throat.

There was a message that read: *How far will you go to save her?*

He sucked in his breath. If this was one of Allie's wild stunts—just a play for sympathy and attention—then it was far more elaborate than anything she'd done before.

Then he focused on the numbers. Under the current day/time stamp—superimposed right above Allie's head—another clock was counting down fast. It read *18 hours, 12 minutes, 53 seconds*. Then *52, 51, 50 . . .*

*Is this real?*

He did the math in his head. That was noon tomorrow. When the parade was supposed to end.

*45, 44, 43 . . .*

A ticking clock.

# Chapter 11

## American Museum of Natural History

Eve Rossi stood in the rotunda of the American Museum of Natural History and let her eyes drift up to the south mural—the one illustrating how Teddy Roosevelt had negotiated the treaty that ended the Russo-Japanese War.

Roosevelt had won the Nobel Peace Prize because of it.

But the man she'd been observing—a police captain—wasn't going to earn any prizes. This man was a bully; she saw it in his body language. It was clear from the way he swung his arms, like he wished he could throw a punch instead of a question. It was signaled by the rise of his blood pressure, which had settled in his hot, flushed cheeks.

He was also a poor interrogator. He was questioning a group of men—her own agent among them. Rounded up as a suspect in firing the paint gun that had injured Commissioner Logan Donovan earlier that afternoon. He was also moving too fast, taking no time to observe. He hadn't learned that getting information from people wasn't a test of wills—or even a matter of intimidation. You had to be smart about it—which involved much more than words. People revealed themselves in hundreds of different ways. Hands. Eyes. Gestures. Expressions. Movements.

It was even easier when they were in trouble. Because then you could see what frightened them. Nothing laid human motives bare more effectively than fear.

She wished she didn't have to deal with the bully. She'd prefer to simply show her badge, flash some paperwork, retrieve her agent, and go. Normally it wouldn't be an issue. In this post-9/11 world, the FBI and NYPD coordinated and cooperated and basically got along.

Except tomorrow was the Macy's Thanksgiving Day Parade, long the province of the NYPD alone. They would not welcome involvement smacking of interference. Especially not from the FBI.

She squared her shoulders and walked over to the officer.

"Excuse me, Captain—I'm Special Agent Eve Rossi."

He glanced at her badge and ID before eyeing her suspiciously. "Captain McDonnell. What do you want?"

Mace was on his feet, ready to go. She shot him a warning glance. *Don't screw this up.*

He sat back on the bench.

"I've come for Julius Mason. He's with me," she said.

"He's staying right here. I haven't questioned him yet." Irritation sparked in McDonnell's voice.

"If you need a statement, I'll be sure he provides one. But he's not the man you're looking for."

"It's our jurisdiction. He stays. I question him."

"Not this time. He's FBI." Eve kept her tone reasonable. Conveying with her words and her tone: *This isn't personal. Nothing to do with me or you. It's just business.*

McDonnell cackled like she'd just said something funny. "Maybe you got your paperwork mixed up, Special Agent. 'Cause I've got this guy's rap sheet right here." He tapped on his clipboard. "Almost didn't have enough paper in the mobile fax for this baby. It's at least two miles long."

Eve nodded. This one couldn't really be explained. Not to someone without a top security clearance.

Her team of ex-convicts was unique. Unusual.

What was she supposed to say to this beat cop with no imagination?

That Julius Mason was part of a team that was the brainchild of the FBI, dreamed up shortly after the First World War? A secret unit that was created after the model of Eugène Vidocq—one of France's most notorious late-eighteenth-century criminals, who had been convinced to use his considerable talents working *for* the police, not against them?

That now the FBI's Vidocq team brought together a group of ex-cons—men and women with extraordinary talents—who could solve crimes using methods that ordinary agents never could?

That they had joined the good guys based on a choice that wasn't much of a choice: put their skills to work for the government—or do hard time in jail?

*Right.* McDonnell was just the type to sign off on that.

Once upon a time, Eve had felt completely unsuited to lead her team of ex-cons and barely reformed thugs. She'd believed she had absolutely nothing in common with them.

Then they'd worked a handful of cases together, and she'd figured it out: She wasn't suited for anything else. They were extraordinarily talented, unpredictable, and strangely loyal. They were also her responsibility.

McDonnell's face twisted into a grimace. "You aren't joking, are you?"

"I'm not."

He poked his clipboard. "I've got cops testifying he was on the street. Just blocks away from the hit."

"Did you ask him what he was doing?"

He ignored her question. "He's the right height and the right weight. He's wearing the right clothes. He was carrying a gun."

"He was in the area on official FBI business. And I have his license to carry right here." She pulled the paperwork out of her bag.

McDonnell's face contorted with a tic, and his cheeks went from flushed to bright red. "You don't have the authority to take him—"

She cut him off. "With all due respect, Captain, I assure you that I do."

His clipboard flew into the air. Eve didn't know if he'd launched it intentionally or simply let it slip from his waving arms. She didn't really care.

Mace caught it like it was a pass. "Please tell me we're done with this bull—"

She froze him mid-sentence with another look. Returned the clipboard to McDonnell. "I'll sign whatever you need," she said calmly. "I take full responsibility."

"You want to take Julius Mason out of here? Fine. But I need to protect myself. Before you can do it, I want *my* boss's authorization. The commissioner's right over there."

*Henry's favor.*

Eve saw him immediately. He had just entered the museum and was hunched over a cellphone, conferring with one of his deputies. Donovan's figure still gave her a sense of his immense physical size—as well as the extent of the stress he must be under. She had remembered that he was a tall man—but when she'd last seen him, almost a year ago, he had been at least forty pounds heavier. It had been a tough year; his department had been embroiled in a series of ugly cases. Numerous cases of excessive force. Too many unarmed suspects shot by cops.

And was there something else? Yes . . . he was widowed now. She'd read an article blaming the NYPD's recent issues on his own personal losses. The media could be cruel.

But he would recover. He was young for the job—mid-fifties—and he was a climber. Every time she had seen him, she had noticed his confidence, ambition, and charm. A combination of traits that, frankly, she had never trusted. Ambition and confidence often led to bad choices. Too much charm covered up mistakes.

The commissioner turned and Eve caught sight of his face, still faintly streaked with red paint. She noted his rage and desperation—and also the way the officer next to him cringed when the commissioner spoke.

"Yeah," McDonnell repeated. "I won't let your man go without an okay from the top cop himself."

# Chapter 12

## American Museum of Natural History

"Commissioner Donovan?" Eve asked, splashing into his path just as he exited the museum. She got a whiff of the chemical stink coming from his hair and face—from the paint that he'd yet to wash off.

He barely acknowledged her with a half-nod. Then he paused and stared at her like he could almost place her—but not quite.

He had a once-busted nose that had healed slightly crooked. Eve found herself thinking that—along with the paint—it created a welcome anomaly to his pretty-boy look. If anything, it made him more interesting.

"My name is Special Agent Eve Rossi. We've met once before, briefly." She held out her hand—a gesture that he ignored, brushing past her.

Not completely out of rudeness, Eve decided. He was obviously preoccupied. "I need to speak with you, Commissioner. It's important."

"Sorry, I'm busy right now." He kept moving. The paint in his hair started running again, mingling with the rain. He pushed it away from his forehead, creating a shower of red.

"I only need thirty seconds." She flashed her badge. "As I said, Special Agent Rossi. FBI. You're holding a member of my team without cause. Your captain insists on your personal authorization before letting him go."

"My captain's not in a position to insist I do anything. Now, I've got work to do."

"He's *your* captain, not mine. I just want the man you're hold-ing." She shoved McDonnell's clipboard with the paperwork in front of him. "Won't take you more than a minute."

He brushed it aside, then turned to face her. "Guess you didn't hear me the first time. Elvis has left the building. Now *get out of my way.*"

He was very nearly shouting. Fully agitated, moving his hands from his hips to his shirt pockets. "Are you all right?" Eve demanded.

"Debatable, but none of your concern. Goodbye, Ms. Rossi."

*Ms.*, *not Agent or Special Agent.* Annoyance surged through her.

He was obviously used to giving orders, always getting his way. She thought of what Henry had told her—and decided to shake his confidence. "Guess this is why your friends are talking. Worried that you're distracted and unfit for duty."

That got his attention. He glared at her. "My *friends* know the truth—not to mention how to mind their own business. Unlike you." There was not even a trace of the charm Logan Donovan was famous for. He was ice cold and ruthlessly determined. "I don't do paper-work. Even if I had the time."

"I came to get my man out—and that's what I intend to do." Eve didn't like being disrespected by men who believed they owned the world.

"Listen, lady—you need help, call Saint Jude or something. Now get out of my way."

"Saint Jude? You make it sound like a lost cause, Commissioner," she said quietly. "Of course, if you're not interested, maybe one of those news crews will be."

He turned—and she watched as recognition washed over him. "I remember you," he said, his voice husky. "From the crisis at Saint Patrick's. You picked apart the hostage taker's motives, tunneled deep inside that bastard's mind." He was now seeing her for the first time—and his eyes locked onto her own. "I liked that about you."

There was no sarcasm in his tone, but Eve knew better than to as-sume he was being sincere. Still, his eyes had just sparked alive, like a firefly on a dark summer night.

He studied her face with an intensity that surprised her. "I saw your team in action at the Cathedral. You were fast and nimble. You cut through the red tape, ignored the bullshit."

"Exactly what I'm trying to do now, Commissioner." She offered the clipboard again, like a peace offering.

"You're just the one to help me! You can find my missing daughter. She disappeared this afternoon."

"Sign my man out and I'll give you some free advice about your daughter."

"I don't want your advice. I want you to find her."

"Because you think she ran off."

"Not anymore. And I need help. You have to understand: I have a city to protect, not to mention thousands of police officers who are the target of a specific threat during this parade."

"It would make sense if she ran off. Maybe she saw you get shot. Maybe she got mad when she noticed the bright pink lipstick on the left side of your mouth. Right now, it blends with the red paint, but it must've stood out earlier. You're a grown man, and I'm sure you're lonely now that your wife is gone, but possibly your daughter's not ready to see you with another woman." Eve kept her last point short and businesslike.

He stepped away from her. "What the hell?"

"I'm good at figuring things out about people." She continued to hold the clipboard. Waited.

He shook his head. "It's settled. You're the perfect person to find my daughter." He reached for the paperwork, scrawled his signature hastily.

"You have almost thirty-five thousand NYPD officers at your disposal."

"Thirty-five thousand NYPD officers with jobs to do. I want you to do *this* job for me. Together with your man inside, who's now free to help you." He gave her a crooked smile. "I'm sorry we got off to a bad start," he apologized. "It's been a helluva day."

She took the paperwork back, saying nothing. The commissioner had just decided that he wanted something, and his instinctive behavior had defaulted to charm. She knew it was in his nature to flatter—the better to win friends and stymie his enemies.

"I understand, of course," she said. "But—"

"Please do this for me. For my daughter. Her name is Allie. She's thirteen. She was last seen in the chaos after I was shot."

That was the moment she made the mistake of looking into his eyes. They were a deep blue and filled with something that impressed Eve in spite of herself: a mix of empathy and sadness. The kind that came from having seen the frailty and flaws of too many people. From having survived failure and loss. From having *lived*. And the only other man she'd ever known to register such depth of understanding was her stepfather, Zev.

"You must already have officers searching," she managed to say. "Interviewing eyewitnesses. Screening video. Calling her friends."

"I want it done outside the department. Nothing can jeopardize my focus—or that of my people—on tomorrow's parade. That has to be my priority." He balled his hands into fists. "I'm no Superman. Right now, I can't be both a father to Allie and the police commissioner this city needs. If I focus on Allie, I risk giving in to worry and panic—and being no good to anyone. The only choice I can make is to do what nobody except me can do: Protect this city. Which is why you have to help me."

Eve noted the set of his jaw and the flash in his eye. She knew she was witnessing the side of him that charged the hill no matter the obstacle. That never took *no* for an answer. The side of him that had made him a leader—but earned him no small number of enemies along the way. That strength, too, reminded her of Zev. "You believe she's been kidnapped. Have you received a ransom call?"

"No. I've got proof of life. And—a virtual ticking clock." He fished a phone out of his pocket. It had a pink case with purple hearts and a jagged scratch across the front. "It doesn't really look like my daughter. I mean, it does—but . . . you know."

Eve studied the photo of the frightened, wet girl that was the lock screen.

Took in the message. *How far will you go to save her?*

Took in the timer above the girl's head: *17 hours, 48 minutes, 23 seconds.*

She did the mental math quickly. "Your ticking clock: It's a countdown to the parade's finish."

"I've sworn to protect the millions of people who are coming to the parade; I'm obligated to protect my fellow officers. This is my professional duty. Will you help with my personal duty—and protect just the one?"

The dark blue eyes challenged her.

*Damn him*—but he was right. She couldn't say no when a girl's life was at risk.

Besides, she had dealt with plenty of powerhouse types over the years. She would do her job, find the child—and make sure Commissioner Logan Donovan kept his distance.

# Chapter 13

## Gramercy Park District

The rain that had been teeming all day soaked the city. Corey Haddox stood outside Durty Nelly's, cupped his hands over his lighter—waited 'til it sparked—and lit up a Marlboro Red. He thought for the umpteenth time how ridiculous it was that the city smoking ban applied to the kind of Irish watering hole that billed itself as a *shebeen*. His mouthwatering dinner was going to go cold. All because he so desperately needed this smoke.

He'd spent the first half of the day recovering from the mother of all hangovers, trying to deaden the darts of agony that shot through his head. First he'd tried plenty of Tylenol and water. Now he'd moved on to cigarettes, booze, and what passed in his life for a home-cooked meal.

He examined the bandage on his left thumb. It had been expertly applied—but he only vaguely remembered the injury beneath it. Just like he didn't quite remember the woman he'd suffered it for.

*Her name is . . . Janie? No. Jennifer? Not quite.*

*Jenna.* She'd been at a bar in the East Village with some bloke who claimed to be her boyfriend. Haddox hadn't particularly wanted to get involved. He believed in the principles of *keep your nose clean* and *mind your own business.* But Jenna looked barely of legal age. And a lass that young didn't deserve to be mistreated.

It was always some version of the same old story. Same plot. Same characters. An utterly predictable ending.

*Time to get out of here,* he decided. But not 'til he enjoyed the hot meal waiting for him inside.

His phone buzzed three times before he answered it. The caller ID was blocked—but only a couple people had the number to this cell line. It was a burner that he'd purchased only thirty-six hours ago at an electronics shop in the Twelfth Arrondissement, shortly before hopping back on a plane to New York. His motto was "one and done." Every day or two, depending on usage, he recycled his throwaway phone with a temporary, anonymous number. It was a way of life for drug dealers, mobsters, and anyone who resisted having their movements tracked by Big Brother. Which more or less described Corey Haddox to a T.

He calculated the odds and decided that his caller must be Eve. So he hesitated only a split second before answering, "Knew you'd miss me, luv."

"Welcome back," she replied lightly, "but I'm not your *luv*. As much as I appreciate your great work on Falcon. I gather all his French associates are now in custody as well?"

"Together with about twenty million dollars' worth of art treasures." Haddox blew a puff of smoke; it floated above his eyes.

"I know I said after this case wrapped, you'd have a free pass—but something's come up."

"Something *always* comes up."

"In the mood to visit the natural history museum?"

"Nope. Don't care for old bones."

"This one involves a missing kid, a tampered iPhone, and a parade. I need your help."

"Then say it like you mean it, luv. Because nobody can track down people like me." Haddox knew he sounded arrogant, but it was true. Sometimes he found out people's secrets by using his considerable charm; other times he used his technological skills and hacked into their private lives. He was the expert when it came to gathering information.

Her silence was meant to be neutral, but he could tell she was struggling to overcome her exasperation. He heard a sigh, then a reluctant "Nobody can track down people like you."

"That's why you can't live without me."

"Haddox," she warned.

He shrugged. "Had to try. So one more case."

"One more case."

"That's it."

"Unless you want more."

"Isn't it *you* who doesn't want more? Which I still don't get. We're good together. Pretty feckin' amazing, in fact. And when something happens that's great, *usually* people want to repeat it."

"We've had this conversation before."

"And we'll keep having it until I understand it." Haddox took a long, final draw on his smoke—and then ground it under his heel and pushed open the door to the pub. "Imagine you've had a glass of wine that's just brilliant. I'm saying it's so good it will blow your mind. The waiter asks if you'd like another glass. *Most* people would say yes."

He took his seat at the bar. His eyes searched the pub's cabinlike interior for his favorite waitress—Colleen, the stunner of a redhead who normally took care of him. She was nowhere to be found.

"Always a flip side to the coin," Eve said. "Sometimes you experience something spectacular: maybe that same wine, but from a different bottle. It's never quite the same. Experiences are diminished when they're repeated. That's why they're called once-in-a-lifetime. So you can remember them, perfect and untainted."

Colleen burst out of the kitchen; Haddox flashed her a smile and motioned for another Guinness. "Thank goodness for Guinness. Perfection each and every pour."

Eve's sigh was exasperated. "There's this guy I know. He's not like anybody I've ever met. Basically lives in his own version of reality. It's about as real as the bits and bytes he hacks into."

"*My* version of reality? You say it like there's some other kind. You know something else I don't get? You're searching for Zev's killer, but you won't accept my help."

"Maybe I don't need your help."

"Maybe you need me—and that's what scares you." Colleen set his pint of Guinness in front of him. "This is grand, luv." He appreciated how the head rose just proud of the rim.

Haddox took a sip, then said to Eve, "So tell me about this case."

So Eve told him. About the commissioner and the balloon

inflation–turned–flash mob. About Allie Donovan and the grainy film footage and the phone.

Haddox didn't say anything. For several moments, he stared at Colleen—who was all smiles for him—and pushed his shepherd's pie around with his fork. He almost asked Colleen what time she finished work.

He didn't. He couldn't resist Eve's invitation. Because the case was intriguing—and there was always the chance of twice-in-a-lifetime. So he told her, "I'll be there in thirty."

"Make it twenty," she replied.

"You ever see the Eiffel Tower at night?"

"Sure."

Haddox stretched his legs over the side of the barstool and threw on his waxed Barbour rain jacket, pushing his brand-new pint of Guinness and barely eaten serving of shepherd's pie to the side. He didn't mind giving up the pie; he wasn't that hungry and he'd been craving another smoke, anyhow. But it was always a shame not to finish a decent stout.

"The metal lady twinkles every half-hour with over twenty thousand bulbs and what they call fairy lights," Haddox told Eve. "I must've seen it over a hundred nights. Still gets me every time."

**VIDOCQ FILE #Z77519**

**Current status: INDEPENDENT CONTRACTOR**

**Corey Haddox**

Age: 39
Race/Ethnicity: Caucasian/Irish
Height: 6'1"
Weight: 178 lbs.
Eyes: Blue
Hair: Brown
Prominent features: cleft chin

**Current Address:** Unknown.
**Criminal Record:** Convicted under the Gramm-Leach-Bliley Act of multiple counts of computer hacking, bank record pretexting, and identity theft. Sentence: twenty-five years.

*Related: Though never charged, Haddox was suspected of killing his brother-in-law—a habitual drunk, wife-abuser, and leader of the splinter paramilitary Real IRA (RIRA). In retaliation, the RIRA has issued a death warrant for Haddox in Ireland.*

**Expertise:** A rare talent in the world of computer hackers. Combines personal charisma with cyber-genius to become the ultimate skip tracer and con artist.
**Education:** Trinity College, Dublin, B.Sc. (honors), Information Systems.

**Personal**

> **Family:** Father, Duncan (in Dublin nursing home with multiple ailments), and sister, Mary. Mother, Emily, deceased.
> **Spouse/Significant Other:** None. Commitment issues.
> **Religion:** Catholic, lapsed.
> **Interests:** When not immersed in the cyberworld, plays guitar with whatever Celtic blues band he can find.

**Profile**

> **Strengths:** Motivated by the need to expose hidden secrets and codes—the more complex, the better. Follows the thrill of the chase, which takes him job to job and place to place.
> **Weaknesses:** Unpredictable. He resists being pinned down to anyone or anything. Deep-seated fear of flying.
> **Notes:** Haddox is extremely comfortable in his own skin and extraordinarily perceptive. He cannot be motivated through traditional means. He'll be more likely to stay in the game if he's kept off-balance.

*\*Assessment prepared by SA Eve Rossi. For internal use only.*

# Chapter 14

350 Riverside Drive, Vidocq Headquarters

Eli Cohen's stomach didn't growl so much as it groaned. He was at his computer in the back parlor office, desperately trying to focus. First, he sat up straighter—though his chair squeaked in protest under his weight, which was now an embarrassing sixty-five pounds greater than his doctor preferred. Then he took a great gulp of piping-hot coffee from his mug—scalding his tongue, causing him to dribble down his perpetually stained denim shirt. Finally, he concentrated hard on the task at hand.

*The money.*

Eve's takedown, Tony Falcon, was a skilled thief, but he was even more adept at unloading his bounty. He'd sold a Picasso last month for five million dollars at nearly fifty percent of its auction value. That was no small feat when the typical black-market price of a stolen piece was capped at ten percent.

Normally Eli would've been in the zone, thanks to his obsession with finances. It wasn't only that he liked tracking the ins, outs, and potential hiding spots of the U.S. dollar—though he did find the process kind of like a kid's scavenger hunt. And like any kid, he enjoyed a fun and challenging game.

But in a world where everyone constantly lied, there was truth in that old adage: *Put your money where your mouth is.*

When Eli was a boy, his grandma had told him that his education was the greatest gift she could give him. Other kids got toys and vacations. Not Eli. And he noticed.

But he also noticed how, after his father died, his grandma had worked two different jobs with long shifts—and that every penny that didn't go to food or rent went to making sure he stayed in school and went to college.

Viewed this way, money was more than a science of the mind. It was the ultimate polygraph test—where individual choices spoke volumes about behavior, values, and truth.

In other words, people might lie with their lips but not with their wallets.

So what did Falcon's money trail reveal about him? Eli was very close to knowing. But he hadn't nailed it yet.

Not with the distraction from the mouthwatering aromas wafting out of the kitchen downstairs. *Pumpkin. Spiced apples. Sausage. A hint of sage.* His stomach growled again.

He shut his computer—followed the aroma straight down to the kitchen at 350 Riverside Drive—and stopped short.

Eli could've said that was because the smells were so intoxicating.

Or that his stomach was now in outright revolt.

But in reality, the moment he saw the chef, he felt his knees go shaky and his words stick in his throat. The man was young, right about thirty, with platinum hair spiked up in all directions and tattoos running down his arms. He wore a black T-shirt and jeans under his apron—and he wasn't moving so much as he was practically bounding across the large stainless-steel kitchen. He noticed Eli, but it didn't matter. He was enjoying himself too much to stop.

"Want to try?" He pointed to a tray of sausage-and-apple stuffing.

The man's voice was a little high-pitched. It wasn't what Eli expected—but he quickly decided that he liked it.

"Sure." Eli could hardly get the word out. He felt like such a schoolgirl.

"My name's Tyler Whitt. Friends call me Ty." He grabbed a fork and lifted the tray, revealing biceps that advertised his regular dates with the weight room.

"I'm Eli." He noted Ty's long fingers. Clean, scented with a potpourri of spices. Eli took the fork, poked it into the highest corner, where hopefully nobody would notice a missing bite. "What's in this?"

"A fresh baguette. Apples, sausage, and celery—a little sage, bound together by eggs and cream. A savory bread pudding."

Eli managed to bring the heaping fork to his mouth without dropping any morsels. Let the flavors come together. Closed his eyes. "Hands down. Best stuffing I've ever had."

"I'm top of my class at the CIA."

Eli stared, saying nothing. Eve's stepfather, Zev Berger, had spent a long career in the CIA—and this house had served as a secret intelligence outpost until his death last year. When Eve inherited the stone mansion, she had transformed it into a state-of-the-art workspace for her own team.

Part of the government, too. FBI, not CIA. But also secret. Off the books. Not part of the bureaucratic machine at 26 Federal Plaza.

Eli was about to make a comment about Zev, but he must've looked confused because Ty added, "You know: Culinary Institute of America."

*Of course.* Eli felt stupid all over again. Maybe he should just think of a good exit line. Get out of there before he really put his foot in his mouth.

Ty covered the stuffing tray and hoisted it into the air with one hand. Miraculously, it didn't drop. "You live here?"

"I only work here. Though some days, you'd never know the difference." Eli's eyes followed Ty as he stored the tray inside the warming oven.

"So when Eve hired me to cook dinner for a small army, does she have a large family—or am I cooking for all your coworkers?"

"We're not a family—but take it from me, we're just as dysfunctional."

"Your own family doesn't care that you spend Thanksgiving at work?"

"My parents have passed," Eli explained. "Rest of the family's too messed-up to deal with. My sister's married to a real asshole who makes fun of my 'lifestyle choices.' She's got a junkie for a son and they treat me like *I'm* the depraved one in the family. But the small army you're cooking for isn't us. Eve volunteers every year, apparently, for a gathering of the homeless at Saint Agnes. I'd told her I wouldn't join her, but I've changed my mind. It'll be worth it, just to sneak a taste of your food." He fidgeted. "But enough about me; where do you spend Thanksgiving?"

"I usually volunteer down at Saint Matthew's." Ty opened the Sub-Zero, pulled out a bag of potatoes. Dumped them in the kitchen sink.

"Healing through food?" Eli leaned on the center island, popped a stray carrot in his mouth.

Ty shrugged. "Food always makes people feel better—no matter what's wrong. I learned that as a kid."

"Me too." Eli pointed to his belly. "Story of my life." Except now Eli was conscious that he'd just advertised the coffee stain on his shirt.

Ty opened a drawer, found a peeler. "Want to help?"

Eli shook his head. He was all thumbs and didn't want to embarrass himself. "I've got to finish something upstairs. But my grandma would've agreed with you. Every time she wanted to make me feel better, she made potato latkes with applesauce. I've never tasted any better. Crispy. Not too thick."

"Is that a challenge?" Ty shot him a sideways glance.

"If you want it to be. She *always* had latkes at Thanksgiving. Every holiday, in fact—just because I loved them. Much better than mashed potatoes."

"Then I'm going to make latkes to rival your grandma's. Got to find a grater around here. Probably requires a thumbprint to use it." He started opening drawers. "I had to stick my eye in a retina scanner to open the freakin' knife drawer. Everything's buttoned up tighter than Fort Knox. Exactly what kind of business are you running here, anyway?" Ty stared at him curiously.

The answer stuck in Eli's throat. He never knew what to say. And when he got nervous? He talked way too much.

Eli wouldn't have lasted a month in the regular FBI; the bureaucratic machine would almost certainly have chewed him up and spit him out. It still might—if he crossed the line and broke their confidentiality rules. Because this was a clandestine division that gave him freedom—what fancier people called carte blanche. He settled for saying, "It's kinda secret. But the work's not too bad."

Then he hoped that was enough, as he stood there, awkward and tongue-tied.

Ty opened a bottle of wine: an Oregon pinot noir. Eli expected a couple glasses to follow—but, to his dismay, Ty drained half the bottle into the sauté pan and began scraping the sides with a wooden spoon. Then he asked the follow-up question Eli always dreaded. "How do you interview for this secret business?"

Again, Eli had no good answer. *Since I was arrested for insider trading eight years ago? Since I got lucky and was offered a sweetheart of a deal: help the government stalk criminals and get out of jail free?* "Stumbled into it, really," he mumbled.

Ty tilted the half-empty bottle of pinot in the air. "The rest is fuel for the chef. Want some?" Now the glasses came out. One was poured. Offered.

Eli desperately wanted that drink. It would loosen him up. Help keep the conversation moving. But he hadn't finished unraveling Falcon's financial trail. "I'll take a raincheck."

Ty rolled the wine around in its glass. Savored its aroma before taking a drink and returning to the potatoes. "Healing through food," he repeated.

Eli scrambled for something to say next. He wondered if they'd made the connection he'd been hoping for. Sometimes shared values forged friendships. He'd seen it happen.

Just rarely with him. But you never knew. This could be the start of something incredible.

It didn't matter at the moment.

Because Eve was calling to him from the hallway, saying, "Hope you've wrapped up Falcon—because it looks like we've got a brand-new case."

## VIDOCQ FILE #A30888
## Current status: ACTIVE

**Eli Cohen**

Age: 53
Race/Ethnicity: Caucasian
Height: 5'8"
Weight: 237 lbs.
Eyes: Hazel
Hair: Red

**Current Address:** 122A Orchard Street (Lower East Side).
**Criminal Record:** Multiple felony counts for embezzlement, tax evasion, and money laundering. Sentence: thirty-five years.
**Expertise:** Corporate financial systems and the clandestine movement of money.
**Education:**
City University of New York, B.S.
Fordham University, MBA

**Personal**
**Family:** Parents deceased. Estranged from extended family after coming out of the closet in March 1990. Remains in touch with sister, Elaine.
**Spouse/Significant Other:** None.
**Religion:** Nontraditional Jewish, devotee of the mysticisms of Kabbalah.
**Interests:** Comics and fantasy baseball.

**Profile**

> **Strengths:** Enjoys the challenge of deciphering complex financial models.
>
> **Weaknesses:** A loner who doesn't bond well with others. Excessive preoccupation with his health (non-diagnosed hypochondria) compromises his abilities and work habits. History of depression. (In 2010, he was hospitalized for seven weeks following a failed suicide attempt.)
>
> **Notes:** Isolated and misunderstood. Will attach himself to someone who understands him. His fundamental insecurity makes him vulnerable.

*\*Assessment originally prepared by SA Eve Rossi. For internal use only.*

# Chapter 15

## Unknown Location

This was *not* how her afternoon was supposed to go. Allie sat alone, shivering—unable to shake the feeling that things had just spun entirely out of her control.

Now she was stuck: mouth dry and cottony. Absolutely parched with thirst. Feeling like a knife had been thrust into her brain. All thanks to the God-only-knew-what her kidnapper had drugged her with.

She blinked away an image of her dad—shot, falling—and rocked forward, curling her knees to her chin. Her chest heaved with a long, unbroken sob. She couldn't believe that her father was gone. She had never felt so sad—or so alone.

The thought steeled her: *Time to focus.* No one was coming to save her.

She had no memory of her journey to this place. Still, she thought she knew where she was.

She was inside a rock.

The rock had a concrete floor below—and a solitary sixty-watt light dangling above. She thanked God it was the new energy-saving kind that was shaped like a spiral. Mom had bought those at home, and they were guaranteed to last five years. At least she wouldn't have to worry about it burning out.

There was also a door—and the door had a lock.

Allie walked over to it and listened, putting her ear to the crack. She hoped for any sound of life from outside, but there was only dull silence and the whistle of cold air blowing in.

The room was secure, because workers stored things here.

She looked around and saw garden supplies. Plastic buckets with the NYC Parks maple leaf logo stamped on the side. Bags of fertilizer. She imagined she smelled mulch, and for the briefest of moments, she thought of spring and pink crocuses and daffodils and experienced a weird emotion that was happy and sad at the same time. Everything here was spring, summer, fall. No snow shovels or salt, which meant no workers would be checking this room.

One bucket was not part of the stack. She walked over and checked inside, where she saw a blue Gatorade and three protein bars.

*Is this my dinner?*

She'd kept it together 'til then, but she lost it when she saw the protein bars. Her mom—who was all about farm-to-table and fresh, organic food—had hated protein bars.

She was so cold she didn't feel the tips of her fingers or toes. Her throat started to close. Then her breathing became very shallow and fast.

She knew she was having a panic attack—even though she'd never had one before. She fought it the same way she did her grief: by closing her eyes and trying to picture a moment when she had been happy and relaxed. She remembered a Sunday dinner before Mom got sick when they were all laughing. Mom had made spaghetti primavera and served it with two loaves of French bread—and Dad had downed an entire baguette, all by himself. People always talked about how family events were important, like birthdays or graduations or weddings. But the ordinary moments—the ones just like these—were the ones Allie thought were the most special.

So she stared at the food in front of her—the food she couldn't possibly eat—and remembered that spaghetti dinner. It comforted her.

It took eight minutes for her panic to subside; then she started to breathe normally again.

She accepted the fact that she was stuck—for the moment—in a stone closet. That no one was going to notice she was gone.

Sam was off duty until school started back Monday.

Jackie, their housekeeper, would call the police by bedtime, she decided. But they would assume she ran off, because she'd done it before. And also—what happened to Dad. They'd say she went over the edge. That she couldn't bear losing her other parent.

She fought her rising panic by finding a different image. Something to hope for.

Her mom had said Allie had *premonitions,* though Allie only called them a hunch. But she'd had powerful ones, all of her life.

They came as colors.

Purple meant something good was going to happen. Green meant someone was about to die. She'd seen green around Mom for eleven days before she died.

She'd seen no green aura for her dad. Maybe because she wasn't close enough to him to sense it. Maybe because he was right—and she'd only ever imagined these premonitions in the first place.

Dad had always scoffed, in the disapproving voice that cut right through her: *That's BS and you know it!* He was a charmer—to everyone but her.

He thought she always did the wrong thing. Like when her mother was first diagnosed, and Allie had given her the Lord of the Rings trilogy instead of hugging her.

Allie had done that because Tolkien always made *her* feel better. Everybody else just thought it was weird.

'Course, everybody else also said Mom's best friend Carrie had been an absolute saint to deliver twenty-nine precooked meals after the chemo treatments started. Even though her mom couldn't eat—and her dad had lost his appetite—so why was all that food going to waste a great thing?

Maybe, Allie thought, no one ever understood anything except their own wants and needs. Well, at least she knew: If Carrie ever got cancer, she'd want ten lasagnas, ten broccoli quiches, and nine Tupperwares full of homemade spaghetti.

All foods Allie would kill for right now. She was *starving.*

So hungry that she didn't even notice the noise at the door—right before it burst wide open.

She turned—and terror blossomed in her chest.

The man was wearing a yellow latex mask that entirely covered his head, except for slots exposing his eyes and mouth and ears. It was so tight, and it distorted his features so completely, that she could only think of a giant yellow wax candle—misshapen and melted.

*Candlestick Man,* she dubbed him.

He reached behind him with hands also covered in tight yellow latex gloves. And forced inside a stumbling boy about Allie's age. He had a smudge of dirt on his forehead and Harry Potter–style glasses that slid, off-kilter, down his nose. He looked scared half to death.

Allie's heart froze—and its icy cold stretched deep inside her.

"I brought you a present," the Candlestick Man said in a distorted, computerized voice. "Misery loves company, right?"

# Chapter 16

West 80th Street Between Columbus and Amsterdam

Jackie Meade had worked for the Donovan family for exactly three years, two months, and eleven days.

Not that she was counting. Not when she was basically happy. Not when the job paid so well.

The Donovans had even given her a fancy job title—one that Jackie used on her annual tax return as well as her résumé. They called her their *household care professional*. Which she thought sounded a whole lot nicer than *nanny* or *cleaning lady* or *housekeeper*.

They'd behaved decently toward her, which was why she'd been sad for Mrs. Donovan in particular. She'd even gone to church thirteen Sundays in a row to pray for divine intercession once Mrs. Donovan had exhausted all available conventional medical treatment. She hadn't deserved to be sick. Jackie wouldn't wish all that kind of suffering on anybody—even somebody she didn't like.

Jackie felt even worse that Allie had gone missing. The girl might not be easy to connect with, but she had been through a lot in the past year. More than any child ought to bear. It was only natural that witnessing another traumatic event might cause her to have a breakdown.

But she also knew: Her every nerve was now tingling with excitement.

Sure, she had plenty of chores still to do. There were two loads of laundry to finish, a dishwasher to run, and assorted items to pick up at the grocery. But now there was the prospect of more.

Police interviews, for sure.

And maybe the commissioner's lady friend would put her on television. If she did well enough, then Nancy Grace and Anderson Cooper—reporters from the big networks—would come calling.

Someone who worked as a *household care professional* wasn't supposed to admit it, but there were only so many times she felt she could unload the dishwasher or make the beds or listen to Allie proclaim that dinner was not edible.

It was important work, taking care of a family. But God—it was boring.

Allie always described things in colorful terms, maintaining that Fridays were purple or that listening to the last movement of Beethoven's Ninth was like watching a confetti of Skittles.

Was it so bad that Jackie craved a splash of red to enliven the beige of her life?

Then she thought about it again.

More than boredom was at stake. When the police and the media invaded this home—as they certainly would, once the investigation unfolded—they wouldn't be content with what Jackie would tell them. They'd have their own agenda.

They'd be looking for all kinds of secrets. Secret hiding places. Secret motives. Secret regrets.

Jackie would never lie to the police. But there were certain things she thought she'd keep to herself.

She went quickly into Allie's room. It was a typical teenaged girl's room—equal parts stuffed animals, trinkets, and technology.

She found the diary that Allie hid under her mattress cover. She stuffed it into her bag.

She found the envelope filled with photos. Those joined the diary, too.

There was an eleven-inch MacBook Air in Allie's usual hiding spot.

Jackie opened the computer. Loaded Safari. Erased the browser history.

Then clicked on a series of files.

She worked fast—because she knew she didn't have much time.

One by one, she examined them. Pressed the delete key where required.

She didn't particularly like being inside Allie's world. It was like knowing too much. Witnessing too many events. Feeling too much pain.

But it was a trip she had to take. So she went there—and back again.

Taking care to destroy all the souvenirs.

# Chapter 17

## Near the Parade Route

Cops. Cops swarming everywhere.

But it's like I'm invisible. They don't notice me. They look right through me.

Not a bad day's work. The commissioner has been shot, I've brought his daughter someplace safe, and I even happened upon another special prize.

People are always in a rush to move on to the next thing. Not me. Savoring the victory is part of the game.

It takes mere seconds to find online footage from the riot at this afternoon's balloon inflation. All the news channels have it running on a continuous loop.

The video captures a guy standing near Molly the Mongoose. He's Mr. Happy Families himself—and he looks like he wants to puke his guts out. Any second, he'll lean over the huge red puddle stretching in front of him and let loose.

Hello, Breakfast. Hello, Dinner.

Not Hello, Lunch.

'Cause it's just a guess, but I think he's the kind of guy who's so busy he skips it.

Watching him, I can't blame him for wanting to toss his cookies. For the better part of an hour, he's been part of the discussion about family values and the importance of community. How all we need is to take care of one another. Asking, in the words of Rodney King, "Can't we all get along?"

If only he meant it.

The news footage keeps running, and I listen to the hypocrites keep talking. I hear how these values are reflected in the Macy's Thanksgiving Day Parade and the company sponsors they choose to work with. There's talk of giant balloons and marchers and singers.

People are swarming across Central Park West. Some are angry, fists raised in protest.

Suddenly fires are burning. A shot rings out.

My, what a show!

I gave them all quite the performance, a riveting first act, something that will pack in the audiences for days. Did you see how the top cop crumpled and fell? Did you see the way people descended on him with the force of a human tsunami? He was lucky that he wasn't trampled to death.

I reach for my cup of coffee and take a sip. Its aroma—and its heat—they comfort me.

I inch closer to the TV screen and watch the strobe effect created by flashing lights. Raindrops are dripping long lines down the camera lens.

I wish I could see more than I do. I'd have liked a close-up view of him, sprawled on the ground. Like a beached seal in a pool of its own blood.

I wish I could know more than I do. Like what he was thinking when he fell. Did he remember his child? Did he think he was dying? Did he worry his secrets would all come out, if he wasn't around to protect them?

I do my best to imagine it all.

Some of us have the ability to put ourselves in somebody else's shoes. To try and understand how somebody different from us feels. Get inside their heads.

We don't need a degree in psychology to do it.

We just have to care.

## PART TWO

# THE RANSOM CALL

Fourth Wednesday of November

7 p.m. to 9 p.m.

## WJXZ REPORTS

This is WJXZ News with Gwen Allensen reporting from the Upper West Side of Manhattan at the Macy's Thanksgiving Day Parade staging zone, where I'm talking with Art Booker, official spokesman for Macy's department store. Art, what can you tell us about the latest plans for tomorrow's parade?

*ART:* Well, I've got some great news for everyone watching. Mayor Kelly and Deputy Police Commissioner Kepler have just informed me that the staging grounds for the parade will soon be reopened to parade workers. This means that overnight, our preparations for all floats and balloons will be under way.

*GWEN:* This afternoon's unfortunate events were obviously a real setback to your planning. Fan-favorite balloon Spider-Man was even attacked and seriously damaged. Do you have enough time to complete repairs and resume preparations?

*ART:* Absolutely. We're lucky to have the finest, most dedicated volunteers and workers on hand. Each one of them is one hundred percent committed to making tomorrow's Thanksgiving Day Parade our best one yet. And kids at home shouldn't worry: I promise you that Spidey will be just fine by tomorrow morning!

# Chapter 18

## American Museum of Natural History

Seven-oh-eight p.m. Unrelenting rain and gridlock.

What Haddox had thought would be a simple twenty-minute cab ride up the West Side Highway took almost forty. It wasn't even Thanksgiving yet, but the city was already in the throes of bottleneck traffic. He immediately regretted his decision not to take the subway, as the bumper-to-bumper taillights, large crushes of people, and frantic atmosphere were enough to drive the pleasant memory of his recently departed pint of Guinness deep into the recesses of his mind.

Horns barked. Sirens blasted. Cab drivers cursed one another in a dozen different foreign languages.

The perpetual motion that was New York City had come to an utter standstill.

And no one was unhappier about that than Haddox. He was the kind of guy who needed to be constantly on the move. Hated the feeling of being trapped. He'd even developed a rule about it: He never made a commitment eight hours, eighteen minutes in advance. That used to be how long he could stay inside a top-security government database unnoticed—and it created a habit that stuck.

So after he used his credentials to get through the security cordon, eventually reaching the NYPD's makeshift headquarters at the museum, Haddox exploded from the cab, dashed up the stairs so fast he didn't even get wet from the rain, and found the acting desk clerk right away.

He kept his first request short and to the point.

The officer's bored gray eyes scarcely acknowledged Haddox. The man checked his ID and authorization, then frowned before tapping a sequence of keys on his keyboard. "Did the video files transfer?" he asked.

Haddox's phone buzzed four times in succession. "Aye," he confirmed. "Are they passcode protected?" Not that his skills weren't up to hacking anything some rank-and-file copper had put on a file, but sometimes the legitimate way was the fastest.

The officer made a face of annoyance, but wrote down a code. Slid it over to Haddox.

Two seconds later, it was in the Irishman's pocket.

When Haddox didn't move on, the officer glanced at him like he was about as inconvenient and annoying as a nosebleed. "Is there something else?"

"Funny you should ask." So Haddox explained that, too.

The officer's expression turned uncomfortable as he scraped his chair back. "Top-level authorization or not, granting that kind of request could end a career."

Haddox knew that his request had a stark cruelty about it. But a girl had gone missing, and that meant nothing was off-limits. Not even the commissioner himself. It was the only way to counter the odds.

Because those odds weren't great. Thousands of children went missing every year in New York City. There were plenty of ways their stories ended, most of them tragic.

"Just routine," Haddox explained. "Part of the process. Better you give me what I need than call attention to yourself by slowing my investigation down."

Another hesitation. The officer looked Haddox up and down, assessing. Evaluating.

"And if there are any questions, I promise to leave your name out of it." Haddox offered the magic words the paper-shuffling bureaucrat was looking for.

"You're barking up the wrong tree." The officer's voice was like gravel, but he yielded to what he determined wasn't worth arguing over. He picked up his phone and did exactly what Haddox wanted.

# Chapter 19

En Route: 350 Riverside Drive,
Vidocq Headquarters

The ticking clock read *16 hours, 49 minutes* to go. Logan Donovan knew, even though he had handed Allie's phone over to Eve.

Before he could head uptown to meet with her team—as he decided he must, just to make sure she had everything under control—he initiated a series of briefings. He reviewed protocol with Critical Response Command and his elite Hercules teams and the K-9 units. "I need all of you to inspect your posts now, while there's still room to maneuver," he instructed. "We want to identify anything suspicious now, before the crowds arrive."

Afterward, he didn't call his department-provided security detail. The men from the day shift were still on the hot seat, playing twenty questions with investigators. There was no reason to call in the night shift early.

Instead, he snuck out of the museum unobserved and called Sam, the part-time driver he had hired for his family six years ago after a political kerfuffle. Donovan had been accused of using city resources for personal use—and even though he received security protection as part of the job, it was questionable whether the city should provide for his family, too. The commissioner had decided it was better to sidestep the issue with private arrangements. Avoid the appearance of impropriety. Sam was former NYPD; Donovan had known him forever; and best of all, Allie liked him.

Sam had been on his way to a Thanksgiving Eve church service, but he assured the commissioner he would pick him up en route.

Fourteen minutes later, when Donovan turned onto Eighty-first Street, the first thing he spied was the aging Lincoln Navigator with Sam behind the wheel, eyes closed, resting his bald-as-a-cue-ball head against the doorframe.

"Sam?"

Sam's eyes flicked open. Despite being well past middle age, he still had a boyish face and gentle brown eyes. Climbing out, he shook Donovan's hand. Held it. His throat worked a moment, then he managed, "You doing okay, Commish?"

"Yeah, doing okay."

"You need a shower, Boss." A deep vertical worry line grooved between Sam's eyebrows.

"Not to mention a handful of aspirin and a change of clothes. Just get me uptown."

Sam moved to open the door. Donovan noted that Sam, wearing a suit that was two sizes too big, moved a little stiffly; the damp was probably making his arthritis flare up. But he'd no more take medication to alleviate the pain than he'd alter his ill-fitting suit. Sam took life as it came and bore up. It was a skill Donovan tried to emulate.

He ducked into the backseat of the car and was instantly reminded of Allie. The pocket in front of him was filled with the flotsam of her life: Gum wrappers. Empty pretzel bags. Cookie crumbs. "I need your help, Sam."

"You name it, Boss," Sam said agreeably. "You know I'd do anything for Allie."

"Yeah, let me know if you hear from her. But I need to know: Is this car still radio-equipped?"

Sam shrugged. "Far as I know, it's rigged out just like the old days, when you drove yourself." Squeezed behind the steering wheel, eyes ahead, Sam drove as casually as though he were out for a Sunday drive. But in reality, he was weaving in and out between cars, making short work of heavy traffic.

"Can you connect to the secure channel and pass it back here?" Donovan popped a piece of Allie's gum in his mouth. *Cinnamon.* He chewed vigorously.

"Don't remember how, Boss, but I expect you can figure it out." Sam tugged on the radio mount. It dislodged—and he passed it back to Donovan. The wire just managed to reach.

Within moments, Donovan had remotely rejoined the meeting he'd just skipped out of.

His deputy, George Kepler, was making noises of frustration. "Who the hell knows? We've got a man in custody, but he's just one of a passel of cop haters—each of them a threat to tomorrow's parade. I'm gonna have an ulcer before this night's over."

The cop was a damn drama queen.

"Time to man up, George." Donovan broke into the conversation. "What's the status on surveillance and tactical?"

A different voice answered. Donovan recognized it as Graham, his best tactical officer. "I've got one team combing area footage. Another is positioning a team on every rooftop along Central Park West."

"Snipers?"

"Our best."

"What if the media notices?" George fretted. "We don't want to publicize any threats."

"The media already knows we're amping up security for this year's parade," Donovan said. "They also know I was assaulted. No one's going to question a forceful display of security."

"And the public?" George asked. "How are they gonna feel when a sniper's got his rifle trained on Little Susie, who just wants to watch Dora the Explorer passing by?"

Donovan laughed. "If anything, it makes them feel better. Like nothing bad's gonna happen with a cop standing next to them. Besides, their eyes are going to be on the balloons and the floats. Not the members of New York's Finest who are working their asses off. The only people we'll piss off are the residents along Central Park, when they realize their rooftop box seats to the big event will be off-limits."

Satisfied the situation was under control for the moment, Donovan clicked off the radio. His eyes fell on another packet of Allie's gum. *Watermelon.*

Under control *professionally,* he corrected with a pang of guilt.

Sam pulled up outside a house on the corner of Riverside Drive and 107th, which was lit up like a Christmas tree. A large white van was parked outside; two uniformed men were carrying metal boxes inside through gaping doors.

"You need me again, just call," Sam said when Donovan ducked out of the backseat. "Otherwise I'll see Allie at eight o'clock Monday morning. Back to school as usual. I've got faith."

"Enjoy your Thanksgiving, Sam."

"You, too, Chief."

Donovan strode up the steps toward the main door, checking his watch. He'd give this fifteen minutes—twenty at the most. Never mind that his own reality had tilted askew. NYPD business—and the parade—both had to go on.

# Chapter 20

350 Riverside Drive, Vidocq Headquarters

Mace took the stairs at headquarters down to the lower level two at a time. He dumped his wet and dirty clothes in the corner, and stepped into a long, hot shower in the living space he periodically shared with the other members of the team—using extra soap and plenty of shampoo to scrub away every trace of the afternoon. Afterward he shaved, brushed his teeth, and started to pull a lucky No. 17 jersey, a bright blue T-shirt, and warm-up sweatpants out of the closet where he kept clean versions of the exact same clothes he had at home.

He checked himself out in the mirror. Let his eyes take in what he saw. The small gold hoop earring. The fact that his jet-black hair, shaved tight to his scalp, had not even a hint of gray. The ropes of muscle, honed by hours in the gym and high-stakes ball, that still drew most ladies' eyes. Including Céline's—and she was one damn fine woman. Smart enough to dominate the boardroom, with a body made to play in the bedroom. The kind to hang on to, if he could. He might be the wrong side of forty, but he was driving hard, making up for the lost time his dumb-assed younger self had squandered.

Maybe his new lease on life ought to have put a permanent shit-eating grin on his face, but there was something wrong that still bothered him. More than his tough guy exterior would ever admit.

Mace knew who and what he was: a troublemaker with two standout talents. One for hoops and one for dealing. He'd made a fortune trading whatever was hot on the black market until a weak link betrayed him—and he'd ended up doing time in the state penitentiary. Being behind bars was no picnic, but the worst thing about it was that he couldn't play ball. Mace was a raw talent who'd enrolled in gangbanger university before he was a teenager. Never had a real chance to polish his skills. Otherwise he'd be sporting championship rings for the Bulls or the Cavs—not winning Benjamins off pickup games down at the Cage.

And Mace didn't just lack skills. His problem was more basic. He might get a thrill from the game, but he was never part of the team. He didn't join things. He never hung out with the guys. He might talk trash with the best of them playin' ball—but he didn't have the patience for the small talk off the court.

*Lies. Disrespect. Nothin' he hated more.*

Mace shoved the No. 17 jersey back into the closet. Time to man up.

He passed by a checkered orange shirt so old that the stitching was frayed and bleached-out stains had faded certain areas pink. Had to be Eli's.

He found three old army-green T-shirts next to a camouflage vest—originally thick and stiff, but now so well worn it was soft. These were lined up next to silk shirts that were red and purple. García's shit.

Behind all that, he found a long-sleeved shirt that was pale blue. The fabric was a hefty grade and it was monogrammed *ZB*. Meaning it had once belonged to Eve's stepfather, a man who stood well over six feet like himself. Mace hadn't known him except by reputation—but he was told Zev Berger had inspired the full range of emotions, from fear to awe to loyalty. And most important of all: respect.

He put the shirt on, hoping Eve wouldn't mind, rolling its sleeves up to his elbows. Since it was tight across the chest, he left the top buttons undone. He didn't bother tucking the tails in after he put on a pair of jeans. Faded but no rips or tears.

Next he pulled on a new pair of Nike socks and a dry pair of Air Jordans.

He looked all right now. Like a guy who had his shit together.

He dumped his wet, stinking clothes in the bin for the laundry service, left the room, and started up the stairs for the kitchen.

Thanks to the commissioner and the cowboy culture he'd created in the NYPD, Mace had missed dinner—and he could eat a horse.

The guy in the kitchen had platinum hair and enough tattoos to rival the look Dennis Rodman had sported with the Bulls back in '95. He was all over the six-burner Wolf, where each flame was contributing to the insane smells in the room. He reached his left hand to grab the handle of a deep sauté pan, giving it a good shake.

Mace stepped into the room involuntarily. Raised a suspicious eyebrow. "What's that you're making?"

The chef grabbed a spatula. Flipped the golden concoction. "Potato latkes. Just practicing for the big day. Want one?"

"More than that. I'm starving, man." Grinning, Mace grabbed a plate, spun it around on his fingers. Stopped it right when four crispy potato pancakes landed on it. He devoured two before the other guy spoke.

"You with the police?"

Mace scowled. "Why'd you think that?"

The cook shrugged. "Maybe you look the part."

*People and their stupid-ass assumptions.*

"If I was with the police, don't you think I would have asked who you were? Even though *you* look like you had a narrow escape from some punk-rock band. But since the only tune you're playing has forks and knives, I'm guessing you're the chef." He downed another latke.

"Sorry—let's start over. Name's Ty."

"Mace."

They shook hands. Mace could smell the different herbs Ty'd been chopping.

"I know the police commissioner just arrived. I thought maybe you were with him."

Mace rattled his now-empty plate as he put it down on the table. His hands turned into fists, with his knuckles pressing so hard that circles of pale white formed against ebony black skin. "Now why'd you have to ruin a perfectly good fried potato with a reference to that bastard? You better stick to cooking. Don't put your nose where it don't belong."

Ty ignored Mace's orders and smiled. "Chopping vegetables can get boring. Been here only a few hours. Seen more action than I have the past month." He let his eyes wander out of the room, across the hall to where Eve was talking with the commissioner.

Mace followed his gaze. Had the big man been made any smaller— any more humble—now that he'd been wounded? Mace didn't see it.

He reminded himself that this wasn't about bad cops—or even the top cop who protected them. It was about a little girl. That the commissioner's daughter had been missing for hours. Despite the simmer of anger still burning at his core, Mace felt a flash of sympathy begin inside of him—and it worked like a sharp knife, whittling away part of his darkness.

But not enough to dispel it. The top cop was still a bastard. The fact that his kid had been taken? That was a case of chickens come home to roost, as his momma would've said.

He trusted Eve about as much as he trusted anyone. More than he'd trusted even his brothers in the Queen's Bloods. But still.

He couldn't do this. He needed some air.

"What's wrong?" Ty asked nervously.

"Nothin'," Mace said, turning to leave. His eye caught the sack of potatoes next to Ty—still unprepped, unpeeled. "Hey—don't get too fancy with these fried pancakes. 'Cause most people think it just ain't Thanksgiving without plain mashed potatoes."

He went down the hall, grabbed his jacket, and slipped out the door—disappearing into the darkness of the street.

He had almost made it to Broadway when a voice came out of the shadows behind him.

"Just where do you think you're going?"

NEWS NEWS NEWS NEWS NEWS

## WJXZ REPORTS

This is WJXZ News with Gwen Allensen, reporting from the parade staging area on Seventy-seventh and Central Park West. Right now, I'm talking with bystander Liz Newman from Washington, D.C., who came with her three kids to see the balloons inflate.

*GWEN:* Liz, I gather you ended up with a ringside seat for the violent police protest that erupted.

*LIZ:* My kids were crying. They were so scared when they saw Commissioner Donovan shot and those cars set on fire. It was horrible. We just came to see the balloons, and we ended up with the whole experience being spoiled for my kids.

*GWEN:* What would you say to all these people who came to protest what they see as unfair police practices?

*LIZ:* Well, I believe that Thanksgiving is about putting aside our differences and grievances for just one day. So we can give thanks for the good things we have.

*GWEN:* Maybe Delores Brown, who answered a social media call—#stoptheparade—to attend the protest, can respond to that. Delores, why target the parade?

NEWS NEWS NEWS NEWS NEWS

*DELORES:* We're not going to sit around on our butts and enjoy some parade when a teenage boy was just killed in a racist attack. The world is watching this parade. So when we take action, we get them to watch *us*—and notice how much we hurt.

# Chapter 21

350 Riverside Drive, Vidocq Headquarters

The rain had stopped by the time Haddox reached 350 Riverside Drive. Apparently, Mother Nature had drowned her sorrows enough for one night.

Unlike the commissioner, who looked like he had sorrows to spare. Haddox wished he could give the man a pint of Guinness—or two—to take the edge off.

Logan Donovan stood at the front of the tech room, staring down at his daughter's phone on the center of the table. Its ticking clock read *16 hours, 34 minutes* to go.

He seemed to dare it to ring. When it didn't, he returned to his own phone and began typing furiously.

Haddox started talking to Eve and Eli, since they were the only ones listening. "The footage of the commissioner's shooting has been catalogued from half a dozen different angles. Three videos come from the Beresford's surveillance cameras. I obtained a download of the feed from the forensic tech on duty at the museum." Haddox moved next to the fifty-eight-inch high-definition screen that was the centerpiece of the tech room, where fast processors and state-of-the-art analytics coexisted with watercolor paintings and a plush gray-blue carpet.

It was like NSA meets HGTV. Even in a room dedicated to function over form, Eve couldn't abide a workspace that was sterile. Haddox inserted a remote drive into the USB port in the wall.

"The first was shot from the Beresford's Central Park West entrance." Haddox thumbed the remote. For thirty-four seconds, they watched rapidly growing crowds transform into an angry mob.

Haddox exchanged uncomfortable glances with Eve and Eli. No one said anything.

The commissioner ignored them, typing. Eve seemed to study him, her brow furrowed.

Allie's phone still didn't ring.

The countdown read *16 hours, 29 minutes* to go.

Another click. "The second Beresford shot was from a camera across from the Eighty-first Street subway entrance." Twenty-two seconds of video showed the commissioner turning toward Molly the Mongoose, walking onto a small podium, and taking the microphone.

Donovan glanced up from his phone and frowned. "My men already combed through that video and came up with bubkes. Unless you've got something new, don't waste my time."

Eli's eyes widened. "Jeez. Seriously?"

"Commissioner, if you feel your men can do it better, then by all means, they should," Eve said smoothly. "There's no need for us to be involved." She reached out, turned the video display off.

That got Donovan's attention. Suddenly he wore a hangdog expression. He put his own phone down. His hand brushed against her arm and came to rest at her wrist. "Please."

Haddox felt a sense of perverse satisfaction when she shook off his hand. The commissioner had made the wrong move. Eve was not the touchy-feely kind, especially with someone she didn't know.

"Sorry," Donovan said. "Like I said, it's been a helluva day. My men are targets themselves, but the city's relying on us to keep everyone safe. You know it's never easy—which is why I need *your* help with my daughter."

Eve's face softened.

*Manipulator.* Haddox had met cops like him before. Blokes who thought the rules they enforced never applied to them. He could already feel his jaw tightening and his knuckles itching to punch the top cop. Bullies had that effect on him.

Haddox spoke up loudly. "Guess the NYPD is nothing but a bunch of feckin' idiots if they didn't find what I did."

Eve flashed him a warning glance: *Be nice.*

"What did you say?" For a brief moment, the commissioner's self-control threatened to break—but he reined it in the moment Eve spoke.

Eve met the commissioner's gaze with a cool one of her own. "Let's get back on track here. The faster we get through this, the faster you can return to city business."

Donovan nodded stiffly.

Allie's phone remained silent: *16 hours, 25 minutes* to go.

*Was he imagining this?* Haddox watched Donovan's eyes linger on the V-line of Eve's sweater as she stretched to flick the monitor back on.

*What an arsehole.* Haddox clicked the remote again. He'd met Commissioner Donovan not half an hour ago, and he already hated the guy.

Everything about the commissioner rubbed him the wrong way. The way he looked at Eve. How his voice boomed too loud. His belief that if he snapped his fingers, then the world would follow his bidding. Most of all, Haddox hated how Eve was actually kind to the guy. What was wrong with her? She'd never been the type to be fooled by a charming smile or to fall for a man in uniform. Couldn't she see the two-faced son of a bitch for what he was?

Definitely time to get through this. *Fast.*

"The third Beresford angle," Haddox explained, "was shot from the mid-block camera that was behind the helium truck. Though it's a partial view, you can see five different Macy's workers racing to finish inflating Spider-Man. I want you to remember them; they become important later."

The seventeen-second video played.

Unimpressed, the commissioner picked up his own phone again. Cleared his messages.

"The next two videos are from the museum itself." Haddox skipped to them immediately. One near the museum's western entrance to the circular driveway focused on five kids eating cotton candy and laughing at the SpongeBob balloon. The other, from the stretch of trees nearest the dog run, showed the girl: Allie Donovan, the commissioner's daughter.

The final video captured the chaos in the crowd following the shooting. The camera had captured Allie, standing amidst the crush, bewildered.

Eli leaned forward, squinted. "That's Allie?"

Donovan looked up from his phone. Took a step forward, craned his neck—and it struck Haddox that Donovan was standing unnaturally close to Eve.

"The image is too blurred to recognize her face," Haddox admitted, "but I identified her from her stance. It's the same as from the previous footage. Now, better fasten your seatbelt; you may just learn something new." Haddox couldn't help himself. "I've taken all six videos and created my own master recording." He hit some keys and a large panorama view filled the screen—with all the players onscreen.

Every angle shot had been blended into one. And though the image was still grainy, Haddox had managed to sharpen the resolution significantly.

"There's the son of a bitch." A red arrow appeared onscreen, following a moving figure. He entered the area from Central Park West. He was hooded—like many others, given the rain. He kept looking down. "There's no direct camera view of his face—and even if there was, the distance would be too great for a positive ID. But watch what he does," Haddox directed.

The time stamp was 1:52:13.

He disappeared behind the helium truck at the 1:52:46 mark.

At the 1:54:03 mark, a new man appeared in a Macy's yellow slicker. Haddox clicked keys and the frame froze.

"You believe it's the same guy?" Donovan leaned in, suddenly immersed in the video.

"Aye," Haddox confirmed. "Same body build. Same gait when he walks. See how he slightly favors his left foot over his right?"

"So he's familiar with Macy's and their procedures." Eve circled to Haddox's right.

Haddox focused the screen. "Now watch this."

The man in the Macy's yellow slicker moved forward. His face was still obscured—but his body movements were those of a hunter stalking his prey.

Slow. Measured. Stealthy.

When he was within eight feet of the podium, he stopped. Waited.

"When did Commissioner Donovan start speaking?" Eve asked.

"He begins moving toward the podium at one-fifty-six p.m.," Haddox replied. He hit some more keys and zoomed in on the area surrounding Molly.

The guy in the Macy's rain slicker waited on the left.

The commissioner took the stage in the middle.

The crowd began rumbling to the right. They continued until the 2:11 mark. A guy in a hoodie raised his hand. It *looked* like a signal to the crowd. Because the moment the fist pumped into the air, shots rang out, the commissioner was hit, and rioters took over.

Something else happened, too. At the same instant that the guy's fist pumped into the air, the man in the yellow Macy's slicker sprang into action. He closed the gap between himself and his prey in 4.8 seconds.

Allie was standing there. Frozen. Stunned.

She didn't seem to notice when this man approached behind her. Then enveloped her, taking her into his arms, before they vanished into the crowd.

"Amazing how a change of perspective can change the story." Haddox waited for the implication to sink in. Not just for the commissioner—but for everyone in the room.

The single frame had shown one man. Striking alone. Taking advantage, in the midst of the chaos.

Haddox's video, which had been created by merging multiple frames of view, showed something else entirely. The fist pump had been a signal. Allie's kidnapper had expected it. The assault on the commissioner and the taking of his daughter had been linked.

"My God," the commissioner breathed. "The bastard knew *exactly* what was going to happen."

# Chapter 22

350 Riverside Drive, Vidocq Headquarters

Donovan looked at Eve like he'd just received a sucker punch, right in the gut. Then he swallowed hard. Recovered himself. Mumbled, "Excuse me a moment. I have to take care of something." Started furiously typing a message into his phone.

Eli whistled under his breath. "That job's going to cost you your child. Sure hope it's worth it."

Donovan stared up at him, unbelieving. "Three and a half million people are depending on me tomorrow. How many are depending on you?"

Eve was aware that it was suddenly becoming hot in the room. Even she was having difficulty breathing. "Allie's kidnapping was choreographed, perfectly timed to coincide with the attack on you. Which raises the question: Is it personal? Or is it tied to the parade?"

"We have multiple credible threats against tomorrow's parade. But the primary ones targeted my own officers. Certainly not the public. Not my own child."

"Based on the evidence we've seen so far, my opinion is that it's personal," Haddox ventured.

Donovan surrendered to the instincts that were ingrained in him after more than two decades as a professional. "Opinion? I've got no use for opinions. But I can envision multiple *reasons* why Allie may have been targeted."

Eve's jaw tightened. She understood the tremendous pressure he was under, but there was something about his manner that Eve found vaguely patronizing, if not outright bullying. He wasn't used to being questioned—and it was beginning to show. She ticked the reasons off on her fingers. "He's looking for ransom. He's looking for revenge. Or he's looking for any young girl, and Allie fit the bill."

The commissioner flinched.

Haddox arched an eyebrow. "Meaning he's a greedy bastard, a cop hater, or a pervert."

"With a solid working knowledge of Macy's inflation zone procedure as well as the police protest," Eli added.

"It's got to be a cop hater," the commissioner decided, "based on the timing of the protest. The people who showed up were angry. I personally heard shouts about the Binta case, where that twelve-year-old boy was beaten—*allegedly*—by four cops in the Bronx. Then there's the Johnson case, which has just started jury selection; the shooting victim there was fourteen."

"Allie's kidnapper may well hate cops," Eve agreed coolly. "But motives can be complicated. We'll know more when the ransom call comes."

"*Ransom?* I thought we just agreed this was a cop hater." Donovan draped his arm over the top of the empty chair next to him. The move made him appear relaxed, but by now Eve had figured out that it was all an act. His mind was razor sharp, always working six different angles, but he liked to pretend he wasn't much of a thinker. It helped him fit in, be just one of the guys, even if he was the top cop.

It also tricked people into underestimating him.

"*We* didn't say anything. You jumped to that conclusion all by yourself," Haddox pointed out.

For a brief moment, the commissioner's self-control once again threatened to snap. But he kept it in check, shoving his hands into his pockets. "I've got to get back to the parade zone; my own officers—and this city—need me. I just want to know you have this under control. And that you promise to bring me back in the moment there's a significant development."

"You have an important job to do, Commissioner." Eve walked to the window. Cracked it open half an inch. "This arrangement will work best if you do your job—and we do ours. We'll call you when Allie is safe."

"That's unacceptable."

"This is going to take awhile," Eve said.

"Also unacceptable. You must work faster."

"I wish we could," Eve agreed. "But the next step is to wait."

"WAIT?" His question was a wounded roar. Then, as quickly as he had erupted, he defaulted to charm. "Eve, you know I want you to find my daughter. I trust you implicitly." Warmth flickered in Donovan's blue eyes as they searched her own. "But in all my decades of service—in Operation Desert Storm and then as a police officer—*waiting* is one strategy I've never used. I don't intend to start now."

"The kidnapper is going to ask for ransom," Eve said. "He'll call or text his demands any moment."

Four pairs of eyes stared at Allie's phone.

It remained stubbornly silent. Still at the center of the table. Still not ringing.

"That infernal ticking clock, timed for the parade's end." The commissioner ran his hand through his salt-and-pepper hair. Lingering flecks of red paint fell like confetti. "Probably because that's when the security cordon lifts and normal activity resumes."

Eve decided he sounded like he was trying to convince himself. More or less arguing for the scenario he could cope with best.

"How can you possibly know this is just about ransom?" the commissioner challenged.

Eve breathed in the cold air from the window—and it calmed her. The air was definitely too hot in here. "I could tell you it's because of my master's in psychology from Yale. Except you don't learn this from the textbooks or in the classroom, only from experience. After a decade in the field, I've developed a sixth sense for human behavior." Eve delivered the line with as much confidence as she could muster.

When it came to reading people's motives, she was one of the best. She understood that the commissioner was a professional used to being in charge. To playing by his own rules and no one else's. She liked his strong sense of self; in no small measure, it reminded her of Zev. But if he didn't stop second-guessing everything, she was going to end up seriously disliking the man.

"Let me make it simple," she said. "He returned Allie's phone—

complete with a ticking clock. This tells us two things. First, he wants to communicate. And second, he has a specific deadline."

No one made a sound.

"People don't initiate contact like that unless they want something," Eve said.

"No one's called," Donovan said to Eve. "And we need this to resolve fast."

Eve understood. It was a rule of thumb for law enforcement: The faster the process, the better the chance for an early resolution. And the earlier the resolution, the better the odds that the victim would survive the experience unharmed.

"They're waiting just long enough for you to feel desperate. To make it more likely you'll do whatever they ask," Eve told him. "That's a good thing."

"I don't follow." Eli scowled.

"I do," the commissioner said tersely. "Whoever this is, if he wants something from me, then Allie is more valuable to him alive than dead."

# Chapter 23

## Broadway and 104th Street

Mace froze. Then he turned in response to the voice.

Eye contact was made.

Then Mace said, "No way."

"No way what? I haven't asked you anything yet."

"No way to anything you're going to ask me."

"Man, don't you think it's hard for me to admit I need help? Especially from you."

"Not gonna happen. Find someone who cares."

"I need you to come to the natural history museum area with me."

"You mean the parade zone? Why the hell would I do that? I'm going nowhere with you. Especially not there. Not after they just tried to lock my ass up."

"It ain't a request. What if I give you a good reason why?"

Mace sighed—long and deep. "Better be a damn good reason."

So Frank García gave him one.

Mace listened despite himself, focusing first on the stupid red bandana García always wore for luck. Then on the intersection ahead of them.

Smudges of smoke drifted out of storm sewers in the street. He could smell roasting nuts from the vendor another block south. Some homeless guy, a neon-blue plastic bag on his back, was rustling for tin cans and plastic bottles as a frazzled woman got out of a cab, hauling grocery bags from Zabar's. Fairway. Citarella. The Upper West Side trifecta of gourmet goods.

Different people, different lives, different problems. But nothing like the real problem he'd just heard.

*Dammit. What kind of guy was he, anyway?*

Apparently not the kind to walk away. "I'll come with you, Frankie," Mace found himself agreeing. "But we have to bring Eve up to speed first."

# Chapter 24

350 Riverside Drive, Vidocq Headquarters

Commissioner Logan Donovan disappeared in the blink of an eye, summoned downtown for a police emergency. Eve had known from his tone that something was wrong.

She, Eli, and Haddox were alone. They stared at Allie's phone. Its clock was ticking down.

*Fifteen hours, 46 minutes, 58 seconds.*

Haddox cleared his throat. "So you think it's about money. Ransom. Simple and uncomplicated."

"It's the motive in the vast majority of kidnapping cases, and it comes with a deadline—which he's already given us," Eve pointed out.

"Why haven't they called?" Eli had found apple cider in the fridge downstairs. He took a sip—then paused, mug still in mid-air.

"Maybe because they're busy talking with Allie, trying to find out where the commissioner vacations and what kind of car he drives and what he bought her for Christmas last year. Details to give an idea of how much cash to ask for." Haddox arched a brow at Eli, seemed amused.

"Does make me wonder." Eli took a seat. "Why would they think the commissioner has much to offer? I know he has an important job, but in terms of salary? He's just another civil servant. An administrator appointed by the mayor. I've had plenty of buddies who worked for the city, and not a single one of them had two nickels to rub together."

"His salary's a matter of public record," Eve said. "Easy for anyone to find out."

"Which I already did, and Eli is right," Haddox said. "The commissioner makes decent money but not enough for anybody to call him a rich man. He's certainly not pulling in a wage sufficient for a significant ransom."

Eli looked up from his screen. "I admit it's not my expertise, but I thought cops—or, more typically, the FBI—handled the ransom money in situations like this. That they kept funds on hand to use for the kidnapper's demands."

"They do," Eve agreed. "They've got suitcases of it. But if they use real bills, they're marked. Even more commonly, they just use blank paper. And in my experience, either option can make kidnappers fly off the handle. Nobody likes being tricked."

"So what's the alternative? Actually give them the real stuff?" Eli brushed away a couple crumbs stuck to his shirt from a mushroom tart he'd sampled downstairs.

"Any reason this kidnapper would think the commissioner's good for serious dough?" Haddox asked casually.

"I can check." Eli popped a stick of gum in his mouth. "See if he came into money recently. Maybe won the lotto? Maybe had a rich uncle die?"

"Or, I believe, a wife," Haddox surmised, looking at Eve.

Eve noticed how his blue eyes were so different from the commissioner's. The latter's were bright with energy but layered with sorrow. Haddox's were nothing but irrepressible mischief. The kind women fell for in an instant, in spite of themselves—though they suffered a broken heart when those eyes invariably strayed. It gave Eve an idea.

"Maybe there's even a more personal reason—and he wants Donovan to pay?" she offered. "Somebody Donovan pissed off. He fired them or didn't hire them or gave them a puny Christmas bonus."

"He's spent the last decade working for this city in one capacity or another—and I'm positive that he's made his share of political enemies," Haddox said. "If there's a dark secret or skeleton in his closet, then I'll find it. Frankly, I'll enjoy digging through the git's dirty laundry."

Eve opened her mouth in retort—but never actually said a word.

Because in that instant, Allie's phone started ringing.

# Chapter 25

Allie's phone continued to ring.

Haddox hit a button and his program promptly initiated a trace—but they still scribbled down the number all the same.

It was ten digits. The first three of them 347. A local cell number.

Eve picked up the phone and passed it to Haddox. "Be Donovan!"

"Who's this?" He tried to flatten his Irish vowels as much as possible.

Silence. Finally, a girl's voice, hesitating. "Um, who's this?"

*Allie?* He mouthed to Eve.

She shook her head as if to answer *Don't think so.*

"This is Donovan," he answered.

"Allie's father?" Shy. Uncertain. High-pitched. "Can I talk to Allie, please?"

"What's this about?" Haddox asked.

"I'm Sara. Allie's lab partner in biology." There was a nervous tremor in her voice. "I know Allie's busy with family stuff, but we've got an assignment due Monday after Thanksgiving, and I wanted to ask her—"

Haddox cut her off. "You haven't heard from Allie today, have you?"

"No . . . not since Spanish class yesterday."

He peppered her with more questions. Allie's routines. Friends. Habits.

But Sara called Allie the "lonely girl." No real friends. Unknown habits.

A dead end.

Eve watched as Haddox placed Allie's phone back in the center of the table. He slowly let his fingertips rest lightly on the device. As though his touch might spark some connection to the missing girl.

His thumb inadvertently hit the home button, activating the lock screen—where the image of Allie, bound and frightened, taunted them from afar.

The phone remained silent.

Its clock was still ticking down.

"What about blackmail?" Eli hazarded.

"Someone takes his daughter because they want to stipulate what deputies get hired? Dictate his policy on stop-and-frisk? Don't think so, mate." Haddox shook his head.

"Or, going back to the shooting, who might benefit if the commissioner had been taken out of commission? No pun intended." Eve closed her eyes, considered the different threads.

Some people were highly visual thinkers who had to see possibilities to believe them. Others could only think in chronological steps. Eve thought in terms of connections. She collected details and possibilities—and worked to spin them into a pattern that made sense.

The phone still didn't ring—or trill to announce a text.

"The NYPD's got threats on file from everybody," Haddox said. "Political activists with a grudge against city officials. Celebrity hangers-on. Former employees of corporate sponsors who ended on bad terms. Individuals who've been hurt by rogue balloons. And the commissioner's particularly worried about telephone threats against police officers this year. We've got too many options. Not enough time."

The phone still didn't ring. Its silence was now downright maddening.

"Haddox, I believe you've pulled everything there is to know about the parade route and the security surrounding it?" Eve asked. She was dashing off notes and talking at the same time.

"I've got full details," he confirmed. "No help from the commissioner. And I still think it's fishy he doesn't use his own resources to find his daughter. It's like he doesn't even care."

"And that attitude," Eli burst in. "I mean, who died and left him in charge?"

"He's got his hands full, between threats to the city and threats to his own officers," Eve said. "It's never easy balancing family and career in moments of crisis. I get it."

"Maybe we oughta call in a psychic," Eli grumbled. "Be more helpful than the commish, I'd bet."

"Maybe we ought to learn everything there is to know about Allie," Eve replied. "Her likes and dislikes. Her friends and frenemies and habits. Did she dance or play soccer? Did she do her homework with friends or alone? Did she like movies—and what did she do for fun? Whoever took her spent significant time learning all about her."

"We'll want to talk with Jackie Meade," Haddox said. "She's been Donovan's housekeeper for years—and a de facto babysitter for Allie. And he's got a personal driver for family business. Sam has driven Allie to school and lessons and playdates for the last couple years."

Eli's eyes snapped up as the door opened.

Mace walked into the room. Sized up the situation within seconds. "Everybody's just standing around, waiting for that damn phone to ring, huh?"

"Shut up, Mace," Eli said.

"Well, I've got a theory why it ain't ringing. 'Cause the commissioner's kid ain't the only game in town."

"What are you talking about?"

"We don't have one kidnapped kid. We got two."

# Chapter 26

## 350 Riverside Drive, Vidocq Headquarters

There was no sound, except for the hiss and clang of the steam radiator—and the clatter of pots and pans that drifted up from the kitchen below.

All eyes warily focused on García.

He held himself perfectly still, hands balled into fists in a stance that made Eve imagine an unexploded grenade sitting in the middle of a minefield: highly charged and ready to detonate. Any misstep would be dangerous.

"So you're saying this is a *double* kidnapping?" Eli stared at García over the can of Dr. Brown's celery soda he was drinking.

"Mace said it, not me. I'm just saying that Frankie Junior's missing," he replied coolly.

"And I said it 'cause I'm smart enough to know: We got two related kidnappings," Mace put in. "Second kid disappears from the balloon inflation area. Not too long after Allie disappeared from the same area. Just think: What are the odds?"

Eve tended to agree with Mace. She didn't like coincidences. And when something didn't make sense, she knew they didn't know the whole story.

García proceeded to bring them up to speed. How he'd sent Frankie Junior underground into the subway to escape from the riot. How he hadn't returned home. And how neither he nor Teresa had heard from their son since.

García had been angry, then concerned, and then outright desperate.

"Frankie Junior's phone has stopped transmitting," Haddox confirmed, looking up from his screen. "I traced its last signal to the underground area beneath the Museum of Natural History—which was hours ago."

"Just so we understand," Eve said, "Is Frankie Junior usually on time? Does he answer your texts right away?"

García didn't hesitate. "Yes. He knows the rules."

"He's familiar with the subway?" Eve asked.

"Frankie's taken that line dozens of times. This is the only time he's ever gone off the grid. Something's wrong."

There was a loud crash downstairs in the kitchen. Then a tinkling of metal as more items fell to the ground. A few choice words soon followed. Eve had almost forgotten entirely about the Thanksgiving prep under way.

García sucked in air through his teeth. "Have you heard from the kidnapper?"

Eve shook her head. "Not yet."

García's eyes lit on Allie's phone. Still in the center of the table. Still silent.

He picked it up. Checked the timer still counting down on the screen: *15 hours, 18 minutes, 57 seconds.*

"Is that a deadline from the kidnapper?" García demanded.

"We think so," Eve said.

"That timer's counting down until twelve noon *tomorrow*? I can't wait that long. Not with Frankie's medical condition. What if he got separated from his backpack, which has his medication? If he gets hurt, then he's at risk."

Eve nodded. "It's a blood-clotting disorder, right?"

"Von Willebrand disease—scary as shit. Whenever he bleeds—and he can bleed spontaneously, even if he's not injured—it's life-threatening. Unless someone gives him the injection he needs to help his body produce clotting agents."

"If his medication's with him, can he self-administer?"

"We've taught him how. He's never actually done it." Desperation trembled in his words. "So I need you to do what you do. Get inside the bastard's head—and find my boy. While I join the team that's searching the area."

Eve didn't give an answer. Not then.

Because at that very instant, Allie Donovan's phone rang once again.

# Chapter 27

When the phone trilled, it was 8:43 p.m.—and Allie had been missing for six hours and thirty-two minutes.

This time, Eli snatched the phone off the table. In his best imitation of the commissioner, he said, "Donovan speaking."

Eve heard a faint voice on the other end. She signaled to Eli to switch the connection to speakerphone. Meanwhile, Haddox's fingers danced across keys, initiating the process that would record the conversation with the kidnapper as well as run a trace on his location.

"*Commissioner Logan Donovan?*" The caller's voice boomed loud—though it was also robotic, distorted by a machine to shield the true voice of the kidnapper.

"Put Allie on the phone."

"*We have business to discuss.*" No inflection. No tone. No energy or urgency or panic. When the voice was a robot's, all that projected was steady and calm.

"Now," Eli insisted. "Or this conversation's over."

"*I expected you would want proof of life. I have arranged to provide it.*"

There was a seven-second pause. Then a girl's voice came on, high-pitched and panicked. "*Help me! Come get me, please!*" Then an ugly scream.

Eve watched the blood drain from Eli's face. He opened his mouth, but his confidence—and his words—had deserted him.

Eve's hadn't.

What they'd just heard was too choreographed. She was pretty sure it was a recording, not a live sound.

She closed the distance between herself and the phone in five steps. "My name is Eve," she said. No mention that she was with the FBI. Not even a last name.

Just Eve. Because it made her sound easy, more approachable, willing to help.

"I'm here with Commissioner Donovan," she continued. "He only wants to bring his daughter home safely—"

The robot voice interrupted her to bark its instructions.

*"This is a test, Commissioner. I'm wondering: How far will you go to save her? I have three demands you must satisfy before the end of tomorrow's parade. The first is a ransom; you have until midnight. You will place the money in a marked garbage can by the natural history museum on the northwest corner of West Seventy-seventh and Central Park West."*

Even though the line was being recorded—even though all five people in the room were hanging on to the caller's every word—and even though there was no chance of her forgetting what she'd just heard—Eve jotted it all down. Looking at the words steadied her.

"How much?" she asked.

*"The commissioner knows how much."*

"Excuse me?"

*"Ask the commissioner if his daughter's life is worth as much as his wife's."*

"I don't understand—"

*"Tell him this is old-school justice. He's gotten away with things, and now it's time to pay up. That is, if he wants to see Allie again."*

"You're not making sense—"

The robotic instructions interrupted her. *"Commissioner Donovan must obey these instructions to the letter. If he wants his precious snowflake back."*

Eve tried a different angle. "Once we put the money in the marked garbage can, how do you get us the girl?"

*"The money must be in cash. Hundreds, packed tight. Unmarked bills. This may be blood money, but I want it pristine."*

"We're talking about a cop. Cops don't have much cash in hand."

*"You have exactly three hours, thirteen minutes, and counting."*

"One more thing. If you're also holding a boy, you need to know: He's got a serious health condition. He needs medication."

There was no response.

García snatched at the phone and shouted into it, "YOU SICK, SICK BASTARD!"

The words echoed back at them. The line had gone dead.

# Chapter 28

## Near the Parade Route

The ransom call was a success. My darling would be proud.

I reach into my pocket and pull out her letter.

*Page One.*

*My dear,* she writes.

> To understand what I'm asking, you should know how I realized there was a problem.
>
> When I first came to New York, I worked with a woman named Holly, a blond former cheerleader from South Carolina who kept a goofy smile on her face all the time.
>
> It wasn't an act. She truly believed that the glass was always half full. That there was good in everybody. That, given the chance, they'd do the right thing.
>
> She begged me to pick a Saturday and show her around the city.
>
> I did. We settled on the "real" Little Italy in the Bronx. And since this was before the Android and iPhone era, she brought her brand-new Sony camcorder. Walking beside her, I felt like a damn tourist.
>
> So best I could, I made sure we hung back from the crowds that mobbed Arthur Avenue that morning—shopping for oysters and cherrystone clams, pork and sausage, fresh pasta, and what were arguably the city's best Italian pastries.

We crossed over to the east side of the street.

I admit it: I let Holly move a little ahead of me. Frankly, I was embarrassed to be with her, since she couldn't stop looking around, filming everything. It was like after spending a lifetime thinking New York City was nothing but Broadway marquees and neon lights and skyscrapers that blocked out the sun, she couldn't get enough of a real neighborhood.

Everything she saw interested her. The old men smoking hand-rolled cigarettes. Women in floral dresses haggling for bargains. And hustlers hawking parking spots to tourists.

One of those hustlers was African American, stocky, with solid-cut muscle, wearing a T-shirt that said DAMN RIGHT I'M SOMEBODY. He was built like a linebacker and gave the impression that he'd been born to play ball; standing at least six-foot-one, he made rough, jagged moves like he was about to flatten whoever got in his way. It was intimidating, but the effect was broken the moment a silver BMW crawled by— and he flashed a rehearsed smile at the driver. "Hey, nice wheels you got there. Car like that deserves a special spot, like this sweet one I've been saving."

At the same time, two beat cops turned the corner. Security, working to keep the neighborhood safe.

They gave the hustler a sour look.

He stared back, just as displeased.

Holly was filming.

"What are you doing?" The cop on the left glanced at the hustler's scruffy jeans and mud-stained sneakers. "Harassing tourists again?"

The BMW driver wanted no part of whatever was happening. He closed his window. Slowly, carefully, began driving away.

The hustler put his hands up in the air. As if to say Who, me? "Just minding my own business."

He turned and started walking.

"Stop!"

*He stopped. Didn't turn around. The two cops closed the gap between them.*

*Suddenly one put his hand on the hustler's arm.*

*He yanked his arm free. Snapped, "Don't touch me like I did something!"*

*The other cop stepped behind the hustler. Pulled his head back. Hard.*

*Holly's jaw had dropped so low that I worried the flies swarming the nearby fish market scraps would make themselves at home. But she was transfixed. She couldn't stop filming.*

*The other cop doubled the hustler over with a savage punch to his gut.*

*The hustler lurched over a storm sewer.*

*The cop delivered another bone-crunching blow as his partner gripped the hustler tight around the neck.*

*There were great, gulping, rasping breaths.*

*The hustler went limp.*

*"Let's take this piece of shit in," the first cop said, wiping the sweat that dripped from his brow. "Book him on disorderly conduct. He threatened us, right? That menacing stare. The way he brandished those fists."*

*The hustler looked to be unconscious as they dragged him away.*

*Had they choked all the life out of him?*

*Holly's camera dropped to her waist. "I didn't see any threat, did you?" she whispered.*

*Later, Holly called the Forty-eighth Precinct to report what she'd seen. To let them know that there were two bad seeds in the Big Apple, hiding in the ranks of New York's Finest.*

*When they weren't interested, she took it to the media. The big three—CBS, NBC, and ABC—all aired her footage repeatedly.*

*She went on* Oprah.

*Those cops went to jail. The hustler's family went to court.*

*Later, the experts called Holly's video one of the first examples of sousveillance. That's a fancy word for when somebody in the community records something that turns out to be significant.*

*Who fixes something wrong by making sure it's public.*

*Because sometimes that's the only way.*

## PART THREE

# THE DROP

Fourth Wednesday of November

9 p.m. to Midnight

# Chapter 29

## 350 Riverside Drive, Vidocq Headquarters

The tension in the room was stifling. García was shaking like a leaf—though not from fear. From anger.

Haddox watched as Eve opened the window another inch. Cold air drifted in like strands of smoke—and revived him almost as effectively as a jolt of nicotine.

*"The commissioner knows how much."* Eve repeated the kidnapper's words as Haddox dialed the commissioner's secure line on speaker. Its ringing filled the room.

No response. Even though Haddox dialed three times in succession.

"We'll keep trying. We know he was called away by an emergency. Now, what data did you manage to collect from the ransom call before it dropped?" Eve asked him.

The location of any caller was now easy to trace, thanks to an FCC order requiring all cell networks to track GPS locations to aid 911. Any disguise would say volumes about the sophistication of the criminal they were dealing with.

"It was made from a 347 number belonging to a Donna Galtrow." He pointed to his computer screen. "Ms. Galtrow reported it stolen five days ago from an outdoor café in Chelsea; she had her phone on the table and someone swiped it."

"Not a surprise: He's smart enough to disguise his ID. But can you triangulate the signal?" Eve asked.

Haddox's monitor was a virtual map, covered in numbers and dotted with triangles. Each corresponded to the signal strength and location of the kidnapper's call, relative to the cellphone tower picking up its signal. From the series of pings it regularly emitted, looking for cell towers within range, someone like Haddox could pinpoint the phone's location, right down to the block.

"Not tonight." Haddox shook his head. "Not reliably. There's too much traffic."

"Thought New York City was built to handle traffic." Mace was looking over Haddox's shoulder, trying to make sense of the screen. Strings of numbers were flashing by fast in a psychedelic yellow blur.

"It's built to make sure you always have cell reception, not necessarily to fix your location. When there's too many users, the nearest local cell tower will overload—forcing your cellphone to find a tower somewhere else. Or sometimes a tall building blocks your signal. If either of these things happen, then a call in Manhattan might cross the Hudson River and get picked up by a tower in New Jersey. Which is exactly what's happening tonight. Not just for Ms. Galtrow's stolen 347 phone—but for the huge population of phones that are on the West Side of Manhattan to celebrate Thanksgiving. Sure, it's possible the kidnapper did indeed call from the Jersey side of the river. But it's equally possible that he didn't. Tonight, we just can't tell."

No one said anything until Eli spoke up. "So this is just an educated guess, but looks like the commissioner magically got two million dollars richer shortly after his wife's death. Probably her life insurance payout."

"And you think *that's* the payment the kidnapper wants delivered by midnight? Impossible!" Haddox moved his left hand—the one with the bandaged thumb—more gingerly.

"Can't be sure, but it's the only thing I see that makes sense. And it raises a big problem: Where are we going to get two million dollars cash? In just three hours, no less? Two million dollars wired into an account, no problem. But cash? No chance." Eli scrunched his eyebrows into a deep V.

Mace shrugged; then something else occurred to him. "How come nobody's mentioning Frankie Junior?"

"We know now: This is a kidnapping for ransom," Eve answered. "It's about money. Frankie Junior's medical condition is probably more than he bargained for. Maybe he decides Frankie is a huge liability and just releases him. Kidnapping is one thing, but felony homicide is a whole 'nother issue."

Mace chortled. "Besides, he probably already figured out that Frankie Senior is no high roller. Can't get blood from a stone."

"Enough," García snapped gruffly.

"Sorry, Frankie, bad choice of words."

"How many times do I have to tell you: Don't call me that!"

"We have what we need," Eve reminded them. "A ransom demand with a drop-off point. If we handle this right, it's the opportunity we've been waiting for to retrieve not just one—but hopefully two—kidnap victims."

"I repeat, he wants two million dollars. Cash," Eli said, exasperated.

"The FBI keeps an emergency stash," Eve reassured them.

"No way," García insisted. "It's marked bills. The bastard notices? He gets mad, which puts my son in harm's way."

"So NYPD, then. We'll involve Donovan, just like he asked. NYPD's the largest and most sophisticated law enforcement organization in the world, with a budget running into the billions of dollars. That's some pretty deep pockets," Haddox said reasonably.

"Not an option." García glared at Haddox. "NYPD marks bills, too."

"Can't law enforcement invent a mark nobody can decipher?" Haddox glanced over at Eve. "And if you don't use Agency money or NYPD money, either marked or fake, then what exactly do you have in mind?"

"I repeat: Beyond going to the Bureau or NYPD for help, how do you get *any* money, other than a few hundred bucks from an ATM, the night before Thanksgiving?" Eli demanded. "I couldn't lay my hands on two thousand dollars if I wanted to. So two million? Forget about it!"

"The fastest way will be to involve Donovan," Eve decided.

She dialed the commissioner's private number again. There was still no response.

"There's something squirrely about the guy." Eli found a toothpick in his pocket. Began trying to clean something stuck between his teeth. "Maybe there's some truth in that talk about blood money."

"I think we just heard half of a story," Eve said.

"What's the other half?" Haddox looked intrigued.

Eve didn't hesitate. "The side the commissioner's not telling us."

"He's like Jekyll and Hyde," Eli continued. "He's nice to Eve, but with us, he's a son of a bitch."

"Can't say I blame him. I like Eve better than you any day," Mace said.

Haddox found himself counting how many times he'd caught the top cop's eyes lingering on Eve—specifically, on the curve of her hips or the neckline of her sweater. He drummed his fingers on the table. *One, two, three, four.*

"Big men have big personalities." Eve's eyes wrenched toward Haddox.

He thought he understood what she was asking. "My cursory review of his NYPD classified files looked clean."

"And you're able to monitor the NYPD chatter, right?" she asked.

"So little faith."

"Your Level One hacker skills aren't infallible. The kidnapper just called. We didn't get a trace."

"That's Manhattan cell traffic for you, luv. Has nothing to do with my *skills.*"

"I'm just saying: Things happen."

"I slip in and out of NSA on a daily basis—and they never know what's hit them. I think I can handle eavesdropping on a little cop talk."

"Assuming you can stay out of a fight." Eve shot a pointed look at his bandaged thumb.

Haddox shrugged. "Some things are worth fightin' for, luv."

"Things?" Eli raised an eyebrow. "Or people?"

"Or women." Mace grinned.

"Okay, now the important details," Eve said, ignoring them. She reiterated the various tasks they each needed to accomplish, finishing with, "We need the identity of the fist-pump guy at the riot—the one who appeared to signal the kidnapper. But no need to reinvent the wheel on that one. The NYPD'll be all over him. We just need to loop in."

"Got it." Eli drummed his fingers on the desk, impatient to get started.

"We also should requisition sufficient fake paper money as a fail-safe. Access the area's security cameras. Confirm what police surveillance is already in place. Mace should handle the drop—then make his way to Eighty-first and Central Park West, where he'll remain on alert. Haddox, you take the area immediately in front of the natural history museum. I'll take the area opposite the garbage can drop. Eli, you can be the point person from here, and García should monitor the west side approach to Seventy-seventh."

Eli made a note of it all. He gave the impression of sucking down the information faster than one of his favorite celery sodas.

"You know," Eve warned, "the ransom drop will be our best chance to catch this bastard. Otherwise, we're going to be stuck playing his game, with his rules, for several more hours. Especially since this guy is telling us that the ransom is only his first of three demands."

"I only like playing by my rules," Haddox agreed.

"García, why don't you go back to the parade zone?" she continued. "Scope out what you can on Frankie's disappearance. Get ready for action. The rest of us will join you by eleven-forty-five p.m. sharp."

"Hey, what am I? Chopped liver over here?" Mace interrupted. "García doesn't own all the moves. I think I may know a way to get our hands on a few million dollars cash. And, Eve, I'm gonna need a get-out-of-jail-free card for this one. May need to cut a few corners."

Eve merely nodded. It was all the affirmation Mace needed. He bolted out of the room, right on the heels of García, before anyone had a chance to ask him what his plan was.

Haddox thought it was probably better that way. Plausible deniability.

Haddox went into the hall and pulled out one of his cigarettes. Rolled it between his fingers. Suddenly Eve was at his side, saying, "I need another favor."

"I only do one a day, luv." He found his lighter.

"Can I get an advance on tomorrow's?"

"It's your lucky day." He held the lighter still.

"I'm sure it's nothing, but—"

"I know. You want the commissioner checked out. More than just what's in his file. You want his secrets laid bare."

"Since when do you read minds?" Inside the tech room, Eli had turned on some music. Ella Fitzgerald, crooning about Paris.

"It's the obvious question. Most people don't get to his position without leaving a trail of bodies behind." He lit his cigarette, hoping his expression betrayed none of his concern.

Her eyes temporarily clouded. Then she said fiercely, "He's a cop. A professional who believes in the law. Which is more than I can say for you."

Haddox could only shrug. "I'll get you the facts, but I'm telling you now: He's not a good guy."

There was a bark of warning downstairs. Something had spooked Bach—and Haddox thought that he had more in common with Eve's German shepherd than he ever expected. He'd also been set on edge by a stranger—one who raised his hackles with suspicion.

She set her jaw. "Why are you doing this? To make sure I dislike him?"

"How about 'professional distance'?"

Eve glared at him. "That's a given. I'm still going to help him find his daughter. Because somewhere there's a frightened thirteen-year-old girl whose life is in danger. And whose kidnapping may signal a larger threat to tomorrow's parade."

"Save the girl. 'Cause he's so busy keeping the city safe. I understand." He blew a ring of smoke. "To do that, though, I think you need to answer the even more obvious question."

"Motive. The reason why someone took her."

"Wrong answer, luv. Maybe you ought to ask: *Why doesn't he care?*"

Haddox watched her go, trying to read the woman he had not quite gotten over. To intuit some explanation from the lift of her chin or the tone of her voice. It was like trying to read tea leaves in a cup, or divining the future from a set of tarot cards.

He gave up.

All he knew was that she was a smart, strong woman. And he wished that she'd let him protect her. Because he had a bad feeling: This bastard of a commissioner was going to be trouble in more ways than one.

### VIDOCQ FILE #N356239

### Current status: SUBJECT

**Logan Patrick Donovan**

Age: 55
Race/Ethnicity: Caucasian
Height: 6'2"
Weight: 217 lbs.
Eyes: Blue
Hair: Gray

**Current Address:** 132 West 80th Street (Upper West Side).
**Education:** John Jay College of Criminal Justice, B.A. Criminology.
**Expertise:** Seasoned law enforcement officer. Relevant job experience:

New York City Police commissioner—*current*
New York City Police (NYPD)—patrol officer, Sergeant, Lieutenant
United States Air Force

**Personal**

**Family:** Mother, Deirdre, and Father, Sean, deceased. Daughter, Alison Rose, age 13.
**Spouse/Significant Other:** Jill, deceased.
**Religion:** Catholic.
**Interests:** A workaholic with little free time, he passionately follows the Jets and the Yankees.

**Profile**

    **Strengths:** A team-builder and master manipulator—skills developed after a demotion early in his career. Under his tenure, crime has dropped for the seventh straight year.

    **Weaknesses:** Has a hair-trigger temper. Charges of ethical lapses ranging from responsibility for instances of police brutality to his acceptance of unauthorized gifts.

    **Notes:** A lifelong New Yorker, he feels great responsibility for his city. Strong advocate of community policing. Details still being gathered on suspicious circumstances surrounding Jill Donovan's death.

*\*Assessment prepared—and updated—by Corey Haddox for SA Eve Rossi. For internal use only.*

# Chapter 30

## The Parade Staging Zone

Frank García was back in the Frozen Zone. He made his way down West Eighty-first Street, surrounded by deafening sounds. Officers barked orders through megaphones. Motors revved. Directly overhead, a chopper was circling.

The area had been reopened to non-police personnel. So much activity, so many vehicles, so many people put his normally wound-up nerves into overdrive.

*Thank you, Uncle Sam,* he thought. Four tours overseas and this was how he'd ended up: a changed man. With his hair-trigger temper and paranoid nature, he had no tolerance for crowds like the one growing around him now.

And so far, only the vendors and true locals had arrived. A boy wearing a green Jets sweatshirt, maybe six years old, whined for hot chocolate. His sister, a few years younger, was throwing a full-fledged tantrum next to Hello Kitty.

In an unprecedented show of force, there were just as many cops as civilians. Men and women in uniform—NYPD and FDNY and Homeland Security—were all standing around, waiting and jumpy. Covering each inch of the parade zone tighter than the New York Giants defense—even if that wasn't saying a lot these days.

García stayed hyperalert for whatever might lead him to Frankie Junior. That was his primary mission, but he figured his best chance of finding Frankie was through the bastard who had taken the commissioner's daughter. So, he began his surveillance of the area, prepping for the ransom drop in a few hours.

He sniffed. Detected an unpleasant odor that seemed like a cross between grease and transmission fluid.

Not explosives, he decided. Just unpleasant.

He breathed in the mix of smoke and exhaust from the generators that powered multiple street vendors—and had just recently been re-started to meet the demand of hungry crowds. He felt bad for the street vendors, knowing they only had a few major holidays to make much of their income for the year. And, thanks to the hit on the commissioner, they'd be lucky not to *lose* money today.

He noted the familiar guys. The ones he'd already vetted and checked earlier in the day. The pretzel and hot-dog stand that normally occupied this corner was joined by a handful of traveling food vendors, here just for the evening's festivities. The popcorn and cotton candy cart. The drinks station.

On West Seventy-sixth Street, there was a toy vendor. Selling crappy plastic figurines of Snoopy, SpongeBob, and Molly the Mongoose. She was next to the cart where Jews for Jesus were giving out hot chocolate.

On West Seventy-fifth Street, the popcorn cart had been joined by the hat-and-noisemaker crew. Bazookas, party hats, and giant sunglasses—the junk he normally associated with New Year's Eve—had Thanksgiving-themed varieties for sale. All catering to the thousands of tourists expected to choke the streets starting at about six o'clock the next morning.

Less than eight hours away.

Cops manned every street corner—at both the Central Park West and Columbus Avenue sides. The message was meant for the public, and it was clear: a visible show of force that said these streets were safe.

The most significant law enforcement presence surrounded the museum. They'd even assigned one officer to stand behind a concrete blockade on the West Seventy-seventh Street corner. His sole job was to guard a collection of about thirty-five empty garbage cans, all harvested from street corners along the parade route. *A garbage can graveyard.* They had to be removed and contained; the NYPD couldn't risk their being used to house a bomb.

García was all too familiar with the practice. Since coming home from Iraq, he hadn't been able to break the habit of keeping a six-foot radius before passing by a trash can. Even now, seeing this can collection that he knew to be empty, he could feel his heart rate accelerating.

The cop gave García a sour look.

"I'm with the Feds," he said, producing his ID. "Searching for a missing kid." He fished his phone out of his pocket. Cleared the latest round of unanswered calls and texts with a swipe of his thumb. Pulled up a recent picture of Frankie Junior. It was one they'd taken during the subway series at Yankee Stadium last summer—Frankie grinning from ear to ear, a blob of mustard on his cheek.

"Haven't seen him." The officer peered at the photo. "Looks like you."

"No shit. Except he's better looking."

The officer chuckled. "You can say that again. I'll keep an eye out."

# Chapter 31

350 Riverside Drive, Vidocq Headquarters

"Everything is under control. I'll have Gwen get in front of the media announcement. She can make clear this is a separate incident, unrelated to tomorrow's parade." A pause. "Of course not. She's putty in my hands—"

"Commissioner?"

He hastily ended his phone call. Slipped the phone back in his pocket.

"I've been trying to reach you. I was just in the kitchen—and heard you talking." Eve Rossi was standing in front of him, carrying a thick manila folder stuffed with paper and coffee in a fat hand-painted mug.

He hadn't heard the library door open. He hadn't heard footsteps. He wasn't used to being surprised—no, not even when he was in the midst of a conversation. No doubt the incessant roaring in his head was the culprit. The noise was a tremor constantly vibrating inside him.

Eve offered him the mug. "Have some coffee. Do you good." She set it down on the table beside him, and took the opposite seat. Clearly expecting a conversation.

*Not now,* he thought. *I have decisions to make. A job to do.*

"Do you happen to know a six-letter word for *conundrum*?"

"What?" His head was pounding. He couldn't deal with this nonsense.

She pointed to the daily *New York Times* crossword puzzle that was folded into the side of his chair. He was practically sitting on top of it.

Not that he'd noticed.

"I tried *puzzle*," she said. "But the *z*—the fourth letter—doesn't work." Then, without warning, she changed the subject again. "I thought you'd left. Had an emergency."

"I'm dealing with it from here, until my security detail arrives. They're stuck in Thanksgiving traffic—but they don't want me to leave. Bunch of worrywarts."

"Because something else is wrong." She made it a statement, not a question.

*What, exactly, did she overhear?* For a split second, he couldn't think what to say. He was normally master of the polite truth and the white lie, but for some reason he was struggling to manage it around Eve. There was something about her that he couldn't put his finger on. As though she could see right through him. Still, he was coming to like her, he realized.

He settled on what was mostly the truth. "I just lost a cop in Brooklyn. Gunned down while on patrol. No suspect in custody."

"I'm sorry."

"Normally, I'd be with his family right now."

"But you have other challenges," she acknowledged, then made the transition into business. "Speaking of family, there's something I need to discuss with you—"

"Everyone means well." He picked up his coffee, slurped thirstily. "One friend called to tell me to check myself into a hospital. One told me to eat something. The third said he'd pray for me. But I don't want anybody's prayers or thoughts or good wishes. I just want Allie home."

"We heard from her kidnapper. He's made a ransom demand."

"Is she all right? What did he say?" The commissioner's hand shook as he set his mug back on the table.

"He asked if you valued Allie's life as much as your wife's."

He stared at her. "I don't know what the hell that means."

She opened her manila file, shuffled through the top pages. "We thought it probably referred to her life insurance policy. You know, the one that made you two million dollars richer? But that you didn't bother telling us about?"

*How the hell did she learn about that?* "That's private," he said flatly.

"But relevant. In fact, he called the ransom *blood money.*"

"Jill and I had two million dollar policies on each other," he admitted, after a moment. "Got them right after we married. I never share personal information—so I don't see how Allie's kidnapper could have known."

"Wasn't hard for me to figure out." She thumped the massive file. "Anything else in here that you're not telling me?"

"I'm an open book."

"Until the moment I ask questions about your wife's life insurance policy. Or why the kidnapper calls it 'blood money.'"

He gulped his coffee again. "I'm no mind reader. Who knows what Allie's kidnapper is thinking? But I have to assume that the ransom he wants is the two million. I can think of nothing else."

Eve waited.

"What do you want from me?"

"I want to know if there was anything suspicious about Jill's death."

"Based on something a *kidnapper* says? My wife was sick. Don't be ridiculous."

She stared coolly at him. "Unless you're honest with me, I can't do this." She indicated her manila file, stuffed with paper. "Getting information is easy, but putting it together is hard. It requires trust. Find someone else, Commissioner." She stood, headed toward the door.

"Wait. You can't leave!"

"Watch me."

"I'm sorry. I don't mean to be rude. Just the stress of it all . . ." He needed to appear more vulnerable, more concerned about his child. It was what she expected.

She turned back. Her eyes were clouded with indecision. "I prefer honesty to playing nice."

"Playing nice greases the wheel. You catch more flies with honey. Want another adage to explain it?" He recognized this opportunity for what it was. He needed this woman to like him and trust him. Didn't hurt that she was also easy on the eyes.

"No adages, just honest answers. Did you have a happy marriage?"

He swallowed the sharp retort that was at the tip of his tongue, knowing it was important to satisfy her concerns. He'd always admired tough, take-charge, smart women like Eve—and he knew the coming hours would go easier if she was on his side. "Happy enough. Jill knew about the policy, if that's where you're headed. Maybe we'd grown apart at the end, but still, we were family—we looked out for one another—and watching her fight breast cancer was one of the hardest things I've ever done."

"What about Allie?"

"She's a great kid. She's had a tough couple years, and I'm not the most hands-on father," he acknowledged. "Don't always understand what she needs."

Then he waited, pretty sure his admission had changed her perspective. It was hard to dislike people when you thought you understood something about them. Sympathy created the strongest sort of human bond.

"Think hard, Commissioner, about anyone who knows you're good for two million these days."

"I will. Please stay. I need this operation lean." The words came out rougher than he intended. He offered her a rueful smile. "Your specialty."

Her face softened. "Look, I know something about tragedy, though I'm no role model for dealing with it—even if I am a trained psychologist—"

"With a decade of experience and a master's from Yale," he said, adding, with his most sheepish look, "Sorry I was such an ass about it earlier."

"Honesty over flattery," she warned. "Anyway, I found that nothing the experts recommended—nothing I'd learned myself as a psychologist—actually helped. I didn't want to spend time with people. Or talk about my feelings. Or take care of myself. There was only one thing that actually worked for me. That actually kept me sane."

"What was that?"

"To keep working—and to feel my work somehow made the world a better place. That's what you need to do. See if your security team has arrived—go downtown—and I'll find your daughter."

He got to his feet, too. "I saw your men looking at me. I know I don't react like your typical distraught father. But you remember what it was like last year at the Cathedral? The pressure of so many lives depending on you. The stakes when you knew the world was scrutinizing your every move."

"It's impossible to forget."

"Of course I'm worried sick about Allie. But if I give in to that? I can't be the leader this city needs. Or the role model my own officers deserve."

"The ransom drop is by the museum at midnight. We have it covered—but you said you wanted to be looped in to major developments."

He quirked an eyebrow. "So you have a strategy—for getting two million dollars by midnight?"

She reached for her cellphone. Offered it to him. It looked heavy and clunky, balanced in her small palm. "I have a plan—and a backup. Meanwhile, I need you to call your housekeeper. Let her know I'm coming down to ask her some questions and search Allie's room. Plus, I need to speak with your family's driver."

His conversation with Jackie lasted all of ten seconds. He left a voicemail for Sam.

When he clicked off, he tapped the crossword. "How about *riddle*?"

"No. The fourth letter can't be *d*." She shook her head. "The most important person in my life so far has been my stepfather. Zev was a lot like you: Stubborn. Used to getting his way. A dedicated professional with little sense of what it meant to be a father—and no idea how to balance his personal life with his professional obligations. But eventually he figured it out."

"Is there a magic formula?"

"I remember the first moment I came to love Zev like a father." She fumbled, clearly uncomfortable revealing personal details. "It was winter, and snow was coming down hard, blanketing the city. My mother called it a slippery mess, but I thought it was beautiful. Zev finished his dinner, put on his coat, and announced that he was taking me ice-skating. He ignored my mother's protests—that it was dark, that the paths weren't safe, that I might get hurt. He'd overheard me say I wished I could ice-skate, and so he was going to teach me to skate under the stars. That was the instant I knew: Zev was on my side. He always would be."

He watched her for a moment, silent.

He liked her attitude. He also liked how she looked in the soft evening light. Her subtle perfume was clean, a mix of vanilla and cotton. And she was slim and toned in all the right places. When this was all over, he wanted to spend more time with Eve Rossi.

"*Enigma,*" he said suddenly.

"What?"

"The six-letter word for conundrum. To complete your puzzle."

Her eyes seemed to rake through him. "Yes, that's it. *Enigma* will work perfectly."

After she left, he went to the side table and picked up the manila folder Eve had left behind. Easily a couple hundred pages of material.

*What the hell did she find out about me?*

He leafed through its contents. Once, twice—just to be sure. After all, there were at least a couple hundred pages here.

Every single one was blank.

Haddox watched Donovan get into his car, flanked by his security detail. Then he sat on the steps in front of headquarters. Waited for Eve.

"I didn't ask for company," she said when she came out the door.

"Just looking out for you."

"I look out for myself." She started to move past him. He stopped her with his hand.

"There's a lass I know. She's not like anyone I've ever met. Tough as nails, but she's got a soft streak for the bad boys."

"Lucky for you she does."

"Are we ever going to talk about us?"

"Haddox, we don't belong together. You get counseling from bartenders, you change your phone number more frequently than most people change their socks, you break every privacy law on the books, and worst of all?" Eve grimaced. "You never make plans."

He gave her a crooked smile. "Got to keep life interesting, luv."

# Chapter 32

## American Museum of Natural History

Donovan entered the museum through the West Seventy-seventh Street entrance, where Tactical was setting up a staging area. He returned a flurry of salutes—and instantly felt his adrenaline kick in.

It was a relief to be back here.

*This* was where he belonged. Where he was meant to be.

They were checking their equipment: Communications. Cameras. GPS. Explosives containment lockers. And especially their weapons.

He approached the Tactical Management Team, which consisted of five men and three women, all hand-picked, all wearing black jeans and matching weatherproof jackets. They were different ages, different ethnicities, different physical builds. What they had in common was their ability to hit a target with complete precision from a thousand yards away—and their absolute loyalty to Commissioner Logan Donovan.

Donovan ignored the roaring in his ears. He modulated his voice, making an effort to speak in the tone they expected. No one was going to suspect anything was wrong with him.

The lead man stepped forward. "This is a full ID and background report on everyone who was standing in that crowd this afternoon. We've reviewed it—and we'll be on alert, should any of the same faces return to the scene."

The commissioner gave a thoughtful nod as he leafed through the file. "Good work."

"And these are blueprints: They outline every nook and cranny of what runs below us, including the subway, the plumbing, electric, and sewer lines."

"What about threats against NYPD officers?"

"We've received sixteen additional threats. However, we've also been unable to link the man in custody with the anonymous calls."

"The key thing between now and noon tomorrow?" Donovan reminded his elite team. "Be alert. Keep an eye on your position. We've got plenty of high-tech tools to detect any danger to ourselves or the public tomorrow—but not a single tool is more effective than the eyes and ears of trained officers like you."

"Sure thing, Boss." The team leader saluted.

"Roger that," a senior man agreed. "What else?"

Donovan stood straighter. "We're New York's Finest, and we'll never be intimidated by enemies who want to hurt us. People are going to come out in droves to celebrate what's great about this city and this country. They're relying on us to protect them. Let's do our job for these next fourteen or so hours—and do it right. Then let's go home and celebrate Thanksgiving with the people we love."

It was a hell of a pep talk. He wasn't sure whether he'd spoken the words for his team—or for himself. Maybe it didn't even matter.

# Chapter 33

West 80th Street Between Columbus and Amsterdam

Another short burst of rain showers. Water gurgled down gutter spouts, slicked sidewalks that were already dangerously slippery, and flooded the clogged storm sewers on West Eightieth between Columbus and Amsterdam.

An hour and thirty-four minutes until the ransom deadline.

An hour and thirty-four minutes to uncover Donovan's secrets, Haddox decided.

He lit a cigarette and drew in deeply, staring at the activity a block away as he inhaled. He saw a circus of police cars, equipment vans, and unmarked government sedans.

The vehicles created a secure perimeter around the museum blocks—which were dominated in part by the crime-scene investigation and in part by the renewed parade preparations. With all evidence secured, and the mayor determined to have the parade go on, the staging area had been reopened for parade business. Soon the floats would arrive, lining up along Central Park West.

Meanwhile, the balloon inflations had resumed. In the distance, Haddox could see Papa Smurf rising high. Even Spider-Man had his wounds patched up; now he was up in the air, all set to fly, constrained only by a massive net pinned down by sandbags.

Somewhere over there, Logan Donovan was back at work in the chaos.

Here, just west of Columbus Avenue, however, it was as if Haddox was in another world. Chaos to the east of Columbus; quiet to the west.

There was only the rain. A stray passerby. And the security detail in charge of guarding the commissioner's home—which consisted of two ragtag rookies, slouching by the curb, wet and bedraggled in their rain slickers.

Neither was making much attempt to disguise the unspoken truth of their situation—which was that they'd drawn the most boring assignment possible. Safeguarding a high-profile target's home might be important work, but standing around waiting for something unthinkable to happen is more tedious than exciting. And worst of all: They were in it for the long haul, with no replacements in sight. Round-the-clock surveillance was a drain on manpower. Between the parade and the riot, these guys were all the department could spare.

Walking beside him, Eve said little, too preoccupied to make conversation.

Haddox didn't push his luck. Call it Karma or Kismet or Fate, he'd always believed in the importance of being in the right place at the right time. He was Irish, after all. That meant he'd been taught from birth to trust in fate or humanity or God—and he'd learned quick that when he was stuck in a tight spot, only luck ever saw him through.

Good fortune played favorites, like it had done with Frank Tanaki—a man who walked away from seven major plane, train, bus, and car disasters before going on to win the lottery. Luck could turn on a person, too, like it had done when Ginny Hoff lost four houses to four different hurricanes. Bob, Andrew, Ike, and Hugo. Like the scorn of jilted lovers.

They stopped in front of the commissioner's home.

"Charming," Haddox remarked. "Guess nobody told the commissioner that a wall full of English ivy will make his stone crumble and crack." The nineteenth-century brownstone where the Donovans lived was straight out of an urban fairy tale, with wrought-iron gates and thick, twisted ivy framing the front door, stretching all the way to the roof.

"Since when do you care about practicalities? On the grand scale of things, a little ivy pales in comparison to those death sticks you keep inhaling."

Haddox crushed his cigarette underfoot. "You know, my grandda loved his smokes all his life. Lived to be a hundred and one."

Eve headed up the stairs leading to the front door. "And since when do you know anything about taking care of a home? You've always refused to maintain one—'cause then you'd have to stick around in one place, and people might find you. Specifically, the *wrong* people might find you." She ticked off examples one by one. "The heavies you stiffed. The friends you offended. The women you didn't call."

"You'd be surprised. I worked a construction job once. Taught me everything I ever wanted to avoid about home ownership."

"So *that's* why you're allergic to settling down in one place." Eve rang the bell.

Haddox knew that the woman who answered had to be the Donovans' housekeeper. Except she wasn't anything like he had expected.

Growing up, his family had occasional help from Mrs. Ryan—a fortysomething-year-old woman with meaty hands that reeked of bleach. She wore size-extra-large T-shirts to cover an indeterminate bulge from her stomach. Haddox had spent the better part of a year trying to figure out whether she was pregnant or not. He'd been twelve and more curious than he had a right to be about these things.

*This* housekeeper was a stunner. Her short blond hair was off her face with a white headband, and she was wearing an oversized light-blue T-shirt that said YOGA IS TWISTED over purple spandex shorts that showed off toned legs.

They stepped into the dim entrance hall. There was a coat rack with umbrellas propped beneath it. Just beyond, they saw that the brownstone had polished wooden floors, tasteful furnishings, and high ceilings framed by elaborate plaster medallions.

The first thing Haddox noticed was how the place was scrupulously clean. Vidocq headquarters had smelled of the preparation for Thanksgiving dinner; here Windex and Pledge were what scented the air. No question, Haddox knew where he'd rather be.

Eve said, "You must be Jackie Meade? Commissioner Donovan will have told you to expect us."

Jackie nodded. Then she glanced at Haddox and a smile lit up her face. "I was headed to barre class, but I guess I can skip."

"We'll need a quiet place to talk," Eve told her. "And is Sam here?"

"He's the Donovans' driver, you know. Almost never spends free time in the house. But here's the cell number where you can reach him." She passed a scrap of paper to Eve.

"Maybe you could point me toward Allie's room," Haddox suggested.

"Allie's room is upstairs. I'll show you." Jackie fiddled with the purple sweatband she wore around her wrist.

Eve shot him a look that said *Not again.*

With a shrug, he tried to convey *What can I do?* Problem was, he liked women—and most of the time, they liked him, too.

Walking upstairs, surveying the décor, he decided that this was definitely a woman's home: There were too many items he couldn't imagine Logan Donovan choosing for himself. Fresh flowers in glass vases. Furniture upholstered in light pastels. Knit throws with delicate lace patterns.

The question was: *Which* woman's influence? That of the commissioner's dead wife? The housekeeper with the legs that didn't quit? Or some other lass that had staked a claim on Logan Donovan?

Jackie slowed just a bit as they passed a wall of photos.

Haddox saw three formal photographs of the commissioner, posing with three different presidents—Obama, Clinton, and Bush 43. It also looked like he'd earned a Distinguished Flying Cross for heroism in the Persian Gulf War. Haddox scanned the framed commendation letter; it made clear that Donovan had rescued a downed pilot in the early days of Operation Desert Storm.

*Who the hell is this guy?*

"Allie's room is over here." Jackie led him straight down the hallway. Then stopped just outside the doorway, lingered awkwardly.

He entered the room. Turned back to her. "You like the Donovans?" he asked. "They're nice people?"

"Of course. They're terrific. A lovely family."

"You've worked with them long?"

"Three years, two months, and eleven days."

"Of course, who's keeping count?" Haddox teased.

A bright red flush spread over Jackie's face.

"I just always expect to leave, so I can do something else," she offered feebly. "Like write the great American novel. Backpack around the world. Or maybe go back to school."

"So why do you stay, counting down the days? Why not leave now?"

She tugged nervously on her wristband. "First it was because Jill was sick. I guess now it's because of Allie."

*A lie.*

"Or maybe because you're in love with the commissioner," Haddox commented.

"What?" Jackie looked mortified.

He'd touched a nerve, so Haddox laughed like he'd just made a funny joke. "Only kidding. Had to think of some reason to explain why you're still here."

*And why you lingered by those photos. I bet he has no idea.*

"I already told you; I stay for Allie." She sped away on deft barefoot feet. Maybe she'd liked Haddox at first—but he'd ruined the moment. Now she couldn't get away from him fast enough.

That was fine. He had work to do.

# Chapter 34

## Near the Parade Route

fumble awkwardly in my pocket. My fingers find her letter, and I continue reading:

*Page Two.*

*The question that kept tormenting me was: Why?*

*I came to know different officers, call some of them friends.*

*How could the same officers who regularly performed selfless, heroic acts—delivering the baby at the side of the road or saving the shooting victim—also behave like monsters?*

*The problem was more than a couple bad seeds.*

*I remember the day I figured that out. It was years ago, before I met you, outside the natural history museum. The crowds were thick and security was tight because the president was in town. I was making my way down Central Park West, fighting my way through a crush of blue uniforms. The thin blue line was fat and wide.*

*Two cops were yelling at a homeless guy who was rifling through garbage cans. "Hey—you! What are you doing?"*

*The homeless man pulled a half-open pizza box out of the trash. He shook it. Something rattled inside. "I'm hungry."*

*If I close my eyes, I can see it all again, just like a movie reel.*

"*What's your name?*" *the cop on his right said. He had tufts of gray hair sticking over his ears, and moved as stiffly as DeVito in* Batman, *so I nicknamed him Penguin.*

"*I dunno.*" *The guy watched warily as Penguin snatched the pizza box out of his hands.*

"*I've seen you before. Hey, Logan—haven't we picked up this guy before?*"

"*Yeah. His name is Jones, right? Ain't that your name?*"

*The homeless man only mumbled.* "*I forget.*"

"*Yeah, I forget, too. But it makes sense if I forget, since it's not my name. You got any ID to tell us your name?*"

"*No. You wanna search my bag?*"

"*If you don't mind.*"

*A shrug.* "*I don't care.*"

"*Okay. Go stand over there, will ya?*" *Penguin stopped. Reconsidered.* "*Actually, have a seat right there. Right there on the curb.*"

*They didn't sound angry. Not yet, anyway.*

*But twenty feet away, I could already feel the crackle of tension in the air. I had a sixth sense for these things. I wasn't born with it—but sometimes life forces you to develop skills you don't want to have.*

# Chapter 35

West 81st Street Subway Station—B/C Line

García renewed his search at the last place he had known Frankie Junior to be: the B/C subway station underneath the Museum of Natural History. He knew as well as anyone that had Frankie caught an uptown or a downtown train, it could have whisked him anywhere throughout the city. On the B train, he could've gone as far as Bedford Park in the Bronx or Brighton Beach in Brooklyn. On the C, he could've hopped on a Brooklyn-bound train to Euclid Avenue or a 168th Street–bound train to Washington Heights. And hundreds of places in between.

But now—knowing the commissioner's daughter had been taken—García asked a different question. *What if Frankie Junior never got on a train?*

He walked the length of the platform, quickening his pace as he approached the opening to the tunnel. He was already feeling uncomfortable. It would feel even worse if a train passed through before he cleared the narrow ledge.

He knew two things about his son: Frankie Junior liked to explore, and he was curious if he saw anything—or anyone—who interested him. It was possible these impulses had got the better of him, leading him into trouble.

García went in deeper. Grit and debris crunched underneath his feet. Concrete turned to steel.

Then—just as he felt the whoosh of air that would announce the next train's arrival—he reached an opening to the right, with access to a room beyond. Within seconds, he was through it and inside the switch and electric system, surrounded by steel.

He gulped. Felt too much like he was in a metal cage.

*Breathe in. Breathe out.* He was going to keep a tight lid on the PTSD-induced panic attacks that always threatened, just below the surface of his resolve.

He had no choice. Not today. Frankie Junior needed him to be strong and in control.

His footsteps echoed loudly as he kept moving.

No sign of life. No sign of Frankie Junior.

Just a lot of stray electrical wires that construction workers had dropped.

He must be getting close to the end.

The noises weren't far now. Maybe twenty feet.

It was darker just ahead. García was approaching a sharp corner. There were stairs. And an all-too-familiar object at their foot.

Then the realization: Someone was there. *Could it be the man who'd taken his son?*

García sprinted toward his target. He bent low and grabbed hard. Caught his target around the waist and brought him down. Slammed him against the wall.

Looked the guy square in the face.

He was filthy, his hair slicked with grease. He didn't smell good. He had the gaunt face of someone malnourished.

"What are you doing?" García demanded.

"I hang here. It's my turf."

"You see anyone else here today?"

"I ain't been here all day."

"You haven't seen a boy? Thin. Dark hair. Eleven years old."

"You don't want to be here," the street bum said, wiping blood from his chin. "It ain't a great space. It leaks water. There's no heat. Plus, we got thousands of rats. Nasty little bastards."

"You're right," García agreed. "I don't want to be here. And I'll leave the second you tell me how—if you haven't seen my son—you ended up with his backpack?" García pointed a finger at the navy blue North Face pack.

"That thing?" The bum chuckled. "Found it right here. More or less exactly like you see it. While I was out hustling this afternoon, some other squatter was using my turf."

# Chapter 36

## The Donovan Brownstone

Allie's room was all done up in shades of purple and blue. There was a low bed with three drawers tucked into each side, its duvet perfectly made, not even a crease. There were two bookcases, their contents neatly stacked and books arranged alphabetically by subject.

*It had to be Jackie.* Unlikely a thirteen-year-old kid was this anal-retentive.

Maybe it was Jackie's job, or maybe just her personality, but she kept Allie's room organized and spotless.

There were plenty of stuffed animals. Fuzzy bears, bunnies, elephants, and dogs lined the window shelf—with the apparent favorite of the day given a spot of honor on the bed. Not to mention other kid stuff. A stack of cards, with Uno on top. Board games, including Clue, Apples to Apples, Harry Potter Monopoly, and Lord of the Rings Trivial Pursuit. A few scattered dolls.

The remnants of Allie's childhood.

A birthday party invitation had been tossed into the garbage. Gemma was turning fourteen; there would be pizza and movies at her building's party room on West Fifty-fourth Street. Allie either couldn't make it—or just didn't want to. The invitation was lodged next to a movie ticket from the latest Bond flick. Friday night's showing.

Her desk had an algebra book on top. Otherwise, it was littered with pencils of all shapes and colors scattered over papers filled with doodles. There was a box filled with gum—a dozen flavor varieties, from strawberry and fruit punch to spearmint and bubblegum. Judging from scattered photos on her wall, Allie's braces had recently come off and she was making up for lost time.

He walked over to the window, which overlooked West Eightieth Street through a trio of maple trees. Glanced outside. A few red leaves dangled precariously; the rest of the branches were bare. The trees would provide a nice privacy screen in summer, but this time of year, nothing was hidden. It would be easy for someone to watch this room—either from the street or from one of the many brownstones that lined the opposing sidewalk.

*Who are you, luv?*

There was a limit to what he could learn poking around her room. What he really needed was Allie's computer. Between that and her iPhone, he'd have the modern version of a teenage tell-all. Because what most people thought of as a cellphone was actually a tracker; what most people thought of as a computer was actually the ultimate spy machine. An archive of all past activity, where files could be deleted and browser history erased, but in the right hands—*his hands*—no information ever truly disappeared.

The fact that it felt a little weird applying his investigative tactics to a thirteen-year-old kid didn't mean they wouldn't work. They'd just work differently.

Haddox peeked into the purple backpack at the desk's edge. *No computer there.* Only a smattering of notebooks, a half-eaten bag of PopCorners, and a pair of headphones.

He checked the main desk cabinet. Came up empty. Just an assorted mess of papers had been stuffed inside. Most of it schoolwork, judging from the algebra test on top with a 97 written in red—and the Latin verb conjugation worksheet poking out from the bottom.

*Where is that computer?*

His eyes scanned across the room. Fell upon the drawers underneath the bed. The first contained sweatpants and fleeces. The second contained heavy sweaters, not yet in use. The third and fourth had summer clothes—neatly folded, stored for the season.

*What now?* She *had* to have a computer. Schools required it these days.

He ought to just ask for help. Given Jackie's organizational prowess, it was impossible that she wouldn't know.

But there were two reasons he didn't—at least, not yet.

First, Haddox never liked getting help when he could do for himself.

Second, the place Allie kept her computer was a choice that would reveal something about her personality. Specifically, what she valued—and what she feared. When he found Allie's hiding spot, he'd also begin to understand a thing or two about the lass.

Haddox was a Level One computer hacker—someone with expert coding skills, an intuitive understanding of how machines operated, and a unique ability to pierce impenetrable targets. But he hadn't gotten where he was solely because he understood technology so well. He was a rare breed because he also understood the human element—IQ combined with EQ.

When he wanted to crack the toughest program, infiltrate the strongest firewall, he always remembered that it had been created by a human being—someone flawed, with likes and dislikes and bad habits. That principle had served him remarkably well, so he applied it here, too.

"If I were Allie, where would I keep my computer?" he asked himself.

He scanned the room. Let his eyes settle on the closet.

The double doors to a large walk-in revealed a California closet organization system. He began searching.

He lifted up a folded quilt. Found nothing underneath.

He ran his hands behind a row of coats. Still nothing.

As long as he was there, he checked the coat pockets. Gum. Mints. Loose change. Raspberry-flavored lip gloss.

He slid open three built-in drawers. One for socks. One for underwear. One for scarves.

*Think.*

He remembered the backpack, with its random assortment of papers and jammed notebooks and candy. The cabinet, with past homework stuffed every which way. Haphazard. Reflective of Allie's personality.

There was a built-in hamper at the base of the closet.

Not a natural place to find anything other than dirty clothes. But he thought: *Allie's personality.*

He pulled open the bin. It was half full, with a towel, washcloth, and what Allie must have worn yesterday: a graphic tee, a pair of jeans, and a sweater.

*There you are.* He saw the telltale silver gleam of Allie's laptop, half hidden under the rolled-up pair of jeans.

Haddox grabbed the device—it was an eleven-inch MacBook Air—and settled in at Allie's desk. He slid her iPhone out of his pocket. Then he popped a piece of her bubblegum in his mouth, reached into his bag for his own laptop—and started to focus.

*Who are you, Allie, luv?*

He flipped open the screen and her computer hummed to life, revealing a map of Tolkien's Middle-earth. Emblazoned across it was a message: KEEP OUT! YOU WOULDN'T UNDERSTAND, ANYWAY.

But Haddox thrived on navigating a world of information. One hour, thirteen minutes to deadline—and he had everything he needed.

# Chapter 37

350 Riverside Drive, Vidocq Headquarters

One hour and twelve minutes to deadline.

Eli sat at his desk for a moment and looked out the window of his office in Vidocq's unmarked headquarters. Through the darkness, he could see the fog rising over the Hudson River. He stared at Riverside Park in front of him. The ghostly mist mingled with the shadows, infiltrating it like an invading army. Creeping through a mini-forest of trees, wrapping around their thinning branches. Sandwiched in between was the Henry Hudson Parkway—still packed with bumper-to-bumper traffic heading north out of the city.

He didn't know why everybody was so desperate to leave. Home was nice during the holidays. Your *own* home. Where you didn't have to satisfy or disappoint anybody else's expectations.

His eyes returned to a scrap of paper on his desk. An Amtrak ticket stub that he'd discovered in the pocket of his jacket—exactly where he must've absently tucked it a year ago. Last Thanksgiving. Which was probably also the last time he'd worn this particular coat. He'd found both this morning—a memento of a whirlwind trip to Vermont with John during the crazy, head-over-heels beginning of their doomed relationship. In other words, the last thing he wanted to be reminded of.

He wheeled back his chair. Kicked on the shredder to his left. Stuffed the ticket stub into the opening; let it transform into confetti.

With a feeling of satisfaction, he opened his laptop. Watched it come to life. His glasses—already secured on one side with a safety pin—slipped down his nose, and he didn't even bother pushing them back up. His computer wouldn't care. Not for the first time, Eli thought how he actually got along much better with computers than he did with people. Computers responded to codes and data, never complaining that he was overweight. Or that his socks didn't match. Or that he'd just said the wrong thing—for the third time the same night.

So he settled in with his laptop and refocused exclusively on getting to know Commissioner Logan Patrick Donovan.

Eli was nothing like Eve. He couldn't read personalities and get inside people's minds. And he certainly couldn't touch Haddox's ability to piece together the jigsaw puzzle of people's digital fingerprints. Couldn't create a compelling narrative of their habits, desires, and secrets.

Still, Eli had a few skills. He was an expert at following the ins and outs of financial transactions—and figuring out what they revealed. You looked at the numbers. You figured out the pattern of what somebody did and what it said about his values. This was the science of the mind that Eli understood—where fiscal details and monetary choices spoke volumes about personality, behavior, and values.

So what did the commissioner's fiscal life reveal about him?

A lifelong New Yorker, Logan Donovan had joined the NYPD straight out of John Jay College, rising from police cadet all the way to police commissioner, with a short stint in the U.S. Air Force along the way. After he came home from Operation Desert Storm, lauded as a war hero, he'd skipped over a few ranks. Some people called it a "meteoric rise." Donovan hadn't spent enough time on the streets, his critics alleged. Hadn't put in the time as a beat cop that was necessary to learn how the city really worked.

But no one really complained. Crime was down in the city. Donovan unveiled a new community-policing program, grounded in his belief that it was important for the community and the police to respect each other. Some people called him the Great Humanitarian because of his approach to outreach: He attended minority church services in order to recruit new policemen—and he put extra cops on the streets, telling them to get to know the local residents.

Then came a particularly shocking incident of police brutality—

especially for the Big Apple, which, under Donovan, had redoubled its efforts to recruit diverse officers. And that was followed by a series of unarmed police shootings. What was happening throughout the nation was happening in New York City, too.

People blamed the commissioner. All of his accumulated goodwill dissipated overnight. They called for his ouster. Alleged that he'd sanctioned racial profiling, stepping up stop-and-frisk. That he had violated people's civil rights. He'd received death threats—though Eli noted that he'd also refused extra security. An odd choice for a widower with a thirteen-year-old child. Did he feel that invincible?

The commissioner's personal history followed a similar trajectory. He'd married a journalist immediately after returning home from the Gulf War. Jill had been a feature reporter assigned to write about his dramatic pilot rescue in Operation Desert Storm—how he'd swept out of the sky to pick up the stranded airman, just as Iraqi trucks raced toward them.

Career had come first, for both of them. Allie had come second. Then Jill had gotten sick—battled cancer for the better part of two years—and been rewarded with remission. A clean bill of health. Things were looking up.

Donovan's financial history actually mirrored his personal and professional one. Funny how things either went completely a man's way—or not.

His career on the rise, a young family in tow, their personal savings had filled his and Jill's bank accounts at a steady rate—for everything was held jointly. Logan and Jill Donovan had socked away and saved. They had no debt—and when the commissioner's father died, he inherited the brownstone on West Eightieth Street that he'd grown up in.

The commissioner was a tough guy's guy. Eli felt absolutely nothing in common with him. Except, apparently, this: They both had gained their own small piece of Manhattan island, thanks to family. In Eli's case, a rent-controlled apartment on the Lower East Side where, he was sure, he was going to live 'til they buried him.

Eli ripped open a bag of pretzel rods, put the end of one in his mouth. Stretched his arms, flexing his hands together and cracking his knuckles. The popping sound relaxed him. Then he toggled the screen, launching new windows of credit card and bank account data.

Jill's illness began a downturn in their financial fortunes as well. Their checking account balance plunged. BC—before cancer—they kept about eight thousand dollars in checking at a given time, backed up by substantial savings and retirement funds. AC—after cancer—their checking account dipped perilously low. There were three overdrafts. They were seventy-eight thousand dollars in credit card debt. They traded in a late-model Audi for a secondhand Lincoln Navigator, and a space at the garage two blocks away for the hassle of alternate-side street parking. All these changes were a sign of how badly they needed cash.

Their spending habits changed—almost overnight. They used to do their weekly shopping at Whole Foods and Citarella. Instead, they frequented Fairway and Gristedes—in the process, cutting their grocery bill in half. Dinners out every Friday and Saturday night—at places like Bistro Rouge and Oxtail Farms—abruptly ceased. They ordered occasional take-out fare from Szechuan Kitchen and Fajita Grill. All charitable contributions stopped.

There were no more trips to the Bronx Zoo. No movies out. No Broadway shows. None of the fun things that parents tried to do with their kids. With illness in the house, they'd not been able to afford it. With illness in the house, they'd likely not felt up to it.

It seemed that every spare dime they had was sucked into Jill's treatment. Her health insurance covered only a fraction of it.

It was a tragic story—but a perfectly normal one. Then Jill had died. The life insurance policy—taken out at the time of their marriage—had paid out the two million Donovan had admitted to receiving. And the money problems ended.

Eli closed out the window. In the interest of thoroughness, he checked whether Allie had any accounts. Parents tended to be split on how they handled their kid's financial education. Some—his own dad among them—set up checking and savings accounts the day their child was born, stashing every gift, every dime of summer job earnings, into the account. Others waited, preferring to manage things themselves.

It took three clicks of the keyboard to figure out that the Donovans had favored Eli's dad's approach. Allie had a checking account, a savings account, and a credit card. Obviously her parents were named on the accounts as well—but Allie was an active account user.

The checking account had regular deposits and ATM withdrawals. The credit card racked up balances approaching seven thousand dollars some months.

Suddenly he felt a niggling sense of disquiet. Thirteen-year-olds didn't spend money like that.

He checked the itemized charges on Allie's Visa card.

Definitely not made by a thirteen-year-old girl.

Dinners out at different restaurants—located everywhere but the Upper West Side.

Purchases at Cosabella. Azaleas. La Petite Coquette. Places that Eli quickly figured out were high-end lingerie shops.

Then there were the hotel charges. The Mandarin Oriental. The Waldorf. And a few boutique places on the Upper East Side.

Eli never had an intuitive understanding of people—but he understood how they got and spent their money. How they earned it, where they stashed it or spent it, all reflected decisions that were the key to who they were. If he knew about their money, then he knew what motivated them. What frightened them. What they clung to when they were in trouble.

He started with the simple figures. Slowly, they would grow clearer. And the moment they fell into patterns of behavior, then Eli *knew.*

The person whose finances he was studying would no longer be a figment of his imagination. No longer a mystery.

His problem right now was: The pattern of spending—filtered through Allie's credit card and checking account—had started three years and two months ago.

It was clear that someone had been having a long-time affair. Perhaps multiple affairs.

They'd been pretty sloppy about disguising it. And the affair had stopped—rather obviously—at the time of Jill's death.

But the card numbers didn't reveal the culprit.

The charge card in question didn't issue unique numbers. Logan, Jill, and Allie each had an identical credit card number.

So who was having the affair? Had it been the commissioner—or had it been Jill, despite her illness?

And whatever the answer, did it figure somehow into Allie's kidnapping?

# Chapter 38

## Public Courts, East Harlem

Fifty-eight minutes to deadline. Mace was taking it down to the wire.

He had left Vidocq headquarters in search of the only person he knew who might actually be able to lay his hands on two million dollars—cash—on the night before Thanksgiving. While he'd talked a big game in front of Eve and the team, now that it was put up or shut up time, doubts began to creep in.

He didn't bother calculating the odds that this guy might actually loan him the money. He knew they were long.

The guy's name was the Professor. He was forty-two, rail-thin, and five-foot-nine. He wore a faded navy hooded sweatshirt, his sneakers were caked in dirt, and his jeans were so thin they were almost transparent. So seeing him sitting courtside at the public hoops on East 115th and Lexington, which was more or less his working office, you'd never know that he had millions tucked away in a vault inside his Harlem brownstone. Or that he was the brains behind the Queen Street Bloods—one of New York City's most powerful gangs.

Maybe the Professor was bad company, but Mace had spent plenty of time in bad company.

Besides, life was complicated. Kind of like Queen's Bloods themselves. They made most of their money from the drug trade, but they also had legitimate business interests that even the most stuck-up social reformers admitted were good for the community. Hip-hop.

Streetball. And nightly patrols, to keep the neighborhood safe—and not just from outsiders.

*From the police.*

Mace had known the Professor since his own stint with the Queen's Bloods over twenty-five years ago. The guy hadn't changed: He still wasn't much of a talker, but his nickname was no joke. The Professor might not be the official leader of the Queen's Bloods, but Mace knew one thing: Anything the Professor wanted, the Professor got. Further evidence that the quietest guys could be the most dangerous.

The thin figure in the navy hoodie was guarded by Afrika, who sat with his legs splayed, fingers locked behind his head. It was his best *don't mess with me* pose—and he had about two hundred eighty pounds of muscle to back it up.

Mace approached. Afrika looked at the Professor. A particular kind of nod was exchanged.

Then Afrika grinned. His gold tooth gleamed. "Shit, man. Almost didn't recognize you in those white-man threads. You ain't dressed for hoops."

"I schooled some guys down at the cage this morning. Now I'm dressed for the holiday," Mace answered with an easy shrug.

"More like you're dressed for church with your grandma," Afrika returned.

The Professor had eyes as sharp as a fox's. They narrowed now. "You ain't here to play ball."

In other words, *Why are you wasting my time?*

Mace got to the point, explaining what he wanted and why. He was careful to point out the significant political upside from helping the commissioner of the NYPD, if the Professor agreed.

Then he waited, his body tense.

The answer was some version of what he'd expected. Two giant hands seized his wrist.

Mace might have plenty of muscle, but he knew Afrika was even more lethal—and could snap his wrist like a dry twig. So Mace didn't move.

196 / STEFANIE PINTOFF

"I've got questions. Lie and I'll break your wrist."

"I ain't no liar," Mace said quietly. He wasn't even breathing hard. He knew how this was supposed to go. The key was to man up. Not panic.

"First question: You alone?"

"C'mon, man, show me a little respect. I know the rules. No one here but this beautiful, six-foot-seven-inch Adonis."

"Okay, smartass. Second question: If the commissioner don't even know about this visit, how can you make promises for him?"

"Technically, guess I can't. But I can tell you this is a guy whose only child is in the hands of a lunatic." Mace gave that a moment to sink in. "If you ask me, our neighborhood's seen too many brothers dying."

Mace didn't point out that one of them had been the Professor's nephew. Some things didn't need to be said.

"The commissioner's my enemy. Not somebody I'm gonna loan money to," the Professor stated without emotion.

"That's one way to look at it," Mace acknowledged. "Then again, strikes me this is an opportunity: a partnership between a grateful police commissioner and the local boys in the hood. A game changer to turn things around. Save lives, make things better."

Afrika shook his head. "You're a regular do-gooder now, huh? First you save a few mangy dogs; now you're gonna save all of East Harlem. Third question: How do we know the Professor's gonna get his money back?"

"The Professor's a gambler. Puts up money and risks it. This time, it's for a win-win situation."

Afrika considered it. "What if you don't catch the kidnapper, recover the money?"

"What if pigs fly and fish climb trees?" Mace countered.

"Cocky bastard," Afrika muttered.

The Professor and Afrika considered that, too. But there were obvious advantages to what Mace was proposing.

"Play for it, under the streetlights," the Professor finally said.

"Excuse me?" Mace played competitive ball all the time. Usually for the occasional Benjamin. Not two million dollars.

"One on one," the Professor decided. "Against my pick."

The Professor was actually a master manipulator. This wasn't the equivalent of a coin toss to decide whether Mace could or couldn't borrow the money. This was about making sure Mace still understood who he was. That he remembered where he came from. Where—ultimately—his allegiances ought to lie.

"I ain't dressed for ball," Mace pointed out.

"No kidding. You look like a damn one-percenter who just escaped Wall Street."

"I also don't have much time," Mace said.

The Professor shrugged. The implication was clear: *Not my problem.*

Ninety seconds later, Mace was back on the court, matched up against Deacon—a player built like a tank, nicknamed for the tattoos of different crosses that lined his forearms.

Mace focused on defense, but Deacon got off a fade away from the left block that banked in for the first score.

"That all you got?" Deacon smirked. "Ain't no match for me."

"In my church, deacons don't talk smack." Mace blocked his next shot, caught the ball one-handed—then dribbled, spun 180 degrees, and arched the ball straight through the hoop with a swish. They were evenly matched, taking turns with the ball. It was close—but Mace sent the winning shot through the net.

No one moved for what seemed to Mace like an eternity. Then the Professor nodded. "Better get home and get ready. Afrika will stop by your crib with a car and your dough."

The Professor didn't like cops. But he understood the situation: A hero cop was being targeted by a batshit-crazy nutjob. That gave him the chance to make a power play. Take advantage of weakness. Meanwhile, maybe a kid or two would get home alive.

So Mace didn't bother thinking about favors owed.

He was halfway off the court when the Professor raised his hand, waved Mace back. "You can't ever fool me, Julius Mason. You're still one of us. Don't forget," the Professor said. His voice was quiet. Intense.

"I think about it every day," Mace replied—and was actually sincere. Not a day went by that he didn't thank God that he'd escaped his former life before he ended up dead. But now all he could think of was how he was going to plant two million dollars cash in a can and take down this son of a bitch. At the moment, that felt pretty good.

The commissioner had better goddamn appreciate it.

# Chapter 39

## Parade Staging Zone

"Have you seen this boy?" García approached a cotton candy vendor at the corner of West Eighty-first Street and Columbus. Showed him a photo from just that afternoon, of Frankie Junior sitting tall on one of the metal bleachers along the parade route.

"Sorry." The vendor was scrubbing down the sidewalk in front of his cart with bleach. "Only kid I remember from tonight is the greedy punk teenager who ordered three pinks and a blue, then hung around and got sick. Vomit ain't good for business, you know?"

García noticed the five-foot radius in front of the candy man was now spotless, reeking of bleach, but the sidewalk was still a mess of litter. Candy wrappers. Mustard-stained napkins. A half-eaten hot dog. And a gooey substance that probably was gum.

Junk that reminded him: He needed to keep his strength up. He pulled an energy bar out of his pocket.

The vendor wrinkled his nose. "Man, that smells nastier than the shit I just cleaned!"

"Peanut butter, banana, kale, and flax." García chewed the last bit of the dark brown energy bar. It was fuel to him. Nothing more.

The vendor screwed up his face in disgust. "Nobody needs to be that healthy."

So far, no one had seen Frankie Junior.

Which only meant García had to look harder.

# Chapter 40

## The Donovan Brownstone

KEEP OUT. YOU WOULDN'T UNDERSTAND, ANYWAY.

Maybe not—but Haddox at least intended to try. He decided to check Allie's public records first, so on his own computer, he ran through a series of password protocols and called up a master database managed by the FBI. Called DIVS—Data Integration and Visualization System—it drew from a multitude of data sources.

Haddox relied on this directory. He was a skip tracer extraordinaire, capable of tracking down people others failed to find. People who'd gone to extraordinary lengths not to be found. He clicked at the keyboard, his fingers moving at their usual 120 words per minute.

His goal was simple. Identify the kidnapper. Put a name to the person who had targeted Allie and the commissioner. Whose primary objective—at least on the surface—was the two million dollars in insurance money the commissioner had just received.

Right now the kidnapper was invisible. Entirely cloaked by a stolen Macy's rain jacket, pilfered cellphone, and computerized voice box. So Haddox turned his attention to the flip side of the problem: the kidnapper's target.

*Allie, luv, when I know about you, then I'll know more about him.*

Allie—Alison Rose Donovan, officially—was an only child, thirteen years old, and in the eighth grade at PS 334, a school just blocks from her home. Apart from her birth certificate and school records, New York State kept a copy of her speech therapy diagnosis and treatment reports. Early intervention, the state called it. Her address had not changed since birth: This brownstone on West Eightieth had always been her home.

She had a U.S. passport. Her travel records on it were normal: A brief trip to England, Scotland, and Ireland. Another to Mexico and some Caribbean islands.

Haddox scanned all available documents in the database. Allie's name popped up on a few documents that her father had been required to file as a senior police official. Before the commissioner had gained access to classified information, he—and those closest to him—had been stringently vetted. The family attended a Catholic church two blocks away. Allie's grandparents on both sides were deceased. An uncle—Jill's brother—was on the English faculty at the University of Montana. There had been some concern within government circles about his radical socialist agenda, but ultimately he had not been deemed a security threat.

Not a lot of information on the official databases. Which for a thirteen-year-old girl was more or less what Haddox would expect.

So Haddox turned his attention to Allie's computer. There were plenty of games on the hard drive: Minecraft, SimCity, and a role-playing adventure based on *The Lord of the Rings*. There were homework folders for each of her academic subjects. He found a lab report in the folder titled BIOLOGY. A term paper on *Julius Caesar* within ENGLISH. A project on Rosa Parks and the Civil Rights movement within HISTORY.

Once again, exactly what Haddox would expect.

Next he checked her Internet browser for bookmarks and history.

The first odd thing: They were empty. No history whatsoever. No bookmarks other than the factory default settings: CNN. AOL. Google and the like.

Nothing personal. Too clean. Someone had wiped the cache.

Of course, he had software for that. A program designed to bring bits and bytes back from the dead. It was effective—but it took time to work its magic. So for now, he moved on.

He skimmed her music. Allie had eclectic taste—everything from Imagine Dragons to Adele to the Beatles. He scanned her photo files. She liked animals, apparently; she took shots of dogs, puppies,

202 / STEFANIE PINTOFF

kittens—none of them her own. She'd created an album of her mom. She had a smattering of photos with friends. One showed her in a set—a strip of four shots, taken at someplace like Six Flags, where she and a friend had posed with bunny ears. She was grinning, happy in the moment.

He felt no closer to uncovering her secrets, so he turned back to her most personal device: her phone.

He no longer needed the passcode the commissioner had given him; Allie's kidnapper had altered the phone's lock screen and deleted the security code. It was certainly possible—even likely—that he had tampered with more. So Haddox implemented his own check-and-balance system; he cross-checked all data on the phone against that collected and preserved by her carrier.

He found her cellphone records easily enough. Checked her pattern of calls. There wasn't much; only a handful of calls home. Allie was part of the generation that texted. Her thumbs could probably move at lightning speed, but her fingers rarely dialed.

There were three friends she texted often. All standard stuff. Homework. Running late to school. Planning a Friday night movie.

*How did the kidnapper target you so easily, Allie?* Nothing Haddox saw could explain it.

He knew instinctively that something had to be missing.

He delved deeper into her cell records. Because what most people thought of as solely a communication device was also a sophisticated GPS unit, tracking and storing its travels—with a precise location marker—for months on end. He mined the easy data first, going into Allie's privacy settings and checking her location services. She hadn't disabled the tracker, so he learned that within the past week, she'd left home to:

Go to school.

See a movie at the Eighty-fourth Street multiplex.

Get take-out at Shake Shack.

Buy winter shoes at Harry's.

Visit the Museum of Natural History block.

His computer hummed in front of him as he downloaded the data to a special program he had fine-tuned over the years. Manipulated it according to certain variables. Crafted a flexible algorithm to decipher his subject's movements.

Between built-in GPS technology and a proliferation of smartphone apps, Allie's phone had captured a hoard of data beyond who she texted and called. It offered a record of what she ate and where she ate it, how many miles she walked, which routes she preferred to take. When Haddox was tracing a mark, he used this data—and could easily figure out whether his target was a church worshipper or a yoga practicer, a drug addict or a philanderer. Companies angling for marketing strategies called it "predictive modeling"—and shamelessly used the data to forecast a person's habits. Haddox called it "finding his mark."

But he'd just learned something new. Data modeling wasn't as useful when the subject was a teenager. Specifically, one who apparently lived most of her life online. Because she'd used a staggering amount of data in the past month.

But what had she been doing with all that data? Assuming Allie Donovan was a typical teenager, then she'd be active on social media. But there was no Facebook. No Twitter. No Snapchat or ASKfm.

He kept trolling through the apps on her phone. Came up with Instagram—where she was logged in as AnimalLover856. It was a public account with 2,318 followers and more than six hundred photos posted: Dogs out walking in the city. Close-ups of squirrels, birds, and chipmunks in Central Park. The occasional stray cat.

Who did she follow?

Again, nothing but animals. Specifically, twenty-six puppy accounts, fourteen breeders, and five animal-rescue organizations.

Nothing personal. Not much there.

*Keep out. You wouldn't understand, anyway.*

Allie's screensaver had delivered a message, predicting that Haddox wouldn't understand. So far, she had been exactly right.

# Chapter 41

Just Outside the American Museum of Natural History

Nine hours, forty-one minutes until the parade began.

Six hours, forty-one minutes until the crowds assembled.

Only forty-one minutes until the ransom drop.

Video footage had been combed through. Suspicious individuals had been isolated. The resulting photos—however grainy—were being circulated throughout the NYPD, FDNY, Homeland Security, Counterterrorism, and Tactical Response Units all the same.

Donovan dialed the leader of Gamma Team on his secure line. "So every rooftop along the parade route is now covered?"

"I'm sending my units in groups of two—Team Alpha through Team Omega."

"And there's coverage on the blocks surrounding the museum?"

"Affirmative. No one's making trouble on our watch."

"I'm about to head down to the corner of West Seventy-seventh and Central Park West. I need you to cover me. But if you see a specific threat, you do *not* shoot to kill. We need any suspect alive and kicking."

"Acknowledged." Donovan heard the team leader take a deep breath. "I remember what you did for me two years ago, when I was shot in the line of duty. I won't let you down, sir."

# Chapter 42

350 Riverside Drive, Vidocq Headquarters

Thirty-one minutes to deadline.

When his phone began vibrating, Eli picked it up right away.

"Guess what, Einstein? You can get your panties out of a wad. I got the money," Mace gloated on the other end of the line.

Eli closed his eyes and groaned. "What money?"

"I knew you were an awkward, no-fashion homebody, but since when did you get stupid?" Mace demanded. "The ransom money."

Eli was sure he couldn't be hearing things right. "You're telling me that you got two million dollars—cash—to use for Allie's ransom?"

"Right here in my favorite extra-large New York Knicks duffel bag. I'm almost at the museum now."

"Damn, Mace. How the hell did you pull this off?"

Over the line, Eli heard police bullhorns and the *thrum* of helicopters. Mace was inside the Frozen Zone.

"Anyone follow you?"

"Nah, I'm still Joe Public. Our surveillance set up yet?"

"I'll let García know you're en route. Don't show yourself. Not 'til you get the all-clear."

"Nobody's gonna make me. If I can do the impossible—namely, getting my hands on a huge chunk of cash the night before National Turkey Day—then I can stay hidden from some lowlife."

"I'll tell Haddox and Eve to head on over," Eli said.

"Guess you can thank me later," Mace replied. "Twenty-nine minutes 'til showtime."

. . .

García walked briskly past the garbage cans on West Seventy-seventh and Central Park West. Keeping a close check on the scene.

He stopped. Jumped the low fence. Quickly looked inside each one.

Thirty-seven cans, he counted. Each one empty.

*It all looks okay.*

But he could've sworn: Last time he came through this way, he hadn't noticed a yellow smiley face painted on that one in the back.

# Chapter 43

## The Donovan Brownstone

*You wouldn't UNDERSTAND,* Allie's laptop had taunted.

Haddox was up for that challenge. In fact, he almost grinned with anticipation. This was a girl who averaged nearly eight gigabytes of data usage in a given month. Nobody did that unless they were glued to their Web browser. He just hoped that the avalanche of content didn't obscure the nuggets of information that would lead him to Allie's kidnapper. With her iPhone now connected to his own computer, he started digging, sifting, analyzing.

He took the Instagram account that he knew to be Allie's as his starting point. Ran a series of algorithms. Cross-referenced the data that resulted. And saw something key: Allie didn't run and manage just AnimalLover856. She had one other account where she posted her art: doodles and emoticons, punctuated by drawings, all decorated with loops and swirls. Maybe Instagram was for photos—but between image capture and the comments feature, Allie had found a useful medium for language. She used her second account to post the virtual equivalent of essays and diary entries.

Her username listed a fanciful alias: Monique Morgan.

*Where have I heard that name before?* A memory hovered briefly at the edge of his mind before flitting away.

He kept going. Hoping he'd learn something. Understand more.

For the next sixteen minutes, he read Allie's stories and poems and posts. He felt a pang of guilt, like he was eavesdropping on a life he shouldn't. Sure, she'd posted this material online—but under the belief that her username offered her a blanket of anonymity.

The entries began shortly before her mom's death. April 18—which he noted was around the time Jill received news of her cancer's recurrence. The entries were brief. They had to be, with Instagram as a medium. It offered a photo-sized text opportunity—with a limited opportunity to post text in the comments section.

They also grew progressively more secretive. Even with an online alias, she had preferred using code words and nicknames he didn't always fully understand.

One of her teachers was so boring he was Mr. Snooze—represented by a picture of a person's gaping yawn. A classmate was Gollum, someone who'd have been better off living under a rock.

She wrote letters to herself and to the world.

She felt she had no true friends.

Sometimes she found relief when she made herself bleed. She claimed it made her feel something, instead of just numb.

He could feel her sadness, her misery, her anger—even more intensely, sitting in her room, among her possessions.

Still, she wasn't all doom and gloom. Reading more, Haddox discovered Allie's likes and dislikes. She loved fantasy books and movies. She debated what music was coolest. Imagined what career would suit her most. She listed the top ten reasons she despised math. A boy code-named Burrito Boy had made fun of her in gym class; he ought to be drawn and quartered, if not boiled in hot oil. There were five reasons why Gwen Allensen was a grown-up mean girl. Her dad's haircut made him look like a dork. A teacher at a middle school concert had burped like an erupting volcano.

That last observation made Haddox laugh out loud.

The worst was the one she wrote the day after Jill died. Underneath the picture of a tombstone, he read:

*Mom is gone, and Dad's to blame. Our priest read a poem about life's seasons, saying "childhood is the sweetest one."*

*Seriously?? Someone believes that crap?? I think I'm going to puke.*

Haddox fought the urge to feel self-satisfied. To rush down to Eve and tell her *I told you so. Your commissioner is not a good guy.* After all, he was reading a teenager's grief-stricken ramblings.

He was absolutely going to find out the details, but first he checked the identities of those who entered a dialogue with Allie. Who was MojoMan? Soccer856? The_Crusader? ForgottenHero?

He never finished the job.

The ringing from Allie's phone pulled Haddox out of the depths of Allie's online world—and into the urgent problem at hand.

# **Chapter 44**

Parade Staging Zone

García tailed a man in a hooded sweatshirt who emerged from under the parade bleachers on Central Park West, just a block south and east of the museum.

*Had he been sleeping there, or had he come from the park?*

He had a slow walk—like a guy who was trying to be too careful. Suddenly, he broke into a run. Heading straight for the collection of garbage cans north and west across the avenue.

García stayed right behind him.

The guy stopped in front of the first garbage can in his path. Not the one with the smiley face. He paused, grabbing either side of the top in both hands. Then proceeded to vomit into it.

Afterward, he stayed in place for a minute, panting like an overheated dog.

*Not our guy.*

"Move along, move along!" Sweatshirt guy finally attracted the attention of one of the cops.

García continued to watch as the cop hustled the man away. His heart rate returned to normal in precisely twenty-one seconds.

*Not our guy,* he repeated to himself. But he was out there.

Somewhere.

And García was going to find him and make him pay.

# Chapter 45

Enough watching Blondie and Rambo.

I'm back to *her* letter—and I even take a moment to admire her script. The beautifully proportioned loops, the elegance of her *T*'s. I read again:

*Page Three.*

*Guess I shouldn't have been surprised by those cops. Did I ever tell you my earliest memory?*

*It's of my father shouting.*

*"This place is a pigsty. You think I want to come home to this?"*

*From where I was cowering behind the living room curtains, I could tell he was in the garage. Things must've been in his way, so he started throwing them. From the window, I saw a flash of yellow and orange as my plastic Big Wheel tricycle slammed into the concrete. Mangled, it slid down the driveway toward the curb.*

*Tears burned my eyes, but I never made a sound.*

*In the kitchen, I heard my mother putting dinner on the table. The dishes rattled because her hands were shaking.*

*His dinner, because I didn't eat with them. Not anymore. I was always spilling my drink, and that made him mad.*

*I remember hoping the chicken wouldn't be too dry or too cold. Maybe the salad would have the right amount of* dressing—and the potato would be the right degree of soft. Maybe she'd read his mind and knew whether he was in the mood for a cold beer or a Coke. Maybe she'd even put it in the right sort of glass.

She tried—and my five-year-old self kept hoping that, just once, she'd get it right.

Except she never did. Everything was always wrong—and there was no pleasing him, ever.

That's how I knew, years later, that there would be no pleasing the cops by the museum.

"PUT YOUR FEET IN FRONT OF YOU." Penguin was still harassing the homeless guy.

"Hey—he's got a driver's license in here that says his name is Ronald Case. Does he look like a Ronald Case to you?" His partner, Logan, held it up to the light.

Penguin circled the homeless guy. "PUT YOUR FEET OUT IN FRONT OF YOU. PUT YOUR HANDS ON THOSE KNEES NOW."

"What?" The homeless man's hands were shaking. Maybe he was on something. Or maybe he was just nervous.

"PUT YOUR FEET IN FRONT OF YOU AND KEEP YOUR HANDS ON YOUR KNEES."

"I can't do both at once." He definitely had a case of the shakes.

"Next thing you know, Dumbass here's gonna say he can't walk and chew gum at the same time," Logan said.

"You better wise up real quick." Penguin pulled a pair of latex gloves out of his pocket. "You see my fists? They're getting ready to mess you up if you don't start listening. SO PUT YOUR DAMN HANDS ON YOUR KNEES RIGHT NOW!"

"All right, all right." The homeless man stretched his shaking arms in front of him.

Watching, I already knew that it wouldn't matter.

First came the fists. Then the batons cracked down.

*Soon he was bruised and bloody, lying on the sidewalk, in need of medical attention that he was never going to get.*

*I was the only one who wondered, "Why?" Who wanted answers.*

*Because the victim himself? He was well past the point of caring.*

# Chapter 46

## The Donovan Brownstone

Eve found a plain laminate table tucked into a small room off the kitchen. She pulled out the stool underneath—it was the ergonomic kind. She sat on it, pushing aside a memo pad and pencil placed next to a corded landline.

*Dentist appointment—Allie—12/2 at 3:45 p.m.* was written on the first page.

Eve wanted neither the paper nor the house phone. She dialed out from her own secure line.

Donovan's driver picked up on the second ring and said, "Yes?"

"Mr. Heath? This is Special Agent Eve Rossi."

"Call me Sam. The commissioner filled me in, told me to expect to hear from you. Any progress finding Allie?"

His voice was quiet but warm. A little bit husky with concern and worry.

"Not yet. But maybe you can help with that."

"I told the commissioner I'd do anything I could. I volunteered to join the search party, man the phone lines, whatever he needed. But he wouldn't hear of it. My mother's in a home on Long Island, her health's pretty bad. He worried that if I disappoint her this year, I might not get another chance to make it up to her." There was resignation in his voice. The kind of tone that said *I've fought battles with Logan Donovan before—and lost.*

"Just telling me about the Donovans will help," Eve reminded him.

So he did. He detailed Allie's daily routine, listing her favorite

shops and naming her friends. He talked about Jill Donovan, too—
how he'd driven her to chemo appointments, how worried she'd been
about Allie. He didn't sugarcoat the problems that complications like
Gwen sometimes caused. But he painted a picture of a family who
stuck together despite it all. He also talked about his history with
Donovan, starting when they were in the Academy together and then
later in the same precinct before Sam retired from active duty. And he
detailed the typical sort of threats Logan—and his family—received.

Eve listened not just to his words but to the thoughts and images
behind his answers. The Donovans were complicated—but so were a
lot of families.

"Your primary job was to provide security for Mrs. Donovan and
Allie. Were there any threats that stood out—or that recurred?"

"There's lots of lone nuts in this city, Agent Rossi. But I don't re-
call a single incident involving Donovan's family where the perpetrator wasn't caught. The commissioner made it a priority, you see. He
always looks out for his own."

"But he's no Superman," Eve replied. "He can't do it all."

"If he can't do it personally, he finds somebody to help. Just like
he found me. Just like he found you," Sam pointed out.

Eve next spoke with Jackie Meade in the living room downstairs. She
was far less helpful than Sam had been.

Still, Eve knew how to compensate.

She just listened, watching, letting Jackie reveal herself in hundreds of different ways. Hands. Eyes. Gestures. Expressions. Movements. Eve knew her observation skills were her most powerful tool.
To be a good listener, she worked to understand more than words.
She paid attention to what excited people—as well as what frightened
them. She noticed where they hesitated and where they raced ahead.
Until she could figure out almost exactly what someone was really
saying. Even if that person never uttered the right words.

What Eve figured out was that Jackie was saying the same things
as Sam—even when she was lying. For example, she claimed that the
Donovans had been Disney-family happy; her body language practically screamed a different story.

And it only took a slightly different angle to reveal the truth.

"Allie is a good kid," Eve summarized, "but not particularly invested in the real world. Her head's always in the clouds. Actually, in *the* cloud. She was happier online than in real life. That was why she didn't want to go to her father's speech at the balloon inflation ceremony—"

Jackie interrupted her. "I wouldn't say that. She didn't want to be around Gwen. Gwen was always the issue. More than how much time Allie spent on the computer or why she didn't hang out more with her friends or couldn't have a puppy." Jackie picked at her fingernails, finding some flaw with her cuticles. Embarrassed that she'd said so much.

But nothing Eve hadn't already figured out.

She opened her mouth to ask more but stopped when she heard the racing of footsteps. Haddox burst into the room.

"You found something?" she hazarded.

"Kidnapper's on the line. You need to talk with him."


Eve couldn't help it; her heart trip-hammered as she took the phone.

"This is Eve. We spoke earlier, when you made your ransom demand." She forced a note of intimacy into her voice that she did not feel. But she wanted to attempt making a connection.

Except it wasn't the kidnapper who replied.

It was Allie, her voice high-pitched and scared. "He wants me to tell you that he will not walk into your trap. You have exactly six minutes for your assault teams to vacate the roof of the natural history museum. And the buildings on West Seventy-seventh Street."

"Will you ask him to talk with me, Allie?" Eve urged.

The girl was sobbing. "If you don't do what he says, he's going to kill—"

"Hold the phone so he can hear me—"

*Click.* The line went dead.

# Chapter 47

## Donovan Family Brownstone

Eve pulled out her own phone and dialed Donovan. He picked up on the second ring. "Allie called with a message from her kidnapper. You have exactly three and a half minutes for your rooftop assault teams on West Seventy-seventh Street to reverse course."

Donovan didn't answer her, but she immediately heard him on his radio. "Stand down! Stand down! I repeat, Cerberus, stand down! Hydra, stand down! Typhon, stand down!"

There was a crackling noise on the secure radio.

"Do you copy?" Donovan asked.

"Roger that." In the background, the Cerberus Team leader repeated the order.

"Copy that," Typhon leader echoed.

"I need confirmation, Hydra," Donovan insisted.

No response.

"Hydra?"

"Egress, Hydra. Egress."

More crackling noise in the background, and the *pop-pop-pop* of gunfire.

Eve heard shouts. Curses. "Officer down! Officer down!"

"Cover them. Mind innocents," Donovan barked.

Another crack as the connection dropped.

Seven minutes later, it was over. The shooter had been in an apartment window of the building one block behind. Its residents were away for the Thanksgiving holiday. Now forensics was combing every inch of the apartment, the building, the block.

The shooter had escaped. His target had suffered non-life-threatening injuries. And Donovan had made the only decision he could in a dense urban environment: He had ordered his men to retreat, as fast as possible.

Eve, hearing all this, exhaled the breath she hadn't realized she was holding.

She had tried to reverse the call from Allie's phone, but of course it did not work.

Still, she could only assume that the kidnapper knew the retreat had been effected.

That the original plan for the ransom drop was still in place.

And something more. That hurting Commissioner Logan Donovan—personally and professionally—was the real goal.

# Chapter 48

## Garbage Can Graveyard

At precisely three minutes 'til midnight, Mace began to stroll down the museum side of West Seventy-seventh Street.

The vendors weren't an issue. They were gathered in a circle, bored, shooting the shit.

Wearing his white-man threads, Mace didn't attract much attention. Still, he waited until he was certain no cop was looking.

Then he circled to the rear of the garbage can graveyard and shoved his New York Knicks duffel bag into a can at the back.

The can with a yellow smiley face painted on it.

Eve held her breath when she saw Mace make the drop.

He'd been right on time. Now he was walking briskly away.

At the corner of West Seventy-seventh, he looked like he was about to stop, spin, and play defense. But he kept going, crossed Central Park West, and went north along the perimeter of the park until he reached West Eighty-first Street.

Playing his part.

Trying to keep a kidnapped kid or two alive.

Haddox waited in the shadows of the press van, just by Teddy Roosevelt's statue at the front of the museum.

He noticed the commissioner across the street. The lying git was finally taking a personal interest in his daughter. Probably wanted to be there for the news cameras the instant she was recovered.

He saw García amble down West Seventy-seventh, covering the rear approach from Columbus.

Each one of them: Watching. Waiting. Ready.

At the southwest corner of West Seventy-seventh, Eve kept her eyes on the garbage can with the smiley face.

As soon as Mace was out of range, someone would make a move.

It wouldn't be long. Two million dollars was too much money to leave lying around.

Eve kept her distance, but she watched every shadow. Never took her eyes from the can.

No one approached the garbage can graveyard.

Cops came and went, carrying cups of coffee. The street vendors chatted among themselves. The floats were beginning to line up, north of Eighty-first Street.

Five minutes stretched into eight, then twelve.

Eve asked herself: *Could we have missed something?*

"García," she murmured into her headset. "Do you see anything?"

*Nothing. Too quiet,* he replied.

"Haddox—what about you? Anybody unusual?"

*Nothing here, luv.*

Mace had the same response.

Nothing happened. Not a damn thing.

Eve gave up after nineteen minutes. She raced across the street. To the can with the yellow smiley face.

It was empty.

No money.

No message.

*Nothing.*

"What the hell?" the commissioner fumed. "You had multiple sets of eyes on the can."

"Man, he must have figured out a way to go fishing. Did it like this." Mace knelt on the pavement. The garbage can access door had been turned to the rear, left ajar. The interior bin had been removed already, to accommodate the size of Mace's bag. A sidewalk paver had its leaves disturbed. A path tunneled through them. It led to a small area behind the fence, obscured by a hulking tree.

A good hiding spot for squirrels, chipmunks—or stalkers.

"I see where the leaves are crushed," Eve said. "Somebody was lying here. What I don't understand is how we missed him."

Her gaze was caught by an odd shape stuck in a mesh of leaves and branches. A sturdy pole with a hook on its end. "Let's hope when he went fishing, he left us with fingerprints and other trace evidence," she muttered. Locard's principle—that with every crime, there was a transfer of material between perpetrator and scene—had solved thousands of otherwise hopeless cases.

Haddox let out a low whistle. "Two million dollars, gone—right from under our noses."

"Task One complete. Total fail," Mace grumbled. "Now we gotta keep dealing with this asshole."

Only the commissioner wasn't complaining.

Eve turned to follow his gaze.

"Allie!" Donovan shouted.

She saw a small figure emerge from the shadows of the park.

A *child*. Wearing a bright purple rain slicker.

Donovan shouted "Allie!" again—and exploded into a sprint.

Eve was right behind him. Thinking: Not *a total failure*. A ransom had been traded for a life. The exchange had worked, even if the culprit wasn't yet caught.

Now Allie was walking toward them. And she was carrying something in her arms.

# Chapter 49

I see the commissioner's been making friends.

Blondie was keeping a close watch on the ransom can.

Rambo was right behind; he circled that block more often than a sick dog with the runs.

And Knicks fan wanted me to think he left the area after dropping the money, but he didn't go far.

Who are these people? Muscle for hire? Definitely not fans of authority. It's fun watching them scatter when a real cop comes near.

Now I'm watching the boy.

He's stiff with fear, locked in a statuelike stance. I feel bad, since after all, how many times have I been in the wrong place at the wrong time? Life's a bitch that way.

Maybe it's because I've been rereading her letter, but I flash back to a time when I was his age.

I was eleven when I met Josh Geller. He was a year older than me, in seventh grade, not sixth. He had whitish-blond hair that he gelled so it stuck straight up. He was thin, but he walked as though he was a sumo wrestler. He was a kid who acted bigger and tougher than he really was.

He was class president, and on the debate team, and poster boy of the principal's FAB program. Friends Against Bullying.

I still don't know why Geller and his friends picked on me. I didn't have red hair or bad acne. I didn't wear glasses. My parents hadn't saddled me with a silly name.

I remember the day I met Josh. He was looking around the cafeteria, expecting to see somebody else. Then he slouched loose. Pulled a paper bag out of his pocket. Walked over to me, flanked by two girls and a boy.

"Got anything good for lunch today, moron?"

It was my first day at a new school. I was sitting by myself.

"What's wrong? Cat got your tongue?"

"No. Leave me alone." I could feel my jaw tightening. I've never liked bullies. I despise the way they have a sixth sense for those with shaken confidence and bruised egos. They target the vulnerable to make themselves feel more powerful.

"Hey, just answer the question: yes or no. Unless you're so dumb, you think this is a multiple-choice quiz." Josh pulled my ham-and-cheese sandwich closer to him. Inspected it. I thought he was going to spit on it.

Instead, he pulled a bottle of hot sauce out of his own bag. Proceeded to empty it onto my bread, until the plate was nothing but a sodden, sorry red mess.

That was just the beginning.

I never stood up to them. Didn't have the stomach for conflict. But every day they played their stupid games, making me more and more miserable until I wished they were dead.

Josh Geller got his karmic payback. After high school graduation, he went out drinking with one of his birdbrained friends. They decided to go subway surfing on the back of a 6 train bound for Parkchester.

I can imagine it now: him clinging onto the outside edge of a closed door, his face pressed against the window, his horror as he slipped and fell onto the tracks.

I think of him every time I see that MTA ad: *Surf the Web, not the train.*

And I smile.

I'm pretty straightforward. I've learned that things are simple if you think about them. That the situation is always the root of the problem. That people are so stupid they need to experience something big to understand a point.

Like the equivalent of a neon sign in Times Square.

## PART FOUR

# THE BREAKOUT

Fourth Thursday of November

Thanksgiving Day

Midnight to 9 a.m.

# Chapter 50

Corner of West 77th Street and Central Park West

Streetlights shone on her bright purple rain slicker. The hood was tight across her head. Logan Donovan could make out a backpack in the shape of a plush bear slung over her right shoulder, with ears and a goofy grin.

He took off, running in tandem with Eve, sprinting toward Allie.

He had worried after that last phone call. But in the end, it had been easy.

That was how it worked when you had nerves of steel—and were determined to get your own way through sheer force of will. That was how he had orchestrated the meteoric rise that was his career. How he had won over Jill as his wife. And how he had secured his daughter's release today.

He'd be hailed as a man who took care of business. A hero.

"Allie!" he yelled. "Over here!"

He could feel his hands shaking as he reached for her. He stared at her through thick tears of relief that didn't fall—but blurred his vision, refusing to be blinked away.

He reached for her. Crushed her into his chest.

And knew the instant his touch registered: *This is not right!*

He blinked hard and focused. The child was Allie's height—and had Allie's slim build. The child wore Allie's purple raincoat. Carried Allie's panda backpack.

But when Donovan pulled the hood off the child's head, even his tears and desperation couldn't disguise the truth.

*This* child was not Allie.

This child was unwell.

He was pale. Blue in the face.

And Donovan caught a whiff of the sickly sweet scent of blood before the child collapsed into his arms.

*What have you done, you sick bastard?* he whispered into the shadows.

And knew the fault was his. Because he'd been nothing but a damned fool.

# Chapter 51

## Southeast Corner of West 77th Street and Central Park West

The shock and silence lasted for three long heartbeats.

Eve called for help. Two paramedics joined them from the first-aid tent that had been set up in advance of the parade.

She and Donovan helped them lift the boy—who was bleeding profusely from an injury to his arm—and carry him to the nearest metal bleachers.

There was an angry howl behind her. García was pushing through the growing crowd. Stopped short—and looked at the boy lying on the bleachers. *Holy Mary, Mother of God,* he whispered. Then he knelt down beside his son, and in a stronger voice, he said, "Hey, Frankie, Dad's here. You're gonna be okay."

Mace and Haddox fanned out to search for any sign of the kidnapper. Any trace he might have left behind or any witness who might have seen him.

The blond paramedic looked Frankie Junior over. Seemed concerned that his skin was so blue, his body temperature so cold.

García fumbled in his vest; then shoved a plastic packet toward the medic. "He needs this injection! He's got a blood-clotting disorder—Von Willebrand."

The vials came out of the packet. The injection was administered.

The paramedics' hands lifted up Frankie Junior's thin frame. They carried him into the light and placed him on a stretcher. Everyone's flashlight shined on him, making his body appear a ghostly silver.

"How bad?" García clutched the panda backpack that had dropped, like it was the most precious treasure he'd ever recovered.

"Pupils dilated. His abdomen is cold. Pulse is weak!" the paramedic yelled to her partner.

"How long until the injection works?" García demanded. "Until the bleeding stops?"

"It's not that easy. We have to get him to a hospital." The blond paramedic was working to create a tourniquet. It wasn't helping. "His heartbeat is erratic."

García reached down, grabbed Frankie's hand tight. His lips moved, and Eve thought he might have been praying. Or bargaining. Or maybe just hoping that the sheer force of his own will could stanch the endless bleeding.

Frankie Junior wasn't shivering. He wasn't moving at all. But his eyes fluttered.

Donovan didn't let the opportunity pass. "Did you see a girl? Her name's Allie."

Frankie Junior tried to say something.

"What was that?" Donovan demanded, leaning over him.

"Give him some space!" García growled.

"*My* daughter's still out there—with the monster who did this."

"I'm sorry, Commissioner, but this man's right," the paramedic agreed. "The boy should *not* be talking—"

"No!" Donovan shouted. "Look. He wants to say something."

Eve stepped between him and the boy. "He's suffered a deep cut. He's lost a dangerous amount of blood."

Frankie Junior's head moved from side to side.

García leaned down close. All Eve heard was a faint, "Papa."

García's face softened.

Red lights mingled with blue and created a psychedelic blur on the wet pavement as the ambulance arrived.

García clutched at Frankie's arm like he'd never let go.

"Someone needs to ask him questions. I don't care who," Donovan said roughly. "He has information I desperately need. He's met the kidnapper. He's wearing Allie's clothes."

"We've got it covered," Eve assured him, placing a hand on his shoulder.

He brushed it off, running forward when the rear door to the ambulance opened. A medic stepped out of the back, made a series of preparations for his patient inside.

Donovan was shaking with anger and frustration, elemental and deep-seated. He waved toward the great expanse that was Central Park. "Kidnapper's in there, somewhere."

"We should send Tactical in for a search-and-rescue mission," Eve said, also stepping toward the ambulance. "Given the amount of rain we've had earlier, they stand a good chance of tracking the boy's movements."

Donovan's words were thick in his throat. "Easy as pie. Which is why I want your man to handle it."

Eve whirled to face him. She had never met a man more determined to have things his own way. "You mean García? Right now, he's a father who needs to be with his son. You and I, on the other hand, have the resources of two entire departments at our disposal."

Donovan's eyes were blazing. Not with anger, though. Unease, Eve decided.

"I want García," he demanded. "He reminds me of men I trusted my own life with during Operation Desert Storm."

"You don't get to pick and choose," she told him.

"Given what the bastard did to García's boy, I'll bet he's motivated and ready to do it."

"*All* my guys are good, and they all want to make this perp pay," she agreed. "But this isn't about skill or motivation; it's about manpower. Central Park is—what?—over eight hundred acres? In the dark, it would be a fool's errand to send only a couple men. We need boots on the ground."

"It can't be cops' boots."

Eve had let this go on too long. She understood the pressures and the concerns that handicapped Donovan. But in this moment, his behavior made no sense—and it had to stop. "Why *wouldn't* you want all the help you can get? The police commissioner is sworn to protect all citizens of this city. Maybe you've forgotten that includes Allie, too."

"Maybe you've forgotten that my department has been targeted by multiple threats. I already lost a man this evening," he said roughly. "Every call my officers get? I'm aware it could be a trap."

"You'd like it better if a trap ensnared my team," she retorted.

"It won't. I've seen the way García moves. Like he's got eyes in the back of his head."

Eve nodded, finally understanding. She watched Donovan straighten his shoulders, regain control. The flash of vulnerability that she'd seen disappeared in an instant.

The paramedics wheeled Frankie Junior to the ambulance. García followed them into the back.

"Safe to say he's got troubles of his own," she told the commissioner. "It isn't always about you."

But in that moment, García surprised her. He said a few words to Frankie Junior—then stepped back out of the ambulance.

It was true that Eve could usually tell things about people, reading the words and emotions they would never say. Her process was largely intuitive, maybe with a hint of magic—not unlike predicting a future from the palm of a hand.

But the truth of someone else's relationship? Like this father and son? Its texture was far too complicated. Even for her.

García watched the ambulance pull away. Then he exchanged a glance with Donovan. Something wordless passed between them— the faintest trace of a signal. Maybe it was a bond between two fathers. Or an understanding between men who always put their job first.

"The doctors will do their job. I'm going to do mine."

"It's too big an area," Eve told him. "You won't be able to accomplish anything until I send in reinforcements."

García shook his head. "I'm still going to get started. It's like my old commander used to say: You eat the elephant one bite at a time."

García was still holding the purple raincoat and soggy panda backpack. Now he offered them to the commissioner.

"It's not even her backpack," Donovan choked, angry again. "Looks like the asshole got it from one of the parade vendors. We ought to check; see if anybody remembers selling it." He indicated a man hawking toys about thirty yards behind, with several animal backpacks—elephants, giraffes, monkeys, as well as pandas.

"So who's gonna look inside it—you or me?" García demanded.

The commissioner didn't open the backpack so much as he ripped it apart in frustration.

He saw what was inside. Dropped it to the ground and gave it a hard kick. It scuttled against the metal bleachers.

Silently, Eve picked it up. And stared, dumbfounded, at its contents.

# Chapter 52

## Near the Parade Route

Reading her letter, I started to understand something: The situation is the key.

That's what I learned back in Psych 101 when we studied the Stanford Prison Experiment. Once people volunteered to be prisoners or guards, they internalized their roles. Guards turned into sadists; prisoners became rebels or victims. Morality went right out the window.

Assuming it was ever there.

It reminds me of the drowning child—another exercise they teach you in school.

You imagine there's a drowning child. He screams for your help—so you think you ought to give it. You're big enough and strong enough; you can lift the child out of the water.

But life's complicated. You imagine how your clothes will get muddy and wet. It will cost time to change them. To call the child's mom. To give statements to the police.

And there are consequences: You'll be late to work. Your boss will be angry. You might lose your job.

Should you still save the child?

It's a no-brainer, right?

But did you know, all over the world, two people die every second from preventable causes? One hundred twenty every minute? Seven thousand two hundred every hour?

So should you donate to UNICEF or the Red Cross? And how often—every day? Every week? Every month?

The abstract is less of a no-brainer, right?

How far will you go to save a child?

And here's a different question: *What if the child is yours?*

# Chapter 53

350 Riverside Drive, Vidocq Headquarters

*Who was having the affair?* The question was driving him crazy. Eli leaned back in his chair, stretching his arms above his head. He had been sitting in front of his computer for well over two hours, tracing the financial details of Jill and Logan Donovan's life. After hearing of the botched ransom drop at the museum, a new urgency had entered his online research.

He considered himself Haddox's technological equal when it came to unraveling asset-protection schemes. What ordinary people called "hiding their money." And he was certainly on par with Eve in terms of understanding how people's money habits betrayed even the most distorted thinking of their psyche.

So what was he missing? Why hadn't he found the answer yet?

And then it hit him: *Because I'm looking in the wrong places.*

He remembered himself as a teenager. How he'd wasted few words on his father or his grandma. He communicated with them in monosyllables, saving his real thoughts for his friends. He's been smart-mouthed and aloof, pretending never to care—but behind it all, he'd been a pretty accurate observer of his immediate world.

Allie had a credit card—and the charges on it fell into three categories. One of her parents was responsible for the hotels and restaurants and lingerie. The iTunes and gaming sites and Fandango charges appeared to be uniquely Allie's. But then Eli had noticed a third category, with unusual names.

He started with the first and worked his way down, his fingers clicking a staccato on the keys.

He uncovered chat rooms with fees.

Forums where you paid for access to a private detective's "expertise."

Something called WebJusticeForUs—which was partly a private forum, partly an advice site for amateur investigators.

Haddox would've just hacked his way in.

But Haddox wasn't here.

Eli couldn't get beyond the login screen without a registered, paid account. So he opened his wallet, pulled out his personal credit card, and ponied up.

# Chapter 54

Southeast Corner of West 77th Street
and Central Park West

Inside the panda backpack were two items that Eve was not expecting. The first was a large block of money—cash, wrapped in cellophane—that contained directions to the current location of the full two million dollars that Mace had dropped off in the garbage can with the smiley face.

Scrawled on it, a message. *Can't buy me love.*

"Check it out." She tossed the block to Mace. But she didn't truly doubt that it was real. It was the ultimate tease from their adversary—throwing their money right back at them. Task One, indeed.

The second item was a flip phone. Nokia brand. Cheap.

Likely paid for in cash. Likely untraceable.

A Post-it note with a message was there, too. *Give this to the blonde watching the can.*

Looping letters with flourishes contrasted with square capitals penciled hard. But jagged—made with a shaky hand. Eve thought that could be from nerves—or the cold—or a mix of both.

"That one's messy. But it's Allie's handwriting." Donovan stared at the paper in bewilderment.

Eve opened the flip phone. Checked that it was active. Then searched its address book.

Only one number was listed. She dialed it.

It rang once. Twice.

García's fury and anguish were so intense they seemed perfectly matched. "I'm tracking down the bastard, not sticking around while you make conversation. Call me if I need to know something. Otherwise, don't bother me."

"Go," Eve said, nodding. If any single person had the ability to find the kidnapper within the vast acreage of Central Park, it was García. Not just because his former Special Ops experience gave him expertise. Because the same paranoia and hypervigilance that had cost García his marriage also made him extremely good at his job.

Another ring. Then another.

Donovan's own cellphone began to trill. He looked down and motioned to her that he was needed elsewhere. "Remember to loop me in when it's important," he reminded her.

Finally, a click. The line was live.

A computerized voice answered. It sounded annoyed—and out of breath.

"Is this the blonde?"

*Great,* Eve thought. *Six years at Yale, an advanced degree in psychology, and first in my training class at Quantico. And here and now, when that all mattered? I have to answer to "the blonde."*

"This is Eve Rossi. You left me this phone—and a message—because you want to talk." Her voice projected the image she wanted to convey: calm and respectful but firm.

She wished circumstances were different. That they had more time. That Haddox was prepared—with the supersensitive equipment that could triangulate this call and record the conversation. Connect to the voice-recognition software that would almost immediately begin to analyze the kidnapper's speech patterns and word choices.

Instead, she would need to rely on her own powers of observation.

"We're going to talk about my second demand," the kidnapper said.

"Because the two million dollars wasn't enough?" Eve remarked. "It's a lot of money. It would satisfy most people."

"Yeah." A chortle. "Obviously, I'm not most people."

"I can see that. Most people also wouldn't have hurt the boy." She held her breath, knowing how he handled the accusation would tell her a great deal.

He struck a petulant tone. "It wasn't my fault. I didn't *want* him to get hurt."

Definitely not the response she was hoping for. No admission of agency. Not *I hurt* the boy. But the boy *got hurt*.

It marked him as one of the delusional ones—what the FBI called an *injustice collector*. A person who remembered every slight, who believed that everything was anyone's fault but his own.

Eve had long believed that these people were the most dangerous. Because it was hard—impossible, really—to reason with somebody whose reality was a fiction.

"You didn't want him to get hurt? We did exactly what you asked and you didn't keep your end of the bargain. All we want is Allie back."

He ignored Eve's last statement as if she hadn't spoken. "I never wanted to hurt the boy. Why would you think I did?"

"He was hurt. Are you saying it was an accident?" Eve was still working to figure out how this person thought. To find out what was important to him and establish a common ground. If she could win him over, convince him that she understood him, and get inside his mind, then maybe she could wear him down. Convince him to let Allie go.

The man laughed softly. "No accident. Just self-defense, pure and simple. The kid tried to hit me over the head with a rock."

*Good for you, Frankie,* Eve thought. *Apple doesn't fall far from the tree.*

"So how about holding up your end of the deal?" she asked. "We gave you two million dollars. You were supposed to release Allie Donovan."

He laughed—but it was harsh and cruel, not a sign of rapport. "By parade's end, Eve—parade's end. The money was just your first task. A down payment, if you will, to prove we can deal honestly with each other. Remember, there are two more."

"Then let's be honest with each other, Mr. . . . ?"

"Call me Bob."

She didn't answer.

"C'mon, Eve."

"Fine. Bob. What I want is simple: for you to let Allie go. Immediately."

"Actually, that won't work for me. *Immediately* implies a kind of urgency that I just don't feel."

"Since you're holding a frightened thirteen-year-old child as your prisoner, I'd appreciate some urgency." Out of the corner of her eye, she watched Donovan, pacing along Central Park West, scanning the perimeter of the park. His phone to his ear. His right hand trained on his gun. Back in uniform, consumed by the job.

"Well, Eve, maybe you can put some of that urgency to work for me. Remember Gregg Burke?"

"The cop killer," Eve confirmed. Gregg Burke hadn't just shot a cop on a street corner in Queens—allegedly in retribution for an unarmed police shooting in the same neighborhood. Burke was also a jihad sympathizer who used racial turmoil as an excuse to kill. Right now he was being held in a secure location downtown, arraigned on charges including first-degree murder and possessing weapons of mass destruction, as investigators gathered sufficient evidence to slap him with terrorism-related charges.

"I want him."

"You and over half the civilized world."

"He was drawing attention to a real problem."

"There are problems everywhere, Bob. Killing people doesn't solve them. Neither does kidnapping a child."

"You want the kid back? You'll bring Gregg Burke to me. This is your second task; your deadline is nine a.m."

"Impossible."

He ignored her objection. "You need to bring Burke to Columbus Circle, right as the parade begins and the first few floats make their way by."

"Even if I could bring you Burke—which I can't—Columbus Circle during the parade will be a madhouse. There'll be thousands of spectators. There'll be hundreds of police."

"Which is exactly why no one will notice our business."

"I cannot spring a cop killer and suspected terrorist out of jail. The idea is preposterous."

"Do you not understand that I'm willing to kill the commissioner's daughter? Remember the ticking clock? You have two more tasks to complete; you need to stay on schedule."

"We need more time," Eve said quickly. "We're talking about a high-profile maximum-security prisoner."

"You'll think of something, Eve. The commissioner will help you. After all, this is his test. I need to know exactly how far he's willing to go to save his child."

"Why do you care?"

"Maybe I have something to prove."

"I want to talk with Allie."

"I'll be monitoring the news, to see if you succeed."

"I need to make sure she's all right."

No answer. Just a click.

And he was gone.

# Chapter 55

Central Park, near 72nd Street

García sighted his path with a Maglite beam, retracing his son's tracks back into the park. He had trouble at first. The tracks weren't neat. They were ever-changing, suggesting rapid, haphazard movements. Frankie Junior had been dizzy from blood loss—and García could detect traces of that, too, on the leaves along the narrow, wooded path.

And, he soon realized, they were going to dead-end into the loop, the paved road that circled around the interior of Central Park. He made an educated guess: The tracks were leading into the Ramble.

Just north of the lake, the Ramble was a thirty-eight-acre maze of twisting trails and winding streams, large rocks, and dense woods. It was probably the one place in Manhattan so remote that it was possible to get lost.

Except García had been trained to navigate the harshest of trails, in the worst of circumstances. If he could track a target in the sandstorms of Afghanistan, blind to the world around him, he could trace a trail in the heart of New York City.

Faint footprints continued on the other side of the bridge, just at the entrance to the Ramble. But just as important, there were additional signs pointing to where Frankie Junior had passed. Mound of leaves recently disturbed. Branches, with their dry side facing up.

A solitary old man was snoring on a bench along the path.

The Ramble wasn't on most tourist agendas this time of year. And within the next few hours, the cops would erect twenty-four-foot-high metal gate barriers at every entrance of Central Park to keep people out during the parade.

Twigs snapped behind him.

García stopped often—turning, checking. The tangle of trails was twisted and the trees were dense. Eventually he reached the top of a small incline.

*Where did you come from, Frankie?*

He shone his Maglite into the trees. No surveillance cameras to help.

He scaled a steep trail. Here, he was surrounded on both sides by Manhattan bedrock; it created a narrow gorge heading east. The air was wet and dense.

He kept going. Passed through the gorge and circled a small pond.

Climbed another hill. The trail twisted left and right and then left again.

Arrived at a clearing above the Seventy-ninth Street Transverse. García turned, surveying the land in each direction. Searching desperately for anything out of place. Realized that he had lost Frankie Junior's trail.

There was a muddy track to the side, weaving until the path surrendered to leaves and undergrowth and crumbling tree stumps.

García forged ahead, moving solely on instinct. His Maglite illuminated what looked to be a stone shed behind a chain-link fence that had collapsed in places, thanks to felled trees and overgrown vines. It was a single structure—though a series of vents and exhaust pipes suggested that the foundation might continue a few feet underground.

The door? Locked.

He took his pick out and considered this deadbolt's personality. It was a high-security lock with six pins. And it appeared to be new—no scratches. Inside the lock's cavity, everything was still set at factory standard—with nothing altered because of the temperature or humidity or moisture.

It was also out of character for a Central Park outbuilding. This kind of lock was rated as a twenty-minute pick job by insurance underwriters. Never mind that people like García could manage it in

seconds; it was far too sophisticated for the contents it surely protected.

He applied the right pressure, measured the pins' resistance, and
worked his magic to each pin in succession.

He felt the click and turned the deadbolt. Pulled the door open, its
hinges surprisingly silent, exposing a small room filled with supplies.
Gardening supplies, yes—plenty of mulch and wood chips and
wrapped-up hoses for watering. But other disturbing things, too.

A wooden bench, bolted to the floor, had a quarter-inch-thick
chain looped around one leg. Four pairs of zip ties littered the floor.

There was a thin blue blanket.

A bedpan.

Tins of food. Protein bars. A couple bottles of Gatorade.

He saw recent disturbances on the dirt floor, where something
heavy had been dragged.

He smelled bleach—like the walls and floor had been thoroughly
doused with it.

He also smelled a scent that took him back to hours-long Sunday
afternoons at his aunt Maria's apartment, where everything reeked of
that pungent, old-sock smell. Mothballs.

He took a hard look. Etched it all in his memory. Then closed the
door, desperate to be away from there.

What stayed with him was that mothball *smell.* And it stirred
memories of a time and place he only wanted to forget.

Strange fragments of images flashed into his mind.

This wasn't just about the commissioner and his daughter. Not
anymore.

He reached for his phone and dialed Eve.

"I've found where he kept the kids. We need tech support to handle fingerprints. DNA. Full chemical analysis." García gazed out at
the west side city skyline, twinkling over the dark canopy of wet trees.

He knew a small army of workers was scurrying to ready the
floats, fill the balloons, organize the bands.

All of them blissfully unaware of what threatened them.

# Chapter 56

Security Tent—Parade Zone

Eve had reason to be unnerved. Though she was used to missing puzzle pieces, something was significantly wrong here. She didn't know why Allie's kidnapper was targeting the commissioner. She didn't know why the commissioner was not more affected by his daughter's kidnapping—never mind the demands of his job. She feared she could not trust him.

So she asked herself, *Who am I doing this for?*

Not the FBI. Not the commissioner. Only Allie—a missing thirteen-year-old girl.

In that case, the only question that mattered was: *How do I help her?*

Eve reviewed the information she had on the commissioner once again. Recognized that he was tough and smart and perceptive. But everyone had an Achilles' heel. She just had to exploit it. Even if it made her feel cheap and manipulative to do so. There was too much at stake here to quibble over matters of conscience.

Including a global threat to the parade.

It was helpful that she and Logan had established a bond of some sort. Their conversation in the library when he had allowed himself to show some emotion—and when she had opened up to him about Zev—had forged the most fragile of connections between them. It might be as delicate as a spider's web—but delicate strands were sufficient to ensnare a spider's prey.

She focused on the ethical lapses in the commissioner's file. A number of trips paid for by others had generated formal censure six

years ago—though it was clear that they were personal journeys, motivated by friendship, with no political advantage. Still, Donovan had
been gun-shy afterward, separating his public and private business. It
was immediately afterward that he had hired Sam to provide personal
security for his family—initially through the Paid Detail Program, in
which uniformed NYPD officers could provide protection when off
duty, and later hiring Sam full-time after Jill had received a series of
threats.

What this told Eve was that the commissioner would bend a rule
he believed to be stupid or unnecessary. She could use that.

Behind her, police in flak jackets and ballistic shields, alert for
signs of protesters gathering in the area, kept a close watch on the few
stragglers out at this hour.

A siren wail sounded from elsewhere in the city. Overhead, a news
helicopter made a wide circle.

The police were watching. Waiting. The crowds would begin to
gather by daybreak. Seven hours, twenty-six minutes until the parade
would start its march down Central Park West.

Under a security tent ten feet away, Donovan was leading a meeting; at least a dozen other officers surrounded him.

She caught his eye, motioned that she needed to speak with him.

Four minutes later, he broke away to speak with her. "I will not
swap that killer for my daughter." Donovan's brow tightened with
concern, but then he took a breath and the taut lines relaxed. He was
never one to let his stress show. "Burke's a bastard who represents
everything that's broken in our society. More to the point, he may be
the source of the threats targeting the NYPD. His release may be the
trigger that fires the weapon."

"Gregg Burke is also the next task of the personal challenge that's
been issued you," Eve reminded him. "*How far will you go to save
her?* He said that specifically."

"Just means we find another way. Even if I wanted to, this guy's a
scourge. He's being held under our most secure lock and key."

She pulled out her phone, checked the time. "I'm thinking there's
a way we can use Burke to draw Allie's kidnapper out into the open
and apprehend him."

"You're not listening to me!" he thundered—or tried to. After hours of bluster and volume, now his voice was failing him. "Gregg Burke is being held at an undisclosed location downtown near One Police Plaza. In a maximum-security cell block with some high-ranking al-Qaeda operatives and drug traffickers from the Los Zetas cartel. And even if I *wanted*—which I don't—I couldn't give permission for him to just walk out of there."

"This is for your daughter."

Something snagged in his throat. "Even for her, I can't put the lives of my officers—and millions of paradegoers—at risk."

Something inside Eve shuddered. It was one thing to say that the lives of the many took priority over the few. "Of course Burke will not walk. But he could be moved. Under secure guard, of course."

"No. Let's give the kidnapper a decoy."

Eve stared at him, amazed. "We can't. For the same reason we didn't risk fake money for the ransom. You know he's monitoring the news. He expects to see reports of a breakout."

"The ransom didn't involve a cop killer. I draw the line there."

"We'd use Mace and García," Eve continued briskly. "They would provide an armed guard at all times. You like García—I think you even trust him. For once, think like a father, not a cop."

The commissioner stared at her for a long moment. "As both a father and a cop: What if it fails? I'd never forgive myself."

Those blue eyes again that had seen too much. What she saw in them electrified Eve—even if she didn't trust him. "You and I both like getting things done and taking decisive action. We can do this, together." Eve felt the heat in his gaze—and knew she had him, even before he finally agreed.

"Only because I trust you." He placed his hand on her arm, a solemn gesture.

"No flattery, remember?" There were so many layers to his personality, she couldn't help but be intrigued.

"I'm trying to be honest. I have no agenda. At least, not a political one."

"I'm not looking to make new friends, Commissioner."

"Bullshit. I have friends, and I'm just as much of a workaholic as you." He noticed his deputy frantically waving at him. His head snapped up. "I've got to go."

"Custody transfers happen all the time. That's how you should view this," she explained. "Because it's our best chance to flush out the kidnapper. And save not just Allie but potentially thousands of paradegoers."

"It's a complete cluster," he muttered. He signaled *one minute* to George.

"Which is exactly why my unit—Vidocq—was founded. To do the impossible in moments of crisis."

"Or failing that, to shoulder the blame?" he challenged.

Before she could reply, Donovan steeled himself, took out his phone—and dialed as he walked.

NEWS NEWS NEWS NEWS NEWS

## WJXZ REPORTS

This is WJXZ News with Gwen Allensen, reporting from Columbus Circle, where despite the events from yesterday evening, parade preparations are going full-speed ahead throughout the night! I'm talking with Manuel Vega, an electrician who works for the city. He's part of a crew that is systematically removing every street lamp along the parade route. Manuel, can you tell our viewers at home why this is happening?

MANUEL: Well, when high winds are a problem for the parade, there are two things that parade organizers do to protect the public. First, the balloons will fly just a little lower. And, my crew and I, we take down all the lampposts. We've done it every parade since 1997, when the Cat in the Hat ran into a lamppost and injured a spectator. And when the parade's over? We'll put 'em right back up!

GWEN: Better safe than sorry, that's for sure! Stay tuned right here for even more coverage as we get closer to our nine o'clock start time.

# Chapter 57

## 350 Riverside Drive, Vidocq Headquarters

QuestingForJustice. SolveAColdCase. WebJusticeForUs.

One hundred and seventy-five dollars later, Eli was a fledgling member of each. He signed up with the username Mookie Wilson. After one of his favorite Mets baseball players—because who couldn't love a guy who battled through life with a name like that?

First, he worked to get a sense of what the different sites were all about. All were devoted to crimes. Missing persons. Cold cases. Conspiracy Theories. Crimes Against Children. Crimes Against Women. Black Lives Matter.

*Who Am I?* was dedicated to unidentified victims. QuestingForJustice had seventy-four thousand registered members. SolveAColdCase had thirty-six thousand. WebJusticeForUs was the largest at one hundred three thousand.

Next, he delved into certain threads. A manicurist at a nail salon in Burlington, Vermont, had left her place of business two Augusts ago, intending to pick up her six-month-old son at daycare. Her car was found the next day abandoned on I-91. Purse, cellphone, and money intact. But no sign of the woman.

Another thread involved people trying to identify a child who had washed up on the beach last June. She'd been wearing a pink Hello Kitty T-shirt and white shorts, and she'd recently lost her two front teeth.

The number of people tracking both cases was nothing short of astonishing. Eli was having a hard time figuring it out: Were these people curious thrill-seekers, looking to satisfy their prurient interests by digging up more information than CNN would report? Or were they wannabe detectives who actually thought they could help solve a crime?

Knowing what he did about the police commissioner, he couldn't help but investigate the Black Lives Matter thread. It made for depressing reading. A fifteen-year-old shot in the back. A man with autism who'd been restrained in a chokehold; he'd gone into cardiac arrest and died. A racially motivated traffic stop that led to a jail-cell suicide.

Eli punched variations of Commissioner Logan Donovan into the thread.

Came up with seventeen hits.

Kept reading.

# Chapter 58

## Security Tent—Parade Zone

"You're the boss, Commissioner. But this is highly unusual."

"Unusual times call for unusual measures," Donovan pointed out smoothly. He had emptied the security tent before making this call to the downtown detention center. "We believe the prisoner may have information about today's riot—not to mention an urgent threat to the parade. Are you ready for my authorization code?"

"Of course, sir." The way he said it let Donovan know that he had secured his full cooperation.

After the necessary authorizations had been transmitted, Donovan asked, "Can you repeat back my instructions?"

"We are to prepare Prisoner number 06498-111, Gregg Burke, for immediate questioning. A man from your office is en route to speak with him now." Another hesitation. "Commissioner, are you—"

Donovan didn't let him finish. "Transfer him within the half-hour. Time is of the essence." Then he clicked off.

As he walked to rejoin the meeting, a man rode past on a bicycle with newspapers slung on his back.

A woman walked her golden cocker spaniel at the edge of the park, apparently roused from bed, pajama pants peeking out from the bottom of her coat.

Two cops watched carefully as city electricians removed a streetlight, taking it out of commission before the parade.

Everyone doing their job. Just like Logan Donovan.

He quickly studied the street and the edges of Central Park. Searching for anything out of the ordinary. Anyone standing in the

wrong place or wearing the wrong clothes. Anybody who didn't belong. Or anybody trying too hard to belong.

The problem was: This was New York City inside the Frozen
Zone, in the silence before the whirlwind of crowds arrived. Except
for maybe the dog owner, nobody around here could exactly be described as "belonging."

Eve first called Mace, then conferenced in García to explain what she
needed.

Both protested and complained, listing all the reasons why it was
a bad idea. The reasons they didn't want to do it. The reasons they
especially didn't want to do it *together*.

Then both came to the exact same conclusion.

It was a crazy plan.

It was also their best, fastest hope of catching this kidnapper—and
securing the parade route.

"How's Frankie Junior?" she asked before closing the line.

"Stabilized," García replied. "The doc promises he's gonna be
okay."

When Eve spoke with Eli three minutes later, she almost couldn't
believe her ears. "You—asking for Haddox?"

"Don't get me wrong: I still can't stand the guy. Don't *really* want
to work with him. Or breathe the same air as him. But he's the only
bastard I can think of who can help me make sense of something I've
found online. Something I think is important."

"I'll ask him to head uptown right away."

Eve fell into step alongside the commissioner. They followed the line
of silver bleachers on the park side of Central Park West. Empty for
now—but in coming hours, to fill with an array of people lucky
enough to score reserved seats for the parade. VIPs and Macy's employees and corporate sponsors.

"Are you sure you don't want me to handle this, without your
fingerprints all over it?" Eve asked him.

"I told you: When it's significant, I need to be pulled in."

"Then we need to talk."

"Words that usually come right before *it's not you, it's me,*" he joked.

"And that's something you hear a lot?"

"'Course not. Women like me." A smile played on his lips. "Even *you* would like me, given half a chance."

*Cocky and full of himself.* The truth was, oddly enough, she did like him. She liked his energy and strength—even if he did sometimes act as a bully. She respected his total commitment to his job and desire to make a difference. How he let her see the occasional flash of vulnerability.

They passed another crew taking down streetlights. "We need to talk again about your enemies," she said.

"I told you already. I've got plenty of enemies; none that I believe hate me enough to take my child."

"The kidnapper's working very hard to tie the plot against you to protests against police brutality. But he's also asked you a question— *how far will you go?* And his 'tasks' have forced you to cross boundaries. He must've known you couldn't come by that much money legitimately the night before Thanksgiving."

He arched an eyebrow. "You mean those millions we gave him weren't kosher?"

Eve ignored the question. "Now, he's asked for Gregg Burke's release from custody. He may or may not actually want Burke. But it seems important for him to make you cross the line."

"The hell if I know why."

"He isn't a traditional kidnapper. He's unmotivated by millions in ransom. His 'tasks' have us engaged in a cat-and-mouse game as he makes a point about police brutality—and targets you, the top cop, in particular. He took your daughter; he shot at your sniper team; now he wants a suspected cop killer released. He claims he wants 'justice'— and given how big a stage this parade is, I'm concerned about the bigger message he may be after."

"Should we be looking through NYPD files? Searching for a political zealot? Re-interview Burke?"

"Political beliefs don't usually take people this far, no matter how strongly they believe in a cause," Eve said. "There's got to be some deeper connection to you—something he perceives as a personal injury—behind all this."

"And you base this idea on?"

"Whoever took Allie knew things about her. Not just her name and age but details about her life and yours. That's personal: He's been watching the two of you; may have even found reasons to meet you in recent weeks."

"He certainly found the one reason that would motivate me to do these crazy things." Donovan cleared his throat. "Reminds me how everyone has a price."

"Not everyone," Eve disagreed, thinking of Zev—whose integrity had been rock-solid.

"You know, a few years back, a group of us went overseas to Afghanistan. We needed to learn some of the latest explosives techniques, and there's no better place to learn than in the field. There was a man who'd been friendly to our troops there, helping out on several occasions. Everybody trusted him. The insurgents got hold of his family. Slit his son's throat right before his eyes. Said they'd release his wife and daughters if he'd put on a suicide vest."

"What happened?"

"He detonated just inside the base; killed eighteen troops."

"And his family?"

"We found them on a roadside—shot, execution-style. But if you're the father, you pay the price and take the chance. You do exactly what they say. And pray that they'll keep their word."

"And if you're the perpetrator, you use whatever advantage you find, to compel the father to act. Are you sure no one wants something from you, Commissioner?"

"Almost everybody I know wants something from me, Eve."

Eve wasn't a believer—and she knew that *hope* was not a plan. She opted for an approach that combined out-working and out-thinking her adversary.

She found a seat inside the operations tent at the museum that Donovan had secured for them. She began firing off a series of calls.

To Eli, she directed: "I need full blueprints of the facility where Burke will be transferred for his interview. Complete details of the security plan they have in place."

To Haddox, she asked for a temporary shutdown of the surveillance cameras and other technological obstacles at the site. She also requested a full dossier on Burke—from which she'd generate a psychological profile. Even if he was only bait for their kidnapper, they would still need ammunition to handle him for a brief period of time.

To Mace and García, she instructed them to gather the supplies they'd need for the physical extraction.

Her final call was to Jan Brandt, the FBI forensic tech. "No fingerprints or fibers from anybody except the kids," she informed her. "But your man García definitely found something interesting in that storage shed. It's headed to our facility in Jersey for testing now."

"Is it what García feared?"

"You'll know soon as I do," Jan said tersely.

Eve stared at the ticking clock on her phone. She'd set it to mirror the countdown on Allie's.

Still six hours, fifty-six minutes to go until Task Two deadline.

Nine hours, fifty-six minutes until the parade's end.

## WJXZ REPORTS

This is Gwen Allensen, reporting from the parade staging area on Seventy-sixth and Central Park West. Right now, I'm talking with Lawrence Cox, a spokesperson for Macy's.

*GWEN:* Larry, can you tell us whether you anticipate today's weather forecast causing any problems for the parade?

*LARRY:* Well, current forecasting calls for sustained winds of twenty miles per hour and gusts of thirty-three miles per hour.

*GWEN:* What does that mean for the balloons' ability to fly?

*LARRY:* We work very closely with the NYPD in making that determination. Basically, the city rules put in place after a paradegoer was injured by the Cat in the Hat in 1997 mandate that balloons may not fly if sustained winds exceed twenty-three miles per hour and gusts exceed thirty-four miles per hour.

*GWEN:* Sounds like we're right at the cusp of what's safe.

*LARRY:* I'm optimistic—though the balloons may not fly quite as high as in years past. Don't forget: Balloons have only been grounded one time, back in 1971, since this parade started in 1924.

*GWEN:* So the odds are on our side. Let's hope those winds cooperate.

# Chapter 59

## Chambers Street—an Unidentified Secure Location

The past few hours had accelerated by in a blur of frenzied preparation. Now it was two hours, thirty-five minutes until the Task Two deadline. Known to the rest of the world as the starting time of the parade.

García didn't like it.

Still, this was an opportunity to flush out the bastard who'd nearly killed his son. He wasn't about to screw that up.

First light was starting to spread over lower Manhattan, but García felt he was still in the middle of a nightmare. In part, because of the ordeal Frankie Junior was going through. The doctors assured him that Frankie was out of immediate danger. And Teresa was right there by Frankie's side. Still, García remained racked with guilt. His fault for sending Frankie home alone.

But the other part of his nightmare? Going inside this prison. That would be enough to give him the creeps, even if he didn't already suffer from claustrophobia.

It didn't look so bad from the outside—just an ugly gray building. A fortress of concrete and steel. In fact, it didn't look so different from the high school he'd gone to. Which, he reflected, had felt like its own kind of prison at the time.

But this place held some of the most high-profile criminal defendants in the United States. There were no guard towers, but there was a security hutch outside and enough surveillance cameras to keep an electronic eye on every square inch within its walls.

García watched the two guards at the outdoor sentry station.

They were drinking coffee, joking, gossiping. They had the early-morning Thanksgiving shift; they were anticipating a quiet day, making it through their eight hours, then heading home to their turkey dinner.

Inside, seventy-nine prisoners were housed in a series of escape-proof cells, including a Lock-Down Unit—LDU—for those prisoners deemed the most dangerous. Or, García suspected, those prisoners who were simply the most hated: including a handful of al-Qaeda and ISIS terrorists. A government traitor. A Madoff-style swindler. And, of course, Gregg Burke, alleged cop killer.

"Ready for showtime?" Mace's booming voice sounded in his ear. His least favorite tag-along companion. Nobody he got along with worse.

"C'mon, Frankie," Mace was saying. "It's just you, me, a beautiful sunrise, and a baker's dozen of America's Most Wanted. What could be better than this?"

"Me. Anywhere but here. Now put a sock in it. We don't have the signal yet."

"Speaking of socks—I see you're wearing your lucky red socks and bandana to ward off the bad juju," Mace retorted.

García bit his lip. Sure, he'd changed into his lucky red socks and bandana, like he did every mission. He'd also said a few Hail Marys. Some called it superstitious, but García was convinced it had helped him to survive the IEDs of Fallujah, making it home in one piece.

"Hey, I'm not the one who's losing his edge, totally whipped by his new woman."

"Sounds like you're jealous, Frankie. I've got plenty of edge—not to mention a lady well endowed with the three B's: brains, beauty, and bucks."

"Just being perceptive, man. Tell me the last time you dropped an f-bomb? She wants you for another kind of B. Bounty—all dark chocolate outside but white coconut inside."

"Frankie, you better—"

At that moment, all the lights along Chambers Street went dim. They extinguished one by one, building by building—as though they were a string of Christmas lights on a tree that had just been un-plugged.

It was highly unusual to lose power in the borough of Manhattan. It had only happened twice in recent memory: once in the Blackout of 2003, and again when Hurricane Sandy slammed into the city in 2012. Though it was early on a holiday morning, Con Ed would still get a flurry of calls. And Haddox was confident that he could stay hidden inside their firewall, blocking their recovery efforts, for at least twenty-eight minutes. Give or take a few.

García set the countdown.

He heard the massive backup generator automatically cycle on. It was on the roof—a necessity after the basement had flooded during Sandy—and it fed off a direct supply of Con Ed natural gas. Powerful enough for a building that took up a full city block, it was as loud as a jet engine revving for takeoff.

The guard on duty was distracted by the noise when García stepped up to the sentry hutch. "I'm with the NYPD. Here to inter-view one of your inmates." He flashed his badge.

Until last month, that badge had belonged to one of the commis-sioner's favorite deputies. Now the man had retired to a cottage in the Adirondacks, but the sentry guard here would never know that. When the number ran, Haddox had ensured that the computer would verify it as *active duty*.

Sure enough, the guard ran the check.

"Clear to proceed," the guard radioed to the next security guard—the one manning the primary metal doors. "Say, did anything happen here this morning to make the power blow?"

"Not that I've heard," came the static reply as García proceeded forward.

"I'm here to interview inmate number 06498-111," García said, glancing down at the note on top of the memo pad he carried. No names were used at this secret, generally undisclosed location. Only numbers.

"What authorization code should I give?"

García consulted his notes again. "012235789."

"Wait, please, sir." The guy picked up his radio and contacted someone on the inside.

The wait was a couple heartbeats longer than García had anticipated. But eventually the sentry guard hung up and said, "Go ahead. They'll be waiting for you at the end of the hallway on your left."

García walked on—and as the metal doors clanked shut firmly behind him after only eleven paces, he tried not to stop, not to go insane with PTSD panic.

*There's plenty of air. Plenty of light. This is only a prison for some,* he repeated to himself.

And in case his calming mantra wasn't enough, he said a quick prayer that Mace wouldn't let him down. He needed him to take care of his end of things.

Just thinking about Mace, he didn't feel the press of walls closing in anymore. He felt the dull annoyance and nervous tension he always felt around Mace.

Made even worse by the fact that he needed him. Couldn't complete the mission without him. They were worse than polar opposites. More like fire and gas. Incendiary.

He reveled in that feeling of intense dislike—because it gave him something to focus on. It kept him calm when he went through the cursory security search he'd expected.

He had nothing made of metal in his pockets, except small change, which he dumped into a scuffed metal tray. Took off his coat. Removed his shoes. Stepped through two different metal detectors.

The shoes set off the alarm. They always did.

"Steel toe," García said with a shrug.

The guard checked the shoes carefully. Found nothing. Returned them to García.

When he put his items back on, his fingers couldn't help but feel for his Randall #1 knife, hidden in a special compartment in the sole of his right shoe. Just knowing it was there reassured him—almost as much as being on the outside, breathing free air.

Great huge gulps of smoggy, polluted New York City free air.

. . .

At the same moment, a guy in a Con Ed uniform approached the rear side of the building, where there was a service entrance. With a friendly grin, he approached the guard there. "Hear you've got a bit of a power problem this morning. I'm here to check it out."

"That was fast." The officer gave a cursory glance to the credentials Mace presented. "Try to get it back on quick. That beast of a generator keeps the lights on and the doors locked"—he pointed upstairs—"but it won't power the TV at my station here." He indicated a portable television the size of an iPad. "Should be quiet here today; I was hoping to watch the parade."

"I'll get you up and running soon as I can," Mace promised.

Six minutes later, García was led into an interview room. Two stories below ground.

No windows. Just one air vent. Four blank walls. A table bolted to the floor and two chairs chained to the table.

As he walked, he made sure to keep his face away from the surveillance cameras.

In theory, Haddox had done his magic and taken them out of commission. In practice, García trusted nobody and took no chances.

The floor below was cracked tile. The light above came from a row of fluorescent strips.

He sat down. Waited another seven minutes until the door opened and Burke was brought in. Shoved into a chair. His handcuffs locked to a slot on the table.

He looked to be on the early side of forty, but his short dark hair was starting to show gray. His skin was so pale, pink, and flabby that García was reminded of a plucked chicken.

The door was shut. The two of them were alone.

Footsteps in the hall walked away.

García glanced at his timer. Nineteen minutes left.

*Almost showtime.*

"Hey, asshole. I need you to follow everything I'm going to tell you. To the letter." García issued orders in lieu of a greeting.

He noticed the bruises on Burke's face. The dark bags under his eyes. Burke hadn't done a lot of time yet, but what he'd done had been hard.

"This is total bullshit. I don't know nuthin' about today's riot," Burke retorted.

García pulled a paper bag out of his jacket. Inside was a packet of cigarettes and some chewing gum. He passed them to Burke. Kept one packet of gum for himself.

Burke examined them.

"I know that and you know that," García replied. "But we're going to have a little adventure if you follow my directions. Take the fourth piece of gum from the right. Unwrap it. There's a pill inside you should swallow."

Burke raised his eyebrows. "You're bringing me drugs? I ain't taking something I don't know what it is."

García shrugged. "You want to stay in here—or get out?" Then he passed over his own water bottle.

With a look of self-satisfied mischief, Burke took a slug of the water—and downed the pill.

García resisted the urge to punch him.

All was still silent in the corridor.

So García started talking. Making up one inconsequential point after another. Just waiting for the drug to take effect. Waiting for the next signal.

He tried to relax, counting off the time in his head. Two minutes. Four minutes. Six minutes.

The room started to feel a little warm.

"How're you feeling?" García asked Burke. "Uncomfortable yet?"

"What kind of crap did you give me?"

Mace's voice buzzed in his ear. *"Hey, Frankie, when are we getting this show on the road?"*

They were running out of time. García couldn't afford to wait much more.

In that instant: success.

Gregg Burke threw up the entire contents of his miserable breakfast all over the table.

García sprinted to the locked door, hitting the intercom button, again and again.

When the "yes?" finally came on the other end, he shouted, "Prisoner medical alert. He's having some kind of seizure. He's vomiting uncontrollably!"

Then he waited.

An officer came within twenty-two seconds.

The door opened—then started to swing shut behind him. García shoved his packet of gum into the opening to keep it from closing. Then he moved behind the responder.

A vicious elbow between the shoulder blades dropped him like a sack of flour. A swift kick and he was out cold.

García felt bad about that. He hadn't wanted to hurt the guy too bad.

He grabbed the officer's keys, tearing them right off the frayed belt loop of his pants. He took the ID card clipped to the officer's shirt.

*Breathed in. Breathed out.* No reason to panic.

But definitely past time to get out of there. Burke had retched once more. The stink was beyond nauseating.

García used the keys. Unclipped the handcuffs that secured Burke to the table—though he immediately re-clipped them behind the guy's back. Burke was leaving jail—but he was still García's to control.

They made their way quickly down the corridor, through the door García had propped open. García's hand firmly in Burke's back, propelling him forward.

"Slow down. I don't feel so good," Burke moaned.

"Tough shit." They made it through the next room. Came to an exit door that had no handle. Had no lock. It was secured electronically.

Time for Mace to do his thing.

Eight minutes to go.

In the bowels of the gray concrete prison, Mace made his way into the mechanical room. It was dark, illuminated only by emergency lighting.

Hot and cold water pipes ran above him—painted by color according to where they went in the building. There were water heaters for each wing of the building. Three different oil tanks for the heating system. Huge ventilation shafts.

He crouched forward; the ceiling down here was low for his six-seven frame.

Came to the wall where the electrical and gas supply area was housed.

He shone his Maglite on the main panel. Found where it connected to the emergency generator supply.

It didn't look exactly like he expected. He was going to have to improvise.

García waited impatiently. Burke, behind him, retched again.

He heard the sound of feet on the floor above him.

Six minutes and the whole system would be live.

He would be totally screwed.

"MACE!" he whispered urgently.

Mace hated making a choice. He hated not being sure.

He made his best guess.

It was the wrong one.

García was cursing on the other end of the line.

Mace shut off the volume.

Three minutes to go. The cameras would be up. Full security back in place.

Their chances of getting Burke out? Gone.

García started calculating his odds for getting out via brute force, once the guards came.

They weren't good.

He got his knife at the ready all the same.

Mace thought about Thomas Edison. How he hadn't failed seven hundred times. Instead, he'd discovered seven hundred ways *not* to make a lightbulb.

That had inspired him, learning to play ball. Practicing free throws, day after day. Working to get better.

He tried again.

This time, it was good. It was like when the ball leaves your fingers and you just *know*: It's going to swish right through the net.

The emergency generator made a great cough, and then simply died. All the lights, cameras, and consoles went out instantly—except for a handful of small items on battery backup.

The quiet was replaced by shouts and the sounds of people running.

The door swung open. García breathed a sigh of relief—and pushed Burke through fast.

Cold air rushed in from outside—and García started feeling good. Mace had come through.

There was one more hurdle. A couple guards and a stairwell were between him and the loading dock level.

The guards—two Asian men—could have been twins. They were the same height and build, with similar features. Neither was more than six feet tall, but they were lean, muscular, and deadly serious. They stood at the top of the stairs, shoulder to shoulder.

García went six paces toward them and stopped. Burke remained behind. Hands still cuffed behind his back. Vomit all over his jumpsuit.

"Just where do you think you're going?" demanded the man on the right.

"None of your business," García said.

The other man shook his head. "Wrong answer."

García took another two steps forward. Balled his fists.

The man on the right lifted his leg for a kick; García grabbed him at the ankle and slammed his fist into the groin. Then he tossed the sentry down the stairs like a rag doll. He lay there in a giant, awkward heap.

García took the next three steps forward with a no-nonsense attitude.

The guard on the left snapped to attention. He glared at García and reached inside his jacket for his weapon. Instead of slowing, García took the remaining distance between them in one leap. He head-butted the guy right in the stomach, like a human battering ram. García sent him hurtling down the stairs like a misshapen bowling ball. He landed on top of his partner, his left leg turned at an ugly angle.

It was the element of surprise—of doing the unexpected—that always seemed to work in García's favor. He was smaller than his opponents, and they never expected him to have too much fight in him. Pure grit and expert training—fueled by pent-up rage, and coupled with an exquisite sense of timing—meant otherwise.

"You coming?" García called down. Without waiting for Burke to respond, he ascended the stairs, adjusted his shirt, clipped his Randall #1 knife to his belt, and opened the metal door that the sentries had blocked.

García waited as Burke stumbled toward him, all left feet. Because now that Burke's stomach was empty, that little white pill was going to make him sleepy and disoriented.

That was also part of the plan. This guy was bait for their fishing experiment—but no one wanted the worm to talk.

García hustled Burke inside.

"Taking your sweet time today, Frankie?"

"Don't call me that." García took the Con Ed uniform that Mace offered. Gave him the keys he'd taken from the interview room guard so he could unlock Burke's cuffs.

"Get dressed, asshole," Mace informed Burke, handing him an identical uniform.

The lights were going to come back on in one minute, fifty-five seconds. And three Con Ed guys were about to leave the building.

# Chapter 60

## 350 Riverside Drive, Vidocq Headquarters

Eli felt a tap on his shoulder. Looked up from his computer screen, blinking. Haddox was standing behind him. Bach, Eve's German shepherd, trotted into the room, turned around three times, then settled down at Haddox's feet.

Eli groaned. "Now I've seen everything. Women fall all over themselves to be with you, and even the dog picks you over all that food in the kitchen."

Haddox took the chair beside him with an easy shrug. Put down a cup of coffee. "For you. Light, sweet, and only halfway full—so you don't spill."

"Always inspiring confidence."

"Eve said you needed help."

"I was looking into the financial part of Logan Donovan's life," Eli explained, "while you were learning the rest of it. Did you find anything to indicate whether Logan—or Jill—was having an affair?"

Mock surprise. "Trouble in paradise? That wounds the romantic in me."

"Want some free advice? The romantic in you ought to be warned: It ain't gonna work out."

"What's not going to work out?" Haddox eyed Eli skeptically.

"I've been bingeing on old Hollywood movies lately. I watched *Casablanca* last week, and I thought of you."

"I can see why. Me. Bogart. Massive sex appeal."

"Yeah, but the point is: Doesn't matter that Ingrid Bergman's character had the best sex of her life with Bogart. She still picked the sensible guy. Women are like that."

"Eve would be bored stiff with a sensible guy." Haddox pulled a pack of cigarettes from his pocket, lit one up. "But no worries, mate. I'm not looking to get pinned down."

Eli coughed, waved the smoke out of his face. Then told him about the credit cards and the lingerie. About how Allie's cosigned card seemed to be the depository of all the Donovan family secrets. "I can't figure out the rest of it," Eli said. "Guess that's more your expertise. But I did find something else that's *really* interesting: Allie's Web habits."

"Yeah, her entire cache had been deleted," Haddox said. "I'm running the software that will bring it back from the digital grave."

"Well," Eli explained, "I tried a different approach. She used her credit card to join some online research forums. Like this one."

Eli flipped to a new screen. Showed Haddox the WebJusticeForUs .org site. "It's filled with your standard mix of wackadoodles, crime scene voyeurs, and amateur sleuths. They compare notes, try to solve various crimes."

"I think I know where this is going. Anything on Logan Donovan?"

"There's a whole treasure trove of files on police brutality and Commissioner Donovan," Eli admitted. "And there's a handful of bad allegations in those threads, sure. But that's not what's interesting."

"Go on." Haddox was drawing on his smoke, but Eli could tell that he had his complete attention.

"There's a whole thread on Jill Donovan. A lot of people think her death was suspicious."

"Yeah, I looked into it for Eve. But Jill had cancer. Nothing suspicious about that." Haddox flicked a few ashes onto an empty plate— one that had earlier contained Eli's sandwich, a turkey on rye with brown mustard.

"Might want to rethink that one. There's more to the story. Want to take a look?"

Haddox took a final puff. Then extinguished his smoke without even a trace of regret. Within moments, in spite of the bandage, his fingers were dancing across the keyboard, moving fast.

Eli watched, hopeful. He wanted answers to his questions. He was starting to believe they were relevant to whether they'd see Allie again—or not.

"Have you told Eve any of this?" Haddox asked.

"Not yet. Just the broad strokes. I wanted to have something more solid before I went too deep."

Haddox didn't look up from his screen. "Eve's problem is: She knows most people are full of shite, but she believes she can read their body language, use her skills to see through it all. Protect herself from their influence. Meanwhile, seems to me that the commissioner's playing her big-time."

"I never thought we'd agree on anything," Eli said. "So how do we stop it?"

"We can't. She's smart but stubborn—which means that she has to see it for herself."

"Some damning data would certainly help."

"I aim to please," Haddox said, switching his screen. "What I trust is computers. The commissioner's a lying git or worse, but his digital fingerprints won't deceive. See, if you look at the world according to bits and bytes, you'll see there's a wealth of information out there that's pretty easy to understand."

Minutes passed. Eli watched Haddox follow the digital trail. Then his fingers suddenly stopped.

"Looks like we've stumbled onto Pandora's box," Haddox said with an easy grin. "What do you say we open it?"

NEWS NEWS NEWS NEWS NEWS

## WJXZ REPORTS

This just in! Gwen Allensen here at WJXZ reporting breaking news this Thanksgiving morning.

We're mere hours away from watching the Macy's parade floats begin their journey toward Herald Square, but we're receiving reports that suspected cop killer Gregg Burke has escaped from the holding cell where he was awaiting charges on the execution-style murder of two NYPD police officers.

Burke is believed to have targeted them simply because they were wearing a uniform—all part of the anti-police tensions that have spread nationwide following the deaths of unarmed African American men at the hands of police officers.

To repeat, we have reports of a prison escape.

Suspected cop killer Gregg Burke is considered to be extremely dangerous, and members of law enforcement will be on high alert until he is recaptured.

# Chapter 61

### Columbus Circle

Traffic was pure gridlock as they neared the parade route.

"You get out by the hospital—Mount Sinai on Tenth Avenue and Fifty-eighth Street," Mace instructed García. "I'll ditch the van."

Their plan was to head to a destination that wasn't the *real* destination. One that wouldn't raise eyebrows. And most important, one that was still a few blocks from the chaos that now surrounded Columbus Circle.

They had changed clothes again. Worked to disguise the guy they'd be using as bait. He'd been painted in the media as Public Enemy Number One, his face plastered all over the Internet. But Mace was pretty sure nobody would pay attention to him in the soiled clothes of a homeless man.

Besides, he already smelled the part.

Donovan dialed out, then waited for acknowledgment on his secure line.

He took in the organized chaos around him. Radios were crackling. Officers in full body armor were crouched eight feet away. In the periphery of his vision, he was aware of sharpshooters in position.

"I need confirmation, Gamma Team."

"Roger that." In the background, he heard the Gamma Team leader speaking to his unit.

The roar of the crowds mingled with the roaring sound in his ears.

"Commissioner? We're on red alert. Your instructions are in place. No threat's getting past us today."

Donovan exhaled the breath he hadn't realized he was holding.

Seventeen minutes until deadline.

Mace had ditched the van and caught up with García.

"Stay here with fish bait. If we're gonna be on him like white on rice, we've got to find a spot where he doesn't stick out," García told Mace. "Like maybe over there. I'll check it out first." He indicated where a street vendor was set up on the Fifty-eighth Street side of the Time Warner Center. I LOVE NEW YORK T-shirts and a vast array of hats and keychains were on display. Swag for the tourists.

"Nah. We're coming with you."

García scowled. "I don't need a babysitter."

"That's debatable, Frankie, but you sure as hell need me," Mace said.

They passed vendors selling newspapers, gum, and candy as they muscled Burke—who continued to weave and wobble—past a flustered couple in their thirties, attempting to wrangle their brood of four into a single-file line.

"I'm hungry. Need something to eat," Burke muttered.

Several faces turned in disapproval.

"I'm starving." Burke lurched toward a man with a baby in his arms.

Everyone thought Burke was a falling-down drunk with mental issues. In other words, he was playing his part to a T. Even if he didn't know it himself.

"I'm going to take a six-hour shower when this is all over." García didn't bother to hide his disgust.

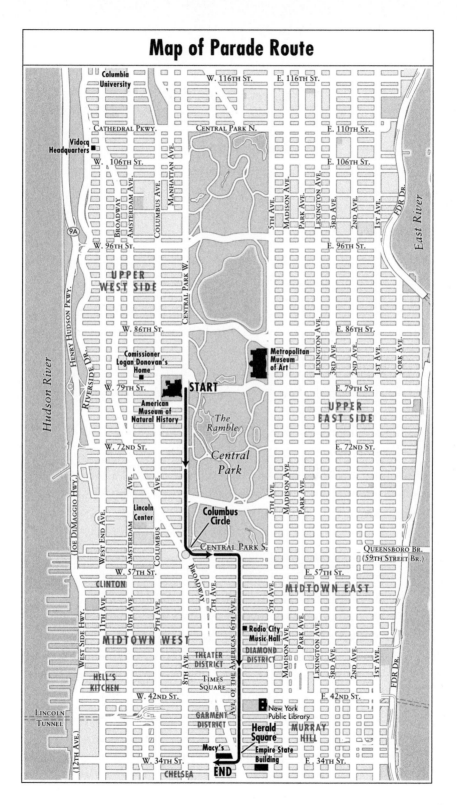

# Map of Parade Route

# Chapter 62

Surrounding Columbus Circle

Deadline hour.

Windy with light fog. So much fog that every image on the parade route more than twenty-five feet away was blurred by gray mist.

Eve looked around her. The crowds were packed in. On the east side of Central Park West, every seat on the bleachers was filled. On the west side, crowds congregated ten rows deep.

On the building rooftops, snipers were in position.

A grandfather in a sweatsuit ambled along, doing his best to keep up with the rest of his family—but falling behind. His two grandsons and their mother, on a mission to find the perfect viewing spot, never looked back.

From several blocks uptown, she could hear the blaring brass of a high school marching band making its way down Central Park West. The tune was "Let's Have a Parade"—in honor of the phrase that had signaled the start of every Macy's parade since 1924.

Eve hurried to position herself between the metal bleachers and the park entrance on West Fifty-ninth.

She and her team were in position. If the area around Columbus Circle was a giant clock, then she was in charge of observing activity in the twelve-to-three quadrant. Donovan had insisted on watching three to six. Mace was handling six to nine. And García—in charge of their fish bait—was watching the nine-to-twelve quadrant.

They weren't going to let this guy get the jump on them again.

The music from the band grew louder.

The surrounding crowds closed together, even tighter, in anticipation. Cellphones still chirped and radios crackled as the uniforms around the Frozen Zone maintained a tight perimeter. But the crowd itself grew largely quiet, staring in anticipation. A lone kid's voice rang out—*When will we see the music, Mommy?*

Eve was aware of her own breath—and of the commissioner's slow, steady breaths, audible in her earpiece. Everyone was trying to keep their nerves in check.

Through the crowds she saw García, standing behind Burke.

Mace on alert at seven o'clock.

Donovan, watching, at five o'clock.

By tradition, Tom Turkey was first in line. The red-and-green top of his hat was barely shy of the low-hanging clouds. Then the marching band passed by—a flurry of noise and color. Music, of course. Clapping and cheering from the crowds.

Behind them, Elmo and Cookie Monster danced on the Sesame Street float. A group of kids behind them sang: *Can you tell me how to get, how to get to Sesame Street?* The crowd listened and clapped and whistled with pleasure.

Eve moved slightly, taking the one-o'clock position.

García dragged the near-comatose Burke to eleven o'clock.

Mace continued on alert at seven o'clock.

Donovan, watching, moved to four o'clock.

Next up was a fan favorite: Snoopy. He bobbed and weaved in the wind and fog, but his handlers kept him low to the ground. A team of Macy's employees smiled and waved.

Eve tensed. It was the right time. She was alert for any signal. *Nothing.*

Another marching band passed by, this time playing "All You Need Is Love."

Another float—the Marion-Carole Showboat, with its paddlewheel and smokestacks, filled with smiling, dancing performers. *Still nothing.*

They all stayed in position. Eight minutes. Ten. Fifteen.

Still nothing but floats and balloons and marching bands.

There was no Allie. No kidnapper. Just like in the garbage can graveyard, the guy hadn't shown himself. Except in this case, the team was still holding the prize.

Whatever the kidnapper was truly after, Burke didn't appear to be it.

She pulled out the flip phone she'd used to reach him earlier. Tried the number again.

It rang incessantly.

No answer. Just another abandoned phone.

Eve radioed her team. "Abort. Go to Plan B."

Hearing that, Donovan's heart sank. He felt his sanity begin to fragment; it was hard to keep hold of his reason.

He cursed his own helplessness.

He cursed himself.

Most of all, he cursed the man who'd taken his daughter—and vowed that, whatever it took, he would not let this bastard destroy him.

"Mommy! Mommy!" A girl with pigtails tied in pink ribbons was shrieking. Her wails even drowned out a chorus rendition of "You're the One That I Want" from Waterbury High.

A grandfatherly-looking man with a thick white beard crouched down beside her, handed her a handkerchief. "Sugar, don't worry. I'll help you find your mommy. Can you tell me your name?"

She stopped screaming. Between sniffles, she said, "Jamie."

"Do you know your last name?"

"Luna."

"Jamie Luna. That's a very pretty name. And what's your mommy's name?"

"Mary."

"Where do you live?"

"At the building by where the fruit guy sells apples."

The white-bearded man sighed. "Well, there's a lot of guys who sell fruit in this city. I think we'd better find a nice policeman to help us find the right fruit seller. What do you say?"

Another sniffle. Then she took his hand, saying, "Okay."

They walked toward the corner of West Sixty-third, where four members of Critical Response, heavily armed, were keeping an eagle eye on the throngs.

The girl balked. Stared. Started bawling again.

"Don't worry, Sugar. They're just dressed to scare off any bad guys. They'll call an officer to help us," the man told her.

Mace didn't like following plans—but he followed this one. He only hoped that it didn't go wrong and land him back in a jail cell.

These were desperate times. Cops were on edge.

He disappeared with Burke behind the crowds. Shoved the creep forward 'til he found just what he wanted.

First, a bench—with a nice view of the Time Warner Center.

Second, a short guy who wore his cop uniform a little uncertainly. Who didn't have a partner within the line of sight. Who'd been relegated to the periphery of the Frozen Zone.

Mace removed the cuffs, dumped Burke on the bench. He'd keep a close eye on him to ensure he didn't move anywhere fast. But he was so out of it, Mace doubted Burke could even move five feet of his own accord.

Mace walked over to Shorty.

"Hey, excuse me. I saw the news reports about how that cop killer escaped prison. Maybe I need my eyes checked, but isn't that him, sitting right there?"

He pointed to the bench.

The beat cop pulled out his phone. Opened his information on the wanted escapee. The cop's eyes grew big and wide. Probably filling with visions of promotions and commendations and a very different future than he'd imagined that morning when he put on his uniform.

He scanned Burke's fingerprint ID. Made a couple calls. And just for good measure, he pulled out his cuffs and wrapped them around the wrists of the insensible man splayed out on the bench.

"I'd better get going," Mace said.

"Wait! I need a statement," the cop said.

"What?" Burke suddenly stirred. "Whaaat?"

"It's all good," Mace assured the cop. "Just smile for the cameras. You can take all the credit."

The cop nodded, unsure.

"Hey, aren't you the guy who broke me outta jail?" Burke gaped at Mace groggily.

The cop maneuvered Burke into a sitting position. "I don't know why you fell into my lap, but you're back in custody, asshole. Take a deep breath, because it's the last gulp of fresh air you're going to have for a real long time."

Psychology was about probabilities and predictors. Eve ought to be able to use that to figure out a few things about Allie's kidnapper. She began an imaginary conversation with him, trying to understand what he thought and felt and ultimately desired. "You knew so much about Allie—her movements, her family. Why her? What had she—or the commissioner—done to you?"

Eve looked around. Saw toddlers on fathers' shoulders. Mothers keeping their broods close. Grandparents holding babies.

"Why did you make the commissioner cross the line for his child—first with a ransom, then a cop killer? Why do you need to involve the Thanksgiving Day Parade? What does this stage symbolize for you that others don't?"

So many people, ten rows deep, cheering and waving. So many families gathered 'round, watching balloons and floats and holiday magic.

He'd chosen the parade.

So this kidnapper's motive had something to do with children? Or with the commissioner? Or simply an event that catered to families, celebrated on a day when most people gave thanks?

Eve still didn't know her adversary. She couldn't yet predict his next move. But if she kept this information front and center, then maybe he would spring into her mind, flesh and blood, with a purpose that made sense to her.

Her phone vibrated. This time it was Jan, her forensic tech—and one of the few people in the department whom she trusted implicitly.

"I've got the test results back," Jan told her. "We have a problem. We're going to need every resource we have for this one, Eve."

# Chapter 63

350 Riverside Drive, Vidocq Headquarters

Haddox and Eli entered Allie's account on WebJusticeForUs.org. Her screen name was Monique10.

Which was consistent. Her Instagram username had been Monique Morgan—a name that still struck Haddox as one he'd heard before.

Allie's first post—titled *I have a problem*—had been about her mom's death. She was devastated. She was shocked. She was also suspicious. "My mom had beaten breast cancer," she wrote. "There was no reason for her to die. And stuff my dad says doesn't make sense."

The_Crusader lent a sympathetic ear. So did Kitty123. They'd both lost people, too.

"I've seen the lowest of the lows," Kitty123 wrote. "Someone gunned down my mom, my sister, and my three-year-old niece. The police think a drug dealer went to the wrong house."

"My pregnant wife had brain cancer," added The_Crusader. "She didn't get the right treatment. When she didn't make it, I lost the baby, too."

Both were on this forum to get amateur help. They wanted more details on their loved ones' deaths. Kitty123 had gotten lots of tips on drug-dealer activity in her mother's neighborhood at the time of her death. The_Crusader had received stats on what better treatment options might have worked.

Monique10 wrote: *My dad has a bad temper. What if he hurt my mom?* She wasn't sure. But he had been having affairs. And he didn't seem too broken up about her mom's death. Worst of all, her mom had died in an alleged accident on vacation. *Where would I look if I want real evidence?*

From there, the ideas flew. *Check the death certificate. Check the police report. Give him a taste of his own medicine.* It was unclear whether Allie had followed up on any of their suggestions. Whether she had become a modern-day Nancy Drew.

"You think this is real?" Eli asked. He poured a bag of PopCorners into a bowl.

"Looks real enough," Haddox said. "But right now, what matters is not just the truth of it—but how people like The_Crusader reacted. Did any of them cross the digital divide?"

"She didn't post anything personal." Eli chewed a chip. "She aired some dirty laundry, sure—but she kept names and details out of it."

"Not completely. Look at her entry on August fifteenth. She mentions that it's the one-month anniversary of her mom's death."

"C'mon. Even these crazed Web sleuths would be hard-pressed to figure out who she was from that. According to WHO, over one hundred fifty thousand people die around the world, every single day."

Haddox looked up. "How do you even know shite like that? Anyway, Allie didn't have to share personal information to broadcast her ID on the Internet."

"How's that?"

"She thought that posting under a screen name made her anonymous. She didn't realize that anyone with a bot—used to roam websites and harvest IP addresses—could find her individual IP, meaning the unique identifier that links her particular device to the Internet. And with a naked IP address, it would take anybody less than two minutes to find out it was a private residence on West Eightieth Street."

"You're worried about The_Crusader or Kitty123? You think an online relationship went real-time and got her kidnapped?"

"Something else. From the commissioner's files." Haddox flipped his own laptop computer screen open. Toggled through a series of files. "His security detail kept a list of the commissioner's affairs, apparently worried that any woman he saw could pose a security risk. And I don't particularly care whether the wanker enjoyed a happy marriage. But there was more, in the internal files," he muttered.

He pulled the files, then stared at the screen intently—as though if he blinked, its contents might change.

"There." Haddox pointed. "You tell me: Does this strike you as suspicious?"

Eli shook his head. "He hired babysitters. Ran a background check on them. Strikes me as pretty normal."

"What about 2006?"

"It was a good year. I saw Barbra Streisand live on her last nationwide tour. I drank fizzy drinks in Antigua over New Year's. I—"

"Not looking for a trip down memory lane. Jackie Meade's background report is right in front of you. Focus on 2006."

Eli scanned it. "I'm still not with you. So what?"

"Three weeks in the loony bin, and all you can say is *So what*?"

Eli stiffened. "So happens that *I've* spent a few weeks at Lochmere Asylum. They have a good treatment program. Don't see why you have to be so judgmental about it."

"Look, *you* pulled yourself together. Went on to orchestrate the white-collar crime of the century. Got sent to jail. Managed to land a sweetheart of a get-out-of-jail-free card. In contrast, what did Jackie do?"

Eli refocused. "Uh . . . looks like she had some trouble. Lots of addresses."

Haddox rattled them off. "New Hampshire. Georgia. Wisconsin. Oregon."

"Lots of dead-end jobs."

"She bounced from McDonald's to Walmart to ShopRite." Haddox leaned over his knees, stretching his back.

"Lots of aliases."

"Including Monique Morgan. I knew I'd seen that name before."

"Maybe that's a famous actress or sports figure—and both Jackie and Allie use her, like I use Muggsy Bogues when I don't want to give my real name."

"Don't think so. When you look to the security detail list in 2006, Jackie was one of the commissioner's affairs."

"So she fell for a man in uniform. It happens. I have to confess—"

"Don't confess a thing. Now look at 2008."

"She took a live-in position taking care of his house and his child." Eli was exasperated now. "That takes balls—moving your mistress right into your house, alongside your wife and kid."

"Not his mistress anymore," Haddox corrected him. "First Diane Ritter, then Kecia Wallace, and finally Cathy Healy take her place on the security detail list as the commissioner's current romantic distractions. Why would he do that? And how did Jackie feel about it?" Haddox grabbed a handful of Eli's corn chips. "I met Jackie. It's like her brain is full of cats; you can practically smell the crazy on her."

"Total conjecture," Eli argued. "We don't have time to chase coincidences just because you like your *Basic Instinct* theory."

"Look, you found evidence on Allie's credit card. It led to this Web account paid for by Allie. Ostensibly written by Allie—and making serious allegations about Jill's death. That's when an idea hit me."

"Sure hope it left a bruise," Eli muttered.

"What if it wasn't Allie?"

"I don't follow."

"Look at the time stamp on Monique10's messages. September twelfth at eleven-forty a.m. September fourteenth at one-thirteen p.m. September twenty-first at nine-thirty-two a.m. Those are weekdays. Allie would be in school. And her last message? Posted at ten-oh-six p.m. last night, after Allie was kidnapped." Haddox let that sink in. "What if *Jackie* was the one who used Allie's credit card and computer—and made those allegations? That would say a lot about how much resentment she harbors against the commissioner."

"I don't know how you come up with this." Eli rubbed his temples. "Maybe you're just smarter than me."

"You ought to put that in writing. Gotta admit: Jackie had a helluva motive to hurt the commissioner."

"Even if I'm convinced, strikes me there's still one important question we ought to answer."

"Go on."

"It's one thing if Jackie's mad at the commissioner. Isn't it another if she's actually *right* about the bastard?"

# Chapter 64

## Along the Upper Parade Route

García pushed his way through the crowds. He hadn't forgotten what he smelled earlier in the room where Allie and Frankie Junior had been held. He also couldn't forget a saying that his first commander had been fond of: "The whole secret lies in confusing the enemy, so that he cannot fathom our real intent."

That was Sun Tzu—from an ancient military treatise.

It was also the idea behind the Greeks' Trojan Horse. The Coalition's Hail Mary in Operation Desert Storm. And—García was pretty sure—the kidnapper's plan today.

If he was right, then he needed to get back to where the floats were lined up. Because *that* was where the bastard was going to make his real move. Right where it had all started. Right where the NYPD mobile units were all set up.

Because this wasn't just about the commissioner and his daughter. Or even what had happened to Frankie Junior—who was now stable and out of immediate danger.

García believed there was a plan tied in to the threats the NYPD had intercepted targeting their own.

He weaved through the crowds. There were too many people.

Young mothers with babies. Teenagers with skateboards. People with scarves and with turtlenecks, high-collared coats. Dads with small kids on their shoulders.

"Nooooo!" a toddler with a mop of brown curls wailed as the paper bag he was holding tumbled to the ground, creating a trail of popcorn confetti.

"It's okay, Leo," his mother soothed. "Look! Your sister has plenty. Sara, share your popcorn with your brother."

Floats and balloons and performers were all passing by.

Mickey and Minnie Mouse. A cheerleading squad from Augusta, Maine. A float with spinning performers from Cirque du Soleil.

A juggler on the side street was tossing six balls in the air, entertaining spectators in back who were stuck with bad views.

There were so many people. Too many people. Like a sea full of moving, bobbing heads.

It was always a miracle when this parade started and finished—and nobody got hurt.

As he pushed his way north, he scanned the faces around him. Stuck to his training. Looked for anyone who didn't belong.

He began to step past the barricade, heading toward the lineup of floats and balloonicles, marching bands and performers. He summoned his paranoia and hypervigilance to recognize the danger. He'd not been this focused on a mission since his last tour in Fallujah.

Suddenly, a man came up beside him. He jostled García hard from the left.

*Stupid idiot.* Man, did he hate crowds.

García glared at the man who'd shoved him. The man moved away, launched into a run. Just like someone who didn't belong.

Behind him—a whiff of odor. Mothballs.

An uncomfortable feeling slithered south in García's chest. Instinctively, he broke into a run, chasing the guy.

He went sideways, toward Columbus, away from the parade route.

Within seconds, García was right behind him, shoving and pushing.

The guy shoved a balloon-and-stuffed-animal cart to block García's path.

García leapt over a mountain of Pokémon. Still gaining.

The guy scuttled an empty baby stroller into García's path. Its spilled cargo of diaper bags and bottles nearly tripped him.

Whoever this creep was, García needed to engage with him. Even if his every instinct warned him not to.

*Bad juju.*

He could feel his breath escaping him. He'd never moved so slowly before. What the hell was wrong with him?

But he'd never been unable to chase down a target he wanted to stop. *Mind over matter,* he reminded himself. *Just do your job.*

That was what trained soldiers did—and they did it on too little sleep and way too much stress.

The crowds became thinner. What crowds there still were, scattered out of his way.

*What's happening?*

García became aware of horrified glances. Of people pulling their children back, making far too much room.

He staggered, fell to his knees.

Looked down.

Registered the red, sticky substance spreading from his ribs all the way down his jeans.

*That's odd. I never felt a thing when he shoved me.*

He looked up, his eyes searching the crowds. Looking for the man who'd done this. Who was now getting away.

He tried to get up. He was finally feeling the pain—the dull throb he'd ignored now flashed with growing intensity.

The problem was: He couldn't breathe.

"Are you all right?" A uniformed cop with a concerned face was above him.

He tried to answer. It was like scalding hot metal had filled up his lungs.

"He's bleeding!" someone shouted.

"Was he shot?"

"Oh my God—"

"We need an ambulance!"

The cop yelled something into his radio.

García thought about Frankie Junior. He thought about his vow to catch the guy who'd hurt his kid—and make him pay. He was absolutely going to do that.

*Later.*

Because right now, he really needed to get some rest.

# Chapter 65

## Along the Parade Route

We make important choices in response to each situation.

I had to kill Rambo. He was too much like his namesake—a man on a mission, determined to interfere with my plans.

He tracked down my storage closet. He seemed hell-bent on disrupting my plan.

So why do I feel exactly like the cop bastards I detest? The bad seeds who think the rules don't apply to them?

I can't deal in the abstract.

I don't want to listen to bureaucrats talk about the general good.

My job is to put a face on the problem. To make the story *personal*.

Otherwise? Nobody cares.

## PART FIVE

# THE PARADE

Fourth Thursday of November

9:00 a.m. to 12 noon

# Chapter 66

Inside the Frozen Zone, Security Tent

*B ad news comes in threes.*

No matter that it wasn't rational. Too often Eve found that it was true.

First: Her forensic tech, Jan, had confirmed the presence of a chemical substance in the Central Park storage shed that García had discovered.

Eve had requested an immediate briefing with the NYPD, FBI, and Homeland Security.

Second: Haddox and Eli claimed to have found troubling evidence of an alleged wrongdoing—and subsequent cover-up—by the commissioner.

They, too, wanted an immediate briefing. It would have to wait.

Because third: Word had just reached her from the Saint Luke's emergency room. Frank García had died of his stab wound, approximately twenty-four minutes after reaching the hospital.

The long, thin blade had slipped in so easily that he told first responders that he never even felt it. It had entered beneath his ribs, piercing his heart and left lung.

The instant she heard, her mind went completely blank and her stomach twisted into a painful knot. She couldn't think. She couldn't breathe. It was as if her entire body had stopped working.

She sat on the steps of the Museum of Natural History, brought her knees to her chin, and hugged herself. Trying to breathe. Trying to think. Praying that she wouldn't be ill.

When she trusted herself to walk, she got up and made her way inside. Found the restroom. She ran a towel under cold water and then pressed it over her face. She stared at herself in the mirror. She was a mess. She washed her face one more time and ran her fingers through tangled curls.

Her brain could not focus, refusing to believe. Her lethal former Army Ranger—the one with eyes in the back of his head—*gone*?

Impossible. If anybody could take care of himself, it was García—who had seemed almost invincible, armed with his lucky red socks and bandana, his absolute self-confidence, his uncanny ability to sense danger.

She forced herself to return to the incident area. To pull up the surveillance from one of the computers.

The film quality was poor—and the view of García, just prior to his stabbing, was obscured by the hordes of tourists. Too many fathers with small children on their shoulders.

She focused on each grainy pixel, freezing the frame and zooming in. The process created something resembling a Seurat. Hundreds of small, distinct dots that, viewed up close, didn't form a pattern at all.

She moved her chair back. One foot. Then two feet. Finally, three.

From that perspective, a clearer image of the man following García took form.

Dark coat. Fedora. Taller than García—so maybe five-foot-eleven? He never looked at the camera, but his gait was resolute.

*Why hadn't García known he had a tail?* she thought angrily.

But that was only her grief talking. She knew the answer already: the crowds.

Her finger pressed a button and allowed the remaining video to play. She watched as García was shoved by the man in the fedora—then gave chase, slowing only when the puncture to his lung made movement difficult, then impossible.

She swallowed her pain, forcing herself to observe the aftermath—and to ensure there was no additional footage capturing the man in the fedora.

She had lost a colleague. A man she respected. A friend.

A boy had lost his father.

All on her watch.

Eve picked up her phone, dialed Haddox and Eli. "Tell me," she said. "Who exactly are we dealing with?"

# Chapter 67

## The Security Tent

Inside the Incident Tent, Henry Ma was livid. "Just what kind of a three-ring circus is this? In theory, you're helping find the commissioner's daughter. Instead, one of your own team winds up dead. If I didn't think it was too ridiculous even for your crew, I would be highly suspicious that you had something to do with a hated cop killer taking a field trip to today's parade."

Eve bested his anger with an intensity that surprised her. "I will not have this discussion. Not now. Not when we just lost one of our own. Not when you don't know the first thing about the real situation on the ground."

"Eve, this is too public a stage to screw up." Henry gestured to the spectators outside the tent. "All I see is you cutting corners. Shattering rules. Doing everything your way."

"You came to me, begged me to get involved—knowing full well what Vidocq is and what we do. We've just received hard evidence that the kidnapping targeting the commissioner personally may be linked to a broader plot against the NYPD and the parade. You need to let me do my job."

"I will NOT have my authority questioned."

"Nor will I." Donovan entered the tent. "This is *my* incident room and *my* investigation. The lives on the line are those of my officers and my child—and I will not be sidelined by the likes of you."

Henry shot him an angry stare. "I'd advise you to calm down. The FBI can take over here at a moment's notice."

"Get out of here!" Donovan thundered, enraged. "The man who has my daughter just went from kidnapper to killer."

Around Eve, detectives gathered, transfixed by the clash of egos. They were members of the interagency support team—a mix of investigators from the NYPD, Homeland Security, and FBI.

"Not when there's so much at stake—and you're screwing it up, Logan," Henry retorted. "This is post-9/11. You have a world of interagency resources at your disposal. Yet you and Eve have run a bare-bones operation. Kept the rest of us in the dark."

"Because I had no choice," Donovan countered. "My officers and I were needed on city business."

"Everybody has a choice."

Henry and the commissioner stood, glowering at each other. Eve stepped between them. "We don't have time for this."

"You just wanted to be in control." Henry never took his eyes off Logan's.

"Why don't we debate the question of control after some maniac has taken *your* daughter and threatened the men and women who work for you?" Logan retorted.

"Remember what's important here," Eve reminded them. "Allie is still missing."

Henry took a step back.

"Her kidnapper poses a serious threat to the parade itself," she continued.

Donovan took a step back.

The tension eased.

"Henry's right on one point, however," Eve told Logan. "Commissioner, we need to put more resources into this. They no longer take away from parade security. This threat involves parade security."

Henry Ma gave Eve a final, incredulous look of warning. "I'm trusting you to handle Commissioner Donovan. Fix this mess now." He stepped out of the tent.

Logan Donovan cursed. "I've never liked that bastard."

Eve shot him an icy stare. "Honestly? Makes two of us. Now, are you going to arrange for more officers? Or should I?"

Yet she was thinking about the evidence Haddox had uncovered on the commissioner: the affairs. The irregularities surrounding his wife's death. Jackie.

*Don't treat him differently,* she reminded herself. She couldn't risk losing the illusion of trust she'd built with him.

Donovan was staring out the opening of the tent, into the chaos of music and noise and wall-to-wall spectators.

A small boy, trying to keep up with his older siblings, had fallen down and skinned his elbow.

"This wouldn't have happened if you were wearing your coat like I told you to," his grandmother said tartly.

His mother offered sympathy and Band-Aids. "Joey, I have one last Yoda Band-Aid left. Remember, last time Yoda made the hurt go away fast."

Donovan was looking at the family, but he didn't seem to register their domestic drama—except as it related to his own. "I should've managed everything better. Allie should have been kept safe. She was my responsibility."

It was an unguarded moment. Eve saw his face reflect raw emotions that he didn't bother to hide. Anger. Disappointment. But most of all—shame.

She had to take advantage of that. "My team's uncovered some questions about your wife's death."

"She had cancer," Logan said roughly.

"You had a number of affairs. Including Jackie—who's still living in your house, caring for your child." Eve kept a straight poker face and an even tone, knowing her emotions had no place in this discussion. She had to be as matter-of-fact as if they were discussing the weather forecast or car trouble—not murder.

He kicked over the chair between them and took a step toward Eve. His blue eyes blazed at her. "Are you going to ask the damn question? Or is it more your style to trick me with a blank ream of paper?"

"Maybe I don't trust you to give me the full story." She refused to back down. "Omissions can be lies, especially when the information matters."

He was inches away from her. She lifted her chin defiantly.

A Hallmark Christmas-themed float was passing by; Mariah Carey was on it, belting out "All I Want for Christmas Is You."

Logan leaned into Eve, so close that his chest pressed against her own. Softly, he whispered, "I'm not a perfect man. I'm not a perfect father, and I certainly wasn't a perfect husband. But I did *not* kill my wife."

He planted one hand on the support beam beside her. With the other, he reached for her arm—held it. The heat from his fingertips seared into her skin. "Last July, I went on vacation in Hawaii with my wife. We stayed on the island of Kauai. I came home. She didn't."

"She died—and it wasn't from cancer."

His face stiffened. "We were hiking the Na Pali Coast. Jill fell. It was an accident. I wasn't a faithful husband to Jill—but I swear to God I had nothing to do with her death."

*A twitch around his eye. One of the primary muscles that cannot be managed. Was it telling a different story?*

There are thousands of automatic human responses the mind cannot control, that give us away. As she herself knew only too well.

"What did the medical examiner say?"

"The medical examiner did not make a determination. I would not authorize an autopsy. Jill wouldn't have wanted her body cut up."

"And Jackie?"

"Jesus, I was trying to help the woman out. Allie, who's picky, actually liked her—and with Jackie's problems, God knows she wasn't going to keep a job elsewhere."

"So you were doing Jackie a favor. You sure she sees it that way?"

"She's moved on."

"Guess we have nothing to worry about, then," she said lightly. And raised her hands, pressed them against his chest, and pushed him away.

One hour, fifty-eight minutes until the parade's end.

Jan Brandt filed into the tent first. Mace, Eli, and Haddox followed—together with an assortment of interagency personnel to provide backup support. The briefing was scheduled to begin in seven minutes.

Eve heard the crack of a can of soda opening and smelled the odor of coffee and a bacon-and-egg sandwich. Fortification for her team—who had been working nonstop throughout the night.

She hadn't eaten in hours. There was no food or sustenance that could distract her from García's murder—and the threat of more murders to come unless they acted fast.

"Looks like we're losing, two–zip. Two tasks done. Presumably one still to go. And we still haven't nailed this asshole," Mace said, suddenly behind her.

"Yeah, it's like being two runs down in the bottom of the ninth," Eli agreed. "We don't have Allie. García's gone. We have to go big or go home."

"What in the name of Saint Francis is wrong with the two of you?" Haddox shook his head. "García is dead, and you guys want to talk like it's only a game?"

Mace shrugged. "Nothing I hate more than hypocrites. And you'd all think I'd turned into one, big-time, if I pretended to be all broken up about García. He and I weren't friends. We couldn't stand each other."

"Geez, that's cold," Eli said.

"Just the truth."

"I don't care how much you guys disliked each other—or hated working with each other," Eve interrupted. "We are a team—and García's death diminishes us."

She turned and walked to the edge of the tent, desperate for air.

Haddox, right behind, pulled a packet of Marlboros out of his pocket and glanced dismissively at the NO SMOKING sign someone had posted. He fixed Eve with soulful blue eyes as he lit up his cigarette. "You doing okay?"

"Not exactly the Thanksgiving I expected," she said ruefully. "You?"

He took a deep drag off his fresh smoke. "There's a lass I know. She's not like anybody I've ever met. Has a thing about wanting new experiences. So I'd been planning to take her advice—and spend the holiday tasting the beef pho at the night markets of Hanoi or para-gliding off Mont Blanc."

"Doesn't sound like anyone you'd ever find in a place like this," Eve said. "There's nothing new about mourning a friend. Working a kidnapping case. Trying and failing to save a city from harm."

"She always surprises me, this lass." Haddox twirled his cigarette between his thumb and forefinger. "Even makes me surprise myself. I like that about her."

A noisy cheer erupted from the throngs lining the street. The last of the floats and balloons, clowns and cheerleaders and marching bands from the staging area, were about to join the parade. The final flank was going to begin their two-and-a-half-mile journey to Herald Square.

The crowd was so loud, Eve barely heard the text message that just pinged the flip phone the kidnapper had left her. She didn't recognize the number, but the message got her immediate attention.

*Demand #3: Commissioner Donovan must take a seat on the final float—Santa's sleigh. NOW!*

NEWS NEWS NEWS NEWS NEWS

## WJXZ REPORTS

This is Gwen Allensen, reporting from Macy's flagship store at Herald Square, where thousands have gathered to watch as the magnificent parade floats and giant balloons make their way across the finish line.

In addition to the 50 million of you watching on television at home, we estimate there are about 3.5 million live spectators here standing along the parade route.

And, just coming into view, you're about to see the rascally Aflac duck with his trademark red scarf!

First making his appearance in the parade back in 2011, the Aflac duck is what Macy's calls a balloonicle—a thirty-five-foot-high balloon mixed with a self-propelled vehicle.

Note that a plush version of this cute white bird will be for sale throughout the holiday season at Macy's. Since all proceeds will go to hospitals nationwide, make sure you find one to take home.

In breaking news, we are just receiving reports that a man has been stabbed on the Upper West Side. We have no information yet on the extent of his injuries—or whether the perpetrator is under arrest.

# Chapter 68

Inside the Security Tent, 77th Street
and Central Park West

"Before Agent Rossi takes you through our specific strategy," Jan began, "I need to explain what we found in Central Park." The forensic tech was short, with no-nonsense hair and an attitude to match. "First, I'm sorry to hear about Frank García."

All around the tent, there were somber nods of acknowledgment. Outside, a high school band was playing "When the Saints Go Marching In."

"As you know, it was García who tracked down the storage shed inside Central Park where the kids had been held for some hours. The commissioner's daughter, of course, is still somewhere under the kidnapper's control." Jan took a sip from her cup of coffee and grimaced.

"We have teams on the ground searching now," Eve added, "but the park covers more than eight hundred acres and has twenty entrances. And that's assuming they're still in the park—and not on the move to an entirely different location. We could have a thousand officers on the grounds, looking under every branch and turning over every leaf, and still not find Allie. More troubling, we now believe her kidnapping is less likely to be a personal attack against the top cop alone. It may be part of a larger plot—involving the parade that millions of eyes are now watching."

The faces around her grew grimmer.

Deputy Commissioner George Kepler walked into the tent. Approached Donovan. "I assume you've been told that you're a damn fool, about to take an unnecessary risk."

"Not your call. You're ready to take control if need be?"

Kepler nodded. "Don't think I don't know how hard that is for you to say."

Donovan shrugged. "It's all part of the job."

"Part of your job is staying safe. This city and this department need you."

"And I know how hard that is for *you* to say."

Jan was still talking in clipped sentences. "García recognized the smell of mothballs in the room where the kids had been held. The smell was suspicious enough that we undertook a full chemical analysis. What we found was Soman—a nerve agent. It's a close cousin of the better known chemical weapon, sarin."

A serious woman with thin-set eyes asked a question. *Are we expecting something on the order of the Tokyo subway attacks?*

"It's possible this agent could be dispensed in a similar way," Jan answered bluntly, "but potentially with a more far-reaching—and deadly—effect. You may remember that a dozen people died in Tokyo. Fifty were seriously injured and nearly a thousand temporarily blinded. That's because the release of sarin in the Tokyo subway was crude. A diluted substance was poured into sealed bags. At the agreed-upon time, those bags were punctured—and puddles of the nerve agent released, exposing people nearby. Had the perpetrators dispensed it as an aerosol—a fine, inhalable mist—there could have been thousands of casualties."

Exposure to Soman, Jan continued, could lead to paralysis—or respiratory failure and then death.

There was an antidote available—but it had to be used within minutes to be most effective. Most of it was held in military storage—and it would never make it to New York City in time to be of help.

A man from Homeland Security with a shaved head raised his hand. *What about the guy under arrest for shooting the commissioner? Or the guy in custody who had been linked to threats targeting NYPD officers?*

Eve accepted the cup of coffee she was offered. It was hot and black, and it steadied her. "Brock Olsen is a well-known anti-police radical. But we don't believe that he's connected with the threat we face this morning; his strategy is to use social media and take to the streets. The man we're after likely has access to the social network that Olsen organized—and used what he learned to orchestrate the kidnapping of the commissioner's daughter—but we believe this perpetrator has greater sophistication. It's not easy to obtain a chemical weapon like Soman—not to mention to weaponize it. So we're looking for someone with the ability to access the high-security storage sites maintained by the U.S. military."

*Maybe the real question is: Should we stop the parade?* A man with a rasping voice spoke up.

"Absolutely not." The commissioner stepped forward. "We have three and a half million people jammed into a two-and-a-half-mile stretch. If people panic—and stampede—there's a risk of significant harm and injuries. Not to mention that the greatest city on earth will look like it can't face down a threat."

"Soman isn't an ordinary threat," Jan disagreed.

Donovan shook his head. "You found what—a trace amount? In a storage shed? With no real indication how long it had been there." He let that sink in.

His eyes seemed to drift beyond Jan's to meet Kepler's—and Eve noticed something pass between the two men. It was a communication that might have been disagreement.

George Kepler turned, stepped outside the tent.

Donovan pretended not to notice. "We have the finest law enforcement team in the world—not to mention the technology to handle this. The parade *must* go on."

"If we stop the parade," Eve added, "we may force the perpetrator's hand. He could release the poison immediately."

Jan picked up the thread. "All officers have been issued tactical response hoods to protect them from chemical attack. Given the evidence of a specific threat, we're also going to dispense additional biohazard detectors. As most of you already know, this tool is the size of a contact lens case—and it can detect any agent released in its vicinity within two minutes."

She continued with the briefing, answering more questions.

Then it was over. Tasks were assigned. Everyone dispersed.

"You guys are clear what to do?" Eve asked Eli and Mace.

"Clear as mud." Eli shot her a grin.

"It's all part of his message," Eve cautioned. "We already know that symbols are important to him—and he's using them to make a point. He asked for money. He asked for a dangerous cop killer. He was like a damn ghost when he attacked García; not even the video cams in the area picked up a decent image for ID."

"And now he wants to stick the commissioner in a Santa sleigh. What's that symbolize?" Mace challenged.

"That he's not done with the commissioner. Not yet," Eve answered grimly.

Santa's sleigh would be leaving the museum area, starting its journey down the parade route, within twenty-four minutes. Commissioner Logan Donovan would be on board.

Donovan insisted that he had no choice; he would follow the kidnapper's final demand. There was no swaying him; no chance of convincing him otherwise.

"Impossible," Eve retorted. "You'll be too exposed."

"Aye," Haddox added. "You know it's a trap."

Donovan shrugged. "Anything on the parade route is exposed. My security detail will be close by."

"Didn't protect you during the riot."

"I'm willing to trust in the wall-to-wall security protecting the Frozen Zone."

"Didn't protect García," Eve reminded him.

Empathy flared in those disconcerting blue eyes again. "I'm sorry about your man. I know what it's like to lose one of your own."

"You've been shot once already," she reminded him tartly. "Next time, they could use real bullets."

# Chapter 69

### Parade Route, Inside the Frozen Zone

The *Phantom of the Opera* float began its journey. Strains of "Point of No Return" filled the air. Noisy spectators were corralled by police officers into sections of metal barricades. And there was now litter blowing everywhere on the streets. A discarded pizza box scuttled by. Empty plastic water bottles rolled. Candy wrappers danced.

*People are pigs,* Haddox decided.

Then he thought about the dangerous threats that those same people were blissfully unaware of. *People are vulnerable.*

He walked toward Logan Donovan, who was waiting by Santa's sleigh.

"Hey, mate. Looks like you have a couple minutes before this thing takes off—and we need to chat," he told Donovan. Then he guided him past the museum, toward the quieter space of Columbus Avenue.

"I've been learning about you," Haddox began. "I dug in deep, trying to figure out how and why your daughter was targeted."

"You've found something. And you disapprove."

"Listen, mate—I'm no priest. I'm the last person who'll ever judge you. Unless, of course, you break the only two rules that matter. Always treat your lass with respect. And always give thanks for a well-poured Guinness."

The older man offered him an empty smile.

"It's got to be hard work, raising a kid. The world's crazy complicated these days, and they get all their information from the Internet—

whether it's social media or instant messaging or online forums. Then you've got porn and cyberbullying and online grooming. You have to worry about their virtual friends as much as their real-life ones."

Donovan didn't seem to be listening. He'd disappeared into his phone again. Where his daughter was concerned, he had the attention span of a two-year-old. *What is wrong with this git?*

Finally, he looked up. "Things used to be all right before my wife got sick."

Haddox wasn't looking for a confession. He neither needed nor wanted to know any of this.

"I get it. We're talking about a rough time in your life. But Allie—or someone posing as Allie—suspected you could be responsible for your wife's death."

"Allie?" He shot Haddox an incredulous look. "No way."

"Or someone posing as her," Haddox repeated. "She posted about it online. Asked for help investigating you. No names, of course. But given what's happened today, it's possible somebody figured it out all the same. One of them peppered her with questions. He made her feel important. He didn't treat her like a child. He took her concerns seriously. He believed her." Haddox passed Donovan his smartphone. He'd taken a photo of the relevant chat.

—Hello. My name is The_Crusader. What's yours?
—Hi. It's Monique.
—Pretty name. You said he had a bad temper. Has he hurt you?
—It's not like that.
—Good. But he hurt your mom?
—I'm scared he killed her.

The commissioner stiffened.

"That gives you the sense of it," Haddox said.

The commissioner wouldn't look at Haddox now. His head was bowed.

"He listened to her," Haddox persisted. "Got inside her head. Took her allegations seriously."

"And this is our man?"

"The thing is, even if he's not, he raises some legitimate questions."

"What's that supposed to mean?"

"I figured your wife's death certificate would lay the question to rest, once and for all. But Hawaii listed no cause of death. Highly unusual, wouldn't you say?"

Donovan was silent.

"I guess that was a pretty treacherous hiking trail you were on, Commissioner. But you can see how it might raise a few questions that your wife fell to her death. Especially since it had been awhile since the two of you played happy family."

"This is none of your business."

"Did you kill your wife?"

"You bastard—"

"Allie's missing. I'm asking you a legitimate question. It needs an answer."

"That's enough."

"Not for me."

"When I say enough, I mean it. Go back to your computer and let real men handle the tough issues."

"Guilty conscience?"

"Wrong again."

"What is your relationship with Jackie Meade?"

"Jackie's my employee."

"She was more than that, once. Any chance she bears a grudge? Because *she* had access to Allie's computer. *She* could be the poster *Monique*. It might not be Allie at all."

Something flickered in Donovan's eye. Definitely not shame, since Haddox didn't think the wanker was capable of feeling any. Discomfort? Maybe. The commissioner had been seen through—and he didn't like it.

"You don't make many wrong moves," Donovan muttered.

"Can't afford to, mate. Neither can you. You ought to stay away from Eve."

"I like Eve. I intend to do something about it. No matter what you say."

"I don't intend to say anything. Eve's smart. She'll see you for what you are."

"She'll see a fellow officer of the law. A man who cares about this city and the cops who work for him."

"Or maybe she'll see a powerhouse type with plenty of ambition but no soul. A philanderer with charm but no heart."

The commissioner swung a punch from the left with a straight right.

It would have landed square on Haddox's jaw if he hadn't ducked two split seconds before it landed. He wasn't one to back away from something worth fighting for. But most arguments weren't worth it—so it paid to have a good exit strategy.

The commissioner spun around like a scarecrow, his elbow whipping back.

Haddox stepped aside with a shrug and a grin. "Enough playing around, Commissioner. You've got a ride to catch with Santa."

*NEWS NEWS NEWS NEWS NEWS*

## WJXZ REPORTS

This is continuing WJXZ News coverage with Gwen Allensen, and I'm talking with Lieutenants Jay Jones and Michael Gabriel of Midtown North Precinct, who just helped one couple celebrate a very special Thanksgiving this morning. Officer Jones, what can you tell us?

*JONES:* I was on patrol near Columbus Circle, just before the parade got started, when a group of spectators on the bleachers started waving their arms. Turned out there was a woman whose baby just couldn't wait for Thanksgiving! We moved her under the bleachers for the delivery, getting her comfortable on some blankets spectators had brought to keep warm—and I called for Officer Gabriel, who's also a trained paramedic. I delivered the healthy baby boy—and Mikey here arrived just in time to clamp the umbilical cord.

*GWEN:* And have you heard how mom and baby are doing?

*GABRIEL:* They're en route to the hospital and doing well. Baby Joseph is seven pounds, five ounces—and he's arrived just in time to enjoy his first Thanksgiving.

# Chapter 70

Mace picked up Melo, the rescue puppy that Céline had just dropped off.

"So you'll ride the *Ace CyberDog* float with your rescue dog, as originally planned," Eve told Mace. "Eli will be right behind you, marching as one of fifty official handlers of the Molly the Mongoose balloon. Molly's corporate sponsor, the *Wholesome Minds* float, will be immediately after, followed by Santa's sleigh, where the commissioner will be riding."

"Eli's marching?" Mace's face spread into a dazzling grin. "Hope they'll let me stay in back of the *Ace* float. Don't want to miss *that*."

"Meanwhile, Haddox and I will continue to search out this suspect's identity. As soon as we have anything concrete—about him or his ultimate target—you'll be the first to know."

"You mean his target ain't the commissioner and the Santa sled?"

"Just in case something even bigger's at play, we have to be alert. Make sure you have your protective gear." Eve was thinking how much she missed García right now. *Can't lose anybody else.*

Mace tugged a soggy, mustard-, ketchup-, and dirt-stained napkin out of the puppy's jaws. "How come nothin' but shit goes in this little guy's mouth?" He nodded to a growing crowd of anti-police protesters, who'd formed a line going down Eighty-first Street, west of the parade. They were matched by nearly as many police officers, keeping them behind the security cordon. "Those guys part of the plan?"

"Maybe. You could check it out. Didn't you used to be one of them?" Eve reminded him.

"I used to be lots of things I'm not anymore. I've given up trying to change the world. I just want to be left alone." Mace rumpled the puppy's head.

Someone had tied one of García's red bandanas around the dog's neck. Couldn't have been Mace. *Or could it?*

She wondered as she watched him, pup in hand, push past the media and police, flash his ID, and hop onto the waiting float.

As she walked back to the Incident Tent, she thought: Maybe Mace was now too world-weary to fight the good fight, but Allie's kidnapper—now also García's killer—wasn't. They were looking for someone who cared deeply about—*what?*

Something that the parade symbolized. Something that the commissioner symbolized.

She needed to *know* Allie's kidnapper. To see the world through his eyes. To understand what excited him—and also what made him most afraid. But with only ninety minutes until the deadline, could she even scratch the surface of this guy's mind?

Her phone buzzed.

Eve read Haddox's message and shivered—as all sense of reality shifted once again.

She closed her eyes. Fought the overwhelming sense of helplessness and disappointment.

Then she opened her eyes and messaged back: *I'm already on my way.*

SpongeBob had joined the parade route—together with fifty-five handlers, two utility vehicles to help anchor the giant balloon, and the solitary police officer who marched beside them.

Inside the security tent, Eve found Haddox pouring a cup of coffee. It was the NYPD's standard swill—so he improved it with a dash of Bushmills.

Eve raised an eyebrow. "Ever consider that you drink too much?"

"Java?" He took a noisy gulp. "Nectar of the gods."

"Whiskey. Bane of alcoholics."

Haddox's eyes lit, amused. "Because of a drop of the hard stuff? Don't think so. Besides, alcoholics are people like my da who take steps, make confessions, and go to AA meetings. I don't do that. Plus, there's the fact that I'm Irish—born with a liver of steel."

"Just like your da," Eve deadpanned. "Now tell me: What did you learn?"

He filled her in with everything he had found online, his conversation with Logan Donovan, and what he'd learned speaking with the commissioner's security detail, made up of rotating three-member teams responsible for his personal security. "They all agreed on one thing: Jackie Meade was sixteen kinds of crazy, and the commissioner was a fool for trusting his child with her."

"Are you still trying to convince me he doesn't care about Allie?"

"You said it, not me." Haddox drained the last of his coffee. He was sorely tempted—but he refrained from mentioning how Donovan had done his damnedest to land a punch on Haddox's perfect white teeth. "I did ask his security detail for their opinion. One of the officers, Casey, goes back a long way with the commissioner—having grown up with him, gone to the Academy with him, served overseas with him. Casey says the commissioner used to have a soft spot for strays. Seems he attracted them by the dozens, kept quite a menagerie at one point."

"Are we talking abandoned dogs and cats?"

Haddox shook his head. "People. The ones who are hurting, damaged. Like Jackie. And don't forget that he felt guilty," he added. "Donovan's Catholic, which means he was weaned on guilt."

Eve began thumbing through a marble notebook, looking for something she'd jotted down earlier.

Haddox put his empty coffee cup down. "Something else. According to Donovan's security team, the man gets over thirty death threats a week—and they're stretched pretty thin trying to keep up with them. One recent threat stands out for its weird factor. Some whacko sent what was basically a manifesto to the commissioner, titled *The Antidote*. The writer said Donovan and the NYPD were a symptom of everything wrong with our society—and that, come Thanksgiving, he was personally going to deliver a cure."

"Did Security ID a suspect?"

"They're looking at Brock Olsen, the same political activist who shot the commissioner with the paint gun."

"So a closed case, in their view. Unless they got it wrong." Eve flipped through the remaining pages of her notebook. Located the profile she'd put together.

❑ Physical: five-foot-eleven, medium build
❑ Probable age: forties or fifties (planning and confidence indicates maturity and experience)
❑ Intelligence: above-average IQ with high verbal intelligence
  ✦ His formal education may not reflect his intelligence. Cat-and-mouse games suggest he is bored easily; he may have dropped out of school.
❑ Background: possible military or equivalent (skill in taking Allie and killing García)
❑ Expertise:
  ✦ Technological sophistication: high level
    * Ability to pierce Allie's online postings to find her true identity
    * Makes calls from stolen cellphones and relies on voice-altering software
❑ Motive: connected to the Macy's Thanksgiving Day Parade
  ✦ A public stage (the world is watching)
  ✦ A holiday celebrating America, democracy, freedom, etc.
  ✦ A holiday celebrating family and the magic of childhood—as favorite storybook and cartoon characters are brought to life through balloons and floats and dressed-up volunteers

She turned the page to Haddox. "If my profile is accurate, it doesn't exactly describe Jackie," she said ruefully. "Maybe she has a new friend? One obsessed with society's ills?"

"I thought of that angle, too, luv. I spoke with Casey from Donovan's detail—as well as Sam, their private security man. We all agree it's possible. Want to pay her another visit?"

Eve felt a prickle in her gut. "Do we have a choice?"

# Chapter 71

Beginning of the Parade Route,
American Museum of Natural History

Mace took a spot at the rear of the *Ace CyberDog* float—looking backward toward the Molly the Mongoose balloon. He was joined by three executives and four kids—all dressed as dog mascots.

"What's his name?"

Mace looked down at the boy and the rescue puppy. "I've been calling him Melo, 'cause I like the Knicks. But when he gets to Herald Square and finds his new family, he'll get his real name."

"Oh." The boy scrunched up his face, thinking. "I'd nickname him Zinger."

"Well, you can call him that. Why don't you take care of him for me for a few minutes? Test out some names; see what he likes. What do people call you?"

"I'm Tom. Like my dad." He pointed to the tallest of the execs—the one dressed in a Dalmatian suit.

The generators behind the float powered up. A police officer gave the thumbs-up. The float began to move—just inches at first, until it picked up speed.

The crowds standing in front of the museum let out a rowdy cheer.

Mace left the boy and took stock of the floats remaining behind them. Beyond Molly the Mongoose, he saw the float of its corporate parent, Wholesome Minds. Santa was going to bring up the rear. The commissioner had taken a seat on the tall sleigh, awaiting Santa.

"I bet you think that Aflac float oughta turn around and pick you up—'cause you're gonna be a sitting duck on that bench, Commish,"

Mace said into his hidden microphone—one that connected all of the members of the Vidocq team as well as the commissioner.

"That's the idea, isn't it?" Donovan retorted dryly. "I'm here to draw him out. And don't worry: I'm ready for him."

Eli stared woefully at the costume the Macy's volunteer had brought him. He picked up a red half-ball at the end of a string. It might have been designed to fit over a human nose. He wasn't sure whether it looked more Rudolph or Bozo.

"This looks like a clown costume," he complained.

The man laughed, exposing a set of crooked teeth. "*Por qué no?* It's festive. And the red cone is your hat."

"I'm not sure it will fit," Eli objected. "I might be a little tall." Because *tall* was a more polite word than *fat*. And he wasn't about to admit that *this* clown costume, which was obviously cut for a man of extremely generous girth, still wasn't big enough for him.

The Macy's volunteer nodded knowingly. "I'll find you another costume. One designed for people who are *taller*."

Donovan checked his watch nervously. Confirmed that the headset and microphone connecting him to Eve and the rest of the team was working. There'd been no further word from the kidnapper.

"Ho, ho, ho! Help me up, will you?" A man in a red Santa suit stifled a belch and sniffed twice before lumbering up onto the sleigh. "You must be the commissioner. I heard we're going to be dance partners this morning. Parade buddies," he said and chortled. "Just you, me, the elves down below, and some reindeer." Santa climbed onto the right side of the bench and stretched, rolling his shoulders in lazy circles.

Donovan glanced at the girth of the man beside him. "I always wonder if that belly's real—or if it's just your costume."

"Just smile and wave, Commish. Smile and wave," Santa instructed with a grin.

NEWS NEWS NEWS NEWS NEWS

## WJXZ REPORTS

Good morning! This is WJXZ News with Gwen Allensen, and I'm talking with Isidore Marone, a World War Two veteran of Patton's Army who's here with his daughters Anna and Lucia, his four grandchildren, and six great-grandchildren. Isidore, you've not missed a single parade since 1945, is that right?

*ISIDORE:* What's that you're saying?

*LUCIA (LOUDLY):* Pop, you've come to the parade every year since '45, right?

*ISIDORE:* Yes. I came home from the war and went with your mother, my Maria—God rest her soul. Haven't missed a one since! It's a tradition.

*GWEN:* Can you tell me what's changed the most since your first parade?

*ISIDORE:* What?

*ANNA:* She's asking you what's changed since that first parade.

*ISIDORE:* Oh, that's easy. The crowds. It's all 'cause of *Miracle on 34th Street*. That movie came out—when? 1947?—and suddenly everybody wanted to be part of this parade.

# Chapter 72

Something was wrong.

When Haddox and Eve arrived at the Donovan brownstone a block and a half away, they found the house silent. Only a humming refrigerator broke the stillness. The house still reeked of Pine-Sol and bleach.

Jackie's cellphone rested on the table in the hallway. A message—unread—lit its screen for a moment.

Eve scanned it in the second before it vanished. Then passed the device to Haddox, telegraphing him with a glance. *Your job.*

Wordlessly, he pulled his computer out of his bag, connected it to Jackie's phone, and began working his magic. He launched the software program he'd designed to unlock first the passcode, then all the device's secrets.

Eve left him and moved toward the stairwell. It was going to be important to proceed carefully.

In the quiet, Eve felt a small tremor expanding inside her, filling her chest. "Jackie? Are you here?" she called out.

Silence.

"I'd like to talk," she offered.

No reply.

It was possible Jackie was gone. That she'd learned of their suspicions and run.

Eve climbed the staircase, reached the second floor. Moved room to room.

All quiet.

"Jackie?" Eve repeated.

Silence.

Another stairwell. The third floor. Only four rooms left to search.

Eve took the two on the left, then those on the right. She gingerly nudged open the last door.

Jackie was sitting on the bed. Her arms were wrapped around her knees, hugging them to her chest.

"Hi, Jackie."

Jackie's hair, no longer in its headband, was sticking out in all different directions. Her eyes were dull, no trace of emotion. There was a pistol on the quilt beneath her.

Eve pressed the button on her cellphone that would summon help. Took a slow, cautious step into the doorway.

"You don't need the gun." Eve edged closer. "Mind if I hold on to it?"

It always surprised Eve how sometimes a direct question yielded exactly the result she wanted. But not this time.

Jackie snatched the gun close. "I am *not* going to jail."

Six words laced with panic, exhaustion, and determination. Three emotions that combined to scare Eve considerably. She thought: *I need to understand what you're thinking.*

"Who's said anything about jail?" She made her voice conversational but concerned. "I'm here because I need your help."

"Liar!" She pointed the gun at Eve. "You're lying to protect that bastard."

*Which bastard?* Eve wondered. *The commissioner—or someone else?*

Eve noted three pill bottles on the nightstand. Each one emptied of its contents. Turned on its side. "Sometimes I'm wrong about things. I make mistakes. A liar wouldn't admit that, right?"

Something sparked inside Jackie's eyes. Shock. Maybe even surprise that someone was truly listening.

Eve put herself inside Jackie's mind: *He lied to me.*

"People let you down. Men, especially, treat you badly. It happens."

Jackie looked at Eve, understanding.

"He lied to me," Jackie said.

Eve imagined Jackie's train of thought: *But I believed him. He said he understood me.*

Jackie said, "He made me feel like he understood me—and would make it all better."

"But the only one who can do that is you, Jackie. I can help you." Eve held out her hand. "Will you give me the gun?"

No response.

The pills, Eve knew, were swiftly being absorbed by the woman's bloodstream.

"I understand what it's like to be attracted to the wrong guy," Eve said. "It happens. It can lead to some pretty stupid choices."

The other woman faltered. "Logan came home alone. He wanted to make believe Jill died in an accident. I destroyed evidence to help him do that." Her words were beginning to slur. "Then I hated myself for it. I started talking to people."

"Talking to who?" Eve sat beside her on the bed. Jackie didn't seem to notice.

Jackie's eyes were blank. Dilated.

"Who has Allie?" Eve asked.

"She's safe." The *S* was extra-long.

Eve took a chance. "A lot of men have lied to you, Jackie. You don't need to protect any of them. Just tell me who has her—and where he's keeping her."

"They say I won't feel a thing," she mumbled.

Eve reached for the gun—and took it. Jackie no longer cared.

Eve picked up the bottles on the nightstand. Read their names. Klonopin. Paxil. Seroquel.

Sirens wailed in the street below. The medical help Eve had summoned was arriving.

"I never meant to hurt Allie," Jackie insisted. Her breath was growing ragged. "He's keeping her in the park."

"I know," Eve agreed sadly, as Jackie succumbed to the pills.

The text message received on Jackie's phone had read: *Anything happens to me, get girl. She's at place we watched the fireworks.*

Haddox waited for Eve just outside the brownstone. Ashen-faced. "Jackie tell you who's holding Allie—or where?"

Eve shook her head. "We didn't get that far. *The place we watched fireworks* has to mean Central Park—so we'll get an expanded search team working. I figure you can handle the ID. Since you had the sender's number and all."

"I downloaded all Jackie's data; I'll search for patterns and suspicious activity." Haddox pulled Jackie's phone out of his pocket, returned it to her. "But no luck on the ID. The text was sent from a burner, luv."

NEWS NEWS NEWS NEWS NEWS

## WJXZ REPORTS

This is Gwen Allensen, with live coverage from the Macy's flagship store at Herald Square.

We're watching as childhood favorite Paddington Bear, that huggable teddy from England, journeys his last few blocks.

He's a big bear: fifty-four feet long, thirty-six feet wide, and sixty feet tall. His trademark suitcase is the size of a typical suburban two-car garage!

He first made his appearance in the Macy's parade in 2014.

There are volunteers waiting on the other side of Herald Square—who will immediately begin breaking him down for the return trip to Macy's Studio in Moonachie, New Jersey.

# Chapter 73

## Along the Parade Route, Inside the Frozen Zone

The *Ace CyberDog* float was passing West Sixty-fifth Street.

Mace took seven steps forward, through Ace's reconstructed doghouse. He stepped around oversized bones and chewies, stuffed fire hydrants, and a life-sized squirrel. He peered inside the float's machine room.

No movement. No sound. No sign of anyone there.

Just the generator that supplied enough power to propel the float forward.

*Where was an Army Ranger when you needed him?* The moment Mace thought of García, he cursed himself. This was no time to be stupid or sentimental.

All around him, there was chaos and shouting, sirens and bull-horns, and the incessant noise from the circling helicopters overhead.

But inside Mace's head? An eerie quiet prevailed.

On the meanest streets of Hunts Point where he grew up, some-body was always mad about something. People got stabbed, windows got broken, and guns went off throughout the night. What he wouldn't ever forget was the sensation of *waiting* for it to happen.

He alternated looking down the dark stairs into the depths of the *Ace CyberDog* float—and looking out into the crowds. His breathing was becoming more labored—which was either nerves or something bad in the air, 'cause he was in top shape—but none of the cops with their biological weapons detectors were worried.

"Anybody there?" he called.

No one answered.

He stopped. Listened.

There it was. A faint whining sound. It was actually coming from the puppy behind him—but it echoed in the wood, bouncing from side to side, until it seemed it came from the depths of the float itself.

Mace wasn't a superstitious man—but right now, just waiting for the unthinkable? It was enough to make a far more practical man go insane.

And Mace had never been practical.

Behind Mace on the *Ace CyberDog* float, Molly the Mongoose had been given the green light to start moving. Eli was doing his best to blend in with the other handlers around him. But the only part of him that actually fit the bill was his carrot-colored hair.

"They want us to look like we're having a great time. It's okay to dance!" The handler next to him, a perky, pony-tailed woman, gave Eli a bright smile. "And if you can't really dance, just kick your legs up high in the air. Pretend we're all Radio City Rockettes!"

"Seriously?" Eli gave a halfhearted kick.

"Try again." The woman smiled even brighter. "Just pretend you can do it. Like you're John Travolta in *Saturday Night Fever*. That's your generation, right? Whatever inspires your best moves."

Eli tried again, knowing he didn't really have a best move.

This time, he kicked his left leg so high he teetered and wobbled. Nearly fell on his face—or, rather, the red ball at the end of his nose.

A cold gust of wind briefly turned Molly into a whirling torpedo. For a moment, Eli was scared—and he remembered why he was there.

*How am I going to keep an eye out for a kidnapper or cop killer or whoever he is if I'm too busy tripping over two left feet?* Eli wondered.

The ponytailed woman had another suggestion. "Maybe you can just wave. Because people in the crowds and the stands? They mainly just want us to look friendly."

· · ·

Jackie's cellphone was a mine trove of data.

It didn't matter that Allie's kidnapper had used a series of burner phones.

Or that Jackie had taken some basic precautions to obscure the man's true identity.

Or that when he went online to communicate with her, he'd protected himself with TOR—or The Onion Router, the most widely used method for staying anonymous on the Web. Multilayered, with no clear center, it relied on a complex network of intermediary relay servers run by volunteers around the world. Political activists in places like Iran, Egypt, and Syria routinely favored it for protection. So did cybercriminals.

It was all too familiar to Haddox.

TOR made identification more difficult—but its shield of anonymity was far from impenetrable. While there was no foolproof strategy for tracing people through TOR, Haddox had one that was pretty close: human error. Because all users—even the most disciplined— eventually made mistakes.

Allie's kidnapper was no exception.

He'd downloaded a series of documents through TOR—documents containing Web links that had taken him outside of TOR—and revealed his naked IP address.

It took three minutes and twenty-two seconds to find him. Haddox flexed his fingers and savored the moment. This was ordinary work. Really no different from what he'd done as a skip tracer— trying every means at his disposal to locate a missing person.

Haddox placed his hands over the keyboard. Then he began speeding through the world of the Web. Fingers flying, he made his way through activity, discovering more and more about his mark.

Haddox continued to work—if you could even call this *work*. Because there was no sensation more intoxicating than tracing the details of a mark, having so much information at his fingertips.

It was the ultimate high.

# Chapter 74

## Along the Parade Route

Santa's sleigh was passing West Sixty-fifth Street.

Donovan scanned the crowds lining either side of the parade route.

Mace was right. Donovan was a sitting duck. Still, he plastered a smile on his face and waved. Focused on the fact that soon he was going to come face-to-face with the bastard who'd taken his daughter.

"Ho, ho, ho!" Santa roared, to the delight of the cheering crowd, as he waved his left hand.

"First time sitting on this sled?" Donovan asked.

"No, sir. Been a fixture at this parade for over a decade. Never had to share my sleigh before with anyone but an elf! Hope you're not auditioning to take my place next year!"

Santa threw his right arm around Donovan's back—and gave another merry and booming *Ho, ho, ho*.

Molly the Mongoose was passing West Sixty-third Street.

Somehow Eli had managed to smile and wave his way down fourteen blocks. It was nothing short of a miracle. He felt like a damn beauty queen.

Molly the Mongoose flew high above, anchored in place by its fifty-five handlers plus Eli, all dressed in clown costumes. The *Wholesome Minds* float followed its famous mascot. And the commissioner was sitting next to Santa on the float right behind them.

Around him, the festivities made for quite a spectacle—picture perfect for the tourists. Lights were glittering, Broadway stars were singing, people were cheering.

And somewhere—a madman lurked.

So Eli smiled and waved, watched and waited. Ready to act when needed—clown suit and all.

*Mace's Ace CyberDog* float approached Columbus Circle. The towers of the Time Warner Center shimmered high above. Significantly closer to the ground, the statue of Christopher himself presided over the ceremonies.

Mace was just watching the crowds. He had a great vantage point. He let his gaze zigzag the way it did when he played street ball. Survey the defense, figure out the weak spots that he could expose, and drive hard to the net.

Except in this case, the defense was an enormous crowd of young mothers with baby strollers; a hooded teenager with a skateboard; an elderly couple, hunched over with arthritis; a father with a newborn sleeping on his beer belly. Hordes of tourists wearing sweatshirts advertising their home states: University of South Dakota. Georgia Tech. UCLA.

Then he saw the shadow slipping among the tourists. A single figure. Dressed in fatigues.

Hands not visible.

Coming right toward the *Ace* float.

It was a moment of truth. Decision time: Live or die.

Mace radioed the Tactical unit on the ground. "My two o'clock," he said. "Camouflage. Possible weapon. *Now!*"

Mace leaped from the *Ace CyberDog* float and ran to intercept the man in camouflage.

Several people screamed. Others ran. Someone yelled at the crowd to step back.

Mace and two tactical agents swarmed the camouflaged man. Mace couldn't say who took him down to the ground; it was a team effort.

They hit him in the chest and at the knees. Then he was gang-tackled by another four SWAT officers.

His wrists were shackled. He was searched. His ID was scanned.

One minute, fifty seconds later, he was pronounced clean.

Michael Deans was a Vietnam War vet who always wore camouflage. Who occasionally had a panic attack when he was stuck in a crowd.

Mace jogged down Central Park South, racing to catch up to the *Ace CyberDog* float before it rolled too far down Sixth Avenue.

Meanwhile, the man who had kidnapped Allie watched from his seat along the parade route as the balloons and floats weaved through the crowds.

He watched as everyone cheered and waved—the crowds on the sidewalks, the marchers, the musicians, the performers.

So many people. All blissfully unaware of what was about to happen. How he was about to deliver an antidote—one designed to counteract the poison infecting them all.

How else could an ailing society get better?

# Chapter 75

Eve brought Haddox a piping-hot cup of fresh coffee, handing it to him like it was a priceless artifact. "No Bushmills this time. Wouldn't want you to end up like your dad, going to meetings."

"You wound me, luv." He passed her a full dossier on Allie's kidnapper—a piece of cake for Haddox once he'd uncovered his IP address—and as she read, what had been gaps in a fractured picture came together.

Eve had built her career on one essential skill: being able to tell when someone was lying. But Allie's kidnapper had played her. His lies had sounded like truths because he had told them in the guise of being helpful. There had been no sense that he was trying to deceive. Not even his unconscious responses had given any clue: His breathing and voice patterns had remained within normal parameters.

She had been convinced this man played no role in Allie's disappearance. She'd thought he lacked any motive to hurt the commissioner.

She had been wrong.

"He was a good liar, luv," Haddox said. "Think about how he took advantage of Jackie, preying on her emotional weakness to make her an accessory."

It was supposed to make her feel better. It didn't. There was an odd fluttering in her stomach; she felt queasy.

Haddox continued. "He's fifty-four years old. Grew up in Alaska, went to the Anchorage campus of University of Alaska on an ROTC scholarship. His major was computer science—which helps explain the technological savvy. He served four years on active duty—and since several of his platoon buddies were on the force, when he returned to the states, he joined the NYPD."

Haddox continued to explain the rest to Eve: how Allie's kidnapper had met his wife through friends at a Yankees game; how they'd married seven months later; how their son Lucas had followed within two years. Then tragedy had struck. Lucas was diagnosed at age three with rhabdomyosarcoma, a cancerous tumor that developed in one of his legs. The tumor was removed in a nine-hour operation—but the cancer returned a year later, in his lung. They soon learned traditional treatments were not working, but there was hope that a new experimental treatment might help.

The problem was: It was crushingly expensive.

He was still on active duty with the NYPD—but their insurance wouldn't cover it. His wife was employed by Wholesome Minds—the corporation behind Molly the Mongoose—but their insurance wouldn't cover it, either.

"So he embezzled the money from an NYPD evidence locker and was caught—by the commissioner himself—who forced him to return the money," Eve said aloud.

"Which is how the commissioner kept his sorry arse out of jail." Haddox nodded. "The commissioner went to bat for him, arguing extenuating circumstances and family pressure. Even managed to let him save face with the NYPD, by resigning rather than getting fired." He gazed beyond Eve to the passing parade. "Donovan definitely went above and beyond. Probably wanted the guy in his pocket."

Eve raised her eyebrows. "Sounds to me like another example of how Donovan looks out for his own. Just because you don't like him, don't assume the worst."

"Call it like I see it, luv." He toggled to a different file on his computer. Opened it. "After the theft, our man's son died. His wife committed suicide nineteen days later. Two tragedies within three weeks. Logan and Jill attended both funerals, on behalf of the NYPD."

"Losing your entire family over the course of a matter of weeks would cause even the toughest man to grieve," Eve pointed out. "But does this really explain why he kidnapped a child, killed our best Special Ops agent, and brought a chemical nerve gas to the Thanksgiving Day Parade?"

"There is no good explanation for that. Nothing more than a co-incidence in his life history—that might explain the access to Soman. It seems Alaska was home to several nerve agent trials—all shrouded in secrecy, of course. But there are a few records. We can thank Congress, since they hauled the Army in for hearings to explain some lost chemical munitions—not to mention the mysterious deaths of fifty-four caribou in the vicinity of Blueberry Lake, where the munitions testing had occurred."

"And our man had access to these weapons, we believe?"

"Aye." Haddox nodded. "He was stationed near Blueberry Lake, at the same time the munitions disappeared."

"And this was how many years ago?"

"Eight," Haddox admitted. "He has a long history with the area. He'd done training near the incident. Grown up nearby. His father still lives there. It doesn't take a great leap of imagination to say that he'd have had an opportunity to take something, store something. And here's the main thing: Two months ago, he took a little trip. Guess where he happened to visit?"

"Blueberry Lake," Eve said.

"She shoots and she scores." Haddox shot her a grin, but his eyes were pools of concern.

# Chapter 76

Unknown Location Inside Central Park

When Allie woke up, she was alone.

Cotton-mouthed and parched—the monster must have drugged her again—but alone.

She ought to have been freezing—especially now that she was without her raincoat—but a huge rush of adrenaline fueled her.

She looked up and could see the city skyline. The San Remo's twin towers sparkled with light, serving as a beacon. Yellow—the color of hope.

She was in a gazebo of sorts. Her hands cuffed in front of her with plastic ties. And this was interesting: She was next to an area where park fencing was piled up. The sort of simple wooden slats that were used for park races like the NYC Marathon a couple weeks ago. She began reaching for a loose stake. And got lucky: She found one with a slightly sharpened point.

She imagined herself, stake in her hand, making a stabbing motion. She didn't feel exactly confident.

Then she pictured the way the Candlestick man had hurt the boy. The way he had lied to her. What she'd figured out about his plans for the parade.

She imagined herself again—and this time, she stabbed the air more easily.

She had a weapon; she played the scene over and over again in her head. Imagining how she could plant the stake somewhere vulnerable: His ear. His eye. His neck.

She had never done any violence to anybody, but she could make an exception for the Candlestick man. She would hurt him bad. Make him pay for what he'd done—and prevent everything he planned to do.

If she could just get out of these stupid zip-tie cuffs!

# Chapter 77

## Along the Parade Route

Donovan, on Santa's *Skyward* float, was passing the stocky white building at 2 Columbus Circle.

"Ho, ho, ho, Merry Christmas," Santa continued to bellow as they made their way along the parade route.

Donovan waved, continuing to focus on the crowd.

"You have kids, Commish? Kids always love a parade." Santa kept waving.

Suddenly, Donovan was furious. He was tired of having to deal with it all. The kidnapper with his cat-and-mouse games. Mo Kelly with her weakness and lies. His deputy, George, for his political greed. Even his own men and women in uniform—because as much as he appreciated the blind loyalty that led them to stand by his side, ultimately they were no better than he was. *Helpless.*

He really wanted to hit someone.

Not just *someone.* The man who'd taken Allie from him. The man who was threatening his city.

Time to end this *now.*

Suddenly he felt his left hand being yanked under the sleigh blanket. There was a click.

He reached with his right hand. It was too late. Metal clicked around that, too.

It was a trap—and it had been meticulously prepared.

"Don't make a sound." Santa's smile never wavered. "Tell me, Commissioner, how do you like my third task so far?" He waved at the crowds.

# Chapter 78

## Somewhere Inside Central Park

Allie was free. Escaped, with the help of a makeshift friction saw.
Those fencing stakes had given her the idea. Because of the wire that held them together.

Last summer, she'd overheard Casey on her dad's security detail talking about how a guy they'd arrested at a protest had used his shoelaces to make a friction saw and escape his zip ties. Casey couldn't stop talking about it. That was why they never used zip ties on gangbangers or military survivalist types—but they'd thought they were safe with a shaggy-haired academic rabble-rouser from Vermont.

Allie had studied her own silver-and-blue Converse sneaker laces—and nearly wept.

But the fencing wire? That was a different story.

So she'd stretched her hands close—started rubbing back and forth—and . . . success!

Now she felt so happy she didn't even care that she was lost.

She was pretty sure this was still Central Park, but it wasn't an area she'd ever visited.

She took her weapon, peered across the open field toward the edge of the lake. There was a figure ahead, lying on the ground, with his head tilted onto a rock. A bandana was tied over his eyes.

He wasn't moving.

Allie crept closer, breathing hard. The cuffs of her jeans and her sneakers were wet. She was starting to feel cold. Stopping about fifteen feet away, she called out. "Hey, mister!"

He didn't respond.

She moved closer. Called out again, louder this time.

This was pretty stupid. Foolish. He was probably homeless or drunk or some pervert. She could hear her mom's voice, saying "Just go tell an adult what you saw. Ask someone else for help."

"Mister—are you awake?"

The man tried to lift his head—flinched. He'd heard her. Seemed to be in pain.

She ran to him. "I'm going to untie this, okay?" Her fingers untangled the knot of the bandana. Then lifted the mask from his eyes.

He blinked at her, struggling to focus. His eyes were wet with tears.

"How long have you been here?" she asked.

"Last thing I remember was . . . walking in the park. I was right over there." His hand indicated the walking path. "Somebody came up behind me . . ."

"Are you hurt? Can you walk?" Allie didn't know her way out of the park, but maybe this guy did. Help couldn't be far away—even if at the moment it seemed as distant as Mars.

"My legs . . ."

He was lying at an awkward angle. Injured badly. But that wasn't what commanded her attention: It was what he was wearing.

A Santa suit.

# Chapter 79

## Along the Parade Route

$M$y third task.

With the words, Santa dropped his act. His voice changed an entire pitch. Modulated its tone. Switched regional accent.

"Hello, Chief. Don't you know me by now?"

*Of course he did.* Santa had put on a decent performance, but the voice—the natural voice—confirmed what he'd already determined to be true.

"Where's Allie?" Donovan strained against the cuffs, trying to launch out of his seat.

Santa waved. "Easy does it. You've got a front-row seat for my final act. And, given that Allie's still under my control, you'd better mind your manners. Lay a finger on me and you may never see her again. People will say the top cop can't protect his own. I think you'll agree: Your reputation can't handle another crack in the armor."

"Why are you doing this?"

"I told you, but hotshots like you never listen." His voice was laced with hatred. "I've created a situation to learn exactly how far you'll go to save her. You didn't show any consideration for my family. I'm curious if you care about your own—or if your power has corrupted you, and you're really the heartless monster I think you are."

"I kept you out of jail. I gave you a job."

"You let my sick child die. All for money nobody would have missed. In my hands, it would've saved a life."

"You broke the law."

"And you haven't? You've crossed the line so many times before. Took a few trips. Had a few affairs. Lost your temper and hurt the poor, the defenseless, the homeless. But when *I* crossed the line, did you lift a finger to help?"

"I did more than lift a finger."

"No one helped enough. Not you. Not the NYPD. Not Wholesome Minds."

The commissioner allowed his gaze to focus on the crowd. There were hundreds of faces. So many of them children.

"Our society is sick with apathy because there are too many people like you. Now, one way or another, I'm forcing you to pay. You have a choice: Let me deliver my antidote—or we can figure out, right now, exactly how far you'll go to stop me. What will you sacrifice, Logan? The hundreds of innocents here today? Or your precious career?"

"You bastard!" Donovan roared so loud that even a few of the spectators heard him over the near deafening din of the parade itself. A child gasped.

Santa coughed in disapproval. "And we were having such a productive conversation."

"I liked you better behind the wheel of my Lincoln Navigator, Sam. You should have stayed there."

# Chapter 80

## A.P.B.

Eve issued an all-points bulletin for Samuel Heath, a white American male, six-one, fifty-four years old, approximately one hundred ninety pounds, dark eyes, with a bald head.

His picture was circulated among all law enforcement personnel.

He had significant military and police training.

The bulletin advised officers to consider him armed and extremely dangerous.

# Chapter 81

## Somewhere Inside Central Park

*Still no bars.*

Allie had left Santa with the promise of returning with help. She was also armed with his cellphone—which at the moment didn't have any service.

Just her luck. She was in the middle of Manhattan, desperate for 911, and all she had was the equivalent of a high-tech brick. *Was AT&T down? Was the parade interfering with cell traffic? Was the phone itself damaged?* She guessed the problem didn't matter. Only the solution.

She was still in the woods of the Ramble. She climbed higher and higher, hoping to get service. Every few seconds, she stopped and checked. A bar would appear—only to blink away and disappear entirely. *No service* always returned.

She kept following the path, up the hill, hiding behind a rock or a tree whenever she thought she heard something.

Finally, she saw a bar—and it held. One second. Then two, three, and four.

Hastily, she dialed 911.

An operator answered. "911 Operator number 638982. Where is your emergency?"

"I . . . I don't know. I'm lost. Somewhere in Central Park."

"Can I have your name, please?"

"Alison. Alison Donovan. Someone's after me, and I don't have a strong signal."

"Has there been an accident, Alison?"

"No, though Santa's been hurt bad. I'm scared he's still out there, chasing me."

"Santa is chasing you? Is this a hoax call?"

"No! I said Santa is hurt. The guy who kidnapped me is chasing me. I don't know his name."

"And you don't know where you are?"

"I'm somewhere in the park. The foresty part."

"You're breaking up, Alison. Can you repeat the location?"

"I said I don't know!"

*Nothing.*

"Is anyone there?"

*No bars.*

*I'm here! Is **anyone around??***

This time, Allie tried texting her own phone number.

This was for three reasons. First, she didn't actually have anybody else's phone number memorized. Second, she was pretty sure her kidnapper had given her phone back to her dad as a communication link. And third, the phone she was using had data reception—but no voice cells.

The reply was almost immediate. *Who is this?*

*Allie. You're using my phone,* she typed.

*Where are you?*

*Somewhere in the park.*

*I'm going to call you—it will help me trace your location.*

Two seconds, and the real Santa's phone rang. A single bar of cell reception had miraculously appeared in time.

The voice on the other end was nice. Strong. Irish. It made her imagine sparkling colors like gold and silver.

"My name's Haddox, Allie. I've been helping a lot of people look for you. Where are you?"

"I don't know—somewhere in the park. I don't have good reception."

"Try to stay still. I'm going to put you on speakerphone."

"Mister?"

"Call me Haddox. I'm still here."

"I need help."

"I'm going to help you, sweetheart. I'm getting your location right now. Tell me what you see."

"The forest. The lake. In the distance, I can see the towers of the San Remo. I'm worried the Candlestick man is still looking for me. And Santa's hurt."

"You're hurt?"

"No—not me. This guy in a Santa suit. I'm using his phone."

"Can you wait a second?"

She could hear him having a conversation. Someone was talking about FBI. The police. Her dad.

"Allie, are you still there?"

"I'm here."

"We have your location. We're sending someone to find you, okay, honey? Two women officers. While you wait, try to stay on the line."

"Okay."

"Listen, I'm with a woman named Eve. She's going to talk with you as well, okay?"

"Hello, Allie."

She had a nice voice, too. It made Allie see sunsets and rainbows, like Mom's voice used to do.

She kept looking around, searching the shadows for movement. Hoping for none.

"Listen, when your kidnapper was with you, can you tell me some of the things he said?"

"He hates my dad. And the NYPD. And one of the parade sponsors, I don't know which one. Says they're the reason he lost his family."

"Anything else, Allie?"

"I don't know. He took something out of the storage room where he kept us. Kept talking about how society had been poisoned and needed an antidote. How's Frankie?"

"He's going to be fine, Allie. Don't worry about him right now. It won't be much longer 'til the officers are there."

"My fingers and toes are numb."

"It won't be much longer, Allie. Help is coming."

The phone slipped from her fingers.

"Allie?"

# Chapter 82

The Security Tent, American Museum of Natural History

The phone Allie had used belonged to Rick Robbins—who had served as the parade's Santa for the past seventeen years. He lived alone on West 105th Street; no one had reported him missing.

Some of the other volunteers—friends of his—who'd worked to prep different floats and balloons had thought it odd that he hadn't stopped by to say hello.

But it had been a weird year. The anti-police riot had started the parade off-schedule, and on an awkward footing.

That was just one more reason why—with proper ID and a full Santa disguise—nobody had questioned the man who hopped onto Santa's sleigh *Skyward* and joined the parade.

The two NYPD officers located Allie—as well as Rick Robbins—within moments of Haddox and Eve losing their cellphone connection with her.

Robbins was taken to Saint Luke's for emergency treatment.

At the parade's medical tent, Allie was treated for minor cuts and bruises.

# Chapter 83

Security Tent, American Museum of Natural History

"Allie says he calls it an *antidote*. That he kept it in the same storage room where she was held. I think we have to assume that's potentially the Soman," Eve told Haddox.

She pressed her face into her hands. She was so tired. Her brain was tired. But she couldn't stop working—not with so much at stake.

"Antidote," Haddox repeated with a roll of his eyes. "What kind of bastard calls a *chemical nerve gas* an *antidote*?"

"His child was sick—and neither his employer nor his wife's employer helped," Eve hazarded. "That's the NYPD and Wholesome Minds. Both of which I believe he's targeting today."

"Not to mention the commissioner. Assuming Sam is the Santa next to Donovan on the sleigh, why don't we just take the bastard out?"

"Let a SWAT team swarm *Skyward*?" Eve started pacing.

"Why not? We've identified him. We can give the networks a heads up to go dark. Then we only worry about the bystanders."

"*Millions* of bystanders," Eve clarified. "Not to mention elves at the base of his sleigh."

"But for the greater good, is there a choice?"

"Depends on whether he's succeeded in weaponizing the Soman. Now that Allie is safe, the right approach depends on how viable a threat we think this is." Eve locked her gaze onto Haddox. "Our key question: Does he have possession of enough chemical to be a threat? Or enough knowledge to weaponize it? Jan's team located only trace evidence."

"Aye," Haddox agreed. "But even if he's a hack, he's still danger-ous. What if he gets lucky?"

"He's no expert," Eve admitted. "So whatever he's managed to obtain is highly volatile. As dangerous as it is unpredictable."

"Do we assume the weapon is with him?"

"Or that he controls it, likely with a detonator. That's why we have to proceed carefully. We don't know for sure that it's in the sleigh."

"It wouldn't be, unless he's on a suicide mission."

"Not necessarily. In Tokyo, those men who disseminated the Sarin? They took an antidote—a real one—in advance."

"I'm making a few guesses. The *when* will be at twelve noon as the parade wraps up. The *where* will be Herald Square, the location the parade officially ends. It's the *how* that I can't figure out."

Eve squeezed her eyes shut, thinking about Sam Heath. Putting herself in his frame of mind.

*I've been injured,* she thought. *Made to feel that those important to me don't matter.* Because of who? She considered all the connec-tions she might make. Between Sam and the commissioner—whom he was now targeting, along with the NYPD. Between Sam and his wife's employer, who hadn't stepped up. How Sam was delivering an anti-dote. Something Allie had said about corporate sponsors. What Eve believed about the importance of a public stage.

One simple motive, really. And it formed one simple, terrifying pattern.

"I think I've got a pretty good idea where he's put the Soman," Eve told Haddox. Then she picked up her phone, dialed Jan, and in-formed her—explaining what was needed to get confirmation.

"I'll put Tactical on it immediately," Jan affirmed.

"The technology will give us a picture of what we're dealing with? Suggest its method of dissemination?"

"It *should*. The device uses infrared quantum cascade lasers—what we call QCLs—to offer hyperspectral imaging for detection of explosives where close contact is impossible." Jan cleared her throat. "This has been extensively tested in military environments—but a pa-rade with moving balloons and floats? That will be a first!"

# Chapter 84

## A.P.B.

ve also sent out an all-points bulletin to every NYPD, FBI, and Joint Terrorism Task Force officer on duty—in addition to the mayor, the governor, and even the White House. It told them that intelligence indicated a potential attack—possibly along the parade route, probably with a chemical nerve agent.

The nerve agent's exact delivery method remained unknown—but it was advised that any vehicle approaching the parade route should be regarded with extreme suspicion. Cabs, delivery trucks, even vehicles belonging to police, FBI, and first responders should be considered dangerous until thoroughly vetted.

The all-points bulletin made clear that anything out of the ordinary, no matter what, should be regarded with immediate suspicion, secured, and isolated.

Officers should also be alert for a camphor or fruity odor.

# Chapter 85

## Along the Parade Route

Twenty-eight minutes until the parade's end.

Eli, still holding on to the Molly the Mongoose balloon, made the turn off Central Park South onto Sixth Avenue, passing the Trump Parc building.

"Careful—don't lose your bones!" The perky handler next to Eli had it all under control. Bones were the name for his individual handling ropes. And yes, he was completely on the verge of losing them every time the wind whipped down Central Park South.

If he weren't just a bit terrified of what Allie's kidnapper had planned, Eli would've said that he couldn't get to Herald Square fast enough.

For now, he walked. Waved. Waited.

And tried to hang on to his bones.

Nineteen blocks uptown, Haddox and Eve were at the computer when the digital image of what Samuel Heath called the *antidote* hit their computer.

Jan Brandt was on the line, explaining what it meant. "Eve, you were spot-on. You're seeing a digital imprint of the chemical Soman, which we've located inside a small plastic bag pinned to the interior of the Molly balloon."

"It's not a large quantity," Jan continued, "but you have to keep in mind: An amount the size of a pinpoint is sufficient to kill one adult. Heath has rigged a small igniter inside—sufficient to rip the plastic bag and release the Soman."

"We have to assume Sam Heath has the detonator. Taking him out with a sniper shot could risk activating the detonator, releasing the gas," Haddox said. "Not to mention sparking a stampede and panic among the spectators—though I suppose that's the least of our worries."

"That's the backup plan," Eve said. "First, I'd like to try a different idea."

Twenty-three minutes until **parade's end.**

Mace and the *Wholesome Minds* float passed Fifty-seventh Street, continuing down Sixth Avenue.

Rue 57's red awnings were decorated with strings of tiny white lights. As he talked with Eve on his headset, Mace watched a gangly teenage boy amuse himself trying to jump up and reach them. Completely unaware of the deadly poison gas that was floating over his shoulder.

"You sure something's about to go down, Eve?" Mace demanded.

*Believe me, I wish I were wrong,* she replied.

"But I'm backup? I just have to get ready and stand by?"

*That's the plan. With luck, I'll never need you.*

Eighteen minutes until **parade's end.**

Santa's sleigh *Skyward* passed Fifty-first Street.

Radio City Music Hall's red neon sign framed a Christmas tree—a virtual candy corn, lit up in blazing tiers of orange, red, and white.

With Evil Santa sitting on his left, Donovan mustered all the strength in his right arm and pulled against his restraints. He was cuffed to a ring that was attached to the inside of the sleigh. He felt it move just a little, which gave him confidence that he could do this. And when he did, he planned to make sure the asshole beside him got everything he deserved—and more.

*Just be quiet and listen; I'm aware of the identity of the man sitting beside you.* Eve's voice crackled in Donovan's headset.

*First, are you restrained in any way? One cough for yes; two coughs for no.*

Donovan coughed once.

*Okay. We believe Santa is carrying a detonator. Do you have a visual on it?*

Two coughs. Donovan had seen no sign of it. His strategy—once free—was to take Santa by surprise and force him to let it go.

He faked a coughing fit. Leaned over until his mouth was almost between his knees. Whispered into his headset, "Give me two minutes. I think I can get free."

Sixteen minutes until the parade's end.

Eli and the Molly the Mongoose balloon were passing Forty-fourth Street.

People were elbowing one another on the sidewalks, straining against the police blockade to get closer to Sixth Avenue. To have a better view.

*Eli, are you there?* Eve's voice crackled in his headset.

"Where else would I be?" Eli marched along. Waving. Smiling.

*Listen, you've got to do something important for me. We've just received confirmation that the Soman is inside your balloon.*

Eve explained exactly what she needed Eli to do.

He wasted no time taking care of the task.

He had no plans to die. Not today.

Fourteen minutes until the parade's end.

Mace hopped off the *Ace CyberDog* float, smiled and waved his way past Eli and the Molly the Mongoose balloon, and easily hopped onto the *Wholesome Minds* float.

As discreetly as possible, he showed his ID to the police officer manning the float—and explained what he needed to do.

The officer pointed to the rear of the float. "Guess you're gonna need to climb that tree!"

The president of the United States immediately ordered into high alert the military's Biological War Defense Center and covert teams who had the job of responding to a chemical attack on U.S. soil.

Hospitals were placed on alert, given the symptoms to watch out for: blurred vision; chest tightness; confusion; drooling and excessive sweating; nausea or vomiting; small, pinpoint pupils and/or watery eyes; convulsions; loss of consciousness; paralysis; and respiratory failure.

## WJXZ REPORTS

This is WJXZ News with Gwen Allensen reporting from Herald Square. Bringing up the rear of the parade, we have right next to each other: the float of Macy's newest corporate sponsor— Wholesome Minds—and our newest balloon, the star of their hit children's TV show *Molly the Mongoose*.

Right now, I'm talking with Robert Chen, a studio worker for Macy's. Robert is one of the carpenters involved in creating Molly and the *Wholesome Minds* float. Robert, can you tell us about that?

*ROBERT:* Sure. I'm a full-time studio employee of Macy's, and it's my job to create and care for the dozens of floats you've seen today in the parade.

*GWEN:* Tell our listeners about the biggest challenge you faced with Molly and her corporate float.

*ROBERT:* Well, we created the *Wholesome Minds* float to honor the values of *home* that we all celebrate this Thanksgiving. So we created a float of Molly's treetop home—where she welcomes all her friends for their learning adventures. It was complicated to build, with that crazy gnarled tree—and since it's three stories high, it took meticulous planning to get it from our work studio in New Jersey, through the Lincoln Tunnel, to the staging area on the Upper West Side.

# Chapter 86

## Along the Parade Route

This was the real moment of truth. The next few blocks were show-time: live or die.

Mace thought the odds were in their favor. Santa was distracted. Speaking urgently with the commissioner.

Drawing his Glock, Mace made his way up the remaining steps of the ladder, inside the trunk of Molly's treehouse. From the recently cut wood, there was sawdust everywhere. He inhaled the scent of it— his fingers scattered it—as he climbed, rung by rung.

He could hear the crowd roaring. Plenty of *Yea!* And *We love you, Santa!* and cries of *Look at the reindeer's nose!*

He peeked through a space between the trunk and the branches.

Now he smelled the roasting chestnuts. Heard the tinny tune "Christmas Sleighbells Are Jingling!" that accompanied Santa's float this year. Saw toddlers dancing on their parents' shoulders and beaming grandparents clapping and awkward teenagers snapping photos with smartphones.

Too many happy people. In fact, if it weren't for all the skyscrapers, it could be a schmaltzy Norman Rockwell moment.

He lifted himself up. Moved toward the most secure branch, positioning himself with stealth and catlike agility.

Now he needed a solid visual to take the shot.

*Should have been García, with his sniper skills.* The moment the thought came, he extinguished it.

*Focus on the game,* he reminded himself.

But for luck, he briefly touched the red bandana that he'd taken from García's things. And tied around his own neck.

Now Mace just needed the right visual.

So he waited—and watched the waving, dancing Santa.

*Five seconds. Ten seconds.*

It took twenty-three seconds before Mace made a clear determination. Santa's right arm continued waving; his left hand must be holding the detonator.

Plus, there was the real risk that the target was ambidextrous: If Mace disabled Santa's left arm, he might activate the nerve agent with his right.

Likewise, Santa's hefty paunch—where it was possible that extra nerve agent could be stored—had to be avoided.

The only shot available to Mace was the kill shot.

Right between the eyes.

Something nobody wanted if there was any other alternative. Not in front of all these people. Not on live TV.

*It was a job so much better suited for García.*

He whispered to Eve through his secure headset: *Do I take the kill shot?*

The reply came within a second: *Stand by.*

Mace listened as the tune continued. *Santa Claus is coming!*

He focused his eyes.

Prepared to fire.

Prayed he wouldn't have to.


Under the cover of Santa's blanket, Donovan put every ounce of strength into his right arm—and pulled.

The loose ring that held his right cuff broke free.

It made a clinking noise as it fell to the ground.

But between the cheering crowds and blaring Santa Claus music, Donovan's nemesis didn't notice a thing.

Donovan was ready for action.

First he turned his face to the masses. Pulled out the earpiece that connected him with Eve.

And tossed it out of the sleigh.

# Chapter 87

## Nearing Herald Square

N ine minutes until parade's end.

Eve had raced downtown to Herald Square. Now she fought her way through the crowds—flashing her FBI shield to the various security detail officers who wanted to stop her. When she reached the sidewalk, she stopped.

Molly the Mongoose was passing Thirty-seventh Street—with *Wholesome Minds* and Santa's float *Skyward* tailing close behind.

Eve's first question was for Eli. "All confirmed?"

Eli answered immediately. *Yes.*

Eve's second question was for Donovan. "Do you have this?"

Silence.

"Donovan?"

Nothing. A technical glitch? Temporary, she hoped.

Her last question was for Jan, who'd been acting as her liaison with other law enforcement. "Everyone's on board?"

Jan's voice crackled in her ear. *All set. We need this to work.*

"Haddox?" she asked.

*I've got the protocol to jam his detonator,* he confirmed. *It will require disrupting all wireless transmissions in the area, including emergency response. Are you sure?*

The music on Santa's sleigh was blaring. "Here Comes Santa Claus" was repeating for the umpteenth time. Children and adults alike screamed in anticipation. In moments, Santa would arrive in his sleigh—and confetti would blanket the air.

On a large screen overlooking Herald Square, WJXZ's live coverage was being broadcast. Gwen Allensen was talking about how Santa's float was the largest in the parade, at sixty feet long, twenty-two feet wide, and three and a half stories tall.

The red star-shaped balloons that hung on Santa's sleigh taunted Eve: *Believe!*

She had three options to secure the Soman and protect the public. Allow Haddox to hack the technology. Rely on Mace to take the kill shot. Or trust that Eli could accomplish the same goal, with the least collateral damage, if the commissioner failed.

She made her decision. "Haddox, stand by. Mace, continue to stand by. Eli, on my mark, we are five, four, three, two, one."

*Mark set,* came his response.

Donovan flung off the blanket that had covered his lap with his now-free right hand. There was a flash of metal as the handcuffs were still attached to his wrist.

He whipped his right arm forward; connected square on with Santa's chin.

Two hundred forty pounds of muscle, fury, and primeval vengeance.

Santa's jaw shattered and his head snapped back; then he went down, hard and vertical.

"Feel good?" Sam managed to ask through a mouthful of blood.

"Feels great. After everything I did to help you, you took my daughter. You messed with my job. Now you're threatening this city with a chemical weapon—and I want that detonator."

Sam balled his hands into fists. "You stupid bastard. You're going to have to fight me for it. *This* is your third task. Showing the world just how far you'll go."

Donovan stopped a moment—and stared. Working hard to make sure he understood exactly what Sam Heath was offering.

*I'm all set,* Eli said over the radio. *Everyone around me is on board.*

Eve heaved a sigh of relief. *Jan—you're confident our next step is the best way to secure the Soman?*

*Affirmative. With this big a crowd, there's not really much choice,* came the forensic tech's answer.

In the background, Henry Ma issued an order that would reach all media. "Cameras up! Due to an emergency situation, we need all media cameras focused on the balloons. Away from the crowds."

Eve made a final decision. *Once the threat is cleared, I'll send SWAT to help Donovan out.*

*Doesn't look like the commissioner needs any help.* Haddox's voice was flat.

*Holy crap!* From his vantage point on high, Mace had a pretty good view of Donovan and Santa going at it.

He'd seen plenty of tough fights in his day. On the courts, after a game gone bad. On the streets, when the Bloods had to defend their turf. He'd seen nothing like this.

For a violent, bloody minute, he watched the commissioner appear to take out all his frustrations. Santa's face was bruised and swollen.

Donovan sure didn't look like a member of the police force—much less its boss.

Rules didn't apply.

A bloody froth had formed on Santa's lips.

Mace wondered: *Should I take a shot? Maybe wound 'em both—and end this?* Then he looked into the crowds—remembered the detonator—and made himself keep still.

But he couldn't help wondering: *What the hell is going on?*

The moment he understood what Sam Heath was after, Logan Donovan dragged him down to the floor of the sleigh. Pinned his hands. "Where's that detonator?" he demanded again.

"If you don't smile for the camera, I'm going to release the poison, commissioner."

Logan scrambled to search through layers of padding and red fur. Found a stiletto knife and pressed it against Sam's throat. "Detonator. Now."

"Better act fast, Logan."

Donovan continued searching until his free hand made it through the last layer of the Santa suit. He found the small device in Sam's left breast pocket.

Next to it was a letter.

Logan went perfectly still. Stared at the handwriting. It was as close as he'd get to allowing himself a gasp of shock.

He was aware of the crowds—screaming, all around him.

"What'd Santa ever do to you?" a voice yelled out from the crowd.

He overheard the answer from some security officer: "Hey, kids—that's a cop dealing with a bad Santa. Like the one Ralphie meets in *A Christmas Story.*"

Logan recovered. Let the letter drop to the floor. Clutched the detonator tight.

"I'll bet you never knew, did you, Logan? Let's take stock: You have the detonator. I swear that your daughter is safe." Sam's words were slurred. "But you don't want to stop, do you? It feels too good." Sam managed something approaching a grin.

Donovan pressed the knife against Sam's left jugular. If he severed it, Sam would bleed out in less than sixty seconds.

"Guess I have my answer," Sam mumbled.

Donovan leaned low. He whispered, "I knew it was you the whole time. It had to be. Nobody else knew about the two million—or how hard I worked to squash the details of Jill's so-called accident."

"But you didn't stop me. Didn't send in the troops to rescue her." The words were garbled, but Donovan understood them.

He pressed the knife harder into Sam's skin. A drop of blood formed—and slid down Sam's neck. "*This* is why I waited, Sam. I'm going to be the hero, not the bad guy. The top cop is about to save the city."

Haddox watched the two figures struggling inside Santa's sleigh. Donovan seemed to have the upper hand. And when Haddox saw metal flash in the sunlight, he got a sick feeling in his stomach.

Donovan didn't look like a victim. Not anymore.

Was he really doing what was necessary to save the city from chemical attack?

Or was Haddox watching a battle without honor or rules?

He saw a final, desperate tangle. Then Santa went limp—and the commissioner held the detonator up high. High enough for the world to see.

*What exactly had just happened?*

There were choruses of screams everywhere. Police took defensive positions, holding their riot shields to keep the crowds in place.

It turned out they didn't have to.

In the same instant, the crowd's collective vision took in the sight of Molly the Mongoose—let loose—flying higher and higher into the air.

There was a chorus of *ooh*s and *ahh*s.

Cameras flashed.

Molly was right by the Marriott Courtyard hotel—where guests pressed foreheads tight against the windows. Molly continued to rise, higher and higher.

She was ten stories up.

Rising to fifteen.

Then twenty, twenty-five, thirty, thirty-five—until she had cleared the top of the hotel, shooting ever higher into the sky.

Logan Donovan watched, too.

When all eyes were focused on the flying balloon, he leaned down and slid the letter Sam had kept with the detonator into his own pocket. It was secure by the time the SWAT team boarded the sleigh—and took the lifeless Santa away.

Molly the Mongoose was a yellow shooting star, high in the sky, heading toward Long Island. At last, too high in the air to cause harm.

People on the sidewalks seemed to cram themselves closer to the metal barricades. Trying to see better, hear better, feel more part of this once-in-a-lifetime finale.

Mace joined Eli on the ground. Now they watched the commissioner—together.

"He's a hero, right?" Eli said. "Secured the detonator. Put down the bad guy."

"Guess so." Mace took the ammunition out of his Glock.

"Do you think Sam could have been taken alive?" Eli hesitated. "I mean, what did *you* see? You had the better view."

"My guess is: Everybody sees what they want to see. For most people, that means a guy fighting to save the public from a dangerous threat."

"But that's not what *you* saw."

"Since when does anybody care what I saw?" Mace growled. "He's the commissioner."

"Yeah." Eli slugged down a gulp of a Coke one of the parade volunteers had given him. "Kind of funny about his radio going out. Right at that moment."

Through the crowds, Mace caught a glimpse of Céline. He waved, then holstered the Glock. "Catch you later, Red."

Eli shot him a sidelong glance. "You ever going to introduce me?"

Mace's boyish grin was slightly lopsided. "Hell, no. I *like* Céline."

NEWS NEWS NEWS NEWS NEWS

## WJXZ REPORTS

This is Gwen Allensen, with live coverage from Herald Square, where I'm joined by Mayor Maureen Kelly and Deputy Police Commissioner Kepler.

*GWEN:* When I spoke with the parade's director earlier, he said that we could expect this year's parade to be unique. Bigger and better, with fabulous floats, superstar talent, and new balloons. But this parade finale is like nothing we've seen before. What exactly just happened?

*MAYOR KELLY:* I feel like we've been transported back to 1929—when all the balloons used to be released into the air at the end of the parade!

*GWEN:* And when people found them deflated in their yards, days later, there was an address card inside for returning them to Macy's. Those who did would receive a prize.

*KEPLER:* Today, we do things differently. Two helicopters are flying right now, determined to intercept wayward Molly's path—and take her to a safe, secure location.

*GWEN:* Molly's release is certainly a news story we'll come back to, but I also need to ask you about *Skyward*. I understand the commissioner was involved in a security incident onboard Santa's sleigh.

*KEPLER:* I'm afraid we can't comment at this time. Our investigation is active and ongoing.

## PART SIX

*The Fourth Thursday in November*

Thanksgiving

12:03 p.m. until 6 p.m.

# Chapter 88

## Herald Square

A press conference was slowly taking form. Mayor Maureen Kelly was headed to the news podium, flanked by her deputy mayor as well as George Kepler. An interpreter for the hearing impaired trailed close behind.

Cops and security personnel surrounded them all. Doing their job; eyes alert for anything amiss. They saluted Donovan as he approached.

The commissioner wasn't worried about Mo or the deputy mayor or any of the host of high-level political officials now gathering. They were lily-livered ninnies who would never take a stand until they saw which way the political wind blew.

Besides, the moment was Donovan's. When he ascended the podium, a half-dozen cameras and mikes turned toward his face, just like flowers stretched to the sun. His heart was pounding, but he needed to make his power play now. Take charge of the media and master the spin.

"Before I'm reunited with my daughter—and we wrap up this parade and go home to our families—I want to give you details on a serious security situation. Fortunately, it was resolved with an outcome we can all be thankful for."

Eve intercepted the commissioner as he broke away from the crowd of police officers who'd swarmed him.

"Thank you," she said—and meant it. "You took on a lot of risk today to save people. You're okay?"

He fell into step beside her. "Nothing's wrong that a hot shower, a good nap, and a maybe a tube of Bengay won't cure. Where's Allie?"

"She's fine. And waiting for you, just ahead." Eve indicated the area right in front of Macy's.

"Listen." He took her arm. "A couple things. First, the knife I found on Santa? When forensic analysis is complete, I'll be surprised if it doesn't turn out to be the same weapon that killed García."

"I agree. What's second?"

"I don't like it when you treat me with suspicion. I'm an open book, if you just ask."

"Any question I want?" She watched his eyes carefully. Those blue eyes again—the ones that had seen too much.

"Anything."

She knew he was working to get her on his side. That was how he manipulated people.

She knew—because she did it herself.

"You knew people would question Jill's death, yet you covered up evidence. Did nothing to allay their concerns."

She was thinking: *Prove me wrong about you.*

"Because there's two kinds of people in this world. Those who want something from me. And those who want me out of this job. To answer them would dignify their suspicions, but I have exonerating proof on file at my attorney's office. Just in case. You're welcome to see it."

"Okay." She understood people well enough that when their words and behavior surprised her, that only made them more fascinating. That was Logan's appeal, she knew.

It was also why she loved her job—right here, in New York, with its variety of cases. The result of so many people from different cultures and backgrounds. Behaving in ways sometimes heroic and other times horrific—but always unpredictable.

He shot her the same brilliant smile she'd seen time and again on television. But today, it was meant just for her. "Jill's illness was hard—but you know something odd? In the end, we started talking again. Real conversations. For the first time in ages. Thinking back, those are some of my best memories with her. Strange, isn't it?"

"Maybe that's love."

"At least maybe friendship." Logan Donovan was looking at her. "Can I see you again?"

"What would Gwen Allensen say about that?"

"Goodbye and good luck."

Eve shifted her gaze to a small figure watching them. "We can talk later. Allie's waiting for you now."

And Haddox was waiting for her.

"There's a guy I know," she said as she approached him. "He's not like anybody I've ever met. He's got this eight-eighteen rule and he doesn't want to stick around. But he always turns up when I really need him."

"Is that a thank-you?"

"Something like that."

"I'm leaving town." His voice became husky, intimate. "Come with me, luv."

She looked into his soulful blue eyes—and was tempted. Then she thought of Allie. García. A fatherless boy recovering in a hospital uptown.

All reminders of a different task she had yet to do.

"Another time," Eve said, turning away. "Right now, there's someplace I need to be."

The commissioner sprinted to where Allie was standing in Herald Square, right next to the *Ace CyberDog* float. She was clutching a small pit bull mix puppy.

The news cameras continued to trail him.

His hands were shaking. Something seemed to have shredded inside of him—and he almost felt tears coming on.

To hold them back, he wasted no time. He enveloped Allie—puppy and all—in a gigantic bear hug. And let it last for a full minute and twenty-three seconds.

"I missed you, Daddy," she whispered.

"It's okay," he soothed. "I'm lucky to have you back."

When he'd been handcuffed, sitting beside Santa, he'd thought of

Allie. He'd pictured her at Jill's funeral—and remembered how help-less he felt, how completely useless he had been.

He hadn't been able to think of anything to say. He hadn't been able to make it better.

"Are we going home now?" she asked.

"Yes," he assured her.

"Just us? Not *her*."

He followed her gaze, assuming she was looking at Gwen, next to the media table. To his surprise, he realized that Allie was looking at Eve.

Eve—trying to leave, but stuck answering questions from the mayor and Henry Ma and Deputy Commissioner Kepler.

"I saw you with her earlier," she said—as accusing as only a thirteen-year-old can be.

"Just making conversation, nothing more." He gave her a crooked smile. "I think the three of us should go home. You, me, and—what's this fella's name here?"

"Sam," she said proudly.

"Sam?" He swallowed.

Apparently Allie didn't know—not yet. How was he going to tell her that Sam wasn't a name they were going to want to be reminded of?

"After Samwise Gamgee," she insisted. "He was Frodo's best friend, you know. And at the end of *The Fellowship of the Ring,* when Frodo is ready to pack it in? Sam refuses to let him quit."

"Sam it is, then." Some arguments could wait.

"Really?" Her eyes were bright with excitement—in a way he hadn't seen since she was a very little girl.

"You've been wanting a dog. How do we make this one yours?"

"A donation to No Bull Pit," Mace answered, coming up behind them. "A *generous* one. 'Cause you owe us *big-time*."

"You got it." The commissioner flashed his signature smile. The one that put everyone around him immediately at ease.

After all, Sam's note accompanying the money—*Can't buy me love*—had been wrong. Everything was for sale, assuming you were willing to pay the price. The man who had died trying to figure out exactly how far Logan Donovan would go ought to have known that.

This city needed someone to protect it. To keep it safe, day after day. Luckily, Commissioner Logan Donovan was strong enough to do what it took.

Hours later, when he was home in his office, and Allie collapsed into bed, he took out the letter he'd stolen from Sam's pocket. He scanned its contents.

She'd had great penmanship, he thought. Those arching *T*'s and looping *L*'s. He supposed others might consider it beautiful.

Then he focused on the final page.

> *It's not just me who's sick, Sam. The cancer is everywhere.*
>
> *You saw that when your son was sick, didn't you? The NYPD didn't care. Wholesome Minds didn't care. The company that rakes in billions selling "family values" could have overridden the insurance decision and funded the experimental treatment your son needed to survive. And Logan? In spite of every line he's crossed, he couldn't look the other way when you were the one breaking the law.*
>
> *And no one notices, because we're all too distracted by our smartphones and busy lives.*
>
> *Someone needs to step up, to make people pay attention.*
>
> *It's got to be you, Sam. I know you can do it, based on the time we had together—which has been the happiest time of my life.*
>
> *You asked me before why I didn't leave him, after I learned what he was capable of. How he treated people. How his ambition had no restraint.*
>
> *The answer is the usual one: because of Allie. He threatened to lawyer up, take her away, and make sure I never saw her again.*
>
> *You have your own issues with Logan.*
>
> *You said you would quit working for him the day I was gone.*
>
> *Don't.*
>
> *The cancer is back and I can't fight it again. I intend to*

*finish this on my own terms—which means that you won't
hear from me again. If you love me, you won't try to stop me.*

*My last request is this: Will you look out for my daugh-
ter? My precious Allie? Maybe he'll grow into the father she
deserves after I'm gone.*

*But if he doesn't? Figure out a way to fix things. Use
whatever means necessary.*

*Just like you did for your son.*

*Love,*
*Jill*

After he finished reading, he closed his eyes. Let the anger and
rage wash over him. Allowed his emotions, smothering and dark, to
crowd his chest until he could barely breathe.

When he came back to himself, he thought: *Get over it. Emotion
will only make you useless.*

This was typical Jill: trying to screw him over, even from the grave.

By God, he would never allow that. Besides, she'd made one major
mistake. She'd written the note before they left for Hawaii. Before her
"accidental" fall.

And those last nine lines? Starting with *the cancer is back*? She'd
actually exculpated him completely.

He took a pair of scissors from his desk. He clipped the final lines.
He could now make a truth of his lie: He'd get her handwriting au-
thenticated, file the note with his lawyer.

Meanwhile, he'd share the important part with Eve.

And the rest of the letter?

He pulled over his metal waste can. Found a box of matches. Set
the pages on fire.

# Chapter 89

## Soup Kitchen—Saint Agnes

It had turned into a perfect Thanksgiving Day. The air was crisp and cold, and the wind whipped the few remaining leaves until they fell off the trees in front of Saint Agnes. They danced in the wind—in a frenzy of gold, orange, and yellow.

It wouldn't last—but in the moment, it was beautiful. Inside the church, pews had been replaced by festive dinner tables. Eve surveyed four hundred people—both homeless and volunteers—who were about to sit down together for a holiday feast.

Eli and Mace had come with her reluctantly. "Nothing we do here's gonna change a thing," Eli groused.

"Maybe not," she said. "It's still worth doing."

And she thought of García. Eating his elephant one bite at a time.

"I don't know what to say," Eli stammered.

"Because they're homeless?" Mace demanded. "You know, it could happen to any of us, with enough bad luck and bad decisions. Besides, you dress like a homeless dude, so you should feel right at home."

Eli flushed as red as his hair. But not from embarrassment.

Across the room, Ty was waving at him, calling him over to help serve.

"What do I do?" He looked at Eve, his voice rising.

"Go. You handle eating just fine," Eve reassured him. "Focus on the food."

"So where do they need the most help serving chow?" Mace

asked—but answered his own question when he recognized an old friend from pick-up games at the Cage on West Fourth Street.

Eve watched him walk away, thinking how, despite all his tough talk, Mace was wearing García's red bandana around his neck. *Always knew you had a soft spot for Frankie,* she thought.

As expected, Haddox was gone. He was—well, who ever knew exactly where Haddox was? He would turn up again when it suited him.

She started work, partnering with Peter, a man who'd become homeless after losing his job as a security officer four years ago. He now volunteered at Saint Agnes, too, while he was looking for work.

Before long, the dinner was served—and it was time to eat. They took seats together at a table near a stained-glass window depicting the Last Supper.

Someone else reached for the seat beside her. Eve noticed, the minute she saw his hands.

People's hands had always fascinated her. And this man's hands were long, but lean and strong. There was still a slight indentation where he'd once worn a ring on his left hand. And today, there were plenty of cuts and bruises. Scars from a hard-fought battle.

She looked up into blue eyes—the ones that fascinated her, because they'd seen too much.

"Told you I wanted to see you again." He lowered himself into the chair beside her. He wasn't in uniform, just an ordinary cream cotton shirt and jeans. The dark circles under his eyes had disappeared, and there was not even a single fleck of red in his salt-and-pepper hair. He looked good.

"Didn't think you meant so soon."

"I figured Thanksgiving was as good a time as any," the commissioner continued. "Besides, I have some time. The city's safe. My department is unharmed. And Allie's finally asleep at home; one of Jill's friends came to watch her."

She raised an eyebrow. "Wouldn't have thought this was your kind of scene. Your department doesn't have the best relationship with the homeless population."

"All the more reason for me to try to change that. Besides, this is nice," he said, looking around.

She saw him take in the red tablecloths. White china dinnerware. Candles.

"It doesn't feel like a homeless event," he added.

"Yeah, it's all civilized. That's why we like it, too," Peter interjected with a grin, passing the commissioner a dinner roll.

An older man next to Peter with a scruffy gray beard—who'd been silent the entire meal—just nodded in agreement.

"I brought you a present. Exonerating evidence." Logan passed her a photocopy of the final lines of Jill's note, starting with *The cancer is back and I can't fight it again.*

Her hand lightly brushed his injured one as she accepted it. She wasn't prepared for the warm surge of electricity in his touch. *Control is only an illusion,* she was reminded.

She scanned the page's contents, raised an eyebrow. "Looks like part of it's missing."

Logan shrugged. "It's all I've got. Found it among her things."

"Who was the recipient? She asks her—or him—to look after Allie."

"I think she meant it for her friend Carrie—who's actually with Allie now. I'm afraid Jill never did think much of my parenting skills," he added with a rueful smile.

Eve felt something uncomfortable slither in her stomach. *Definitely not an open book.* So she'd find the answers for herself.

And she definitely wanted to look at the footage of the commissioner's fight with Sam. Mace—who'd had the clearest view of the action—had questions.

Yet Vidocq had crossed some ethical lines of their own trying to bring Allie home. Were any of them really in a position to take the moral high ground?

That, Eve decided, was a problem for another day.

She'd settled in comfortably beside Logan, talking some more, when the phone in her pocket chirped.

She retrieved it. Haddox's message read: *There's a lass I know, not like anybody I've ever met. If she wants to ditch the cop, I'll help her track down Zev's murderer. JFK. Gate 17. Terminal 4. I've an extra ticket for a friend.*

She typed in reply: *Is that what we are? Friends?*

His answer came in a heartbeat: *All up to you, luv.*

Sometime the simplest things could be complicated.

"Is there a problem?" Donovan was asking.

She flashed him a smile, shook her head. But she didn't put her phone away. She clutched it in her right hand, thinking.

*Something had changed.*

She'd spent most of her life alone, working. Her most meaningful relationships at the moment were with her Vidocq colleagues.

One of whom was dead.

García, like Zev. His death had made her realize: Solving Zev's murder might give her intellectual satisfaction, but it was unlikely to dull her pain. There had to be another way.

*What do I want?*

She'd been working to safeguard a world she'd experienced only a small portion of—the ugly part, having to do with crime and the worst side of human nature. She wanted to experience its better half. Not just to enjoy art and architecture, museums and theater, music and dance. Not just to see historical landmarks and national treasures and scenic vistas. But to meet the kind of people who made the world better. Who created a place where men like García—and Zev before him—didn't die. Where men like Sam did not create terrible threats.

And if she returned to criminal work—to Vidocq—well, she'd do so after having learned something.

*Haddox was waiting.*

*And Logan Donovan, too.*

"Eve, is there a problem?" the commissioner was asking again.

"No," she said firmly and started to type her reply. "Nothing I can't figure out."

# Acknowledgments

M y deepest gratitude to those who have been indispensable in bringing about this book. Thanks to Kate Miciak and Anne Hawkins for your unflagging enthusiasm and support. I'm especially grateful to all those at Random House whose contributions have made this book a reality, including Kara Welsh, Jennifer Hershey, Kim Hovey, Julia Maguire, Alex Coumbis, Maggie Oberrender, Nancy Delia, Amy Brosey, Victoria Wong, and Carlos Beltran. Thanks also to cartographer David Lindroth.

Congratulations to Jan Brandt, who won the honor of a character naming at a charity benefit for the New York Musical Festival. I hope you enjoy your fictional counterpart.

Special thanks to Clair Lamb, MacKenzie Cadenhead, Mark Longaker, and Natalie Meir.

Finally, heartfelt thanks to Maddie and especially to Craig, my partner in every story.

## About the Author

STEFANIE PINTOFF is the Edgar Award–winning author of five novels. Her writing has also won the Washington Irving Book Prize and earned nominations for the Barry, Anthony, Macavity, and Agatha Awards. Pintoff's novels have been published around the world, including the United Kingdom, the Czech Republic, Italy, and Japan. She lives on Manhattan's Upper West Side, where she is at work on her next thriller.

stefaniepintoff.com
Find Stefanie Pintoff on Facebook

## About the Type

This book was set in Sabon, a typeface designed by the well-known German typographer Jan Tschichold (1902–74). Sabon's design is based upon the original letter forms of sixteenth-century French type designer Claude Garamond and was created specifically to be used for three sources: foundry type for hand composition, Linotype, and Monotype. Tschichold named his typeface for the famous Frankfurt typefounder Jacques Sabon (c. 1520–80).